A TEAR FOR THE DEAD

A TEAR FOR THE DEAD

DAVID PENNY

THE THOMAS BERRINGTON HISTORICAL MYSTERIES

The Red Hill

Moorish Spain, 1482. English surgeon Thomas Berrington is asked to investigate a series of brutal murders in the palace of al-Hamra in Granada.

Breaker of Bones

Summoned to Cordoba to heal a Spanish prince, Thomas Berrington and his companion, the eunuch Jorge, pursue a killer who re-makes his victims with his own crazed logic.

The Sin Eater

In Granada Helena, the concubine who once shared Thomas Berrington's bed, is carrying his child, while Thomas tracks a killer exacting revenge on evil men.

The Incubus

A mysterious killer stalks the alleys of Ronda. Thomas Berrington, Jorge and Lubna race to identify the culprit before more victims have their breath stolen.

The Inquisitor

In a Sevilla on the edge of chaos death stalks the streets. Thomas Berrington and his companions tread a dangerous path between the Inquisition, the royal palace, and a killer.

The Fortunate Dead

As a Spanish army gathers outside the walls of Malaga, Thomas Berrington hunts down a killer who threatens more than just strangers.

The Promise of Pain

When revenge is not enough. Thomas Berrington flees to the high mountains, only to be drawn back by those he left behind.

The Message of Blood

When Thomas Berrington is sent to Cordoba on the orders of a man he hates he welcomes the distraction of a murder, but is shocked when the evidence points to the killer being his companion.

A Tear for the Dead

As the reign of Moorish Granada draws to a close, dark forces gather to carve a new Spain. Can Thomas Berrington overcome the plot to destroy not just one civilisation, but two?

———

THE THOMAS BERRINGTON PREQUELS

A Death of Innocence

When 13 years old Thomas Berrington is accused of murder he must enlist the help of pretty Bel Brickenden to prove his innocence. And then another kind of death comes to Lemster.

———

THE THOMAS BERRINGTON BUNDLES

Purchase 3 full-length novels for less than the price of two.

Thomas Berrington Books 1-3

The Red Hill

Breaker of Bones

The Incubus

Thomas Berrington Books 4-6

The Incubus

The Inquisitor

The Fortunate Dead

Thomas Berrington Books 7-9

The Promise of Pain

The Message of Blood

A Tear for the Dead

GRANADA, ANDALUSIA
1491-92

CHAPTER ONE

Thomas Berrington was making scant progress on the list of demands sent by Christof Columb. There were several obstacles associated with the task. First was the rain. It had woken him during the night as it hammered against the canvas roof and sides of his tent. Second was the handwriting of whoever had created the list. It was awful. Scrawled and scratched on a sheet of reused vellum with parts of the original document showing through. Then there were the items, half of which Thomas had never heard of. The note would have been better evaluated by another mariner, but Isabel, Queen of Castile, had demanded Thomas make a judgement on it. Columb wanted to procure supplies, on the expectation Isabel would recommend funding for his voyage to discover a new passage to the Indies. Thomas saw him as misguided, but he was also starting to believe there might be some merit in the mariner's plans.

Thomas glanced at the entrance to the tent, grateful at least Isabel had given him one for his exclusive use. There was a desk of sorts, and a bed, also of a sorts. His clothes, what few there were, hung from a rope attached between two of the posts keeping the canvas roof up. Thomas had rearranged the furniture that morning to move it away from water pouring through gaps in the roof. The rain showed no sign of ending, and he was glad of the meagre shelter. For most of the soldiers and hangers-on arrayed across the sodden ground circling the unimportant town of Ojos de Huescar, scarcely a league south of the Moorish city of Gharnatah, there was no refuge at all.

As Thomas looked out at the rain, he noticed a slim figure running towards the tent, a makeshift cape draped over her head. It did little to protect Theresa, or her clothes.

She dashed into the shelter and shook herself, spraying water from her hair.

"Watch the documents!" Thomas tried to cover them with a hand.

"Is this rain ever going to stop?" Theresa came closer, too close as she always did. "Are they important?"

"Some might consider them so. And this is al-Andalus, so yes, the rain will cease, and then it will be too hot. This land offers extremes and little else." Thomas glanced up at her. "Do you need something, or have you come only to spoil my work?"

"She says she needs you. She wants us to share her midday meal." There was no need for Theresa to mention who. She had been in Isabel's service all her adult life, Thomas for the last year and a half. He was still trying to determine if accepting Isabel's invitation to be at her side had been a sound decision or not. On balance, he believed it was. Staying in Gharnatah would have been more precarious with the unpredictable Abu Abdullah on the throne in al-Hamra.

Thomas looked out from the tent to where Isabel's quarters sat two hundred paces away. They comprised a grouping of larger tents, plus a farmhouse requisitioned from the previous owner in exchange for allowing him and his family to live. That had been Fernando's doing.

"Will the children be joining us?" Thomas asked.

"I don't think so. Juan is walking among the men—he likes to let them see he is willing to share their hardship—and the others are playing house. Juana claims she is too old, as does

2

the young Isabel, but Catherine is happy enough playing on her own while the others pretend. You should have brought your children, Thomas. I think Catherine has set her heart on your son."

"If only he was a prince."

"Princesses and queens can take lovers from common stock, they do it all the time. Kings even more so." She touched Thomas's wrist. "Even serious men take lovers." Her teasing had become a comfortable constant. Theresa was a handsome woman with a fine figure and luxurious red-brown hair. There were times Thomas wondered whether her words carried any deeper meaning.

"We are going to get wet," he said, stepping towards the door as he sought distraction from his thoughts.

"Then come under here with me." Theresa offered the meagre shelter of the length of cotton she had used. Thomas gripped one side and she the other as they dashed out into the rain, laughing so hard several of the soldiers sheltering as best they could stared at their flight.

When they entered the farmhouse, they found Isabel looking out at the rain from beneath a substantial awning raised on solid wooden piers. It had been erected to the rear of the house, now used by Isabel and her children. Thomas shook the soaked cotton before stepping beneath its shelter. He expected Isabel to turn, but she remained where she was. No doubt the hammering of the rain masked the sound of their arrival. She only noticed their presence as Theresa approached from the side. Isabel reached out and touched her hand, then looked beyond her to Thomas and offered a smile of welcome. Thomas had grown used to her presence the last year and a half, but her smile still touched something in him that had been dormant since he had lost his wife, Lubna. He tried to push thoughts of her aside as he crossed the flag-stones, aware he was leaving a trail of water. Lubna had been gone for over four years, but there was never a day he did not think of her. Even in the presence of the Queen of Castile. Thomas kissed Isabel's hand when it was offered. She indicated a table laid ready for their meal. Fine silvered glasses awaited the pouring of wine, and no doubt that too would be fine.

"Will Fernando be joining us?" Thomas asked.

"He rode out at dawn with Perez de Pulgar and two hundred men," said Isabel. "He intends to destroy the fields east of Granada. He said he might be gone a week or more."

Fernando, King of Aragon and Castile, was a man who believed in destroying perfectly good crops. It was a habit that had come back to haunt the army on more than one occasion. Now, a caravan of carts carried supplies from Córdoba and Sevilla, a journey of three or four days.

"He'll be lucky to set fire to anything in this rain," Thomas said.

"I told him I disapproved, but he does not listen to me these days. He says the war is ending and I should be pleased at whatever he does to hasten that day." Isabel took a seat on one side of the table. "I would ask your opinion, Thomas, but know there is little point. He does not listen to reason. Did you read those papers Columb sent?"

Thomas sat across from her as Theresa took a seat at the end of the table. "For what good they did me. I don't understand half of what is written there even when I can read it. I need a mariner. I do not understand what abaft or abeam mean, or even if they mean the same thing."

Isabel glanced at Theresa. "Can you send a message among the troops? There are bound to be mariners in their number. Find one to assist Thomas in this matter."

Theresa gave a nod, knowing the instruction could wait until they had eaten. The servants must have been waiting for them to settle because almost at once, food was carried in on platters. The servants disappeared, leaving them to select whatever they wished. Looking across the table, Thomas saw there was enough food for ten people. No doubt the staff would eat well on what they left.

Theresa poured wine for each of them, starting with Isabel, who gave a nod of thanks. She reached for her glass almost at once and drained it, holding it out to be refilled. When Thomas studied her face, he saw a tension there. It had been present for some time, ever since Thomas had tracked down a killer in Qurtuba and uncovered the extent of Fernando's infidelities. A king was not expected to be faithful to his queen, but Fernando had shown poor judgement in the women he chose. Including one Thomas had once loved many years before. At least he believed he had. Meeting the grown woman, he knew he had been too young to judge her true nature.

"What are you thinking?" asked Isabel. "You look a thousand leagues away."

Thomas forced a smile. "Only Columb and his foolishness."

"Is it foolishness, Thomas? If you believe so, you must tell me. He asks a great deal of us, and his plans may lead good men to their deaths."

Thomas dragged his thoughts back to the present. "I misspoke. I thought him foolish once, but no longer. I am minded to recommend you fund his expedition."

Isabel stared at Thomas as Theresa picked at small items of food. Most of it was familiar, but it was not the food of Castile. The dishes were of Moorish design, containing both more spice and more sweetness than the bland food usually served at Isabel's table when her husband was present. Fernando believed in meat, and a great deal of it.

"Can you make a case my men of God might agree to?" asked Isabel. "You know it is they who have the final say."

Thomas smiled. "Yes, I believe I can make a case."

"Explain it to me." Isabel reached for a round pastry sprinkled white with ground sugar. She popped it whole into her mouth and chewed. "Oh, Theresa, try this one, it is exquisite."

"I will explain it as soon as I have decided what that case

might be." Thomas also reached for one of the tiny pastries. Isabel was right, the balance of sweetness and spice was perfect, the meaty texture of fresh mushrooms sitting in a tart sauce. "I need to think of how to couch my recommendations in terms they will understand."

Isabel tried to hide a smile. "I am not sure you know words short enough for that." Despite her devoutness, Thomas was aware of her opinion on the lack of open-mindedness of most of the Cardinals who made up her advisory court.

"I will see what I can do."

Thomas watched Theresa select another sweetmeat. Her glass was empty and he reached across to refill it. Theresa stroked the back of his hand before he could withdraw it. Thomas saw Isabel observe the gesture, her face expressionless. A sense of intimacy had settled through the chamber, which unsettled him. He knew Isabel was aware of how he loved her, both as a woman and a queen, but he also knew neither of them would ever act on any feelings they might share. She was exalted, and he was … Thomas was no longer sure what he was. Everything he had once known lay in the past, and only an uncertain future remained.

"I need you with me in the morning," Isabel said. "A party of Turks arrived a few days ago and their leader claims he has a proposal to make me." She drank more wine, waited for Thomas to refill her glass. "I suspect they would prefer to talk with Fernando, but they will have to make do with a mere woman."

"No mere woman," Thomas said.

"We shall see. I heard they speak a little Castilian, but some form of Arabic is what they normally use in negotiations. I sent them a message saying I have someone fluent in that language."

"And who would that be?"

Isabel swatted a hand at him.

"I think their language differs from that of al-Andalus, but I will do what I can. Are they in the camp already, or—" Thomas broke off as Theresa gave a loud laugh. Both he and Isabel turned to stare at her.

A coarse grin sat on Theresa's face and her eyes were wide, the pupils dilated.

"I like the sound of Arabic." She reached out, trying to touch Thomas's hand again, but he did nothing to assist her. "I would like someone to whisper it into my ear as we lay—"

"Are you all right?" Isabel asked before Theresa could say exactly what she might like.

"I feel wonderful." Theresa rose and spun around, teetering as her balance failed.

Thomas glanced at Isabel before rising and going to stand beside Theresa. He gripped her wrists as she tried to wrap her arms around him. Turned his face aside when she tried to kiss him. And then, in a moment, Theresa changed from wanton to despairing. Her face paled, and she tugged free of his grip and ran to the edge of the terrace. She was doubled over by the time Thomas reached her and took her arm.

"What is it?"

"Sick."

Thomas pulled her upright and gripped her chin. He stared into her dark eyes, then touched the pulse in her neck. It beat too fast, too unsteady for his liking.

He turned back to Isabel. "Do not eat another scrap of food, Theresa has been poisoned." He tried to examine how he felt, but believed there were no symptoms. He wondered which of the items Theresa had eaten was to blame, but suspected he knew.

Isabel rose to her feet and came across on small steps. "How ill is she?"

"I don't know, not yet."

"Can you help her?"

"I don't know that either." He glanced at the table. "Leave everything where it is. Allow nobody to clear anything away. I want it all left as it is until I come back." He turned and led

Theresa out into the rain, then stopped. "And send one of your women to assist me."

Isabel stared at Thomas, her mouth open. "Who shall I send?"

"It doesn't matter. Anyone. Send them to my tent. Do it now."

CHAPTER TWO

By the time Thomas carried Theresa to his tent, she was barely conscious. He laid her on his bed and felt the pulse in her neck. Still too rapid, still stuttering, and he feared he might be too late. As he stood in indecision, a slim woman stepped beneath the shelter of the canvas. She glanced at Theresa, a frown troubling her brow.

"The Queen said you need me for some task."

Thomas had seen her before but didn't know her name or what her role was, not that either mattered at that moment.

"I have to go out. I want you to remove Theresa's clothes and cover her in a blanket."

The woman stared at Thomas with the same expression Isabel had shown and he shook his head.

"She is sick. Poisoned. I need charcoal to treat her, and someone must be here when I examine her body. I will do the work, but you must ensure propriety."

The woman continued to stare at him as Thomas walked out into the rain. He ran, the growl of thunder following him. The smiths worked beyond the main camp. Their braziers were covered with piecemeal arrangements of canvas and leather which allowed water to pour through the gaps. Thomas ignored the fires and went to the rear of the sheltered area and picked up two handfuls of charcoal.

"Hey, what are you doing?" One smith blocked Thomas's path, but he pushed past without comment and ran back to his tent.

As he entered, he saw the woman Isabel had sent had done as asked. Theresa lay with eyes closed, a coarse blanket covering her to the chin.

"Sit at the table and wait." Thomas did not soften his voice, uncaring whether the woman did as instructed. He glanced around until he found what he needed. Not what he would have chosen if he was in his own house perched on the slopes of the Albayzin, but better than nothing. He tipped an assortment of fresh nuts from a metal plate and laid two pieces of charcoal on it. He searched again and came up with a short dagger. He used the hilt to break the charcoal into small pieces, continuing to work until it was a fine dust.

"Wine," he said. "I need wine." He looked at the woman. "Go fetch some."

"What sort of wine? Do I take it from the Queen?"

"It doesn't matter what kind or quality, whatever you find first." He clapped his hands together. "Quickly. Go!"

The woman raced outside, lifting her skirts to keep the hem clear of the thick mud. Thomas went to Theresa and gripped the top of the blanket. He was about to draw it down when he hesitated, then lowered it to reveal only her shoulders. He leaned closer, examining her skin. He was looking for any sign of discolouration, relieved when he found none. He would examine Theresa in full later once the woman returned and he had forced the charcoal and wine into her. He lifted Theresa's eyelid to discover the pupil even wider than before. Sweat pricked her brow and her skin was pale. Thomas leaned close and sniffed at her mouth as she exhaled. All he sensed was the residue of the spice she had consumed.

"What are you doing?"

Thomas jerked upright, aware it would appear as if he had been trying to kiss the comatose Theresa.

"Did you get the wine?"

The woman held up a flagon. Thomas rose and took it, poured a little across the charcoal and mixed it to a paste. He set half aside, then added more wine to create a liquid. He brought the mixture back.

"Sit her up."

"She is naked," said the woman.

"I am aware of that. I am a physician and have seen a thousand women naked."

"But not Theresa!"

Thomas stared at the woman. "How can you be so sure? Sit her up if you want to see her live the day out."

For a moment, he thought she would disobey him, then she came and supported Theresa. Thomas ignored the display of her breasts and tilted her head back. He poured some charcoal and wine into her open mouth, then held it shut. He waited for her body to do what he knew it would. After a moment, she swallowed, and he gave a smile before pouring more of the liquid into her mouth. Satisfied it would stay down for now, he went for the thicker paste and did the same with that, alternating between paste and liquid until both were all used up.

"What is that for?" The woman accepted Thomas's skill now, her voice softer.

"It will gather any poison still in her belly and prevent more being absorbed. In a short while, I will give her another liquor that will make her bring everything up. Then I will see how she is in an hour." He glanced at the woman. "I need to examine her more delicately now. Sit at the desk and ensure I do nothing inappropriate."

"Is seeing her naked not inappropriate?"

"I have already told you, I am a physician. I have seen the—" Thomas stopped himself from saying what he had been about to reveal. What he had seen of Isabel was none of this woman's business.

Thomas waited until she was seated before removing the blanket covering Theresa. He leaned close without touching, checking for discolouration or rash, relieved when he found none. He turned her over, having to touch her skin. It was warmer than normal, but she had no fever. He checked her back, her buttocks and legs, satisfied when he found no sign the poison had passed into her blood. He would need to check again in an hour and every hour until morning. He wondered if Isabel could find somewhere better for Theresa to recover. If she recovered.

Thomas rolled her onto her side and covered her with the blanket again.

"I need to fetch some things. Stay with her."

Before the woman could answer, Thomas left the tent. He had little time, so Isabel first, he thought, as he made for the terrace where they had eaten. As he approached, he saw three men standing guard in front of the entrance. They moved to block his way.

"Queen Isabel ordered us to allow entry to nobody but one man."

"It is me who asked her to do that."

"You are the one called Berrington?"

"I am. Can I pass now?"

The men stepped aside to allow Thomas entry. "Your name was given."

Thomas was pleased to discover the table left exactly as it had been. There was no sign of Isabel, but he was not expecting her to be here. So much had changed since he and Theresa last walked on these flagstones. Thomas rested his knuckles on the smooth wood of the table-top and surveyed the remains of the meal. He had eaten some, Isabel less, Theresa possibly more than either of them, and he wondered which of the items had caused her sickness. That the cause might lie elsewhere did not even occur to him. Though if that was true, why had it only affected Theresa? He leaned over each of the items of food, looking for anything out of the ordinary. He had eaten the pigeon breast, but saw nothing different to what remained, so pushed it aside. He reached for the glass goblet Theresa had been drinking from and sniffed. It smelled of wine and nothing else. He dipped his finger and ran it along the bottom of the glass, but found no residue. He sucked on his finger. No taint. No bitterness. He set the three wineglasses and the two flagons of wine next to the meat. A significant amount of food remained. Rice cooked different ways, some spiced, some sugared, some mixed with vegetables, more mixed with meat. He closed his eyes and thought back before pushing all the rice away. He had no recollection of Theresa eating any.

Which left the sweet dishes and jellies, but they had not started on them when she showed symptoms, so he rejected those, too. Now only the mixed pastries and nuts remained. Thomas picked up three almonds and tasted each, wondering if the bitter sort had been used by mistake, but all were sweet. Apart from which, Theresa would have needed to eat several handfuls of bitter almonds to see any ill effects.

Thomas reached for the knife he had been using and cut open each of the pastries. He was half way through the task when he stopped and leaned closer. He used the tip of the knife to separate the pastry from its contents, then spread them across a plate. He looked around and reached for another pastry of the same kind. The same as he himself had eaten, as had Isabel. In fact, he recalled it had been she who had recommended the mushroom pastry to Theresa. When Thomas cut into another, he discovered what had poisoned her. He cut each of the mushroom tarts in two and placed them in separate piles. In one sat five containing poison mushrooms; in the other, seven with only the expected benign contents. Thomas had eaten one, Isabel two, and Theresa three. How many of those three had been the wrong kind? He had no idea. One at least, perhaps all.

Thomas reached for a jug of water. He spread the poison mushrooms across the plate, then washed them. He gave a nod. *Amanita*—the slightly yellow flesh and red top pitted with white spots could be nothing else. They were not usually fatal unless consumed in significant quantity, unless whoever had created these deadly delicacies had steeped even more of them in water, then distilled the liquor to increase its potency. Thomas recalled doing the same as a seventeen-year-old on the verge of turning from boy to man. He had been taught about the effects of the mushrooms by someone he had considered an old man at the time, back in the sleepy Marches town of Lemster he had once called home. Until they had accused him of murder, and then the town lost half its number to the pestilence. The old man had been a monk. Brother Bernard—the name came to Thomas in a rush of memory, together with green fields and hedges painted white with hawthorn flowers in the spring. Of the River Lugge and a girl by the name of Bel Brickenden. At one time, he thought they might marry, but that was before death came to the town and scrubbed the innocence from his soul.

The present returned only slowly to him. He smiled and shook his head. The boy he had been then would never have believed he could stand here, looking down at the detritus of a meal shared with the Queen of Castile. If he prayed, he would pray all three of the pastries Theresa ate were not tainted. He pushed away from the table, ignored the guards still positioned at the door, and made his way to the interior of the farmhouse. At least the rain had stopped so the soldiers outside would get no wetter—though it might take them until the morning to dry out.

Thomas saw no one as he walked through corridors dimly lit by small windows. Even on a bright day, the illumination would be scarce enough. Though he lacked someone to ask, he

14

knew where he wanted to be, and his nose led him in the right direction with only one false turn. He came to a forking of ways, hesitated, sniffed and turned right. He was rewarded when he walked into a large room where seven women stood around a table that filled over half the space. Three fires burned, making the air almost shimmer with the heat from them. All the women were dressed in thin cotton, their sleeves rolled back, sweat beading their brows.

"Are you lost, señor?" The largest of the women turned from where she had been issuing instructions to two younger girls. Thomas thought of Bazzu, the head cook in al-Hamra. The girls reminded him of those who scurried to her command. He tried not to think of one whose death he still felt responsible for.

"I believe I have found the place I need to be."

"Are you a cook?" She eyed Thomas up and down, unimpressed with what she saw. No doubt he lacked the girth a good cook was meant to possess. She shooed the girls away. "You know what to do, so make sure you do it well. Now, señor, what can I do for you?"

"Did you cook for the Queen at midday?"

"We all did. There was a great deal of food, but it seems she and her guests must have eaten it all for none has come back." She appeared disappointed.

"That was my doing. Some of the food was poisoned."

The cook stared at him, her mouth working as if trying to swallow a lump of gristle. "You are wrong, señor. I oversaw every single item taken to the Queen. It was of the highest quality, even if most was of Moorish recipe." The gristle appeared to be stuck again.

"I am sure you believe it to be so." Thomas made at least some attempt at smoothing her ruffled feathers, alien though it was to him. He had been forced to learn a whole range of new skills since working alongside Isabel. "Who oversaw the making of the small mushroom pastries?"

"That was Baldomero. In fact, he oversaw most of the dishes because the Queen instructed us to provide Moorish food." She glanced around at her workers. "None of us here are familiar with such … delicacies. We followed his instructions, but as I recall, the mushroom tarts he insisted on preparing himself. He said they were delicate and needed special handling."

Thomas looked around, but he was sure he had seen no man among those in the kitchen.

"Where is this Baldomero?"

"He left soon after we took the food out. He came to do a job, did it, and left."

"Show me where he worked."

For a moment, Thomas thought the cook was about to refuse him.

"I was a guest of Queen Isabel when her companion was taken ill. She has asked me to investigate." It was only a slight stretching of the truth. Isabel had not forbidden him to investigate, which as far as he was concerned was permission enough.

The cook stared at him, a spark of fear in her eyes Thomas was familiar with. "Are you the Berrington?"

"I am Thomas Berrington, yes."

The cook clapped her hands. "Show him where Baldomero worked. Do it now."

A slim girl of little more than fifteen years darted forwards and waited for Thomas to follow, her body quivering from either tension or fear. Fear most likely, the same as he had seen in the head cook. Thomas knew his reputation, even here where he tried to soften his reactions, but old habits died hard. He gave a curt nod. The girl skipped away, and he followed.

CHAPTER THREE

The table where Baldomero had worked was set to one side, separated from the other preparation areas by a good six feet. Thomas suspected the others had not wanted the Moorish spices to taint their dishes. As the girl turned to leave, considering her task complete, Thomas stopped her with a touch against her thin shoulder.

"What was he like?"

"Baldomero?" As if he had asked about someone else. "Kept to himself. Brought his own ingredients with him. Thought he was better than the rest of us."

"What did the head cook think of him?"

The girl shrugged.

"Did you try his food?"

The girl nodded.

"What was it like?"

"You ate it, didn't you? You tell me. You look like a man more used to spices than I am, or any of the rest of us here."

"But you tried it, didn't you?" Thomas nodded towards where the head cook was trying to ignore their conversation. "Your mistress must have done so to employ him."

"I heard he came recommended."

"Who by?"

Another shrug to show she didn't know. Thomas had no other questions, so turned away, but the girl was not quite finished.

"It was good, I liked it—the spice."

Thomas turned back. "So did I." He offered a smile and knew he must have got it almost right when the girl smiled back. She gave a bow and moved away to return to her work.

Thomas examined the few items remaining on the worktable, which had been cleaned when the man finished cooking. Three knives of varying lengths sat in a wooden block, and Baldomero had brought his own pans. A small array of stoppered pots sat on a shelf. Thomas reached for each, twisted the tops loose and sniffed. He recognised the herbs and spices used by Belia when she cooked for them, the same Lubna had used, and which even Thomas himself had used on the rare occasion he cooked for himself.

There was nothing out of the ordinary—at least nothing that would be out of the ordinary a league north in Gharnatah. Thomas turned and spoke loud enough for the head cook to hear.

"Did Baldomero bring his own ingredients?"

The woman made a show of being interrupted. "Most of them. He asked for lamb and beef and we supplied the pigeon and flour, but he brought everything else."

"There is nothing here anymore other than a few spices."

"He took most away with him and we threw the rest out. We would use none of it."

"Threw it where?"

The cook spoke to the girl again. "Show him."

She hurried across. Thomas followed her outside to where two piles sat at a distance from the rear of the farmhouse. Three dogs searched through the discards, but ran off as soon as Thomas and the girl approached.

Thomas ignored the pile the dogs had been scavenging in

and knelt to examine the discarded vegetables. The girl hovered nearby, and he told her she could go before picking up a stick and starting his search. He saw beans, peas, sugar cane, beets and carrots. He also saw an array of mushrooms. These he picked out and set aside. Then he found what he was looking for. The unmistakable red and white cap of *amanita*. There was one entire mushroom and one quarter piece. He rose and took them back inside.

"Did you see Baldomero using these in his tarts?" he asked the head cook.

She examined the mushrooms resting in Thomas's palm.

"Never seen them. Why?"

"Do you recognise them?"

She gave a shake of her head, which made Thomas wonder at her ability as a cook.

"These are what poisoned Theresa."

"Theresa? It was she who was poisoned? You did not say."

"I am saying now."

The cook looked down at the red and white mushrooms again. "Will she die?"

"I don't believe so."

When the cook met his eyes again, she said, "You are the physician, are you not? The one who repaired Prince Juan's leg? The one who assisted at the birth of Princess Catherine? I see now why Queen Isabel has taken you into her employ."

"This Baldomero, do you know where he lives? Among the soldiers or somewhere apart?"

"He comes from Granada whenever the Queen requests Moorish food, but I do not know where he lives."

"So how do you ask him to come?"

"I send a message to the head cook in the palace and she passes it on."

"Bazzu?" Thomas said.

"Do you know her? I heard a rumour you used to live in Granada."

"More than a rumour. How do you know Bazzu?"

"I worked alongside her many years ago, before she went to the palace. She was already well thought of, and I doubt she even remembers me."

Thomas heard something in her voice. Jealousy perhaps, or something else? He knew he lacked Jorge's skill to understand what it was.

"I will remember you to her if you tell me your name." It was irrelevant, and Thomas knew he had more important things to do, but asked anyway.

She hesitated a moment. "Maria de Henares." She spoke in a low voice, as if she didn't want her staff to hear. Perhaps she feared they might start calling her by name.

Thomas returned to find Theresa still unconscious. The woman sat at the table, though her eyes looked heavy.

"Has she moved?" Thomas asked.

"Not a muscle."

He went and checked, but found no change from when he left. At least she was no worse. He took the other chair at the table, opposite the woman.

"I have prepared something that is going to make Theresa sick. You can stay or you can leave. I can manage on my own for this. But I will need you to return in an hour because I have something else I have to do."

The woman stared at him. She was pretty, fine-boned with luxurious dark hair. Her clothing set her apart as one of the ladies who attended Isabel. Most of the time, Thomas ignored them.

"I will help," she said. "I have children, and a husband who likes wine too much, so someone vomiting is nothing I have not seen often enough before. I will stay as long as you need me." She looked around the tent. "I will have another bed brought in, if that is acceptable to you?"

"It is." Thomas rose and went to where the liquor had been

steeping long enough. He swirled the glass jar before returning with it. "Help me sit her up."

The woman knelt beside the bed and lifted Theresa, the tendons standing out in her slim arms.

Thomas put two fingers into Theresa's mouth and opened it. Theresa gave no sign she was aware of what he was doing. Thomas poured a third of the liquid into her mouth, then held it shut. He waited. Waited a little longer. Theresa's automatic response came and she swallowed. Thomas repeated the process until all the liquid was gone.

"Lie her on her side," he said, then went to fetch a leather bucket. "You might want to stand at a distance."

The woman backed off a few paces. Thomas watched Theresa's face and chest. The expected reaction came swiftly. Her throat constricted, and she vomited a mixture of liquid and charcoal into the bucket. Her eyes remained closed, but her chest heaved for air. She wasn't finished yet, Thomas knew, rewarded with a second expulsion of her stomach contents.

"Water," he said without looking around. A moment later, the woman placed a mug in his hand. He sat Theresa up and forced the water into her, waiting to see if that too would be ejected. After a while, he laid her on her side again.

"I have done what I can. Now I need to leave. Give her water, plenty of it, and if you need help, send for someone."

"When will you return?"

"I don't know. Later today, I hope, but it might be tomorrow."

"Tomorrow?"

"I have to go into Gharnatah if Isabel will allow it." He saw the woman's eyes widen at his use of the Queen's name and knew he might have made a mistake.

———

As Thomas made his way towards the farmhouse where they had eaten, the rain clouds had moved north and the heat of the sun raised steam from tents, clothes and the churned mud. He had almost reached his destination when a voice hailed him. Thomas slowed and looked around. A rangy figure strode across the ground as if the mud was not sucking at his boots in the same way as everyone else's. Martin de Alarcón raised a hand in greeting.

"Are you going to the same place as me, Thomas?"

"If you mean Isabel, then yes."

"I do mean the Queen. I hear you ate with her today."

"Did you also hear Theresa was taken ill?" Thomas started to walk again, Martin falling in at his side.

"I did not. Was it something she ate?"

"You could say that. She was poisoned."

Martin stopped abruptly. "How sick is she?"

"She hasn't regained consciousness since I treated her."

"Are you worried?"

"Of course I'm worried. She ate at least one tart containing *amanita*. She might have eaten more. If it was one, she should be all right. If she ate three, maybe not."

"Does the Queen know?" Martin started walking again.

"We were all three at the table, so she knows."

"I mean, does she know how ill Theresa is?"

"That is why I am going to her now. And you?"

"She has a task for me. No doubt the same task I have been working on fruitlessly for the last eight years, but one day, Boabdil might weaken and we can end this war once and for all."

"Not so fruitless, then," Thomas said. "Without you, we would not be gathered here now. You have shortened the war by years, Martin."

"I wish it felt that way. That man is…" Martin shook his head. He had no need to tell Thomas how difficult Abu Abdullah, Sultan Muhammed XII of Gharnatah, could be.

They entered the farmhouse and kicked off their boots, which were caked with thick mud. A guard informed them the Queen was talking with her advisors and they would have to wait. Thomas led Martin to where he had eaten. He saw they had cleared away the food, the table now set for another meal. He wondered how Isabel would feel about eating after what had happened. No doubt the food served at her next meal would be plain Castilian fare.

"You are going to talk to him?" Thomas asked. Both men stood at the edge of the terrace and stared across to where the fabled palace of al-Hamra sat atop its red hill.

Martin sighed. "It is what I do, is it not? It is what Isabel and Fernando see me as doing." He shook his head. "I had another life once, before we captured him."

"Before you turned him to your will," Thomas said.

"Yes, that too."

"You did too good a job. He is your plaything now."

"Once perhaps that was true. Of late, he has discovered his courage again." Martin glanced at Thomas. "Did he have courage before?"

Thomas smiled. "Oh, he did. He was magnificent. A leader of men and a fierce warrior. I have stitched his wounds, both his and his brothers'. He had two, but one died. Now there is only Abu Abdullah and Tarfe. I think sitting on the throne changed him. He is beset by fears and phantoms these days. But you know all this, don't you?"

Martin gave a soft laugh. "Are you not concerned you are revealing secrets? Even if we are on the same side now?"

"Are we on the same side? Yes, I expect we are." Thomas did not feel as if he had switched loyalties, only that he carried no loyalty towards Abu Abdullah. Gharnatah owned his heart, not its leader. And now he had another to serve: Isabel, Queen of Castile. A woman he loved as much as he had ever loved any other than Lubna, and she was beyond his love now.

Thomas was drawn from his thoughts by approaching footsteps. He turned to see Isabel enter behind a guard, who she sent away.

"If they had told me sooner it was you, Thomas, I would have come at once. You too, Martin. How is Theresa?"

"No better, but no worse. I need to go into Gharnatah. The man who made the tarts that poisoned her lives there."

"Will it help her if you find him?"

"It will help me kill him," Thomas said.

"Not again," said Isabel.

"It was not Theresa the harm was meant for. The man wanted you dead."

"What was it?"

"The mushroom tarts," Thomas said. "Some had *amanita* mixed with them. I have purged Theresa and one of your ladies is staying with her until I get back."

Isabel stared at Thomas for a long time without speaking, then her gaze shifted to Martin de Alarcón.

"You are going to see our friend in the palace?" she asked.

"Do you have any last-minute message for him, Your Grace?"

"Tell him I want the war to end without bloodshed."

"It is already too late for that," said Martin.

"Without too much more, then. Is he a reasonable man?"

Martin shook his head. "He is not. Ask Thomas the same and he will confirm my answer. Boabdil is a fool, afraid of the shadows of birds and the muttering of his own citizens."

"As well he should be," Thomas said.

Isabel shifted her attention back to him. "Go with Martin, he will get you inside the city walls. Find this man if you must, but return to me as soon as you can. I will not have Theresa languishing for lack of your attention."

Thomas walked beside Martin in search of two mounts to take them the short distance to Gharnatah's walls.

"She relies on you a great deal," said Martin.

Thomas tried to hear any note of judgement in the words, but failed.

"She needs good people around her. People like you. I do what I can, but fear it is not enough."

"More than if you did nothing. Who is this man you seek? Another of your distractions?"

"Is an attempt on Isabel's life a distraction? I think not."

"No, of course not. But had she eaten those tarts instead of Theresa, you would have saved her, would you not?"

"Isabel is slighter than Theresa, and her constitution not so strong since the difficulty of Catherine's birth."

"It is one reason she wants you at her side."

They came to where several hundred horses were held inside a rough wooden fence. Its creation had taken half the trees from the hillside, the ragged stumps that remained a testament to the work. Martin asked for two mounts and a man went to fetch the first two he could round up.

"Do you intend to talk with Abu Abdullah?" Thomas asked.

"No point my going otherwise. Why—do you want to see him, too?"

"I don't, but I would like to get inside the palace. If I am with you, that will be all the easier."

Martin laughed. "I will tell the guards you are my servant, that should do the trick. Unless any of them recognise you, and then you are on your own."

"It has been some time since I entered there," Thomas said. "I hear he changes the guards often for fear they might turn on him."

"With good reason."

As they mounted the horses and set out, Thomas worried that Isabel was right and his journey was a distraction from helping Theresa. Would finding the cook make any difference? The deed was done now, and even killing the man would not take it back. At least he would never be allowed entry to Isabel's kitchens again.

As they neared the open city gate, Thomas changed his mind.

"When we are inside the walls, I will leave you, Martin. I need to see someone else before I go to the palace. I am sure I can find my own way inside."

CHAPTER FOUR

As Thomas watched Martin climb the slope towards the palace, he wondered if he had made the right decision not to accompany him. There was no guarantee he would gain admittance on his own. But if Jorge couldn't find a way in, then nobody could. Thomas turned away and crossed Hattabin Square, heading for the alleys that would lead him to his old house and the family he had neglected for far too long.

When he entered the courtyard, he heard laughter and stopped in the shade, a strange reluctance filling him. Out on the sun-dashed flagstones, Usaden was teaching Will and Amal how to foil an attacker when you possessed no weapon. Watching them, Thomas wondered if it wasn't more of a game than a serious exercise. If so, it was good. He worried Will was too obsessed with fighting. As the grandson of Olaf Torvaldsson it was understandable, but Thomas didn't want sweet Amal to pick up on the same blood-thirstiness as her brother. He slipped away unseen and entered the house.

Thomas stopped dead in the doorway, unsure whether to back away. Belia sat in a low chair, her robe open on one side to reveal her breast, to which her ten-month-old son was suckling with gusto. Close by sat Jorge, an indulgent expression on his face, and Thomas felt a sense of satisfaction replace his previous reluctance as he observed what he had helped to give this couple. Thomas was Jahan's biological father, but that was little more than a nicety. The boy belonged to Jorge and Belia. He was their son. Just as Will was Thomas's son, despite his mother Helena continuing to deny him the certainty he craved.

As if sensing his presence, Belia glanced up and gave a smile, wide and welcoming.

"Thomas!" She eased Jahan from her breast and drew her robe closed. She handed the boy to Jorge, who placed him against his shoulder and rubbed his back. Belia rose and came across on bare feet. She embraced Thomas. "What brings you home? Did you miss us too much?"

"Always," he said, wondering if he regarded this house as home or not anymore. "I came to see Da'ud, but I couldn't do so without calling here first."

"Did the children see you? They ask all the time when you are coming home. Or when they can come to you. Was the journey far? Where are you living now? Qurtuba or Ixbilla?"

"I live a league south of here in the Castilian camp."

"How long have you been there?" Jorge rose and came across. As he touched Thomas's shoulder, Jahan gave a loud belch then settled.

"Here, give him to me," said Belia. "He will sleep now, I'll put him upstairs in our room."

When she had gone, Jorge said, "The army of Castile has been camped outside the city walls for near two months, and only now you come and see us? Has Isabel got you so much under her thumb she doesn't allow you to visit your family?"

"I have been busy."

"I expect you have. Is that a reason, or an excuse?"

Thomas looked at the man who was closer to him than anyone else in the world and wondered if he deserved Jorge's rebuke. He expected he did. He did not understand why he had not come before. The walls of Gharnatah were as open as a bucket with no sides. People and goods flowed in and out constantly. It was almost as if the Castilian army was not there at all.

"It's an excuse," Thomas said. "I accept I should have come sooner."

"Except you didn't." Jorge shook his head, and Thomas knew he wasn't forgiven yet. He wondered whether he ever would be. "Amal calls Belia her Ma now. You are father to Jahan and he has hardly even seen you."

"No, you are Jahan's father, you know you are. He need never know of my part in his conception." Thomas stared into Jorge's eyes. "I did it for my love of you."

Jorge returned the stare before smiling. "Don't tell that to Belia. She still thinks you are half in love with her after what the pair of you did."

"Perhaps I am, but she is yours heart and soul and we both know it."

"Yes, we do. Now come and hold your children while they still remember who you are." Jorge led the way into the court-yard and Thomas followed. From upstairs came the sound of Belia singing her son to sleep. The tune was alien to his ears, but soft and comforting all the same.

Outside, Jorge was mock punching Will. Thomas watched for a moment, aware his son had grown in the months he had been away. Ten years old now, Will might be taken for a man. He was tall with broad shoulders, his pale hair hanging along his back in a plaited knot, just like that of his *morfar*, Olaf Torvaldsson.

It was Amal who saw Thomas first. She gave a high squeal and ran towards him, arms out. She too had grown. Four years old and already a miniature copy of her mother.

Thomas knelt and scooped her up, swinging her around, swinging her upside-down to peals of laughter. Then he held her to his chest and let her kiss his face all over. All his doubts, all his fears crumbled into insignificance beneath her onslaught of love. They would return, he knew, but tempered by what was happening here.

When he put Amal down, she tried to climb up his leg, but now Will was approaching, more circumspect, as if unsure of the welcome he would receive. He was too big to be swung around and tumbled upside-down. For a moment they stood facing each other, then Thomas opened his arms and Will came into them. The hug he returned almost took the breath from Thomas's lungs. Will was only an inch or two shorter than Thomas and would tower over him before he became a man, just as Olaf did.

Thomas kissed his face and tried to hug back as hard as he could before holding Will at arms' length, his hands on his shoulders.

"Have you been taking care of everyone like I asked?"

"Of course I have, Pa." Even Will's voice sounded deeper, though he was not yet of an age for such to happen. "With the help of Usaden."

Thomas looked beyond his son to the Gomeres mercenary who had turned his back on his old profession to become an integral part of this family.

"Is that true?" he asked.

"Some of it, but I can teach Will little more now. He has grown to be a better fighter than I am."

"Not true," said Will, and Thomas was pleased at the show of modesty.

"He is not as fast, I admit," said Usaden, "but he is stronger. And with an axe he is unbeatable, just like Olaf."

"I see you were teaching Amal a trick or two as well when I came in."

"I saw you watching, but we had not finished our training, so I made no mention of you to them. And yes, a girl needs to know how to defend herself. Are you back for good, Thomas?"

He shook his head. "I have people to see and things to do. I don't know how long I can stay."

Usaden nodded as if he understood and made no judgement.

Thomas felt an arm snake around his waist as Belia came to stand beside him, as though she was his woman, not Jorge's. Thomas glanced to where his friend stood and saw only an indulgent smile. Life had taken a strange turn, but Thomas was growing accustomed to it.

"Stay tonight, at least," said Belia. "I will cook a feast and you and Jorge can drink wine until you cannot stand up, and then you can sleep in your own bed."

"I wish I could, but I have to return to Theresa."

"Don't tell me she has finally seduced you?" said Jorge.

"She lies close to death. Poisoned. It is the reason I am here. The reason I need to visit Da'ud." Thomas glanced at Belia, who continued to lean against him. "I would welcome your advice. You are better with herbs than me."

Belia released her hold and took a step back, her face serious. "What nature of poison, do you know? Have you given her charcoal? What else?"

"*Amanita*," Thomas said. "And yes, I used charcoal, then made a liquor up as you showed me, but still she languishes."

"*Amanita* rarely causes death unless given in large doses," said Belia. "Are you sure there was not something else?"

"It was baked into small mushroom tarts. Most were safe, a few were not. I suspect Theresa ate at least three of the wrong kind."

"Were you together?" asked Belia. "It is strange she ate all the bad ones while you had none."

"We were with Isabel, and yes, it is strange. I believe they were meant for the Queen, not me or Theresa. I doubt their maker even knew we would be there."

"Have you captured the woman who baked them?" asked Jorge, who had come closer.

"It was a man, and no—he has returned to Gharnatah. At least, he lives within its walls. If he has any sense, he will have fled al-Andalus entirely." A thought occurred to Thomas. "He intended the poison for Isabel, he must have done. But I was told this man is a skilled cook and was sought out especially to prepare Moorish food for her. He is known to Bazzu, so there can be no stain on his reputation or he would never have been allowed near the food presented to Isabel. Which means he must have been put up to it by someone else." Thomas stared up at the palace of al-Hamra, illuminated in the late afternoon sunlight. "Perhaps Abu Abdullah sent him. It's the kind of underhand scheme that would appeal to him. What if his instruction was to poison Isabel but not kill her? He might want her weak, but not dead. Or even…"

"Even what?" said Jorge. "It seems you are creating an entire conspiracy on very little evidence."

"I am aware of that, which is why I need to seek the evidence. But not today. Today I need Theresa to recover. Will you come and help me, Belia?"

She gave a nod. "You said you wanted to see Da'ud, too, didn't you? Then you need to know he is unwell. No, more than unwell, he is dying."

"Da'ud?" Thomas experienced a sharp wave of grief. He had always believed Da'ud would live forever.

"He is an old man, you know he is, and his life has been hard. But yes, you need to see him while you can. He will also have medicines you might need."

"Which is why I intend to go to him, but now more so than ever. Is there any doubt? Who has attended him?"

"I have, and one or two others. Not you, obviously, but what ails Da'ud is beyond even your skills, Thomas. I am sorry, I know he means a lot to you."

"When I first came to Gharnatah, he was the only physician who welcomed me. Even now there are few who do. You will come with me? To Da'ud as well as Theresa?"

Belia looked towards Jorge, who had watched the conversation with his usual good humour.

"Belia is her own woman," he said. "She can do whatever she wants, as well you know. But you should not disappear so soon after you arrived."

"Do you think I want to? Theresa needs me. I believe she needs Belia. Let us do this and I will return tomorrow. I need to find this man and your friend on the hill can help with that."

"I have many friends on the hill," said Jorge.

Belia laughed. "You can admit to it, I know you love Bazzu. Just so long as you don't love her more than me."

Jorge stroked Belia's arm. "How could I ever love anyone more than you?" He turned to Will and Amal, who had watched the entire conversation. "You two come with me. I need your help in buying enough food for a feast tomorrow."

"What day is tomorrow?" asked Amal. "Is it an important day?"

"It is the day your father comes to eat with us." He glanced at Thomas. "And he will stay the night. Perhaps several nights. That is correct, is it not?"

Thomas knew he could make no promises, but he could manage a day, perhaps even a night. Provided Theresa recovered. He wished he could return to this house and never leave again, but he had also made a promise to Isabel. She needed him. Perhaps, when the war that once seemed endless did end, she might not need him anymore. Then he could sink back into a welcome obscurity.

CHAPTER FIVE

Thomas offered a puzzled glance at Belia. Da'ud al-Baitar looked healthy enough. Unless he looked closer. He saw the man was thinner, his dark skin paler than it had been. His eyes remained as sharp as ever, but he was slower to rise than he might once have been as he struggled to lift himself from the cushion he was sitting on. Thomas offered a hand, pleased when Da'ud was not too proud to accept it.

"I hear you are the lover of the Spanish Queen now, Thomas. What are you doing here?"

"Visiting an old friend." He did not correct Da'ud, aware half the people who knew of his new role believed the same. The other half considered him a traitor. Neither were correct, but beliefs became too ingrained to change and Thomas could no longer bother making the effort.

Belia kissed Da'ud on both cheeks.

"This one has been keeping me updated on your exploits," he said.

"I am afraid I need your help," Thomas said.

"Whatever I can do, but I am not much use these days. Did Belia tell you what ails me?"

"Only that you are unwell."

Da'ud gave a laugh that degenerated into a fit of coughing that had him leaning over, hands on knees. Thomas waited for it to pass.

"I have a growth on my liver," said Da'ud when he recovered, though a sheen of sweat stood out on his brow. He touched his side through the robe to show the location.

"I will examine you if you allow me. You will not be wrong in your diagnosis, I am sure, but I would like to satisfy myself."

Da'ud stared at Thomas for a long time before nodding. "You will come to the same conclusion, but at least you will come to it for yourself. I know you, Thomas, you trust nobody, not even me."

"Did you not fix me when I was injured all those years ago?"

"I did. But only because you could not fix yourself." Da'ud rose and loosened the tie on his robe before hesitating. He glanced to where Belia stood behind Thomas. "Perhaps Belia should go to my workshop and gather whatever you need. That is what you came for, is it not?"

"It is."

"I like that you never sweeten your words with syrup, just as you never sweeten your remedies. It makes people dislike you, but at least they get the truth, and often as not a cure. Besides, Belia has already seen everything this old man has to offer, and she is unimpressed."

"Do not be so sure."

Da'ud gave another laugh, gentler on his body this time. "You do live with a eunuch, so I expect you have little to compare me with." Da'ud laughed again when he saw the look Belia cast in Thomas's direction. "Oh, I know who the father of Jahan is, though I believe few others do."

"That was duty, nothing more," Thomas said.

"A duty any man would envy. Now leave us, my sweet, so I can talk to Thomas in private. Take whatever he needs, for it is of little use to me anymore." When Belia had gone, Da'ud continued to disrobe. "Send Jorge and that sturdy son of yours with Belia next time to pack up everything here. Not yet, perhaps, but you will know the time. Now, do your worst, I am too old to care."

Thomas examined Da'ud for a moment without touching him. The man's dark skin showed a yellowing, which was more prominent in his eyes. The growth within his body caused a swelling on the right side of his belly, and finally, Thomas traced it with his fingers.

"Does it hurt when I press here?"

"It does. I try to avoid doing such, but these days it requires not even a touch. I use poppy, but it can only do so much."

Thomas stood behind Da'ud and ran his fingers along his spine. Next he felt his shoulders, then beneath his arms.

"It has not spread yet, which is good."

"It has not," said Da'ud, "but that makes no difference, does it?"

"I cannot cut it out, so you are right. How long have you known?"

"Half a year."

"That long?"

"It will not be much longer. Have you finished molesting me?"

"Not quite." Thomas examined Da'ud's genitals, feeling once more for lumps or growths, relieved not to find any. Though, as Da'ud had said, it made little difference.

When he finished his examination, Thomas went to the stone sink in one corner and washed his hands.

"You can dress again now."

"I might not if you send Belia to examine me as you have done."

"I would like you to live a little longer if possible."

"Ah, but what a way to die." Da'ud met Thomas's eyes. "She was fine, was she not?"

"I told you, it was duty, nothing more."

"My memory must be slipping. You will come when I send for you?"

"Yes, I will come."

Da'ud smiled, his relief showing. "It will not be long, though I am not afraid to die. I have started visiting the mosque again. It is strange how the prospect of your own mortality makes you think of the next world more than this one. You do not believe, do you?"

"You know what I believe, my friend. I believe in good men and women. I believe in friendship and family. And I believe in knowledge."

"Yes. Knowledge is good, but family is better. I have sacrificed my own needs in service to others. Do not do the same, Thomas. What is it like, working for the Queen of Castile?"

"Different."

"I expect it must be."

———

"How long does he have?" asked Belia as they climbed the switchback path through the Albayzin.

"You tell me."

"You forget I am not Lubna. I know herbs and medicinal plants, but I do not know the human body like you do and she did. I would guess not long. A few months."

"More like a few weeks." Thomas carried a heavy wooden box which Belia had filled with medicines and liquors. She carried another almost as big. Da'ud was right—he had no need of them anymore.

"Then you have to be close."

"If I can. You know it's not so simple. But I will make up the right mixture for you to give him if I can't be there."

"No."

"You won't help him?"

"If it was help he needed, yes, but it has to be you, Thomas. Da'ud is closer than a father to you. It must be you with him at the end. You know it does."

"I will try."

"You will do it," said Belia, her tone brooking no argument. "Now, do you want me to come to the Castilian camp with you?"

"Would you? I can fix bodies, but you are better for what ails Theresa. I left a woman looking after her, but she knows nothing."

"If I come, the others must as well. You are not to abandon Will and Amal again so soon."

"I only have a small tent."

"Then we will keep each other warm, and I will tell Jorge not to accost me in front of you."

"Why change the habit of a lifetime?"

"Do not change the subject. We all come or none of us come. Agreed?"

Thomas let his breath go. He was surrounded by women, each of who held a great many opinions, almost all of them concerning his lack of duty.

"Yes, we all go. I will see if I can arrange additional accommodation. There must be more in the farmhouse Isabel is using, it is big enough."

"I expect you could always share her chamber. I am sure she would not object."

Thomas turned to look at Belia, relieved to see her smile, for her voice had sounded serious.

———

The day was fading fast before everything was arranged. Jorge wanted to take more clothes than a camel could carry, but Belia persuaded him they were not abandoning the house, only taking a leave of absence. By the time they reached the

Castilian camp, full dark had arrived. Thomas showed them his tent before saying he had to visit Isabel.

"Will you be all right with Theresa?" he asked Belia, and all she did was wave him away with her fingers.

The dark-haired woman he still did not know the name of accompanied him to the farmhouse.

"I must thank you for your dedication," Thomas said.

"I did it for Theresa. We have been friends for many years."

"I didn't know that."

"Theresa tells me you are a man who misses much even as you see a great deal. Will she live?"

"Now Belia is here, yes. She knows more than anyone about cures for what ails Theresa." Thomas glanced at the woman. Her face was pale with exhaustion and he wondered if she had slept at all. "How long have you served the Queen?"

"Queen now, is it, not Isabel?" Her lips tightened as she suppressed a smile. "All my adult life I have served her. My father was in her brother's employ. I was a child in King Juan's court and always knew I would serve Isabel."

Light spilled from the terrace onto her face as they approached. She yawned and stretched.

"I will leave you now, Thomas. I think I may sleep for a week."

Thomas watched her walk away on delicate steps and wondered if he would recognise her again if they passed in a corridor tomorrow or the day after. He hoped he would. He realised he had not even asked her name.

He was taken to a room where Isabel sat in front of an unlit fire, despite the chill of the evening. An unused glass sat on a table at her side, a jug of wine waiting to be poured. When Thomas was announced, she rose, but he held a hand out and she settled back into the chair.

"My advisors stuff my head with too much information," she said. "Where have you been?"

"I did as you gave me permission to do and went into Gharnatah. I have brought Belia back with me. If anyone can help Theresa, it is her."

"Did you see your children while you were there?" She nodded at a chair set against the wall, and Thomas drew it across and sat.

"I brought them back with me. I didn't have the heart to abandon them again after not seeing them for so long."

"I told you to fetch them before. Why did you not?"

"A battlefield is no place for children."

"Mine are here."

"This is not a battlefield yet."

"So you can bring yours."

Thomas knew he was beaten. "Which is what I have done, though my tent is creaking at the seams. Fortunately, Usaden said he would find somewhere nearby."

"He is your mercenary, is he not?"

"He is."

"Pour me some wine, Thomas. And you will find another glass for yourself somewhere over there." She waved a hand in no particular direction.

"Have you done as I advised?" he asked once he had poured the wine and taken a mouthful, the taste rich on his tongue.

"You advise me on so much, Thomas. Which thing is it this time?"

"The food. I told you to find someone to taste your food."

"I cannot do that. I will not endanger another life, but I have given instructions that every item prepared for me is to be watched over by the head cook."

"And if she is the poisoner?"

"She has been in my employ for over a year, so if she intended to kill me, she has left it exceedingly late. I must trust someone, Thomas. Other than you, of course." She reached out a hand as if to take his, but they sat too far apart.

"Do you know where she came from before working for you?"

Isabel's face showed impatience. "I do not interview cooks myself, so no, I do not know, but she would have been recommended."

"Who interviewed her?"

"You are making too much of this, Thomas. You already know who poisoned my food. Seek the man out and punish him. I have too much to concern me at the moment to involve myself in things you are better equipped to deal with."

"Has Martin reported back to you yet?"

"He has not returned. No doubt Boabdil is attempting to turn him against me."

"He will have little luck in that endeavour."

"Martin is like you. Loyal." She reached for her glass, sipped at the wine.

"You need to go to bed, Isabel. You need sleep more than my company." Thomas rose and held his hand out to her.

"Are you offering to accompany me?" She took his hand and he drew her to her feet. She stood with the top of her head barely to his chin, her face turned up.

"When does Fernando return?"

She pulled a face. "When he has finished burning every-thing. And then he will start again here."

"Perhaps Martin will succeed and all this can end."

"Yes. Perhaps." Isabel lifted up and offered her cheek. He smelled the scent of her, heard the creak of whalebone sewn into her clothing. "Goodnight, Thomas. Take good care of Theresa."

"I have to return to Gharnatah in the morning."

"But you have brought everyone here."

"It is the matter of Baldomero, the cook who made the poisoned tarts. I must find him."

"Will you kill him, like you have killed your enemies before?" Something sparked in her eyes.

"I will expose him. If you wish it, I will bring him back to stand before you so you can offer judgement on him. I have grown tired of killing."

Isabel stole another peck on his cheek. "I wish you could persuade my husband of the same."

CHAPTER SIX

Thomas woke before dawn to a grey light spilling through the entrance of the tent. He eased his legs from beneath Will, lifted Amal from where she slept with her head on his chest, and rose while trying to avoid treading on the tangle of limbs. Theresa turned her head at his movement and smiled.

"Thank you," she mouthed.

Thomas went to the low bed she lay on and touched her neck. He held a finger to her lips to stop her saying anything until he was done, then leaned close.

"How do you feel?"

"As if I have been run over by a horse, but I have been worse."

"You have?"

"Once, perhaps. I am mending, Thomas, all thanks to you." She reached out to squeeze his hand.

"Not me. It was Belia was who has attended to you since yesterday, and your friend before that."

"I did not know about anyone else, but Belia told me what you did. You saved my life."

"You talked with her?" Thomas glanced to where Belia lay

43

curled against Jorge. "She said nothing to me about you being awake."

"Because I told her not to. I knew you would only have questions, so I told her to keep our secret. Jorge knew, but he promised as well."

"He did, did he?"

Theresa shifted on the bed, trying to sit up. "If you can help me, I would return to my room. I need to sleep longer, but I am better, I promise."

Thomas gave a quick glance around and knew Theresa was right, she would rest better in her own bed.

"You are sure you are well enough?" He feared the poison might still affect her.

"You are the physician, you tell me." She offered a smile. "I am naked beneath this blanket so it will take you no time at all to check my body for any signs. In fact, I might welcome the reassurance."

"I am sure you would. Yes, I see you are better." Thomas slid his arms beneath Theresa and lifted her, hoping the blanket would protect her modesty, but the warmth of her skin beneath his hands was an unwelcome distraction. He carried her from the tent and across to the farmhouse. "Where is your room?"

"Along the corridor and to the right, provided Isabel has not gifted it to someone else in my absence."

"She was concerned for you."

"Of course she was."

Thomas found Theresa's room and laid her on the bed, then turned his back as she slid beneath her own blankets. When he returned to the tent, Belia was awake and Jorge had taken the cot Theresa had vacated. Thomas kicked him with his toe.

"Get up, we're going to Gharnatah."

"It's not even dawn."

"It will be by the time you're ready. Come on, I need you."

"I know you do, but I need sleep more than I need you."

"Are we going home?" The conversation had woken Will, and his sitting up woke Amal beside him, though she lay on her back, only her eyes open.

"Not yet, if Belia will look after you until I return. And then I will see if I can find a bigger tent."

Will rose to his feet and stretched. "Can I go find Usaden and talk to the soldiers? I'd like to find out how good they are, what armaments they have."

"So you can report back to Olaf?" Thomas tried to hide his amusement. "You will find out nothing because most of these are men of Castile."

"I speak their language well enough," said Will. "And I saw other banners when we arrived. There are men of England, Francia, Germania and Italia. I think I might also have seen some Turks. I admit I don't speak all their languages, but you have taught me a little of yours, Pa. I like to know about different places in the world, about different people. Is there anything wrong in that?"

"No, there is nothing wrong. Nothing at all. Make sure Usaden is happy with the idea, I don't want you wandering around on your own."

"Pa…"

Thomas knew Will was growing up. Soon, if not already, he would no longer listen to his father's advice. Just as Thomas had not listened to his own father's—though he hoped he was a better father than his own had been to him.

The sun was still obscured behind the snow-capped peaks of the Sholayr as Thomas and Jorge made their way back the way they had come only the night before.

"I don't welcome another night in that tent," said Jorge.

"I intend to find us somewhere better as soon as I can."

"If you can't, we might just return to your house on the Albayzin." Jorge looked around. "Where are we going, anyway? I thought you got everything you needed from Da'ud yesterday."

"We need to visit the palace and your friend the cook."

"Bazzu? Why?"

"I want to find out what she knows about the man who poisoned Theresa, and where he lives. Isabel's head cook said she is known to Bazzu and sent a message for the man who baked the poisoned food."

"He'll have run by now," said Jorge. "But I have no objection to seeing Bazzu. You should call on Olaf and Fatima while you are there. They miss you too. You have responsibilities, Thomas. Don't neglect them."

It amused Thomas that Jorge should lecture him on responsibility. How the world had changed.

As they approached the inner gate to the palace, two guards moved to block their path, but when they saw Jorge, they stepped aside to allow them entry. One glanced at Thomas and offered a nod of recognition.

"I didn't expect that to be so easy," Thomas said.

"I come often enough, they are used to me by now."

"To visit Bazzu?"

Jorge laughed. "Despite what Belia says, and what I like the world to believe because it is good for my reputation, Bazzu and I have not enjoyed the pleasure of each other's bodies in over a decade."

Thomas slowed. "Truly? That is not the impression she gives."

"Bazzu likes to tease, you know she does. And where is the harm in a little innocent teasing? You and Theresa have done enough of it these last years, and I suspect it is the same with Isabel, is it not?"

Thomas recalled her playfulness of the night before. "She is always proper with me."

"Of course."

"So why do you come here?"

They entered the outer gardens. Dark yew and cypress ran

46

in perfect lines to frame distant hills. Water shimmered and flowers grew in abundance.

"I like to keep an eye on the harem. The eunuchs Abu Abdullah has put in place are competent enough, but none care as much as I do. And I'm helping Helena."

"Helena?"

"You remember Helena, don't you? Beautiful? Wanton? Scarred?"

Thomas slapped Jorge on the belly with the back of his hand. "Help Helena how?"

"She has returned to the harem, but not as a concubine. I believe she approached Abu Abdullah and he agreed."

"Why?"

"Why did he agree, or why did she approach him?"

"The second, though both are a mystery to me."

"Helena wants to help the women, I believe in two ways. The first is simple enough and even you can guess her purpose, but in case you have grown even more stupid since you went to work alongside Isabel, she trains them in how to act with a man. Nobody knows how to please a man better than Helena, but you are already aware of that. Second, she is advising them on what to do when the war is over. Their choices are limited, of course. Some wish to travel to Africa or the East. Arabia and the Ottoman Empire are Islamic, so they may find places there. Others want Castilian noblemen as husbands or lovers. It's not as if any of them expect fidelity in a man."

Thomas walked in silence for a moment, trying to work through what Jorge had told him before responding.

"All of this was Helena's idea?"

"It was."

They entered the outer corridors, the words of praise for Allah inscribed in a continual line of tiles above head-height. Cold words that might prove false: *There is no victor but Allah.* A claim that was soon to be put to the test.

"Abu Abdullah agreed to it?"

"He did."

"I don't understand. He held her captive for over a year. Mistreated her. Gave her to Abbot Mandana and his son as a plaything. And still she wants to serve him?"

"Not him," said Jorge, "the women. She wants to serve the women."

"We are talking of the same Helena, are we?"

Jorge laughed. "It took me by surprise, I admit. You should talk to her. She has changed. Changed more than I thought possible."

"She is still Helena," Thomas said as they turned into a wide corridor rich with the scent of cooking. "Besides, they would never allow me into the harem now I am no longer the Sultan's favoured physician." They entered the kitchen, passing through it to where Bazzu, the head cook, had her rooms. Bazzu claimed to know everything that went on in the palace. Thomas hoped she would also know where he could find the man he sought.

"Jorge! My sweet!" Bazzu rose from behind her desk and bustled around. She took Jorge's face in her hands and kissed him on the mouth. He appeared to enjoy the experience. "And Thomas—where have you been?" She came towards him and Thomas submitted to the same treatment, knowing resistance was impossible.

"He works for the Spanish Queen now," said Jorge.

"Why?"

"I believe he wants to be on the winning side."

"I do not want—"

Jorge waved Thomas's response aside. "He seeks your wise advice."

"And not my body? Is he of sound mind?"

"I wonder that myself, but you know how he is. Too serious for his own good."

Bazzu continued to stand in front of Thomas, her ample

figure pressing against his. He recalled when she would not have shown him such affection, but it appeared she might have finally forgiven him for the death of a young woman, Prea, many years before. If so, he had not yet forgiven himself.

"Tell me what you want of me, then. Have either of you broken your fast yet?"

"Thomas dragged me from my bed before I was even awake."

Bazzu clapped her hands together loudly. After a moment, a young woman appeared in the doorway.

"Fetch sweet rolls and … what would you each like?"

"Bread is fine for me," Thomas said, but Jorge had a long list which he went to pass on to the woman.

"I seek a man," said Thomas.

"You do? For any specific purpose?"

"As Jorge said, I serve Queen Isabel now. Someone tried to poison her."

Bazzu stared at him for a long moment before saying, "Is she all right?"

Thomas wondered what answer she might prefer, but Bazzu was too intelligent to believe Isabel's death could stop the war.

"Isabel is unharmed, but her servant, a friend of mine, almost died."

"I sympathise," said Bazzu, "but cannot see what help I can be in this matter."

"The cook who prepared the food lives in Gharnatah. His name is Baldomero de Pamplona. Isabel's head cook told me she sent word to you asking for someone who knew spices. She told me to send her regards."

"Isabel's cook? I do not believe I know her."

"Her name is Maria de Henares. She said she worked alongside you a long time ago, but told me you would likely not remember her."

Bazzu stared into space for a while before shaking her head.

"The name is not familiar, but I worked with many cooks when I was young and lithe. Perhaps if I met her, I would recall. How long ago did she say?"

"She didn't, but I got the impression it was some time ago. You made an impression on her, it seemed."

"So why does she cook for the Queen of Castile?" Bazzu patted his cheek. "No matter. Is she happy in her work? Fulfilled?"

"She cooks for Isabel, so I expect she is fulfilled. As for happy, I could not say, but she remembers you. She told me she has asked for your help before when Isabel wants spiced food."

"I have no recall, but my girls protect me from most such requests. They do not wish to trouble me with trivial matters. Did you say she asked for Baldomero specifically?"

"She wanted someone expert with spice."

"That would be Baldomero. Most here know him and would have contacted him directly. He has worked for me in the past, not so long ago, in fact." She leaned against the table and tapped at the pale wood with a finger. "He cooked for the Sultan two weeks since when he had visitors from Turkey."

"Turkey?" Thomas thought of the Ottoman delegation Isabel wanted him to be present for.

"It is east of Greece and north of—"

"I know where Turkey is. Do you know where this Baldomero lives?"

"Not exactly, but…" She rose and went to a set of shelves. Bazzu ran her finger along the journals sitting there. She pulled one out, took a look, then replaced it. "Somewhere here … yes, this one." She withdrew another and brought it back to the table. She leafed through the pages before giving a grunt and turning the journal around. "He lives here. At least he did when I first used him, which was several years ago now. He is a skilled cook in great demand." She glanced up to meet Thomas's eyes. "Are you sure it is Baldomero who prepared this poisoned dish?"

"As sure as I can be."

"Then I have misread him all these years. You cannot trust men, Thomas, I learn that even more the older I grow. You and Jorge are the exceptions, of course."

"Of course."

Thomas read the location of Baldomero's house. He knew where it lay, surprised it was not in the jumble of the Albayzin, but on this side of the Hadarro.

"Is he much in demand?"

"Very much so. He is skilled in many cuisines, but in particular that of North Africa. He is an artist with spice. What poison did he use?"

"*Amanita*," Thomas said, and saw Bazzu nod.

"Then perhaps he meant not to kill. He may only have wanted the Spanish Queen to have visions and change her mind about destroying Gharnatah. I have partaken myself occasionally and it can be a most pleasant experience, especially if shared with the right man."

Thomas made no mention of his own experience with the mushrooms. The girl Bazzu had sent away returned alongside Jorge with an armful of sweet pastries. She scattered the delicacies on the table, oblivious of the papers already there, then ran out.

"And bring coffee for these two beautiful men," Bazzu shouted after her.

Jorge perched on the edge of the table and picked through the offerings until he found one that met with his approval. He took a large bite and chewed, pastry flaking onto his chest.

"I had a woman here recently asking after you, Thomas," said Bazzu.

"Jorge told me Helena had returned to the hill." He reached out and picked up a soft roll. The bread was fresh, still warm, and delicious.

"Oh, Helena comes all the time. And yes, she also talks a

51

great deal of you. I believe she has changed, but this was another woman. She claimed to be a Countess."

Thomas stopped chewing and swallowed with difficulty. "A Countess? Did she give a name?"

"She may have, but if she did, I forget what it was. Do you want me to ask one of the girls if they recall it?"

"Was she tall, around my age, and beautiful?"

"She was all of those things, though I would have put her as at least a decade younger than you."

"I have had a hard life. Are you sure she mentioned me?"

"I am. She came here because she was told I know you." She glanced at Jorge. "She also asked after you, my sweet, but mostly about Thomas. I am sorry. She must be a fool if she prefers him over you."

"Did she say what she was doing in the palace?" Thomas asked.

"She did not, but after she had gone, I asked. Rumour has it she is sleeping with Abu Abdullah, so it intrigued me why she wanted to know about you. She even asked where your house was on the Albayzin."

Thomas felt a finger of dread creep through him.

"Did you tell her?"

"I said I did not know. I think she believed me, but her son may not have."

"Yves was here as well?"

Bazzu smiled. "So you already know their names?" She glanced at Jorge. "Is there some delicious mystery I need to know about?"

"No mystery," said Thomas. "We were lovers once, when we were young. I had sixteen years when we first met, seventeen when she was taken from me. And then we met again less than two years ago in Qurtuba."

"Did you become lovers again?"

Thomas saw no reason to hide the truth, aware Jorge would take pleasure in telling Bazzu his own version of events.

"Briefly … but then she betrayed me."

"She had the appearance of a woman who might betray a man, as well as delight him. She attended the meal Baldomero prepared for the Turks, as a guest of Abu Abdullah. Except she uses his title. She called him Muhammed in my hearing. No doubt he likes her to call him that. I expect it makes him feel important when she lies with him."

"Abu Abdullah is important, he is the Sultan of Gharnatah. You are sure they are lovers?" Thomas examined his feelings about the news, but found he had none.

Bazzu waved a hand at the idea. To her, the Sultan was still the young boy she used to chase from her kitchens and try to keep away from her girls.

"Helena told me they are lovers, and she is the expert in such matters. The son was handsome. He reminded me a little of you. Apart from the handsome part, obviously. It was in the way he held himself. He had a confidence."

"Possessing a title can do that even for a weak man."

Bazzu waited, but when Thomas offered no more, she glanced at Jorge.

"Don't look at me," he said. "If Thomas wants you to know more, he will have to tell you himself."

The girl returned with coffee, set it down with a clatter and ran out again.

"The reason he looks familiar is he is my son," Thomas said. "Eleanor was carrying my child when she was taken from me and I was left for dead on the side of a road."

"Does he know?" asked Bazzu.

"He didn't, but he does since Qurtuba."

"What is he like?"

"Spoiled. Privileged. Lacking in spirit."

Bazzu smiled. "I like that you always say what you think."

"Should I not?"

"No, continue doing so. It is refreshing in a man."

A quarter hour later, as Thomas descended from the palace

53

beside Jorge, he said, "I wonder what Eleanor is really doing here? I thought she had returned to France after what happened in Qurtuba."

"Perhaps she did and has come back, like half the nobles in Christendom. They are here to witness the end of al-Andalus. She seduced Fernando back then, remember? Perhaps she wants to balance things out by seducing a Sultan. You know he likes pale-skinned women, and she does have the most luxurious red hair."

"I don't doubt she could lure him into her bed, or more likely herself into his bed, but for what reason? There is no advantage in it for her. She can't possibly believe Gharnatah will win the coming battle."

"Perhaps she remains Fernando's lover and he sent her as a spy or assassin. I wouldn't put anything past him. He's sly, that one."

"You could be right." Thomas tried to push thoughts of Eleanor from his mind. Other matters demanded his attention. "I hope this Baldomero is at his house and we can get back to living our lives again."

Jorge laughed. "We will not do that until Gharnatah falls."

CHAPTER SEVEN

Baldomero de Pamplona's house sat in a row of identical dwellings that ran south from al-Hattabin square towards the Hadarro. At the far end, a low wall offered a view of racing water, cold with snow-melt.

"What if he puts up a struggle?" asked Jorge.

"Then I will knock him down." Thomas shook his head. "I might be Isabel's plaything, but I can still knock a man down. Besides, he's a cook. He's probably fat and slow. No doubt even you could defeat him, but he will not put up a fight."

"I hope we are not going to find him dead. You have a habit of doing that, you know."

"Killing people? Only when they are trying to kill me." Thomas slowed. There was nothing on any of the identical doors to show which house was which, and he tried to recall Bazzu's instructions. He counted down from the square and moved to a door two further on before hammering on it.

"Not killing people," said Jorge. "Finding dead bodies. I have lost count of how many you have discovered. You are a dangerous man to know."

"You are still alive, aren't you?"

"Thanks to you. But also thanks to you I have been injured and almost died. We should have brought Usaden."

"We can manage between us, I expect." Thomas hammered on the door again, the sound swallowed by the house.

When Jorge stepped past Thomas and tried the catch on the door, it opened to his touch.

"Oh no, not again," he said.

"Many people leave their doors unlocked. I do."

"Then you are a fool. Most people also answer their door when it is hammered on as hard as you have been doing." Jorge stepped to one side. "You go first."

Thomas sighed and stepped across the threshold. A hallway led to the far end of the house. An open door showed a large room where light spilled in from hidden windows. Two doors on each side of the hallway were closed. Thomas opened the first on the right to reveal a sitting room. It smelled of smoke. He went to the fireplace and put his hand over the ashes to discover them still warm.

There was no dead body in the room. Its lack would no doubt please Jorge, but there remained four other rooms still to check. Thomas opened the door opposite to find a large bedroom. The bed had been slept in, but not made. The room smelled of a man. There was also the faint scent left by a woman, but it was not recent. Only one side of the bed had been slept in. The other doors revealed a second bedroom, which appeared to be unused, and an office, but still no sign of the occupants, either alive or dead.

The room at the end was a kitchen. It stretched the full width of the house and was eight paces deep. A large open range sat against the left-hand wall, while a table as large as the one used by Bazzu filled the centre of the room. Shelves and workbenches took up the rest of the space. There was no sign of Baldomero de Pamplona, though it was clear he had been here not so long ago.

"Go and knock on doors," Thomas said to Jorge. "Ask the neighbours when they last saw either of them."

"What are you going to do? There is nobody here."

"I am going to look for poisons. If this man tried to kill Isabel, then there will be evidence of it here."

"Who else could it have been?"

"Go and ask questions." Thomas turned his back on Jorge and crossed to the first of the shelves. Stoppered clay pots sat there, and Thomas removed the tops and looked inside. He used his eyes and nose, but found only spices, herbs, pepper and salt. He continued examining the other shelves, then went to his knees and opened cupboard doors. He found bags of flour and sugar, pots of dried fruit, but nothing that would kill a man or even make him unwell. Belia would be better at identifying what everything was for, but Thomas knew enough to recognise their benign nature. Which raised the question of whether Baldomero de Pamplona had poisoned Theresa or not? Except Thomas knew it must be him. He had made the mushroom pastries she ate. Pamplona was guilty. But where was he?

Thomas took one last look around the kitchen before returning to examine the other rooms. This time, he looked beneath the bed and opened every door, however small, searching for a body. He found none.

When Thomas eventually left the house, he saw Jorge standing on the other side of the street and three doors closer to the river. He was talking with a woman of indeterminate age, not that age ever bothered Jorge, and was using all his powers of promised seduction to draw from her every item of information she might possess. As Thomas approached, he saw her glance at him, and for a moment, doubt showed on her face.

Jorge turned. "Fear not, my sweet, he is with me. Do you not know Thomas Berrington?"

"The physician?" asked the woman. "Only by name. We have

always used Da'ud al-Baitar, but he is unwell, so I may call on your friend in the future. If any of us have one. What was it you asked me?"

"Whether you saw Baldomero returning home two days ago."

"Two days? I heard him come home last night, but two nights since? I cannot recall. I may have, I may not have. Is it important?"

"I don't know," said Jorge. "Ask Thomas."

"Is it important?" she said again, turning to him.

"It is never possible to know what is important and what is not until the whole picture is revealed." Thomas caught Jorge's smile and knew he had set him up, having heard him say the same thing often enough before. Except it was true. "At what time does he usually return?"

"Often late," said the woman. "Sometimes close to midnight. He does most of his work in the evening. He cooks for people, anyone willing to pay. He told me he cooked for the Sultan not long since."

"How long ago?"

The woman gazed off into space, her lips moving silently as though she was counting.

"Two weeks?"

"Are you asking me or telling me?"

"Two weeks," she said with more certainty. "He said he had to buy special spices because he was preparing a meal for the Sultan's important guests. Turks, he said. He told me he knew their food and wanted to impress them with the range of dishes. He gave me some of what was left the following day, but it was not to my taste. Perhaps it was them he was arguing with last night."

Thomas stared at the woman.

"He was arguing with someone last night?"

"He was."

"When were you going to tell me this?"

"I just have, haven't I? It is you asking the questions. You asked if I saw him, not whether he was arguing with someone. Do you think something has happened to him?"

"That is what I am trying to find out. After midnight, you said?"

"Perhaps closer to dawn. The sky was beginning to lighten."

"Do you always rise so early?"

"I did last night because my husband snores so loudly. I punched him on the arm and he stopped, and that is when I heard the shouting from the street. I went to the window and Baldomero was out here arguing with two men. There was a woman standing at a small distance, watching them."

"Are you sure it was Baldomero arguing with the men?"

"There was enough light to see his face. Yes, it was him."

"And the men, did you see their faces?"

"One of them. The other was turned side-on to me."

"Would you recognise the man again?"

"Do you know who they are?"

"Not yet, but if I find them, it would be good to have confirmation of who you saw arguing with Baldomero."

"I might recognise them, I am not sure. The light was poor. But I could hear them well enough."

"Were they speaking Arabic?"

She looked off into space again before shaking her head.

"No. They spoke the tongue of Castile."

"Are you sure?"

"I hear it often enough in the city these days. Everyone wants to speak it because they know what is coming."

"Did you hear what the argument was about?"

"I did not. We have glass in our windows and I was tired. I watched them for a short while only, then went back to bed."

Thomas could think of nothing more, so thanked the woman.

"Who else have you spoken to?" he asked Jorge once the woman had returned to her house.

"Everyone who answered their door, which is about a quarter of them. I have two more to try and that will be it."

"Did anyone else hear an argument?" Thomas followed Jorge to the next house. When he knocked on the door, there was no answer, which left only one more.

"Not that they mentioned, but now we know there was one, it might be worth asking again. You are better at questions than me, even if people like me the more."

As Thomas raised his hand to knock on the door, it was flung open by a woman in her twenties who stood there with an angry expression on her face.

"Why are you back here? Did my husband not pay his debt in full?"

Thomas stared at her. Before he could say anything, Jorge took command.

"I am sorry, but we are not who you think. My companion and myself are looking for a neighbour of yours, Baldomero de Pamplona."

"Oh." The woman looked from Jorge to Thomas, then back, liking what she saw there more. "What do you want to know about him? Baldomero is a good man."

Thomas watched the tension leak from her shoulders and tried to hide his smile. Already Jorge's charm was working its magic.

"Another neighbour of yours said she heard him arguing with two men last night. Or rather, early this morning before dawn."

"I was asleep then. We were all asleep in this house."

"Have you seen any strangers in the street? Apart from us, that is. And we are not really strangers, not now we have been introduced to such a beautiful vision as yourself." Jorge smiled, and a flush of colour came to the woman's cheeks.

"I do not spend my time peering through my windows like some. I have seen nobody."

"Tell me what Baldomero is like," said Jorge. "You said he is a good man. Has he lived here long?"

"My husband bought this house when we married eight years ago, and Baldomero was already living here. He brought us fine delicacies to welcome us to the street. I can still taste them on my tongue. I have tasted nothing like them. He prepares a meal for the entire street twice a year. On Eid Al-Adha, and again at the end of Ramadan when he prepares especially light foods so our stomachs can learn to eat again."

"Baldomero is devout?"

"My husband says he has never seen him in the mosque, so I doubt it. Rumour has it he is Christian. He came from the north. Not that anyone holds either of those things against him, not these days. He prepares the food out of the goodness of his heart."

"Is he married?" Thomas asked.

"Yes, to Cruzita. You should knock on their door. She no doubt knows where he has gone to. Baldomero is much in demand for his skill and is often away, sometimes for as long as a month. Though if he is gone long, Cruzita will accompany him."

Thomas moved away. He had heard enough and knew Jorge would flatter any other minor items of information from the woman and then leave her unsettled. Her husband might enjoy her attentions more than usual tonight. Thomas returned to Baldomero's house and opened the closet doors in the bedroom. He had searched them before, but then he had been looking for a body. Now he examined the clothes. One side held outfits for a man, the other for a woman. When he looked around the room, he saw small signs to show Cruzita had gone. A crumpled linen kerchief sat on a narrow table next to an empty bottle of scent. There was a clean patch on the floor beneath the clothes that might show where a bag had rested.

"Do you believe he has gone away, his wife with him?" asked Jorge as he entered the room.

"Does it not seem convenient for him to be called away only two days after he tried to kill Isabel? I need to know a lot more about the man. We should go back to Bazzu and have her tell us everything she knows."

"Everything? I take it you are planning to do nothing else for a year."

"Everything about Baldomero."

As they reached the end of the row of houses, they almost collided with a man coming the other way, his head down in thought. Jorge skipped to one side. Thomas stayed where he was, forcing the man to slow.

"Do you live here?"

"Why do you want to know?"

"We are seeking Baldomero de Pamplona."

"Another two wanting him, then. What has he done to be in such demand?"

"Another two?" asked Thomas.

"I saw him early today in the company of a man and woman, crossing al-Hattabin square."

"A man and woman? Did he appear to be going with them willingly?"

"I would have gone with the woman willingly enough," said the man, "for all that she was not young. She possessed that fire some women have."

"And the man?"

"I gave no notice to the man. I hailed Baldomero and he hailed me back. He seemed willing enough, though not his usual self. Normally he would have stopped and chatted a while. He was like that."

"Did you see in which direction they went?"

"They climbed the roadway on the far side of the square, but if they were going to the palace, I know not. Baldomero has cooked there before, so it is possible."

After the man had gone, Jorge said, "We need to talk to Bazzu even more now, do we not?"

CHAPTER EIGHT

When Thomas and Jorge arrived back at the kitchens, Bazzu was busy with final preparations for the Sultan's guests. Thomas had never seen her do any actual work before, but now he watched as she moved around the kitchen with surprising speed. Her role appeared to involve tasting and advising, but now and again she would add spice, salt or pepper to a dish until satisfied it was perfect. She caught sight of them standing in the doorway and hurried across to kiss Jorge on the mouth while her soft hand circled Thomas's wrist.

"I will be some time yet. Jorge, take Thomas along the corridor to the room with the views. Wait there and I will join you as soon as I can." She glanced at Thomas. "I assume you have returned with more questions?"

"I have."

"Then wait, and I will answer what I can. Did you find Baldomero?" She shook her head. "No, don't tell me, I have no time now. Go." She pushed them away.

Bazzu was true to her word. The chamber they entered possessed a magnificent view, at least as long as Thomas kept his eyes raised to the towering peaks that marched away to the south. Lowering his gaze, he saw the Castilian camp spread beyond the low rise where Ojos de Huescar sat. Smoke from a hundred fires rose in lazy spirals to be snatched away by a wind that did not blow at ground level. On the level plain between the opposing forces, mounted men rode backwards and forwards, distance lending them a sense of unreality. Thomas knew they would be taunting each other. Now and again one would advance, then turn away. At some point, the taunting would turn into a brief fight and someone might die. It happened every day, all day, and would continue to do so until the forces of Castile advanced on Gharnatah.

"Why do they just sit there?" asked Jorge as he came to stand beside Thomas.

"There are negotiations going on, and Isabel doesn't want Gharnatah destroyed. She asks about the palace all the time. She wants to know what it's like. How beautiful it is. The place is a minor obsession for her."

"And Fernando?"

"He would attack tomorrow if he could, but so far, she has held him in check."

"It will come to that, though, won't it? Eventually she will grow tired of sitting there and let loose her dogs of war."

"She will." Thomas turned as a slim girl entered the room carrying a tray of coffee and cups.

"Do you know how long Bazzu will be?" Jorge asked.

The girl shook her head. "She said she will come as soon as she can."

Jorge went to the table and inspected what she had brought.

"Come and sit, enjoy this excellent coffee. There is nothing we can do until Bazzu arrives."

Thomas stayed where he was, conscious of the passage of time. A tension thrummed through his body, but he was unsure what its cause was. Theresa was on the mend, thanks to Belia. His children were safe. Baldomero de Pamplona had poisoned Theresa, but Thomas was sure the man had fled. The matter was closed. The conclusion might be unsatisfactory, but conclusion it was. He crossed to the table and sat, reached for a cup. It was halfway to his mouth when he stopped.

"I have already drunk it and I'm still alive," said Jorge. "They prepared this in the palace kitchens. Bazzu would not poison us."

Thomas finished the movement and sipped the hot, bitter liquid, its taste filling his senses. He had finished the cup by the time Bazzu eventually entered the room. She sat beside Jorge and poured coffee for herself.

"What do you want to know, Thomas? I do not have long, I have been sent for. Abu Abdullah's guests want to ask me about some of the dishes."

"I need to know whatever you can tell me about Baldomero," Thomas said. "He wasn't at his house, but some neighbours said he had an argument with two people at dawn this morning. He was seen leaving in the company of a man and woman. I don't suppose you have any idea who they might be?"

"Why would I know that? Baldomero is much in demand, so it could have been anyone. There are few cooks that can match him in certain cuisines. I still cannot believe him responsible for what you claim."

"If we ever find him, perhaps he can explain what happened then, but I am sure it is he who crafted the poisoned dish. If he is as skilled as you claim, there is no way he could mistake *amanita* for ordinary mushrooms."

"I expect you are right, as always. In which case he has most likely fled, and if he has fled, you have little chance of finding him. End your search and return to your queen."

Bazzu's words so matched Thomas's own recent thoughts that they came as confirmation.

"You said Baldomero cooked for the palace recently. Did he do so often?"

"Often enough. Perhaps once a month, sometimes a little less, sometimes a little more."

"Exactly when was this last time he cooked here?"

Bazzu stared off into space, her lips moving as if she was counting.

"I would say between two and three weeks, but I can check if it is important. I will have made a record of it."

"No need. Abu Abdullah's guests were Turks, you said?"

"They were. I met their leader when I was sent for." She glanced at Jorge. "He was almost as handsome as you, my sweet, but with an air of danger to him you do not possess."

"Was there anyone else?" Thomas did not understand why he was asking the question. The dinner was too far in the past to be relevant.

"Only the countess I told you about," said Bazzu. "She came to see me a few days later wanting to know how to contact Baldomero. She said she had enjoyed the meal so much, she wanted him to prepare a meal for her and her son."

"He cooked a meal for Eleanor?"

Bazzu smiled. "Nothing passes you by, does it? Was she a good lover?"

Thomas ignored the question. "Do you know where I can find her?"

"She is living in a house in the Alkazaba, conveniently close to the palace whenever Abu Abdullah wants her. If he wants her. You know how fickle he can be. The house is on the southern edge, perched above the slope. It has an arched terrace front and back. You cannot miss it because it is painted pink. Not her doing, I expect, but not to my taste."

————

"What are we doing here?" asked Jorge. "I know Eleanor betrayed you in Qurtuba, but you cannot suspect these matters involve her, can you?"

"The man we spoke to saw Baldomero going off with a handsome woman."

Jorge gave a laugh. "I expect there is more than one hand-some woman in Gharnatah—I could name at least four score. I still think you are making too great a leap."

"Mushrooms," Thomas said. "*Amanita* mushrooms."

"Mushrooms?"

"I taught Eleanor about them when I first knew her. Warned her of the dangers if she ate too many. I know it was a long time ago, but what if she built on the little knowledge I gave her? What if Baldomero is in there and we don't check?" Thomas stared across at the house Bazzu had described. It was indeed pink, but less garish than Thomas had expected. There was a connection between the walls and the red of the soil surrounding it that was pleasing to the eye.

"That's a lot of what ifs," said Jorge. "If Baldomero is in there, she may not let us talk to him, and certainly won't allow us to take him away."

"She can't stop us. Not unless she has half a dozen soldiers in there with her."

"I wouldn't put it past her."

Neither of them moved.

"You don't want to see her, do you?" said Jorge.

"I don't, but I am going to have to or abandon my search."

"What is the worst she can do—seduce you again? And I recall you telling me you enjoyed the experience."

"Once."

"Is once not enough?" Jorge punched Thomas on the arm. "Come on, let's get it done, then we can return to our families."

The door was opened by a slim woman who trotted back inside to see if her mistress was accepting visitors. She did not ask their names, so when Yves accompanied her back to see who was there, he stopped dead in his tracks, mouth open.

"What are you doing here? Mother wants nothing to do with you."

"And I her, but I have some questions. The first you might

be able to answer and we will be gone. Do you know a man named Baldomero de Pamplona?"

Thomas watched Yves take half a step backwards and knew the answer.

Yves decided to lie. "Who?"

"He is a cook. I was told Eleanor hired him to prepare a meal."

Yves shook his head. "We have a cook already."

"Why do you lie to me?" Thomas stepped across the threshold, pushing past the servant who attempted to stop him.

"Who is there, Yves? Don't stand all day talking, bring them in." Eleanor appeared at the end of the hallway, and once more Thomas felt the world shimmer with memory and pain. A beautiful woman now, he still saw details of the girl he had fallen in love with. Except that girl no longer existed. Eleanor had betrayed him in Qurtuba, and her deceit was unforgivable. At least it meant he didn't have to care about hurting her feelings.

"Our son is lying to me." He raised his voice so she could hear him, pleased when he saw Yves wince at the word son. "He is telling me you did not employ a cook by the name of Baldomero."

Eleanor stared at Thomas for a long time. Eventually, she said, "Come through. Your man can amuse Yves while we talk."

"Your man?" said Jorge.

"She's only trying to anger you, but it's not a bad idea. Things will go quicker between the two of us."

Thomas left Jorge beside Yves and strode into a wide room. A second terrace jutted out into what appeared to be thin air, but as he approached the railing, he saw heavy wooden posts set into the slope to support it.

Eleanor smiled at him. "I apologise for Yves. In some ways he is still very young."

"He has thirty-five years. It's time he learned to act like a man."

"He had no father figure for most of those years, and my husband barely acknowledged him. There were times I was convinced he knew Yves was not his son. He said nothing, but he was always cold with the boy." Eleanor reached out as though to touch Thomas's hand, then withdrew before completing the move.

"What are you doing here?"

"Passing the time with an old, dear friend."

"In Gharnatah. What are you plotting now?"

"I am plotting nothing. You know everything that happened in Córdoba was the fault of Castellana, her son, and her mad husband. They deceived me as much as you. It broke my heart to see how much I hurt you. Is it too late to rekindle our friendship?"

"Friendship? Friends don't lie to each other. What did you want with Baldomero?"

"I ate his food when he cooked for the Sultan and his guests. I wanted him to cook for me and Yves."

"You are attracted to power, aren't you?"

Eleanor gave a faint smile. "If that is true, why am I still attracted to you, Thomas? And I am attracted to you."

"You are attracted to a memory, nothing more. We had love for each other once, I acknowledge, but we possess it no longer. Tell me what you know of Baldomero."

"I liked him. He was competent. I like men who know what they are doing, you know I do."

"Did Abu Abdullah eat here or in the palace?"

"Who is Abu Abdullah?"

"The Sultan, Muhammed."

Eleanor frowned. "Why does he have two names?"

"Because he is the Sultan. His father was Muhammed before him, and his father's fathers going back twelve generations. Abu Abdullah is Muhammed XII and…" Thomas stopped his explanation, aware Eleanor had distracted him from his questioning. He wondered if it was deliberate or nothing more than her nature. "I take it there were no ill-effects from eating Baldomero's food?"

"None. It was delicious, though a little too highly spiced. I ate the blander foods and they were excellent. Yves said he enjoyed them all."

"Exactly when did he cook this meal for you?"

Eleanor stared out across the vista.

"Ten days since? Near enough ten days."

"Did he say what other work he had?"

"It never occurred to me to ask. I employed him to cook, not provide conversation. You should ask Yves. He spent time with him in the kitchen. He is interested in food and its preparation. I told him the skill is beneath him, but he doesn't listen to me. Have you returned to Gharnatah now?"

"I am still in the employ of Isabel."

"Should I be jealous?"

"Of what? Did you know where Baldomero lived?"

"How would I know that? Everything was arranged through Fatima. Again, you should ask Yves, he might know. Is it important?"

"Where does this Fatima live? I would like to talk with her."

"She should be easy enough to find. She is the wife of the Sultan's general."

"Olaf Torvaldsson?"

"If she told me his name, I have forgotten it. Is it important?"

"Olaf is my father-in-law," Thomas said. "Grandfather to my children, as Fatima is their grandmother."

"You know so many people of power, don't you? You have changed from the boy I ran wild with, and I am not sure which I find the more exciting."

"That one, I am sure, and he is dead to me now. Baldomero was seen talking with a man and woman early this morning, then leaving with them. There is nobody in his house. His wife is also missing."

"Well, it was not me he left with," said Eleanor, her expression closed. "I was asleep in my bed. Alone. But that state of affairs can easily be remedied." All at once, she was closer to him, her scent enveloping him, and Thomas cursed the weakness of his body as it responded to her. He turned and strode away, angry at himself.

CHAPTER NINE

"Why are we going to the barracks?" asked Jorge.

"I want to talk to Fatima. What did you find out from Yves?"

"Only that he has become intrigued by you since he and his mother came to Gharnatah. He is even trying to learn Arabic, though I told him not to bother. Castilian will be all he needs soon enough. He's not stupid, and he has changed since we met him in Qurtuba."

"He looked the same to me—weak and controlled by his mother."

"You are wrong in that. I believe him more confident, more sure of himself, a man who knows his place in the world. Why he has changed so much, I don't know, and I was not with him long enough to find out the reason. Is it strange to have a son you knew nothing about?"

Thomas slowed as they entered the cobbled barracks yard. It was almost deserted. He had given Yves' existence little thought and wondered if that was a mistake. The boy was his son, after all. Was there at least some small connection that could be forged? In Qurtuba, Yves had been all weak bluster, but perhaps people could change. If they wanted to.

"Did you really think him different to the last time we saw him?"

"I thought him grown into himself. Perhaps he has accepted you being his father and it has changed him. He told me he has learned a great deal about you since they have been living on the hill. Hearing of your exploits. Your skill. Your persistence."

"More like my stupidity, I expect."

"It depends who he has asked. He has spoken to Olaf about you, and Fatima. He told me he heard about Lubna from her. I gained the impression he is sorry not to have been able to meet her. He is different to how he was when you first met him." Jorge chuckled. "Perhaps he wants to turn into a copy of you."

"I can think of better role models to choose."

They reached Olaf's small house, which sat on the edge of the barracks yard. Thomas entered without knocking and stopped dead in his tracks. Helena stood in the middle of the room, half-turned to see who had entered. For a moment, they stared at each other, then Jorge pushed past and went to embrace the woman who had once shared Thomas's bed. The woman he had grown to despise, and then put himself in danger to save, more than once.

Olaf Torvaldsson's second wife, Fatima, emerged from the kitchen. She made a sound and bustled across to Thomas, crushing the breath from his lungs with the strength of her embrace.

"I wondered how long it would take you to call. Too long, but I forgive you." She patted his cheek. "Olaf will be sorry to have missed you."

"Where is he?"

"Off fighting, or watching someone else fight. You know how he is. I barely see him these days and I worry about him." She did not need to explain why. As the Sultan's general, Olaf would be involved in the coming battle when it came. Strong and skilled as he was, he was still only one man, but at least he had the advantage of an army standing behind him.

Thomas took Fatima's arm and led her back into the kitchen. Jorge had already drawn Helena to one side. Now they sat on cushions arranged in the corner where bright light fell through finely glazed windows. Thomas was aware of Helena watching him as he crossed the room.

"Why have you brought me in here?" asked Fatima. "Are you hungry? I was preparing lunch for the two of us, but there is enough for four."

Thomas wondered when his life had started to revolve around food, but had to admit he was hungry. He also remembered how good Fatima's cooking was.

"I expect we can stay. I wanted to ask you what Helena is doing here."

"She is Olaf's daughter, she has a right to be here."

"I thought she didn't like you."

Fatima glanced at the door, then crossed the room and closed it.

"She has changed."

"Jorge claimed the same, but I don't believe Helena capable of change."

"Do not judge her too soon. I believe being held captive by Abu Abdullah changed her."

"She would have to change a great deal before I could forgive her."

"Perhaps she has, and perhaps you will. How long are you staying? Olaf may return tonight. He usually does."

"I doubt we can stay that long. I have a question for you."

"Ask, then." Fatima busied herself with rolling out flatbreads.

"There is a woman staying in the Alkazaba by the name of Eleanor. I know her from long ago. She tells me you recommended a cook to her, Baldomero de Pamplona."

"I did. It was before he went to cook for the Sultan, and she wanted to know whether to attend the meal. I told her there was nothing to worry about. She would enjoy the experience."

Fatima opened the lid of a clay oven and slapped the dough against the inner walls.

"Have you ever had any doubt over his probity?"

"Baldomero? Why do you ask?"

"He was sent for by Isabel to prepare a meal for her."

"Your Isabel? The Queen of Castile?"

"Not my Isabel, but yes. She enjoys Moorish food when her husband is away, as he is at the moment."

"The King is away? Do you think I should pass that information on to Olaf?"

"Pass on what you want, but no doubt he already knows. Olaf misses nothing."

"He will miss not seeing you. Why are you asking about Baldomero? Was there something wrong with the meal he prepared for the Queen?"

"It was tainted. Poisoned."

Fatima left the stew to simmer and turned her full attention on Thomas.

"Baldomero would never do that."

"It could have been no one else. He created mushroom tarts, but used *amanita* in some of them."

"He poisoned the Queen?"

"He meant it for Isabel, but it was her friend who almost died."

"Were you there?"

"I ate the same food as they did, but not all of it was tainted. Theresa was unlucky, but I know he intended the poison for Isabel."

"Baldomero is a good man," said Fatima.

"Who has since gone missing. Jorge and I went to his house this morning, but he was seen leaving with a man and woman shortly before dawn."

"What did his wife say?"

"She wasn't there either."

"Perhaps he has another commission. Baldomero is much in

demand. He cooked for your friend, and yes I recommended him, and he cooked recently for the Sultan and his guests. He has cooked for myself and Olaf. I tell you, he is a good man. An honest man."

"And I tell you it can have been no other." Thomas had no wish to upset this woman who had become a mother to him. This woman whose daughter he had married and lost. But he knew she was wrong.

"If you speak true then he was forced to do what he did," said Fatima. "It is the only explanation. Who were this couple he was seen going with?"

"Nobody knew them. A man and a woman, that was all I was told. Baldomero appears to have gone willingly enough. There was no force involved. I thought they might be Eleanor and her son, but now I am not so sure."

"So they are nothing to do with what you seek, are they? They will be clients taking him to their house to prepare a meal."

"And his wife?"

"She goes with him often enough, particularly if it involves travel. Sometimes he will be away for a month or more. Now, are you staying to eat or not?"

"Is Helena staying?"

"Does that make any difference?"

Thomas was unsure if Fatima had forgiven his suspicions of Baldomero or not, but he and Jorge needed to eat, and he also needed time to think.

"How long has she been visiting?" Thomas perched on the edge of a small table and watched as Fatima fussed over her final preparations, aware of the strong connection between them.

"Ever since she moved back to the harem."

"Jorge told me she is instructing the women there."

Fatima smiled. "She is preparing them for what comes next."

"The end of the war. Have you told the same to Olaf?"

"Olaf isn't stupid. Neither is Helena. The women of the harem are exquisite, and she is teaching them the language of Castile and its manners. In a year, two at most, Olaf tells me, there will be many men of Castile pleased to take a beautiful wife. Particularly one with the skills these women possess."

"Has Olaf said what he is going to do when that day arrives?"

"He has mentioned the north." Fatima gave a mock shiver. "Is it cold there?"

"I only know England. It is warm enough in summer, but the winters are long and wet. Olaf is from further north again, so it is no doubt even colder. He can stay here if he wants. I might even find a place for him under Isabel's command. She will need loyal men."

"Even a man loyal to a Sultan?" asked Fatima.

"Olaf is no fool, he serves whoever rules. I have heard him say it often enough. Let Isabel be his Sultan. Or he can retire. I will ensure she finds him land somewhere, and you and he can while away your years in comfort."

"Are you talking about the same Olaf? Can you see him whiling away anything, or seeking comfort? Olaf was born to lead. Born to kill other men. Born to serve."

"Then he can serve me," Thomas said, not knowing where the words came from.

"You?"

"When the war ends, I will have a position. I have a position now, alongside Isabel. When she triumphs, there will be honours for those close to her."

"She will make you a duke or some-such, I suppose." Fatima looked him up and down. "She has already changed how you look and how you dress. What happened to the Moorish Englishman who married Lubna? What would she say?"

"She told me to serve Isabel when she lived. She would tell

me the same again now if she could. Your daughter was clever. Cleverer than me. She would see the way events turn."

Fatima crossed the room and embraced Thomas, turning her face against his chest, and he felt her body shake. He held her for a time, and when she drew away, there were tears in her eyes which she wiped away.

"I miss her. I miss Lubna every single day. She was my only child and I miss her."

"As do I," Thomas said.

"I know you do. Which is why it is a comfort to me that Helena comes to visit. She is not my daughter, but she is Olaf's, and she is Lubna's sister. She talks of her, you know."

"She does? That is more than she ever did when the three of us shared the same roof. She treated her as a servant then."

"People change. Helena has changed. If you spend a little time with her you will see the same. She has become … good." Fatima shook her head as if the notion came as a surprise to her. "Help me carry the food through. Sit next to Helena and talk to her, see if I am not right. Do you want me to ask questions about Baldomero to see if I can discover anything?"

"Would you?"

"Of course." She reached up and touched his cheek. "I love you, Thomas Berrington, just as my entire family does. Now, go and do as I say."

Thomas picked up the clay pot and backed out into the main room. He sat beside Helena as ordered. Her familiar scent touched his senses, raising unwelcome memories. Across from them, Fatima spooned food into rough bowls and passed them around while Jorge leaned close and regaled her with tales that made her laugh.

"Jorge tells me you are living in the palace again," Thomas said to Helena. "Is that wise after what Abu Abdullah did to you?"

"He has changed." Helena raised a perfect shoulder, the skin as pale as marble. "As I have changed. I went to confront him because it had to be done if I wanted to regain my life. I asked what he intended to do with the harem when the Spanish take the palace."

Thomas suppressed a smile. "What did he say?"

"That he had not considered the matter."

"Of course he hadn't. What did you say to that?" Thomas noticed the scar that had once brought her into his house was no longer visible. There were few signs of ageing to be seen on Helena's face or body, though almost ten years had passed since she had been gifted to him by the previous Sultan after she was attacked.

"I told him he needed to think about it. He said he hoped Castile would allow him to leave with his wealth and harem both. He said he had arranged to move to Tunis."

"I'm not sure Tunis will offer much welcome to a deposed Sultan, particularly one with Abu Abdullah's reputation for making mischief."

"I told you, he has changed. I also told him if he so much as lays a finger, or anything else, on me, he will have to answer to you."

Thomas laughed, almost losing some of the stew he had put into his mouth.

"I expect that scared him."

"It did. He knows you serve Queen Isabel now. Knows you are a man with influence. He also knows how many men you have killed when they crossed you."

Thomas wasn't so sure Helena was right in her judgement. He wondered if she shared Abu Abdullah's bed. It wouldn't surprise him, despite what he had done to her in the past.

As if reading his mind, Helena said, "I have given up on men." She offered a smile, one unfamiliar to him because it carried no hint of scorn.

"And have they given up on you?"

"You have, so no doubt others will, too." She leaned across the table. "Have you given up on me, Jorge?"

Jorge reached out and took her hand. "I never give up on a beautiful woman." He kissed the back of her hand.

"See, Jorge knows how to treat me." In the past, the words would have been coloured by a sneer, but now they were spoken with affection.

Thomas recalled how Helena had once shared her life with another woman when she was carrying Will. If he asked her now, would she tell him the truth, tell him whether he was Will's true father? He wondered how long the apparent change in her might last. He looked across to Jorge.

"We need to go back to Baldomero's house. I examined the spices and herbs he had, but it would be better if Belia saw them. She has far more knowledge than I do."

"Baldomero the cook?" asked Helena. "What business do you have with him?"

"No business, but he is missing. How do you know him?"

"Everyone knows Baldomero. He cooked a meal for Abu Abdullah not long since when he entertained the Turks. Their leader was exceptionally handsome." Helena glanced across the table to Fatima before returning her gaze to Thomas. "Can I come with you? I know his wife."

"Who is also missing. Why do you want to come?"

"Because I want to be of help. You said you need to gather up his spices. I can do that. And you will need a cart or something to take them to your house so Belia can examine them. I know where I can get one of those. And I have a message for you from the Sultan."

"For me? Does he wish you to pass on an insult?"

"He wishes me to pass on a message. He wants to talk with your Queen. He knows there are people in Gharnatah already talking with Castile in order to save themselves. You should call on him and find out exactly what he wants."

"Abu Abdullah told you this?"

"Do you think I am making it up?"

"He wants to see me?"

"He does. I can take you to him. The guards will allow you to pass if I am with you." She reached out and touched his wrist, let her fingers remain there.

Thomas was confused. He gripped Helena's chin, turned her head from one side to the other. Then he leaned across and looked behind her.

She smiled. "What are you doing?"

"I am looking for Helena. What have you done with her?"

CHAPTER TEN

Isabel, Queen of Castile, gave a frown. Thomas sat with her on the terrace while once again rain fell beyond its shelter, the sound of its falling a comfort. There was food on the table, so far untouched. Night had come to the Castilian camp. Its fires sparked away in a seemingly endless wave, rising and falling across the contours of the land until beyond lay only darkness. Thomas had taken the cart of supplies to Belia and checked on Theresa, pleased to see she was recovering. Then he had come to Isabel and told her of Abu Abdullah's proposal, which had brought the frown.

"Is he mad?" she asked.

"There is an argument to be made for such."

"Does Boabdil expect me to trust him?"

Thomas raised a shoulder. "I told him I would convey his message and I have done so."

Isabel stared at him. "Do you have no opinion on the matter?"

Thomas could not read her tonight. Normally he believed he could, but this evening she was both distracted and strangely vulnerable. She had dressed in a Moorish robe, her hair covered beneath a silk scarf, pale red strands escaping to brush against her cheeks. Perhaps she was thinking of the next stage of her reign, once al-Andalus was defeated, concerned that the peace might be harder than the war.

"I do, and if you ask I will offer it."

"Is that not what I just said?" Isabel poured wine into two glasses and handed one to Thomas. It was against all semblance of protocol, but they had long since moved beyond such.

"How soon do you want this war to end, and how many lives do you want to save from being thrown away?"

"You know my answer to that."

"The second part, yes, I believe I do. The first? I have never heard your opinion on the matter."

"I would have it end tomorrow if I could. Tonight. Now!" She drained her glass and filled it once more. "This is not a decision I can make alone. Fernando must agree, and I do not trust Boabdil. Whatever promises he makes now, I expect him to default on them."

"Abu Abdullah mentioned neutral ground when I went to see him. Somewhere close. He gave me the impression he would be satisfied if I were to suggest the location."

"You, Thomas? You have many admirable traits, but I was not aware Boabdil appreciated them as much as I do."

Thomas smiled. "He doesn't. He knows I work for you, but I believe he thinks I might still owe some loyalty to him even after all he has done."

"And do you?"

"There is only one person I am loyal to now."

"I cannot understand his motives. Tell me, is it worth pursuing his advances until we discover what it is he wants?"

"I can deal with him, or Martin, though he mentioned he would rather it not be him. If the war can end sooner, is it not worth some small effort?"

"And this other thing you are doing to find out who poisoned Theresa?"

"I think the matter may be resolved. The man behind it has fled, and if he has any sense he will never return."

"Do you know of anywhere we could arrange a meeting?"

"Not yet, but I am sure I can find something. There is land to the north and east of Gharnatah that, while notionally in Moorish hands, is not subservient to it. They are an independent people and there will be some place there."

"Then look, Thomas."

"Even before you decide?"

"It is not a waste if I say no later, is it?"

Only a waste of my time, but Thomas kept the thought to himself.

"Suppose you agree and he says he will take fifty men, and you are also to take fifty. How many would you in fact take?"

"At least half as many again, but I would not allow him to see them all."

"Take more," Thomas said, "for that is what he will do. And allow him to see them so he knows your forces are equally matched. I believe he makes the offer in good faith, but I will ensure Olaf Torvaldsson leads Abu Abdullah's forces. You have met the man and I know he likes you. Olaf will not allow any double-dealing."

"Then do it. Are you sure this other matter is closed? I know how persistent you can be."

"I identified the man who was brought here to cook. It seems he has already fled his house, his wife along with him, but I have other avenues I can explore." Thomas stared at Isabel for a moment, seeing her attention turned inward, and decided to press her a little. "Abu Abdullah also told me he believes you are discussing terms with others in Gharnatah. Is he wrong?"

"I have spoken with many people, as well you know."

"There is only one man who can hand the city to you. Whatever these others might have promised, only the Sultan has the power to surrender the city. The citizens circulate rumours of betrayal and might rise up against their masters."

"Which is only to my advantage, is it not?"

"You would inherit a city fighting a civil war, so no, it is not to your advantage. These people you might or might not be talking to play a dangerous game."

"They seek to keep their own wealth and will sacrifice people to do so. I sent them away disappointed. Does Boabdil want the same?"

"He seeks an assurance, but I believe he loves Gharnatah and its citizens and would not see either destroyed. You need to give his proposal consideration, Isabel."

She suppressed a smile. "Am I Isabel tonight, Thomas?"

"To me you always are."

"Then I will do as you ask, even if it should be the other way around. Are you not meant to serve me?"

"As I do, in whatever way you ask."

"Whatever?"

Thomas made no reply. He drained his glass and filled it. As he did so, Isabel reached out and touched the back of his hand.

"We should eat some of this food," he said.

"You can be my taster. If you fall writhing to the floor, I will know not to follow your example."

He reached for a sliver of pale meat. Some kind of bird, he thought, as he popped it into his mouth. He made a show of chewing, then choking. Isabel laughed and punched his side.

"When does Fernando return?"

Her face lost any trace of humour. "He sends me no message. It is as if he has fallen from the edge of the world. He will turn up one day and want to burn something, if anything remains." She leaned over to select a small tart and her shoulder pressed against his for a moment. "You are right, I must give thought to Boabdil's proposal. My duty is to save lives, but my duty is also to see Granada fall to Castile. I have come too far to stop this close to victory. If need be, my army will assault the walls. Men will die on both sides, but I will be victorious." She popped the tart whole into her mouth, chewed and swallowed. Thomas saw her thinking about making a pretence of choking before dismissing the idea. It had already been done.

"If you give thought to his proposal, might I make a suggestion?"

"You know I always value your advice."

"Don't take too long. If you meet with him, do it before Fernando returns if you can. Abu Abdullah does not respond well to arrogance or pretend shows of strength and anger. He also likes women better than men. Meet him on your own. If a deal is to be struck, that will be the way for it to succeed."

"And what will my husband say when he returns and discovers I have not included him?"

"If Gharnatah is handed to Castile without the spilling of blood, he won't care how it is done."

"I sometimes think Fernando has no objection to the spilling of blood, as long as it is not his own." Isabel glanced at Thomas, holding his gaze. "But he has other battles to fight once this one is over. There is Naples, and the French are always giving him problems along the northern borders of Aragon. So yes, I will give thought to the proposal you have brought me. I will decide by the morning—is that soon enough?"

"I expect so." Mention of France brought a memory to him. "Do you recall the Countess who befriended you two years ago in Qurtuba? I saw her today with Abu Abdullah."

"Is she his lover too, now?"

Thomas knew Isabel did not want to say as well as who. Both of them knew Eleanor had shared Fernando's bed.

"Perhaps, but she acted oddly if she is."

Isabel laughed. "What, did she want to seduce you?"

"It was a possibility, I feared. I need to ask Jorge, he will know for sure."

"I like his wife," said Isabel. "I went to see Theresa this afternoon and she was there. She is competent, is she not? She reminds me of your wife. She had her son with her. He is so sweet, just like Jorge."

"They are not married, but they might as well be. And yes, she is more than competent. Belia knows herbs and plants far better than anyone else. It is how I first met her, when she lived in Sevilla. Theresa could not be in better hands." Thomas thought it wise to omit mention of Jorge not being Jahan's father, though he knew Isabel was clever enough to work out such a thing was impossible. Perhaps she had already done so and made a connection to the truth.

Isabel sighed and looked at the food remaining on the table.

"I should tell the kitchen to make less. Look at all this waste. It is wrong."

"It is not waste," Thomas said. "They will distribute it among the kitchen staff, even some of your soldiers if they are lucky. Did you not know?"

"I expect I have never thought of it, but now you tell me, it makes sense. Then they are welcome to it, for I need my bed. Even if it is lonely these days." Isabel giggled. She covered her mouth quickly, as if trying to take back the sound, then turned and stared directly into Thomas's eyes. "Do you have a woman now?"

"You are my only woman."

Isabel pulled a face. "Do not say that, Thomas, not even in jest. Do you remember what I asked of you two years ago, on another terrace far from this one?"

"I do." Thomas knew there was no need to state it. One kiss, she had requested, that is all she had asked of him, all she would ever ask. Except he knew it might no longer be enough. For either of them. He held up a finger and touched her cheek. "Do not speak it, Isabel."

She stared at him for a long time, then said, "I do not need to, do I? We both know what troubles me, and has ever since that day."

"Do not say the words, for they can never be."

Isabel rose and walked away on small feet. She stopped at the door and turned back.

"The Turks come after noon tomorrow. I will need you at my side to translate their words. I have another man, but I trust you the more. Say nothing unless my man misspeaks, and then say it only to me. Do you understand?"

"At what time do you want me?"

"Tomorrow?"

Thomas suppressed a smile. "Yes, tomorrow."

"When they are ready. You can do something else for me until then."

"Ask it."

"The Ottomans arrived two days since. They have set up camp on the edge of ours. Go and sound them out for me. Do not tell them you come from me, but see what you can discover. Take Jorge with you, for he is good with people, and he is a eunuch. I have been told the Ottomans are keen on eunuchs."

Thomas laughed. "Perhaps he is better staying away in that case."

"I will send for you when the formal talks start. Spend time with your children. In fact, bring them to visit with mine. Little Catherine is much taken with your son. It is a shame we can do nothing about it. He is a handsome boy, is he not? Just like his father." And then she was gone, leaving Thomas to think about the meaning behind everything she had said.

CHAPTER ELEVEN

Thomas and Jorge worked their way through a melee of men, fires, dogs, weapons, whores, cannons and cooks as they made their way to the Turks' camp. The rain had continued overnight before stopping at dawn. It was a harbinger of the coming winter. Many of the soldiers had rigged stakes close to their fires to dry bedding and clothes. Smoke and laughter drifted through the air as if this was a celebration, not a war. Will walked ahead, the rangy Kin his constant companion. Thomas's son and his adopted dog had become as one over the last few years. Thomas had asked Will which he preferred—to accompany Amal to play with Isabel's children, or come with him and Jorge.

"With you," Will had said. His speech pattern grew more and more like that of his *morfar,* Olaf Torvaldsson. Two words might even be considered a speech.

"Catherine is there," Thomas said, teasing.

"So is Juan."

"I thought you and he got along."

"We did, once."

"And now?"

"He is turning into a prince."

89

Thomas laughed. "He is a prince, and one day he will be King of Castile."

"And he wants everyone to know it. You don't see it, Pa, because he likes you."

Thomas recognised the truth in Will's words, gratified his son could read Juan so well.

"Am I right in thinking you still want to see Catherine? Or does she believe herself a princess?"

"I see her now and again. We—" Will broke off. He dropped a hand to curl his fingers through the long hair on Kin's neck.

Thomas considered pressing Will for more, then thought better of it. Will was a handsome boy on the cusp of turning into a handsome man. Catherine was still a good few years younger than him, but the daughters of kings and queens had to grow up faster than those of ordinary men. Not too fast, Thomas hoped.

He glanced at Jorge, wondering if he should ask him to advise Will. Wise words regarding the ways of men and women would come better from him than Thomas, who had little experience to base any advice on. No good experience, in any case.

"Can I take Kin hunting while you talk with the Turks?" Will asked. "Usaden said there are good rabbits in the woods, and we might even get a boar."

"Boars are dangerous."

"I know." It was clear Will felt no need to point out that he could also be dangerous. It was a judgement Thomas didn't doubt. He would wager his son against almost any man except Usaden, Olaf or himself, and he wasn't so sure about himself anymore.

The last of the Castilian camp fell behind. Ahead, a cluster of tents stood on a low rise. They were of a more ornate design than those used in Castile, with higher peaks, their walls fashioned of silk rather than canvas or cotton. They were meant to impress, and it worked. Thomas wondered if they were also intended to keep out the weather. No doubt those using them would have discovered the proof of that last night.

Three men left the group gathered on the ground and started down the slope. A dozen more remained, together with three women, one of whom stood apart from the others. Already Thomas knew Jorge would evaluate her, though little evaluation was needed. She was achingly beautiful.

"You had better leave now if you want to hunt," Thomas said to Will. "I think my work is about to begin."

"Give them hell, Pa."

Thomas laughed as he watched his son run away—agile as a deer and strong as an ox. Also stubborn as a mule sometimes. He shook his head at the simple comparison to beasts. Will was Will. His son. Unique, as all people are.

"Do you have business with us?" The lead man spoke accented Arabic that differed from the language used by Thomas, but it would suffice. He stopped six paces away. The man glanced to where Will was about to enter the tree-line. "Or are you joining your man to hunt? I like his dog."

"I like his dog, too. You are the Ottoman delegation?"

"Who wants to know? We have no time to pander to casual curiosity. We have sent scores away since we came, but I admit none of them spoke passable Arabic. Where did you learn? You do not look like a Moor." The man glanced at Jorge, then away, mistakenly regarding him as unimportant.

"My home is in Gharnatah."

The man narrowed his eyes as he regarded Thomas.

"So what are you doing here? Is that not the army of Castile spread out behind you?"

"I am a seeker of knowledge," Thomas said. "My companion is a seeker of experience. We search out both wherever we can. I am curious about you and would welcome finding out more."

The man laughed. He looked at his companions, who also laughed, as though an expectation had been placed on them. Thomas assumed the man was their leader and took a moment to judge him. Tall and slim, handsome, with a black beard neatly tended and black hair cut long. He wore a wrap of cloth around his head in the Turkish manner, his clothes fashioned of fine cotton and silk.

"Perhaps I can propose an exchange of information," he said. "I will provide the knowledge you seek in exchange for the knowledge I seek."

"And if I am not a knowledgeable man?"

The man looked into Thomas's eyes.

"I doubt that. I doubt that very much. Your name?"

"I am Thomas Berrington, and my companion is Jorge Olmos. The youth you saw entering the woods is my son, Will."

"And the dog?"

"His name is Kin. He was my dog, but now he is my son's."

"I am Koparsh Hadryendo, and I lead this sorry band of exiles. We too are searchers after knowledge. You are welcome in our camp, Thomas Berrington. You too, Jorge Olmos. Come, we will talk and drink coffee, then you can report back to your mistress." The man laughed. He appeared to laugh a great deal. "Yes, I recognise your name and I know who you work for. I also know who you used to work for. My party spent a pleasant week in Gharnatah in discussion with the Sultan, and he mentioned you. As did his guest, a rather beautiful Frenchwoman."

Thomas fell into step beside Koparsh Hadryendo as they started towards the largest of the tents.

"I suspect Abu Abdullah may have given you the wrong impression of me, as would the woman, if she is who I think."

"It was not flattering, I am afraid, but then I believed little the Sultan said. Perhaps you are a paragon of virtue and not a snake who bites the hand of his betters. I make my own mind up about men. The woman spoke of you only with affection."

They reached the tent, but rather than enter, Koparsh indicated where carpets and cushions were set on the ground. Thomas waited for him to sit first, then followed, his movements awkward. He had been too long in Isabel's service and grown accustomed to tables and chairs.

Koparsh made small-talk until the beautiful woman brought coffee. She was slim, with dark eyes and even darker hair that hung loose. Beneath the silks of her robe, it was clear there lay a body that could offer the promise of delight. Her eyes offered a promise of even more. She wore a scarf, but it hung loosely around her neck rather than over her head. The tails of the scarf touched the ground as she knelt to set a jug and cups on the carpet.

"Is there anything else, My Lord?" She remained on her knees, looking as if she could maintain the position all day. Thomas stared at her because such beauty deserved attention. When he glanced at Jorge, it was to see him also studying her.

"Do we have any of those small cakes you made last night? I always think they taste better the next day."

"I will go and see." She rose and moved away, her movement lithe.

"She is a wondrous cook," said Koparsh. "And she makes the best coffee in the world. Turkish coffee is the best in the world, and Salma's is the best in Turkey."

"Is she your wife?" asked Jorge.

"My companion, but also her own woman. Do you have a wife?"

"A companion also."

"And you, Thomas?"

"She died."

"My sympathies." Koparsh nodded to one of his men, who poured the coffee. Only the three of them would be drinking it, though a fourth cup remained empty. When he had finished, the man retreated to stand at a distance. Salma reappeared with a tray holding sugared cakes, which she set down. Instead of leaving, she settled on the ground between Thomas and Jorge despite there being not enough room, so her shoulders touched against theirs. She reached out and poured coffee for herself.

"Why are you here among the army of Castile?" Thomas had grown tired of small-talk. The day was passing, and soon Isabel would talk with these men. More than likely this man, their leader. He half expected Koparsh to avoid a direct answer, so it surprised him when he did not.

"My master sent me to this land, to this war, to judge what action he should take. Sultan Muhammed sent a request for our help, but the Sultan Bayezid, the second of that name, all honour be upon him, does not make impetuous decisions. He sent me here to discover the truth of the matter."

"Surely the war will be over before you can report back?"

"Which is why Sultan Bayezid sent a man he can trust. A man who can decide on his own. Gharnatah is Islamic, as is Turkey and the lands she now rules. It makes sense that we should support the Sultan Muhammed. But what makes sense does not always make sense." He raised his eyes to meet Thomas's. "You understand this, of course."

Thomas made no reply other than a brief nod. He sipped at his coffee. He hated to admit it, but Koparsh was right. He had never tasted better. He reached for one of the small cakes which Jorge had already consumed two of, and who now leaned even closer to Salma as they whispered together.

"What is your opinion of Abu Abdullah?"

Thomas expected a political response, so it surprised him when Koparsh once again answered honestly.

"He is a fool. Even worse, he is a weak fool. It is only those around him who keep him in power. I met his general, the big Northman. Now there is a man who knows what power means."

Thomas suppressed a smile. "Olaf doesn't care for power. He does what he is told by his master. Whoever that master might be."

"What will happen to him when Gharnatah falls? My

master could find a place for such a man." Koparsh glanced at Jorge and Salma. "I see your friend fascinates Salma."

"She is safe with him. He is a eunuch, but he does so love to beguile a woman. Or a man, for that matter."

"He does not look like any kind of eunuch I have ever seen. Is he clever? Ottoman eunuchs are usually clever. Is it the same here?"

"Jorge is clever enough, but his intelligence takes a different form to that of other men. And I would not approach Olaf with any offer if I were you, he believes in total loyalty."

"He must know the war with Castile can end in only one way?"

"He does. But until that day arrives, Abu Abdullah has his unwavering loyalty."

"Very well. And what about you, Thomas Berrington, are you loyal to Queen Isabel? I hear you are closer to her even than her husband. It is a shame Fernando will not be here for our talks today. He too is a good general, is he not?"

"Fernando likes to fight, which I expect does make him a good general," Thomas said. He hoped Koparsh would not pursue his question regarding Isabel, because he was unsure where his own loyalty lay. "What will you be proposing at this meeting we are to have?"

"For that you will have to wait until we have it. You will be present, I assume?"

"I will. It might help if I had some idea why you are here, other than to observe Castile's forces." Thomas watched Koparsh, looking for some tell on his face, but the man showed nothing. Why he was here was something he was keeping to himself. Why he was here was a matter of confusion for Thomas, because it made no sense. The lands controlled by the Ottoman Empire were too distant to threaten Castile, or for Castile to threaten them. Then an answer occurred to him. He reached for another small cake and popped it into his mouth.

Beneath a crisp pastry shell, sour cherries burst, tart against his tongue.

"Naples," he said. "You want to discuss Naples."

"What makes you say that?"

"Turkey already controls lands east of Italia and south into Africa. It controls almost the entirety of Greece, which has laid claim to Naples for centuries. Roma is home to the Pope. An Ottoman outpost on the same land would send a powerful signal."

"I admire a man who can conjure tales from the air, whether they have any basis in reality. Perhaps you are a poet and not a physician, as I was told."

"I am no longer sure what I am anymore." Thomas rose to his feet, wondering if he had revealed too much of himself, but he liked the man even if he did not understand him. "Come on, Jorge, we have work to do. I will see you after noon, Koparsh."

"Why did we leave so soon?" asked Jorge once they were at a distance from the Turkish camp. "That woman Salma is exquisite, but strange."

"You already have an exquisite woman, and Belia can also be strange."

"Do you think Belia is exquisite? Yes, of course she is. You were a fortunate man last year when I allowed you to share her."

"You wanted a child, didn't you? Both of you wanted a child."

"I would have liked a girl," said Jorge. "I love Jahan, but I would still like a girl." He glanced at Thomas. "Perhaps you can help us again. I expect it was not such an arduous task, was it?"

"What did you think of Koparsh?" Thomas wanted the subject changed. "Despite appearances to the contrary, I know you were watching him, as he was you."

"He is a clever man. Perhaps he is even as clever as you, or more so. Tell Isabel to be careful. He will charm her, for he is a handsome man, good with women, and she is not used to such.

You were right to ask why he is here, but you cannot have expected an honest answer."

Thomas glanced at the trees where Will had disappeared, half-expecting to see him, but both son and dog had forgotten about them in the thrill of the chase.

"I will warn her, but she is no fool. She can see through flattery for herself. Nothing will deflect her from the course she is pursuing."

"Do you think he seduced Eleanor when he was in Gharnatah?" asked Jorge.

"Possibly, for as you say, he is exceedingly handsome and urbane. If he did so, it is no business of mine. Eleanor is nothing to do with me anymore, and I wish she was not here."

They were two hundred paces from the edge of the Castilian camp when Jorge said, "What is all that smoke?"

Thomas looked up from being lost in his own thoughts. Jorge pointed to the right, then again to the left.

"Fire," he said. "Some idiot has been drying their tent too close to a flame. If they're not careful, the entire camp will go up."

Thomas ran, but already he knew they were too late. The fire was spreading fast, the sound of it a deep roar. Flames rose high, smoke already starting to shade the sun. He left others to their attempts at saving the camp and ran hard for where Isabel was.

CHAPTER TWELVE

Jorge leaned close and whispered into Thomas's ear.

"Salma is over there."

"I see her, but you are to stay here beside me. Talk to her later if you must, but I need you at my side. I need your skill in understanding people. Say nothing and watch Koparsh. I want to know when he lies, and I want to know what he is hiding."

"She has already attracted Fernando's attention. Can I at least stare at her while I do your bidding?"

"Not if I want you to watch Koparsh."

Ten days had passed before the meeting between Isabel and the Ottoman delegation finally took place. Once the fires had been extinguished and the damage assessed, the Turks had broken camp. Nobody knew where they had gone, or whether they would return. Isabel decided their current position was no longer tenable, and moved the entire army to where the new town of Santa Fe was being built. Thomas hoped it might confuse Fernando when he found the army gone, but he rode into the growing town four days before the Turks returned.

Now Koparsh Hadryendo sat on a chair, looking as uncomfortable on it as Thomas had on the cushions at their last meeting. Isabel sat in a more ornate chair, not quite a throne but built to impress. Fernando stood a little behind her and to one side. His face wore a scowl, as if his intention was to protect his wife from these heathens. Thomas saw Jorge had spoken true, because the King's eyes drifted often to take in Salma.

Isabel had dressed in one of the Moorish outfits she increasingly favoured, and Thomas suspected it was in deference to their guests as well as her own comfort. There were almost a score on the Castilian side, men of God, statesmen, dukes and duchesses. Theresa stood at the rear beside Martin de Alarcón.

Isabel's interpreter stood to her right, facing the man who would translate Isabel's words into Arabic. There would be no trust from either side. Isabel had told Thomas to say nothing unless one or other interpreter failed to convey her words accurately, and even then not to interrupt unless he heard a major failure. He was to go to her afterwards and tell her his opinion.

The work began with slow progress towards the crucial matters. The rules had to be followed. Those surrounding Isabel would ensure that. They were, in the main, men who valued things done in the correct manner, however much time it added to proceedings. Koparsh Hadryendo showed himself as a man with no patience for such niceties.

"I want to talk about Naples," he said, his eyes on Fernando. He would know Naples was a vassal to Aragon.

"Naples is not a subject open for discussion," said Isabel, after Koparsh's words had been translated, her own words passing back in the same way. "I need to know your intention in coming here." She glanced briefly towards Thomas. "I hear you have already been in discussion with the Sultan of Granada. That I can understand. What interest do you have in Castile?"

"My master, Sultan Bayezid, wishes to offer the hand of friendship to Your Majesties."

"A hand with a sword in it, more like." Fernando took half a pace forward, ignoring a stern look from his wife. "Where is your army, sir? Is it massed in Tunis waiting for us to show weakness so you can invade?"

"I have no army. Who you see here are my only companions. Neither I nor my master bear Castile any ill will. I have gifts for the Queen, fine spices and herbs from the east, gold, silver and myrrh. I have watched events in this land and know there can be only one victor in the long and valiant war you have fought. There are gifts for you also, King Fernando." Koparsh held his hand behind him without looking. One of his men reached beneath his robe and drew a sword. Within an instant, four men of Castile did the same. Martin was the first, striding to put himself between Isabel and Koparsh.

"It is a gift," said Koparsh, smiling. He nodded at the man holding the sword, who placed it on the tiles. Koparsh pushed it with his foot so it slid to lie between the two parties.

Thomas saw Fernando's eyes on the sword, which was a thing of great beauty.

"Martin," said Isabel, and he bent to pick up the weapon. He turned and handed it to Fernando, who raised it to examine the fine script that decorated the hilt and blade.

"What do these scratchings mean?" asked Fernando. "I trust they are not heathen words in praise of your false God."

"They say the blade is a gift from the Sultan Bayezid to King Fernando of Castile and Aragon."

Fernando scowled at Koparsh. "You still don't get your hands on Naples."

Koparsh tried not to smile. "It is not a bribe, Your Grace. It is a gift, freely given, with no expectation of anything in return. The Ottoman Empire wishes only to be a friend to Castile. Perhaps we should move on to the other Sultan who sits not three leagues from here. I would plead mercy for Muhammed when the time comes for him to step down. Also for the people of his city and its lands."

Koparsh Hadryendo approached Thomas and Jorge as they climbed the slope to the house Isabel had assigned them. Thomas glanced at the man, but said nothing, waiting for the Turk to speak first. If it was a conversation he sought and not just his company. There had been little point to the discussion, and Thomas wondered what their purpose had been.

"I would speak with you if allowed to do so without your mistress present."

"That depends on what matters you have in mind." Thomas indicated the sky, a bank of gathering cloud to the south. "If it is the weather, or the growth of crops, then perhaps I can be of assistance. If it is anything to do with where we have just come from, then perhaps not."

"It is the latter, of course, but you have my permission to tell the Queen everything I say. It is only that it is easier said away from the cauldron of her advisers. And her husband." Koparsh peered around Thomas at Jorge. "I would speak with Thomas alone if you have no objection."

"So you can attack him out here without my protection?" said Jorge.

"I believe Thomas can well defend himself, even from someone like myself. I want our conversation to be honest, that is all, and honesty will come easier if there is nobody else present."

The house was three hundred paces ahead, and Thomas could see Will and Usaden on the terrace. They were doing their daily practice with the sword, the clash of metal on metal drifting down to greet them. Hand to hand combat would follow later in the afternoon. Belia and Amal sat to one side, watching.

"Perhaps I can return the favour and offer you coffee? There may even be some sweet cakes. Not as delicious as those baked by Salma, but passable."

"Belia is as good a cook as her," said Jorge.

"Perhaps I can be the judge between them," said Koparsh. "I accept your offer. I would like to meet your family, Thomas. Is your woman with you?"

"I have no woman."

Koparsh smiled. "Perhaps I can assist you in that matter as well. I may have brought more than I seem to need with me."

Thomas made no reply. He assumed Koparsh was making a joke, poor though the effort was. He led the man to the terrace after introducing him. They sat on comfortable chairs set apart.

"How long have you worked alongside the Queen?" Koparsh surprised Thomas when he spoke in Spanish. Bad Spanish, but enough to tell him the man may have understood the whispered conversations between Isabel, Fernando and their advisors. The conversations Thomas had not translated.

"I prefer we use Arabic," Thomas said. "It is easier for me these days, and how long I have been in Isabel's service is a question I will not answer."

Koparsh raised a hand in dismissal. "It does not matter. A little under two years, I have been told. That is good enough. Do you bed her? That is also what I was told."

He looked up as Belia approached carrying a tray with a steaming pot of coffee, two silvered cups and a plate of small cakes. She placed them on the table and walked away without saying a word.

"She is Jorge's woman?"

Thomas nodded as he poured the coffee.

"She is exquisite."

"As is your woman, Salma."

"She is not mine. Salma belongs to no one but herself. But yes, she is beautiful. She likes Jorge, if he is interested. Though I understand if he prefers not to take up any offer she might make. I believe she might also be interested in King Fernando.

She has always been attracted to men of power. Belia and Salma might be cut from the same cloth."

"Except Belia does not lust after power and is loyal to her man."

"I told you, Salma has no man."

"Have you come to make small-talk or do you have something meaningful to say?"

Koparsh sipped his coffee, reached for one of the sugar-dusted pastries.

"Very well. I know you must be a busy man, so I will get to the point. It is to do with the Sultan."

"Yours or mine?"

"Yours, of course. You are aware I have had talks with Muhammed. Unsatisfactory talks, but my master sent me to sound him out, and I always do as instructed. As I am sure you do. We are men of similar minds, I believe. These small cakes are delicious, by the way. Perhaps Salma and Belia should meet to trade recipes. They can talk about Jorge at the same time. Perhaps an arrangement can be made."

"What conclusion have you come to regarding Abu Abdullah?"

"You use his given name, I see. Is that a matter of friendship or a lack of respect?"

"We were friends once, of a kind, but no longer. I am still waiting for your answer. Though as we are apparently so similar, I suspect I already know what it will be."

Koparsh laughed and took another cake.

"Tell me, then."

"Abu Abdullah is a weak fool. You know that because you are a clever man. How much flexibility did your master give you?"

"He trusts me completely. He would not have sent me otherwise. We are many months' travel from Constantinople, so he has to trust me. And, like you, I am exceptionally good at my job. And because we are being honest with each other, I can tell you my decision is to offer no succour to the man. It would be a waste of gold, a waste of men's lives, and a waste of my time."

Thomas ate one of the cakes. He couldn't decide which was the better, this or the ones Salma had baked.

"Which brings us to the question of what you want from Isabel, or can offer her. Do you have an army with you?"

"You have seen who is with me. A score of men."

"A score here, but elsewhere?"

Koparsh's eyes showed amusement. "Oh, I like you. Of course there are more men, but they are not here."

"Nearby?"

"A few days' ride. Too far away, and too small a force, to offer any threat."

"How many?"

"Two hundred, possibly a little more."

"Not enough to make a difference to Gharnatah, not enough to make a difference to Castile. I assume they are your protection, your guarantee of safety."

"I met someone else in Gharnatah while I was there who also told me you are a clever man."

Thomas thought for a moment, but knew it could only be one person.

"Helena has made some odd decision to like me of late."

Koparsh frowned. "Did you say Helena, or did I mishear you?"

"Helena." As he repeated the word, Thomas realised his mistake. The two names, said softly, could sound much alike. "Can I assume you met Eleanor, the Countess d'Arreau? Did she tell you her title?"

"She did. The Countess told me you and she were once lovers, but that it was a long time ago." Koparsh's eyes were on Thomas, measuring him. "I also met your son. He intrigued Salma."

"Did Eleanor invite you into her bed?"

"She did, and I turned her down, despite her beauty and the sin I saw in her eyes. She took it in good grace, despite my obvious charms. Am I not a handsome man?"

"You are asking the wrong person, you should try Jorge. Have you decided what action you intend to take regarding Castile? Two or three hundred men mean nothing. Castile has at least ten thousand under arms. Gunners from France and Italia. Bowmen of England. Seven thousand men of Castile, Aragon, and the other kingdoms of Spain. So no, two hundred, even five hundred men would disappear like a pebble tossed into the great ocean. But the importance of you standing beside Isabel and Fernando would mean far more than almost any other man. You are the emissary of the Ottoman Emperor, an Islamic state. For you to stand with Castile would send a powerful message. It would weaken Abu Abdullah more than any other action you could take."

Thomas watched Koparsh. Watched his benign expression. Looked into dark eyes that hid his thoughts. Yes, he was handsome. Not as handsome as Jorge, but who was?

"You have made your decision, I see."

"I have." Koparsh rose and walked to the edge of the terrace. He looked across the wide plain to where the palace of al-Hamra sat, towering over the city below. He turned and looked at Thomas's children. Will had ended his practice, and Usaden had gone off with Kin to hunt. Amal knelt beside Jahan, playing with wooden blocks. She was trying to show him how to build a tower, both of them laughing each time it fell down. Finally, he turned back.

"You are a fortunate man, Thomas Berrington. You are loved, and you love. Almost everyone who mentions you does so with either respect or love. Even the Sultan Muhammed."

"But without the love, I expect," Thomas said.

"Indeed. Tell Isabel she can count on the Ottomans. My men will stand in the ranks so the entire world can see them."

Thomas watched Koparsh descend the slope towards Santa

Fe. He glanced at the sky, judging how many hours of daylight remained, and made a decision. He would go to Isabel and give her Koparsh's message. Then he would ask for a week to continue his investigation into Theresa's poisoning. Baldomero's absence still rankled.

Thomas went into the house.

"Who wants to come to Gharnatah in the morning? Provided the gate remains open, that is."

Everyone raised their hands.

CHAPTER THIRTEEN

There were six men and a dog who walked through the wide eastern gate into the city of Gharnatah. The approaches had been busy, within the walls it was busier still. Traders continued to buy and sell their goods. Men and women wandered in groups while children and animals ran between them. Only if someone stood beneath the gate and looked towards the smoke of the Castilian fires would they know a war was being fought over ownership of this last bastion of al-Andalus.

Between them, Thomas and Usaden pushed the cart Belia had used to transport the bottles and boxes from Baldomero de Pamplona's house. Now it contained their clothes and Amal, who sat with Kin draped across her legs and the infant Jahan cradled beneath her arm. Will walked to one side of the cart, only a little shorter than Thomas. Come the end of the year, he might exceed him in height. The boy was changing too fast for Thomas to keep up with, and he wanted to spend more time with both his children. Wanted to tease out his thoughts about the future and what he wanted to do when that future arrived. Thomas had only been a few years older than Will when his own life had changed forever, but he had not sought those experiences. He did not want the same to happen to Will. Sometimes life threw events at you and you had to cope with them or succumb. Watching Will, who was unaware of his gaze, Thomas doubted there was much that could make his son succumb. Unless it was Catherine. That was another conversation still to be had.

Thomas wondered if Helena would still be at the house, and if she was, what he might do about it. But that was a decision for later, and as they walked towards al-Hattabin square, he felt a tension leave his body he had not even been aware was present. It felt like coming home. It *was* coming home, but for how long, he knew none of them could say.

"Do you have a plan?" asked Jorge as he caught up with Thomas. He handed him an orange and bit into his own, opening the peel so he could suck the juice.

"I have things I want to do, but no plan. What about you?"

"I intend to sleep in my own bed tonight and make love to Belia for at least two hours."

Thomas smiled. "I assume you have told her of this coming debauchery so she can prepare herself?"

"It was her idea. That place we are staying in is all right, but it is too small. Both the house, the rooms, and the beds. I am a man who needs space. Tell me about the things you want to do. Is bedding Helena one of them?"

Thomas glanced at Jorge, who laughed.

"It is, isn't it? Good. She has changed, and you need a woman in your life again."

"I still need to know what happened to de Pamplona."

"Then I will help once we have taken everyone safe to your house and broken our fast. Could we not have come after noon instead of this unholy hour of the day?"

"And waste time? But agreed, my house first, and then … I have a reply from Isabel for Abu Abdullah."

"A reply? About what?"

"I will tell you later. And I need your advice on a certain matter."

Jorge stopped walking, and it took a moment for Thomas to realise.

He turned back.

"What's wrong?"

"You need my advice?"

"Isn't that what I said?"

Jorge shook his head. He reached out and touched Thomas's brow.

"Are you unwell? Do you need a physician?"

"It's about Will."

"Then you would be better consulting Usaden or Olaf rather than me. Will is turning into a fine young man, but he is not someone I claim to understand. We are too different. I like him well enough, and beneath all that strength, he possesses a sweet soul. What about Will?"

Jorge waited for Thomas to say something, his gaze on him. When nothing came, he laughed.

"Ah, I see. *That*."

"Yes. That." Thomas glanced away to where the others had travelled a hundred paces further on. They knew the way to his house and could find it without him and Jorge, but he would like them all to arrive together. "Perhaps we can talk while we walk, if you are capable of such dexterity."

"It may prove difficult, but I will do my best. If it is a matter of men and women, or boys and girls, how long do we have? Because, as you know, I am a master of such information. Is it Catherine you worry about? If so, she is barely of an age to be interested in Will in the way you fear."

"Catherine worships Will, but I agree, her love is innocent so far. I also hear he attracts the older girls, and they may be more of a problem. Juanna in particular. She is a wild thing." Thomas shook his head. "Why is it I need explain nothing to you?"

"Because you are an open book to me."

"If I was, you could not read me."

"Then you are an entertainment, a song I already know the tune of. Or a dance. Yes, you are a dance, and what you want to talk about is also a dance. Are you worried Will grows too close to Isabel's daughters?"

"I am. He needs to realise the consequences of his actions and the difference in their positions."

"He may be a little young for me to talk to him about positions."

"I believe I already possess a book from the east that contains all of those. I should show it to you."

"As you have already pointed out, I cannot read."

"It has illustrations," Thomas said.

"In that case, please do. What are you going to tell him? Keep it in his britches?"

"I was hoping to be less crude than that, but yes."

Jorge walked on for a while, the sun on his face.

"When did you first lie with a girl, Thomas?"

"Is that relevant?"

"It is, and I am curious. When?"

"I was older than Will is now."

"But you have already said Will is advanced for his age. Were you as tall as him when this wondrous event occurred?"

"I was not. I had thirteen years."

"What was her name?"

"Arabella Brickenden. Everybody called her Bel."

"Was she pretty?"

"She was beautiful, and clever, and sweet-natured. You would have liked her."

"How old would she be now?"

"She was two years older than me, so she would be fifty-three or four. She probably has half a dozen children by now, even more grandchildren. I often wonder if she followed her mother into the same profession."

"Which was?"

"Jane Brickenden was the best whore in Lemster. It was a respected profession there."

"As it is here. I know you have availed yourself of the charms of Aamir's girls in the past, but not for some time, I admit. So you lost your virginity to the daughter of the town whore? At least it would have been an excellent education. What happened? Why are you here and not back in England married to this Bel Brickenden?"

"Disease and war." Thomas realised Jorge had distracted them both from what he wanted to discuss. "What should I tell Will? How hard should I be on him?"

"Not hard at all. Will is as clever as you, I believe. Tell him the truth. Tell him he can never marry Catherine or any of the others, but he can be as close as he wishes as long as he does not take that step we both know cannot be taken back. We don't want any awkward accidents, do we?"

"I can't tell him that. I need him, as you say, to keep it in his britches."

"No, you don't. That way leads only to disaster. Will is a little young yet, but to look at him, he is to all intents a man. I lay with women when I was younger than Will, so it is not beyond the bounds of possibility."

"But then you are not like most men," Thomas said.

"For which I am eternally grateful. Tell Will what I have said, and then tell him to come to me and I will explain the details. It's no good you doing it for I expect you don't know them, or will only confuse the boy. I will take him under my wing."

"That's what I'm afraid of."

"And show me this book of positions you claim to have, perhaps there is something Belia and I have not tried."

"I very much doubt it."

"Yes … you are probably right."

The fact Baldomero de Pamplona's house had so far failed to yield a single piece of useful information continued to nag at Thomas, which was why he and Jorge once more stood within its walls. For how much longer the house might remain unoccupied, he didn't know, which was why he had made it his first task to visit there as soon as everyone was settled in his house on the Albayzin. Belia had told him she went through every item brought from Baldomero's house on the cart, and there was nothing unexpected amongst the tools of trade for a cook. She did comment on the presence of unusual herbs and spices, but none that could kill someone, not even make them slightly ill. Which left papers.

Thomas sent Jorge to examine the other rooms while he searched the kitchen, but the search took barely any time at all. De Pamplona seemed to make no notes. All his knowledge must reside in his head. Thomas searched again, lying flat to reach deep into drawers and cupboards, but with the same result. He was starting to wonder if the cook had not been responsible for Theresa's poisoning. If so, it raised a whole new set of questions. Which of the cooks used by Isabel might be? He didn't even want to consider the danger she was in if that was the case.

He went in search of Jorge, expecting he would have had the same result, but couldn't find him. When Thomas went out to the street, he saw him talking with a woman of middling years with a wash-basket of clothes at her feet. Jorge raised a hand to beckon Thomas over.

"This beautiful maiden collects washing from the street. She told me she saw something you need to hear." Jorge turned to the woman. "Tell him, my sweet. He is not dangerous, despite how he looks."

The woman didn't seem so sure.

"I told you everything, can you not tell him? Baldomero was a good man, and I may have been mistaken."

"Mistaken how?" Thomas watched the woman take a step back and knew he had been too abrupt. He glanced at Jorge to recover the situation.

"Everyone we have spoken with confirms what you say. Baldomero is a paragon of virtue. How old was this woman you saw?"

The woman looked between them before nodding at Jorge.

"Your age, I would say, and almost as handsome."

"You are too kind. How was she dressed?"

Thomas was sure Jorge knew all this information, but he waited to hear it from the woman.

"She dressed in expensive silks and satins. Her hair was dark and shone like polished fire."

"You said you overheard their conversation on one occasion, did you not?"

"I was not eavesdropping, but I called for Baldomero's washing and he invited me in while she was there. He spoke to me in Arabic, but then as I was loading my basket, they conversed in an unfamiliar language."

"Castilian?" Thomas asked.

"No, I would have recognised that, I speak a little of it myself, we all do these days. It was familiar, but I could not say from where."

"Did it sound like this?" Thomas spoke the words three times. In English, the tongue of Naples, and finally the language of the south of France.

"That one," said the woman.

"Which?"

"The last. Speak them again, but use different words this time."

Thomas looked at her a moment, then said, in each of the languages, "How many of the mushrooms do I need to give her?"

The woman's eyes widened. "Yes, that one, the last. And I am sure those are the same words I heard. What is their meaning?"

"You are fortunate Baldomero knew you didn't understand what they were talking about," Thomas said. "My thanks, you have been of great help." He held out a coin for the woman.

"We need to visit the hill," Thomas said, and Jorge nodded. There was only one person they knew who both matched the description given and spoke the language of southern France.

CHAPTER FOURTEEN

Thomas knocked on the door of Eleanor's house, expecting a servant to answer, but instead Yves opened it.

"Is your mother home?"

"She left early this morning. Do you want me to tell her you called when she returns?"

Thomas heard a hesitation at the end of his words, as if he had meant to add something. Father perhaps, though he doubted it. Certainly not sir. He was starting to think Yves no longer hated the idea of an estranged father as much as he once had.

"Tell her, but I would like to talk with you as well if I can."

"About what?"

"That is an excellent question, to which I am sure I will soon work out an answer."

"Do you need me?" asked Jorge, who had stood beside Thomas the whole time. "If not, I would like to visit some people on the hill while we are here."

"No, I don't need you. Go see Bazzu."

"That may not be who I meant."

Thomas smiled and sent Jorge away before turning back to Yves.

"May I come in?"

"If you want to talk, I need something in return."

"Ask, and if it is mine to give, you can have it." It occurred to Thomas that Yves and Eleanor might be running short of funds. They had been in Spain a long time and had no obvious source of income.

"Mother tells me you live in the city."

"I do. Not all the time, but at the moment, I do."

"I would like to see your house."

"Why?"

"Curiosity. I am growing used to the idea of having a father, and would like to learn more about him." Yves met Thomas's gaze, something different in his own. He had grown in confidence since their first encounter in Qurtuba. Thomas wondered how much he knew about his mother's actions.

"Are you sure you want to see the city's sights and charms, such as they are? I could take you to the Hammam baths, unless you are like most of your countrymen and forgo such pleasure."

"Mother bathes in the palace. It might be where she has gone today, she didn't tell me." Yves smiled. "And yes, take me to the baths, and then your house."

"The house will be busy," Thomas said. "Everyone is there."

"Who is everyone? Wait a moment, I will fetch a cloak." Yves stopped and turned back. "Will I need a sword?"

Thomas held his hands out from his sides.

"Am I wearing one?"

"But you know this city, and no doubt its people know you. Both Mother and I keep hearing your name mentioned."

Before Thomas could ask who by, Yves disappeared into the house. Thomas peered along the corridor, half-expecting Eleanor to be hiding somewhere inside, but if she was, she continued to hide. Yves returned within a moment, pulling a cloak around his shoulders. It was dark red, almost black, with a fine sheen. At least it told Thomas he had no need of funds.

Within the hour, they had explored a little of the city and Aamir had found them a private chamber. Thomas led the way through the humid, scented air. Yves followed slowly, his head turning this way and that as he took in the unfamiliar sights.

"You said Eleanor has used the baths in the palace, but I take it you have not?"

Yves shook his head, then stopped in his tracks as a slim girl came towards them carrying a pot of oil. Her shift barely fell to mid-thigh, and the thin cotton clung against her youthful body.

"I have not, but I am not as averse to the habit of washing as many of my countrymen."

"Would you prefer we spoke French rather than Castilian?" Thomas asked in that tongue.

"It would be easier for me, I admit, but no, I need the practice. Mother tells me we will need to be fluent before long. As it seems you already are."

"Better than I was a few years ago, but you are right, it will become the language of the whole of Iberia soon. But won't you be returning home then?"

"Perhaps."

Thomas turned into the chamber Aamir had assigned them, aware he had let his feet carry him without thought. He had bathed here so often, he knew every corner and niche.

"How does this work?" asked Yves as he stood in the doorway. His newfound confidence appeared to have deserted him.

"We undress and stand under that pipe and let hot water cascade over us, then use the soaps to wash ourselves." Thomas pointed to where a round stone pipe emerged from the wall, a slow drip falling. Over many years, that steady drip had created a hollow in the stone beneath. "And then we float in the water here for a time." Thomas nodded at a recessed bath filled with clean water, a faint steam rising from the surface. It was eight paces by four, deep enough to cover a man to the waist if he stood. "But the bath is optional. We will be clean by then."

"I want to try everything." But Yves made no move to remove his clothes. "Is there no door to afford privacy?"

"No, no door. One or two of the servants might pass, but they have seen enough naked men and women to last them a lifetime. I expect you hold no surprises for them. Though a Frenchman might be a cause for curiosity."

Thomas hung his cloak on a peg set opposite the pipe and removed the rest of his clothes. When he turned to face Yves, he did so deliberately. His son had yet to remove his own cloak. Thomas saw his eyes track his body, but felt no shame. He had been naked in front of Jorge and others often enough to no longer care who saw him. It was only flesh, and in this case it was family flesh.

"Stay dressed then, but I intend to wash."

"Where did you get those scars?" asked Yves.

Thomas pushed his leg out and touched a raised line above the knee.

"See this?"

Yves nodded, eyes wide.

"This happened when soldiers sent by the man you believed to be your father broke my leg. I was seventeen years old, the same age as your mother, and she was carrying you inside her."

Yves continued to stare at the scar.

"Did it hurt?"

Thomas laughed. "It was the most painful injury I have ever experienced, before or since. So yes, it hurt a great deal. I thought I was going to die."

"And yet here you are." Yves came to a decision and unbuckled his cloak. He walked past Thomas and hung it on a peg, then removed his shirt, keeping his back turned.

Thomas walked to the spout and pulled the lever. Hot water cascaded over his head. He reached into a niche cut in the stone for soap and washed himself, his eyes closed. He assumed Yves would watch, and when he next opened his eyes, they confirmed his assumption. His son, a man of thirty-five years, stood naked. Thomas shook his head to clear it of water and surveyed him. Yves was as tall as him, with broad shoulders and a narrow waist. He was a handsome man, and Thomas wondered why he remained unmarried. He stepped away from the cascade of water and handed the bar of soap to Yves.

"Pull on the lever and rub hard."

He moved past him and slid into the welcoming heat of the bath itself. He watched Yves wash himself, seeing him grow more at ease with the situation until a young girl entered and Yves covered his manhood with his hands.

"Do you need anything else, Thomas?" She glanced at Yves and suppressed a smile. "Does your friend want a woman?"

"Ask him yourself, though you will need to use Castilian. His name is Yves."

The girl turned to face Yves.

"Do you want a woman when you finish, Yves?" The name emerged with an exotic twist in the unfamiliar language.

He shook his head hard, splashing water.

"No, no woman."

"A man, then?"

"Gods, no!"

"Take a coin from my cloak, Asha," Thomas said.

"You know Aamir says everything is free for you."

"This is not for Aamir, but you. Take something."

"Do you trust me?"

"Should I not?"

She grinned. "Thank you, Thomas. Is Jorge coming?"

"Not today."

When she was gone, Yves straightened up. He used his hands to sluice excess water from his belly and sides.

"Why do you let a slip of a girl like that call you by name?"

"Because she is as worthy to do so as anyone else in this city. She works hard and does her job well. She is no worse than me and I no better than her. Tell me what you have heard about me."

Yves stepped away from the water that was slowing. He looked uncertain about what to do next, even though it was clear what was expected. In the end, he slid into the pool opposite Thomas and sank to his chest.

"That you are the best physician in the city, perhaps in the whole of Iberia and beyond."

"And the negative?"

"That you are arrogant and cold. They call you the butcher, do you know that?"

"I am sure it is a term of affection."

"It did not sound that way when it was told to Mother. They also say you get involved in matters that are none of your business. Like you have done now."

"Where has Eleanor really gone?" Thomas knew an opportunity would come if he relaxed Yves enough and judged now was the time to press for answers.

"I don't know. Truly, I do not know, but I suspect she is with the Sultan again."

"Again?"

"I think she likes him, and he her."

"Are they lovers?"

"Would it make you jealous if they were?"

Thomas laughed. "When we go to my house, you will see why I am not jealous." His smile faded. "I loved your mother once, it is true. Loved her more than anything in this world. But we were wrong for each other. I think we both knew it, but could not accept the truth. I would have liked to have seen you grow up, though."

"I would have been a different man if you had," said Yves.

"Yes, you would. Why have you never married? Have you ever lain with a woman? Or a man? I would not judge you if you had."

"I have. With women, that is. But marriage is difficult for someone in my position. Mother says we must find the right match."

"Perhaps she can arrange something with Queen Isabel. She has a surfeit of daughters, though I believe most are spoken for, and Juanna is not suitable."

"I do not know who you speak of, but a princess would be far too elevated for someone such as myself. Mother says someone will come along, eventually."

"Perhaps you can marry one of Abu Abdullah's daughters. He has several, all exquisite and all young. The single ones, anyway."

"They are Moors," said Yves.

"True, they are. I was once married to a Moor."

"You were?"

"Someone will no doubt have told you that."

Yves said nothing, which was answer enough.

"What business did your mother have with Baldomero de Pamplona?" Thomas was unsure if the time was right for the question, but he had held on to it as long as he could. Soon they would begin the climb through the Albayzin, and he didn't know if there would be an opportunity once they entered his house.

"Who?"

Thomas was disappointed.

"You will meet your half-brother and sister when we go to my house. Neither would ever lie to me. Why do you do so now? I know Eleanor met with Baldomero more than once. I want to know to what purpose."

"Mother never tells me anything." Yves turned sulky.

"How adept is she at using herbs these days?"

"She told me it was you who first taught her about them."

"I did."

Yves smiled, starting to relax again, perhaps believing they were on safer ground.

"She claims she outstripped her tutor. She is called on by a host of people who want her to consult for them."

"In their ailments?"

Yves' gaze shifted away as if fascinated by the bathhouse. He looked up to where openings at the top of the walls were cut in the shape of stars, moons and circles.

"Yes, in their ailments. Perhaps you and she should have stayed together. You would have been a formidable team."

"Yes, I believe we would. Unfortunately, we would almost certainly have killed each other. Is Baldomero staying at your house?"

"No."

"So where is he? I was told he was seen leaving at dawn one morning in the company of a man and woman. Was that you and Eleanor?"

"It was not me."

"But it could have been her?"

"How early in the morning?"

"A little before dawn."

"In which case, I would no doubt have still been asleep. I do not rise early, I have no need to. When was this?"

"It was several weeks ago."

"Why do you want to find this man so much?"

"Because he almost killed a friend of mine. A good friend. The poison was not meant for her, but for Isabel. Queen Isabel. It was only good fortune she didn't eat the poisoned tarts." Thomas splashed his hand into the water, making Yves jump. "Tarts poisoned with the same mushrooms I taught your mother about all those years ago."

"She had nothing to do with what happened."

"But she knew about it, didn't she? She spoke with Baldomero, and she led him away from his house. His wife is also missing. Where are they?"

"I don't know, and neither does Mother. You are mistaken, Thomas, and will be making an even greater mistake if you accuse her without proof of any kind."

CHAPTER FIFTEEN

"He knows something, but I won't get any more out of him today." Thomas sat in the courtyard of his house with Jorge. A jug of wine rested on the low table between them, almost empty now, and it was late. Yves had returned to the house on the Alkazaba. Thomas had sent Usaden to ensure his safety. Gharnatah was normally safe enough, but these were not normal times.

On this side of the Hadarro, everyone else slept.

"Do you believe Eleanor had something to do with the attempt on Isabel?"

"I'm sure of it. The description Baldomero's neighbour gave us matched her well enough. They spoke French. How many other French women can there be in Gharnatah who look like her? We know Baldomero worked in several countries, so it's likely he learned her language—enough for a simple conversation, at least."

"Explain the connection to me again," said Jorge. "I almost understood you."

"That is because you drink too much."

"Tonight we are both drinking too much. And did you say you have hashish somewhere? Do you also own a pipe?"

"I do, but we have both had enough sweet oblivion for tonight."

"You perhaps, not me."

"That is one reason I'm convinced Eleanor is involved." Thomas thought of the hashish he had in the workshop. It was there to ease the symptoms of patients and reduce pain, but it was true he had indulged himself in its pleasures over the years, though not recently. Perhaps it was time to partake again. He needed something to stop the jumble of thoughts that filled his head.

"Hashish?" said Jorge.

"Substances that change perception. Yves admitted to me, before he realised his mistake, that his mother is adept in their use as well as other herbs and potions. And it was me who first showed her the red and white mushrooms that grow in the woods. Me who made a mixture we used many times."

"What red and white mushrooms?" asked Jorge. "Would I be interested in them?"

"I suspect your mind already works the way they make you feel. You are always talking about infinite love, but I will prepare some if you ask me to. For you and Belia. They are best taken with someone close. They can enhance lovemaking between a couple."

"That might be difficult to achieve."

"You may be right, but it is beside the point. Over the years, I suspect Eleanor has turned herself into an expert in poisons and healing herbs. Yves almost hinted at as much, and often enough a cure and a poison are the same thing in different doses. He let slip she has worked for many people over the years. We both know a poisoner can charge a great deal for their services and get away without suspicion. Someone as handsome as Eleanor would find it even easier."

"So Baldomero didn't poison Theresa, Eleanor did?"

"I believe she gave him the mushrooms, but remained at a distance herself. It is almost certainly how she works."

"How did she get him to agree?" asked Jorge.

"We've both heard how his wife hasn't been seen for some time, before he went to cook for Isabel. I suspect Eleanor kidnapped her and held her captive to ensure Baldomero did what she wanted."

"And now? He was seen walking away with her. Why would Baldomero do that if they had returned his wife to him?"

"There are many possibilities. The most hopeful is that his wife was freed and the two of them have fled until it is safe to return. The least that they are both dead."

Jorge stared at Thomas. He reached out and emptied the last of the jug into their beakers.

"Who killed them?"

"One possibility is Eleanor came for Baldomero and told him she was returning his wife. She invited him to her house and poisoned both of them."

"He wouldn't be fool enough to eat anything she prepared."

"Unless they forced him to."

"Eleanor is not that strong," said Jorge.

"But Yves is. I took him to Aamir's bathhouse today and saw him naked. He is strong enough. I want to believe he has nothing to do with any of this, but it is difficult to see how he cannot. In fact, I am sure he knows. Which disappoints me. I was starting to like him."

"A son you never knew about." Jorge's eyes were on the bulk of al-Hamra, the stone walls iridescent in the moonlight. "You are adept at sparking children, aren't you? How many others are there, do you think?"

"A few, possibly. As you have pointed out, I seem to have a talent for setting seed in a woman's belly. There have been many women over the years. More so when I was young. Less so of late, as well you know."

"I would like a daughter," said Jorge.

"You have already told me that. As has Belia."

"And...?"

"Ask me again when the war ends. All our lives might change then."

"Will you continue to work for Isabel? It makes sense. Siding with the victor is always a sound choice."

"What will you do with yourself when that time comes?" Thomas asked.

"Whatever Belia wants."

"Will she want to return to her homeland?" Thomas didn't want to think about what it would be like to no longer have Jorge at his side. He had grown used to his presence. His friendship.

"She was born in Ixbilya, so she may want to return there, but I doubt it."

"Have you had the conversation?"

"It is too soon. Who knows what the next year will bring?"

"Gharnatah will fall before the end of this year."

"I don't want to hear you say that, but whenever it does, I will have the conversation with Belia. She will be with child again by then if you have done your duty for me."

"Duty?"

"I know it is a hard task I ask of you, but you have my permission to enjoy the act as much as you like. If there was any other way, I would seek it, but there is only one way to set a seed in a woman. It is only a pity you appear to find it such a hardship. When are you going to take Helena to your bed? I know you want to. I saw it as we ate tonight." Jorge laughed. "I thought Yves was going to melt when you sat him next to her."

"He was besotted, was he not? They are of an age to each other, so perhaps I should encourage it."

"You told me you didn't trust him."

"I don't, but how much of that is because of what his mother has done? I believe I am starting to like the boy."

"He is no boy."

"You are right, he is a man."

"He looks a little more like you than he used to. He has lost

126

the fine polish of a Count and grown rough around the edges. Though obviously not as rough as you. Do you think Helena would like more children with you?"

Thomas rose and went into his workshop. He came out with a fresh flagon of wine. When he held it up, Jorge nodded and Thomas filled their cups.

"You forget, I still have no certainty she ever has had."

Jorge laughed. "Will is your son, there can be no doubt of it."

"I agree, but is that because he has been raised by me? It doesn't prove he is mine."

"Ask her again, she may tell you the truth now."

The thought had not occurred to Thomas, not recently, though he had sought an assurance from her several times before. Jorge was right—he should ask again. Perhaps he should do more than ask. He was aware of the growing tension between him and Helena. The tension between a man and a woman before it breaks like a storm in a chaos of need and want. Except Thomas knew now was not the time for that storm to break. He had too much else to occupy him. Theresa's poisoning was only one of those things. In the morning, he intended to climb the hill once more to see Abu Abdullah. He had a message from Isabel, and if the man agreed, there would be other arrangements to make.

As he reached for his cup, he heard the door from the kitchen open. It had started to scrape on the floor and he knew he needed to ask Britto to look at it. There were other minor jobs around the house that also required attention.

Thomas turned to see Belia step barefoot onto the terrace. She had drawn a robe around herself, but he imagined she had come straight from her and Jorge's bed.

"Is there any wine left?" She came across silently and sat beside Jorge, leaned over to kiss the side of his mouth.

"I was about to come to bed." Jorge poured wine into one of the empty cups left from their meal.

"I did not come to scold you, but I woke and you were not there. Have you and Thomas been putting the world aright?"

"Thomas has. I am a mere observer of his genius."

Belia cast a glance at Thomas. She smiled.

"It was good you brought Yves here, Thomas," she said. "Now both him and his mother know where you live."

"I have never brought Eleanor to this house."

"I know you haven't. She came here…" Belia stared off into space for a moment, "…probably a month ago, perhaps more. Before you came back that first time."

"How did she know where my house is?" Thomas experienced a sense of unease.

"All she had to do was ask anyone in Gharnatah. Even the Sultan knows where you live, but I believe it may have been Helena. Eleanor told me they had spoken about you in the palace."

"What did she want?"

Belia shrugged. "At first, I thought only to know more about you, but then when we were in your workshop, she changed."

Thomas's unease increased. "Changed how?"

"She was curious about what you have in there. The books. The papers. The herbs and minerals. I realised as she continued to ask questions, she knew about almost everything you have. She was as curious about the items capable of killing someone as much as those that could heal."

Jorge laughed. "Well, if she does turn out to be your poisoner, I expect that's your chance of another reconciliation gone."

Belia slapped her hand against Jorge's belly, which only made him laugh harder.

"Tell me what she knew. How skilled would you say she is?"

"Not as skilled as me, but close. She knew everything you had in there, but I made no mention of the herbs I have. She asked to see the garden and I showed her that as well. She could be your poisoner, Thomas. She has the skill, but does she have the nature? If I had known of your suspicions when she came, I would never have let her in. What was she like when you first knew her?"

Thomas drained his cup and refilled it. He thought he might need to get very drunk before he could tell Belia the story of him and Eleanor.

"I had seventeen years. What does a boy of seventeen know about women, or life, or anything?"

"But you were no ordinary boy, were you?"

Thomas knew Jorge was watching the conversation and would take everything in. Jorge never judged. Jorge never revealed secrets that might be spoken of, or shame confessed to. Jorge forgave. That was his nature.

"She was wild," Thomas said. "As was I. I was not the person you know today. I was a long way from the person you know. You wouldn't have liked me, either of you."

"But Eleanor did," said Belia.

"Yes, Eleanor did. I think beneath our skins, we shared the same dark hearts. I know mine was tainted, but I pretended I could justify it."

"Jorge tells me your father died in battle when you were young. That can darken the soul of a man, let alone a boy."

"I barely remember being a boy. I know I didn't feel like a boy, even at thirteen. I had lain with a girl. I had almost killed another boy. And after the battle at Castillon, things grew only darker. For a long time, I lost myself." He raised his eyes to meet Belia's, then Jorge's. All he saw in them was love and forgiveness, so he made a decision, whether it would prove right or not.

"I killed men. I lay with women I didn't love. Some I didn't even like. I took money from a man to get his wife with child because he could not and took pleasure in both the wife and the money. A band of renegades captured me, and within a month I was their leader. That is how bad I was, how uncaring of others. We stole and cheated, and yes, sometimes when we had to, we killed. Then I found Eleanor. Finding her almost killed me, but if I had not, I would have died soon enough. It was not a way of life for anyone who wants to live to an old age."

"Has Thomas ever told you any of this before?" Belia asked Jorge.

He shook his head. "He has hinted and teased, but no, he has not. It explains a great deal to me. A great deal." Jorge reached out and took Thomas's hand. He raised it and kissed the palm, then passed it to Belia, who did the same. It was their acceptance of who he had been, a confirmation of the love they held for the man he had become.

For Thomas, it had been one chaotic ride through life, as if the madness the mushrooms gave him and Eleanor had never ended. He shook his head and smiled. How strange his life had been from beginning to end.

He pulled himself up short. Why was he thinking this was the end of his life? He accepted fewer years remained to him than he had lived so far, but those years still held a promise, and he knew he was a changed man. Whether it was working with Isabel that had made him so, or losing Lubna, or the love of these two and his children, not to mention a Gomeres mercenary and a dog, it made no matter. It felt like a new start. A second chance. He smiled. Perhaps even a tenth chance, his life had seen so many changes.

He stood.

"Don't let Jorge get too drunk, I need him in the morning."

"I will try," said Belia. She rose and embraced Thomas. Kissed his mouth. "Helena is in the room next to yours."

Which is where Thomas intended to go until there came a hammering on the door to the alley. When he unbolted it and swung the door wide, he knew what the message would be. He recognised a neighbour of Da'ud al-Baitar and held up a hand.

"One moment, I need my bag."

When he came out from the workshop, Belia was waiting for him.

"Is this what I fear?"

"It is."

"Then I will come too."

CHAPTER SIXTEEN

Da'ud al-Baitar perched in a corner of his terrace on a pile of cushions almost as high as himself.

Belia went to him and took his hand.

"Are you not cold out here?"

"I do not want to die beneath a roof, my sweet. Out here suits me better." His eyes sought Thomas and he offered a nod.

Da'ud had faded fast in the weeks since Thomas had last seen him, and he wondered how much pain he was in. At least he could do something about that. He knelt at Belia's side and reached into his leather satchel. It was the old one he had carried for more than half a lifetime, a gift from an old man in the northern mountain range separating Iberia from France. It had been his dying gift—that and a letter of introduction to the infirmary in Malaka.

Thomas drew out a glass phial which held an oily brown liquid.

"Is that it?" asked Da'ud.

"How much pain have you?"

"Enough to send for you, old friend. Give it me and I will drink it myself. I have no wish to make you responsible for my end."

"It will be my honour." Thomas handed the phial to Belia, then drew out a second. This held a clear liquid, only a little more viscous than water. It was the last of the miraculous liquor he and Lubna had made years ago when Thomas healed the leg of Prince Juan. He knew he should make more, knew he should tell others of it, but could not bring himself to do either. It was his last connection to the wife torn from him. It was a fitting end that it would help Da'ud pass from this world to the next, for the man had been a good friend to Lubna.

When Thomas saw Da'ud wince, he unstoppered the first bottle and poured a little into a cup.

"Do you have wine?"

"The fermentation of the grape is against the law of Islam."

"That is not what I asked."

"In the kitchen. Belia, can you fetch some?"

After she rose and went inside, Da'ud caught Thomas's shirt and pulled him close.

"Keep me alive until dawn, old friend. I want to hear the muezzin call me to prayer one last time."

Thomas glanced at the sky. The moon that had bathed al-Hamra earlier had set. Only the spark of stars punctured the dark sky, and there was no hint of the coming day. Thomas had no idea how far off dawn lay, but knew he had no choice.

"If I can."

"Then I will drink the wine. Ah, here she comes. The sight of a beautiful woman will help me stay awake." Da'ud tried to laugh, but it turned into a cough which almost brought a premature death.

Belia wiped his face, then Thomas poured a little of the dark liquid into a cup and added wine. He handed it to Da'ud.

"You know to take only what you need, so I will not offer any lecture. Not to you who taught me so much."

Da'ud drained half the cup, as if greedy for its promise of oblivion. Thomas watched his eyes close, but only in relief as the strong poppy and hashish mixture started to do its work. He reached out and took the cup from Da'ud's shaking fingers.

"I taught you nothing and you know it, my friend. You came to Gharnatah with more knowledge than I have ever seen, and you have only gained more as time has passed." Da'ud opened his eyes and looked at Belia. "How is Jorge, my sweet?"

"Being Jorge."

A faint smile tightened Da'ud's mouth. "Then all is well. And your boy? I forget his name."

"Jahan. He has almost one year now and is as handsome as sin."

"Ah yes, Jahan." Da'ud glanced at Thomas. "A miracle. A veritable miracle."

Thomas was uncomfortable on his knees, but knew Da'ud possessed no chairs. The man kept to the old traditions, even if few of the population of Gharnatah did anymore.

"I want you to have everything that remains here, Thomas," he said. "The house as well, if you wish it. Perhaps Jorge and Belia might like it." He looked at Belia. "Would you like a house of your own?"

"I thank you, Da'ud. I will ask Jorge. It is a fine house, and its position is more convenient than Thomas's."

"He does insist on living high on the Albayzin. Perhaps he likes to look on the palace to keep himself modest."

"Then it has not worked," said Belia.

"I expect that is for the best. The world needs men of wisdom who are not afraid to express it."

"If I find one, I will ask him," Thomas said as he reached out to touch Da'ud's cheek. "Rest, old friend. Sleep a little. I will keep you alive and pain free until dawn, I promise. And then, once the muezzin has finished his call, I will help you pass to paradise."

Da'ud smiled and leaned back into the cushions.

"No wonder people like you, Thomas," he said, his voice so soft it barely carried.

Thomas laughed, as did Belia.

"How much of that tincture did you give him?" she asked.

"Clearly too much."

"You attract people," said Da'ud, his eyes closed. "A woman came to me not long since and told me she knew you. She gave me the impression she was in love with you."

"A handsome woman with deep red hair?"

"And a fine figure, yes."

"Did she tell you her name?"

"Ellen … something."

"Eleanor."

"That might be it. She told me she was once your lover, many years ago when you were both barely older than children, but I did not believe her."

Thomas tided away his bottles and tried to get comfortable. He knew they would be there several hours yet.

"What did she want?"

The corner of Da'ud's mouth lifted in the hint of a smile.

"She wanted to know about you and where you lived. She came on some pretext of feeling unwell, and wished to purchase certain herbs from me, but I knew it was nothing more than an excuse. It was you that interested her." The speech exhausted the man and left him breathless.

Thomas reached out and felt his neck, relieved to find the soft beat of his pulse.

"I am not dead yet," said Da'ud. "How much more of your ambrosia am I allowed? The pain is growing fierce now. It knows I intend to expel it and wants to remind me of everything that lies in store for me if you are not here." Da'ud opened his mouth and Belia tipped a little of the mixture into it. She used a linen cloth to wipe the spill from his beard.

"We are going nowhere, old friend." Thomas watched the man who had been more a father to him than his own. As he did, the thought came to him that he had ended the life of his real father, and now he was about to do the same for this one.

He waited for some sense of shame or guilt to come, but none did. None was required. Thomas knew his own father had been in excruciating pain before he put an end to it. He knew Da'ud would suffer the same fate, but at least he could end his pain with more compassion. He would end it with science instead of a knife.

Belia's touch on his arm drew him back to the present.

"He is sleeping." She leaned across and kissed Thomas's cheek.

"What was that for?"

"You know what. You love him, don't you?"

"Yes."

"He knows you do. It will make his end better." She glanced at the dark sky. "I judge another two hours until dawn. You should go inside and try to sleep. You must confront that woman in the morning. You and Jorge." She smiled. "You make a good team."

"Do we?"

"Do not seek compliments, Thomas." She removed her hand and rose, towering over him for a moment. "Do you think he truly means Jorge and I can have this house?"

"He does. You know Da'ud, he is generous. He has nobody else to pass it on to, and it is too fine a house to leave empty."

"In that case, I will explore a little. Are you staying here or do you want to come with me?"

Thomas wished he was more like Jorge and had some idea of what Belia had in mind. Perhaps better he did not.

"I will stay in case he wakes alone and is afraid. If you find another blanket, bring it back, it will get colder before dawn."

Belia touched his cheek and walked away. He watched her go.

"You do not have to stay on my account."

Thomas turned away from Belia's retreating back.

"I thought you had gone to sleep, old man."

"I wish I could, but I want to experience every last moment remaining to me."

"This does not have to end at dawn."

"You know it does. I cannot bear another day. Dawn will be long enough for me." His gaze moved away, returned. "You can go with her if you wish."

"She is Jorge's woman, not mine."

"But you are Jahan's father."

"It could hardly be Jorge, could it? As you are awake, tell me what Eleanor came in search of."

"Those items that can help a man breathe more easily in small doses, but might steal the breath from him when too much is used. Those that cause a man to die in writhing agony if mixed too strong. Is it true you and she were once lovers?"

"Long ago and far away."

"I believe she still has feelings for you. I do not understand how you attract beautiful women, Thomas, but you do. Make the most of the opportunity before you are too old to enjoy their attentions."

"Did you mean it when you said Jorge and Belia can have your house?"

"Who else is there? I heard you say the same words when you thought me asleep." Da'ud winced, but when Thomas unstoppered the phial, he shook his head. "Any more and I will not see the sun rise. I can bear this much. What are you going to do about her?"

"Who?" For a moment, Thomas was unsure whether Da'ud meant Eleanor or Belia, or even Helena, who he would know now lived in Thomas's house.

What would that be like, he thought, if Jorge and Belia lived here? What if Usaden and Kin went with them? Then there would only be Thomas and Helena and the children beneath his roof. Was that what he wanted? He imagined the end of the war, when Gharnatah became a city of Castile. Isabel might allow him to stay in his house. Might allow him to marry if he asked, for he knew he would need her permission. Would she grant it? He didn't know.

"Eleanor," said Da'ud, who at that moment appeared to be the more rational of them. "Your lover. And not so long ago is what she hinted to me."

"There was a moment in Qurtuba," Thomas said. "An old passion reignited, but it was not what either of us wanted."

"For you, perhaps."

"She tried to kill Isabel."

"Ah."

Thomas waited. When Da'ud kept his silence, he said, "Is that all you are going to say? Ah?"

"Do not forget, I die in a few hours. I no longer need to care."

"Tomorrow I will confront her," Thomas said.

"See, you do not need my advice. Will you punish her?"

"If she has done what I believe, then others will do the punishing. All I will do is expose and capture her."

"But you have inflicted justice in the past, I know you have. What if she flees, will you pursue her?"

"You have said it already—it is what I do."

Da'ud lowered his eyes. "I may sleep for a while after all. Wake me when the sky turns grey."

Thomas sat up, rose.

"Ask Belia if she will prepare my body. I would prefer a pyre if that can be arranged."

"We will do it. Me and Jorge. Perhaps even Will. It is time he learned about death."

"I like Will," said Da'ud. "He comes to visit sometimes. More so of late. He tells me tales of his exploits and what lies in his heart."

"Will doesn't have exploits."

"Fathers are always the last to know." Da'ud shooed Thomas away as Belia returned with a blanket. Between them, they wrapped it around his frail body.

Thomas followed her back into the house, dazzled by the candlelight.

"I like this house," said Belia. "It is compact, but sensible, and Da'ud has a large garden already stocked with many of the herbs and spices I need. I will nurture them and plant more."

"So you intend to live here?"

"If Jorge agrees, and I am sure he will." She touched his arm. "Do you mind, Thomas?"

"Of course I don't mind. It's a sound idea. You and Jorge must make a life for yourselves with Jahan."

"But you will visit, won't you? You are part of our lives now, you know you are."

"Of course I will visit, Will and Amal, too."

"You can even bring your dog. I did not think I would ever like a dog, but Kin is different to any I have ever known."

"He is surely that."

"And Usaden," said Belia.

"Yes, Usaden too." Thomas laughed. "Perhaps we should all move down here. Da'ud did point out I live too high on the hill."

"And it would make it all the easier for me to have the daughter Jorge so wants."

"Ah," Thomas said.

"But it is no great distance, is it?"

"Do I have any choice in the matter?"

"I recall you rather enjoyed the process the last time."

"I did, but … it was strange, and remains so."

"Do you not love Jorge?"

"You know I do."

"And me?"

"I love you both. Just not … in that way."

"We are family. You and Jorge and me. Your children, Usaden, even your dog. And yes, Helena too, once you stop being so thick-headed and realise what is staring you in the face. She loves you, and she is changed."

"Da'ud wants you to prepare him."

"Can you help, or do you have to rush off on some important business?"

"No, I will help. I have important business, as always, but today it can wait."

They sat in the candlelight and talked of all they had experienced together over the years, the three of them, and talked more of what might come to pass. Da'ud had confirmed Thomas's suspicions of Eleanor, but he knew confronting her could wait. His dying friend took precedence over everything else.

When the sky lightened, they went outside to rouse Da'ud as the sound of the muezzin called the faithful to prayer. As the last notes echoed across the city, Thomas unstoppered the bottle of clear liquor. He kissed Da'ud, then Belia did the same. Thomas poured the liquor onto a cloth and stared into Da'ud's eyes, waiting.

"I am ready," said Da'ud.

Thomas held the cloth over his friend's nose and mouth until his body went slack. He reached out and felt his neck, continued to hold the cloth against him as Da'ud's heart slowed … then stopped.

When Thomas looked at Belia, he saw tears on her face that reflected those on his own.

CHAPTER SEVENTEEN

As Thomas climbed the hill to the Alkazaba, it was with a sense he had abandoned his responsibilities. Thomas and Belia had stripped Da'ud and washed him twice, then he had left her to wrap his shroud. He wanted to stay, but was conscious of time passing. He did not want Eleanor to escape his wrath. And wrath it was. All the turmoil of the night, of the last weeks, his own frustration and hopes, grew tangled and sharp. It was as if he had fallen into a bramble bush, each thorn an agony against his skin.

The same slim maid opened the door of Eleanor's house and offered a nod of recognition.

"My mistress is not home, if that is what you want."

Thomas was disappointed, but not particularly surprised.

"Do you know where she is?"

"She left the house yesterday a little after noon, but did not tell me where she was going. She is often away overnight."

"Is Yves here?"

The maid gave a shake of her head. She continued to stand in the doorway, offering no invitation for him to enter.

"Did they leave together?" Thomas wondered if they had

left the city, though Yves had not departed his house the day before until well after dark.

Thomas was annoyed. He had started to like his son, to trust him a little. He wanted to believe some good lay within the man, but was wondering if he had been working with his mother all the time. Da'ud's news that she had visited him, and of what she sought, only confirmed his suspicions of her. He wondered how much knowledge she might have passed on to Yves, and whether he was involved in her work.

"The master returned after dark, but his mother had already left. He went out again early today and has not returned."

Thomas took a step closer, hoping the woman would stand aside. Instead, she crossed her arms and glared at him. He knew he could lift her up, but didn't want to do so.

"You know me, don't you?"

A nod. "Everyone knows Thomas Berrington."

"Do you also know I am Yves' father?"

A frown formed on her smooth brow, and he knew she was wondering exactly how such a claim could be true.

"I need to search the house."

"I cannot let you in without the mistress's permission."

"Do you want me to go to the Sultan and ask him? This is his house, is it not?"

"You know all these houses belong to him, but he never uses them."

"I have no argument with your loyalty," Thomas said, "but I believe Eleanor is escaping justice. She may also be in danger. I need to find out if there is any clue here to where she might be." The claim was false, but the woman would not know that.

The frown returned to trouble her brow and she uncrossed her arms.

"Were you and she married once?"

"I believe marriage is not essential for a child to be set, is it? Will you let me enter?"

"I will not." Thomas was about to change his mind and force

his way in when she said, "My mistress and master may return before long, and they will expect food on the table. I need to visit the market, and will lock the door when I do so."

Thomas listened to her words and heard a different message beneath the surface. He turned away, but walked only a few paces to lean against the corner of a wall when the woman went inside. She came out a few moments later carrying a reed basket and a heavy key. She pulled the door shut and locked it, then knelt and placed the key beneath a pot holding a small olive tree. She glanced at Thomas, nodded and walked away. In deference to her help, Thomas waited until she went from sight before retrieving the key and letting himself in.

Already there was an abandoned air to the house. Thomas walked through rooms touched here and there by Eleanor's scent. He began in the kitchen on the assumption that any poisons might be stored there, but the shelves held barely anything. A few pots of spices and herbs, each of which he opened and sniffed to make sure they were what they seemed.

Yves' bedroom was obvious from the male scent that clung to it. Thomas expected to find nothing here either, but searched diligently, rewarded only with what he expected.

Eleanor's room was more subtly scented, raising a strange sense of loss in him. He searched more thoroughly, but with the same result. He looked around one last time, a sense of being too late at every turn settling through him. He knew that confronting Eleanor might have triggered her flight.

Thomas went outside. He locked the door and placed the key beneath the olive pot. For a moment, he stood on the step, trying to formulate a plan. Any plan. Slowly, something came to him. It wasn't a brilliant plan, but at least it was something. It would do for now.

———

Thomas didn't expect Olaf to be home, so was surprised when he found him sitting at the table breaking his fast. The big general nodded to indicate the chair across from him. As Thomas moved to take it, Fatima emerged from the kitchen. She gave a cry and embraced him, holding his face in her hands so she could kiss him before holding him at arms' length.

"Aii! You are too thin. Sit, I will bring you food. It will do Olaf good not to finish every scrap like he usually does."

Thomas sat. He cocked his head in question at Olaf.

"She forgets my job is fighting, and a fighting man needs energy."

Thomas let his eyes scan Olaf for a moment, but all he saw was strength and health, any sign of the serious injury he had received a few years before now gone. He still had no idea what age Olaf was. He had always considered him beyond age, though he knew from his exquisite daughters he had to be almost a decade older than Thomas himself. How he could still fight the way he did was a miracle.

"What brings you to the hill?" Olaf asked.

"Da'ud died."

Olaf stopped eating and put his knife down. "I heard he was unwell. When? Did he suffer?"

"At dawn this morning, and no, there was no pain at the end."

Olaf met Thomas's gaze and smiled. "You are a good friend to him. If you came to give me the news, I thank you. When is he to be interred? Both myself and Fatima want to be there."

"He has asked for a pyre, so we take him to Valparaíso before sunset." As he spoke the words, Thomas knew it was one more duty he had to discharge before he could begin his pursuit of Eleanor. He could almost hear the drip-drip of a water-clock marking out the seconds, each one allowing her to escape his justice.

"Then I will help carry him. I assume you and Jorge will also do so. Who else?"

Thomas had given no thought to the matter, but now he knew there was only one other person who could make up the four.

"Will," he said, pleased when Olaf nodded in agreement. "But you might have to bend your knees a little if we are not to tumble Da'ud from the pallet."

"Put me opposite Jorge, he is the tallest of you, though Will is catching him up fast."

"He is. Come to the house later, both of you, but Da'ud is not the only reason I came. I need your knowledge."

Olaf laughed. "You know I have no knowledge, Thomas, only brawn."

"If someone wanted to flee the city, and they needed a fast horse, where would they go?"

"You know where the stables are in the city as well as I do."

"I know some, but I never need a fast horse. Advise me, Olaf."

"I will give you some names, but who are you pursuing now?"

"Eleanor. She tried to murder Isabel."

"Is she the woman who came here asking questions about you? The one living in a house on the Alkazaba with her son? If so, I liked her. She is a handsome woman."

"She is. And Yves is my son as well as hers."

For a moment, Olaf frowned as he worked out what Thomas had just said, then shook his head.

"You have too many women. She looked to me like someone who would take a carriage rather than a horse."

"She will want to travel fast, so a stallion suits her purpose better, but I will make enquiries about carriages."

Olaf leaned across the table. "I would ask if you are sure she is guilty of this crime, but I know if you make the accusation, it must be true. What will you do when you catch her?"

"Take her to Isabel. What happens then is up to her."

"Did you love her once?"

For a moment, Thomas wondered who Olaf was referring to. Perhaps he was right, and he did have too many women in his life if he couldn't work out which was which.

"I thought I did. Enough to set seed in her belly."

Olaf laughed. "We both know love has little to do with that act. There is no time now, but one day, when we are both old men, you can tell me the story."

"If either of us get to be old men."

Olaf smiled. "Yes, there is that."

———

Olaf had given Thomas the names of a dozen traders who might have the manner of steed Eleanor would require. He had discarded half because he knew them and also knew their horses would not meet her high standards. The first two he visited were no help, and Thomas wondered if Eleanor might not have used some other means of transport. As he walked to the next stables, he glanced at the sky, aware of the passage of time. Da'ud would be fully prepared by now. Soon people would begin gathering, and Thomas knew they expected him there. Four more stables to visit, that was all. He promised if he met with no success, he would leave the alternatives to the following day, even if it allowed Eleanor more time to make good her escape.

"A handsome woman, maybe ten years younger than me?" said the third stable owner. Thomas had used the man in the past and knew his horses were of the highest quality, even if he was a rogue himself. He claimed many of his stock were those destined for the palace, but excess to requirements.

Thomas looked the man up and down and judged his calculation of Eleanor's age at least fifteen years adrift, but accepted she looked younger than her age. The man continued brushing the grey coat of a young mare. Other steeds filled half the stalls, the smell of their sweat and droppings rich in the air.

"Did she give a name?"

"She did, but I have no recollection of it. There was a title in there somewhere, as I recall."

"Countess?"

"Possibly. Like I say, I have too many customers to remember them all."

Thomas didn't believe the man. He remembered how Eleanor looked, and Thomas expected he remembered everything she had said.

"Do you not keep records?"

The man tapped his skull. "All the records I need are in here. Why pay a scribe when you have a memory like mine?"

"But not for names."

"Countess sounds right, now you mention it. And the name she gave was Isabel."

So Eleanor had used a false name.

"What if she fails to return your horse? You will need both a name and address then, won't you?"

"If she had hired it, I would, and in that instance my memory would no doubt serve me better, but she bought the stallion outright."

"Only the one horse?" Thomas asked.

"That's what I said, isn't it? Though she could have afforded every horse you see here."

"She carried gold on her person?"

"In a saddle bag, as if she knew she would need it. Which she did."

"When was this?"

"Yesterday, half way between Zhuhr and Asr."

"Did you see which way she went?"

"I followed her. She left through the Jaen gate and continued north."

Thomas stared at the man. "You followed her?"

"I was curious. She was a handsome woman, and spirited." The man smiled. "The horse I sold her was spirited, too. I thought she might have trouble controlling him, but she was an expert rider."

"Did you decide you wanted more money for the horse? Or did you want all the gold she carried in that saddle-bag?"

When the man refused to meet his stare, Thomas knew the answer.

"Why did you stop? You did stop following her, didn't you?"

"I followed only long enough to satisfy myself she was content with her purchase. When she met a group of other riders, I watched for a while, thinking they might be brigands about to steal her gold, but it was clear she knew them. They greeted each other like friends and rode away together."

"How many men?"

"Half a dozen. All mounted."

"Describe them to me."

"They were hard-looking. Used to riding, I could tell. They were dressed all the same, though whether it was some kind of uniform, I cannot say for sure. Black, it was."

"Were they Moors or from Castile?"

"Neither."

"Could they be of France?"

"They were men, that is all I can tell you. I was too far away to hear what was said, but unless they spoke Arabic or Castilian, I doubt I would have recognised their speech."

"Which direction did they ride?"

"The same way, north. I turned back to the city then and saw no more."

"My thanks for your time." Thomas considered offering the man a coin. He saw one was expected, but made no move to do so. No doubt he had charged Eleanor more for the horse than it was worth.

Thomas walked fast through the city, not seeing the bustling life that continued all around him. He needed to return to his house. He would take Usaden and Kin and head after Eleanor. She had a good start, but two riders could travel faster than seven. Much faster when one of them was Usaden. Thomas would give him and the dog their head and let them ride fast. With luck, Eleanor would not be expecting any pursuit, so her progress would be slower still.

As Thomas climbed the twisting alleys towards his house, a sense of hope filled him.

CHAPTER EIGHTEEN

"Where have you been? We were about to leave without you!"
Belia's dark eyes sparked with anger. "How would it look if
Thomas Berrington did not set the light for Da'ud al-Baitar's
pyre?"

"I had things to do."

"And now you have a duty to perform. Da'ud is prepared
and lies in your workshop. Usaden has already tied him to the
pallet, and Olaf is with Helena and that man you brought here
yesterday."

"Yves?"

"I believe that is his name."

"Yves is here?"

"I just told you that, didn't I? He'll have to stay here or come
with us, we don't have time for anything else. It will be dark in
two hours and the fire must be lit before the setting of the sun.
You owe Da'ud that. You owe him more than that, Thomas, but
this is the least you can do for him. He was your friend.
Perhaps your only friend other than Jorge."

It was clear Belia did not include herself in that list. Thomas
knew he had no choice, and nodded.

He went into the workshop crowded with people. Olaf stood beside the pallet. He glanced up as Thomas entered.

"When I die, I want to be burned. Set me on a boat and send it out to sea with the flames crackling high. It is the northern way. Will you do it for me, Thomas?"

"I hope I never have to."

"But if I should die, I want you to give me a fitting journey to Valhalla."

Thomas shook his head. "Let's get this burning over with first, shall we?"

The four of them carried the pallet up through narrow alleys until they widened into a square, Thomas and Will at the head, Olaf and Jorge at the rear. People lined the streets as they passed before falling in behind. By the time they reached the burning grounds of Valparaíso, a line of men, women and children snaked backwards for half a league. Thomas doubted even half a dozen would turn out for his own funeral. Other pyres stood in stark relief against a lowering sun, and Belia had found an Imam who recited the prayers for the passing of a soul.

Jorge pushed something into Thomas's hand, and he looked down to find a burning torch.

"It has to be you, Thomas," said Jorge, echoing Belia's words.

"I know. I loved him."

"Everyone loved him. He loved you too, though why I cannot tell. Do it. Do it now before that man of God finishes his words."

Thomas didn't want to set the torch to the pyre. It felt too final. But he knew he must. This is what Da'ud had asked him to do, and he could not turn his back on the man now at the last.

He stepped forward and thrust the torch into the pile of dry wood beneath Da'ud's pallet. He held it there as the pyre began to smoke and crackle, held it there until the ferocity of the heat forced him back. He bumped into someone, expecting it to be Jorge, but when he turned, it was to find Helena standing beside him. She reached out and took his hand. He grasped it within his own as tears filled his eyes. Later, he would pretend it was the smoke that caused them, but everyone would know the truth.

———

It was dark by the time they returned to the house. Thomas wanted to bathe the stink of smoke from himself, but when he went into the small bathing chamber, he discovered it was already in use. Helena turned to him, unashamed to display the perfection of her body.

"Do you want to join me?"

"I smell too much."

Helena laughed. "If that is the only reason, I can probably put up with it while I wash the smell from you."

"There are a thousand people in the courtyard." Thomas wondered why he was talking to her instead of leaving.

Helena began to soap herself again. "I suspect you exaggerate."

"Only a little. There must be a hundred. Belia has sent to the neighbours for more food, but most of them are already here. There will be no wine left by the time they've finished."

Helena tugged at the lever set into the wall and allowed warm water to cascade over her. When it stopped, she came towards Thomas, but he moved aside and handed her a linen towel to dry herself.

"Belia and Jorge washed when they came in, so the water will be cold before you finish."

"I have worse problems than cold water." Thomas waited for Helena to leave. The damp linen cloth wrapped around her hid nothing. Once he was satisfied she had no intention of

152

returning, he removed his smoke-tainted clothes and stepped under the water. Helena was right. It was cold.

———

It was close to midnight before they managed to get everyone to leave, but one intruder remained. Yves sat beside Helena on the low wall that ran around the sides of the courtyard.

"He's besotted," said Jorge. "Perhaps you should let him sleep with her tonight and get it over with." He had found a flagon of wine from somewhere and poured it into their cups. Thomas suspected he had hidden the prize before everyone arrived.

"It's not my decision. If she wants him to, she can ask him herself."

"It is your decision, you know it is."

"I thought…"

Jorge smiled. "Thought what?"

"It's too late tonight to start the pursuit of Eleanor, but we need to organise it so we can leave at dawn."

"Dawn again?"

"I know it's a hardship for you. Stay here if you wish. Me and Usaden should be enough."

"You should ask Yves. I heard you talking with him earlier. You told him his mother had fled. You accused her of being the poisoner to his face."

"I wanted to see his reaction."

"He already knew," said Jorge. "Tonight he acted like a young man besotted with his first girl. He was uncertain, shy, and sweet. But I sensed something else beneath the act. A hardness. A coldness. A strength of will."

"So do you think I'm right, and he knows what his mother is involved in?"

"I'm not saying that, only there is something else there,

something he is hiding. It might be nothing more than lust for Helena, but he made that fairly clear, didn't he?"

"Oh yes, I think he did. So what should I do?"

"Take him with you and see how he acts."

"In that case, I need to wake you at dawn. I need another pair of eyes and your skill to see the truth within him."

"Then I will come. Have you asked Usaden?"

Thomas did not need to say whether the man had agreed. Any chance to escape the city in pursuit of someone was always acceptable to Usaden.

"I think he went to sleep in the workshop."

"And you?"

"I have more planning to do."

"And then?"

"I will try to get a little sleep."

"And Helena?"

"What about Helena?"

"Don't make me say it, Thomas. She has changed. You have changed. I don't know why you fight it when you are going to submit in the end."

"Because I don't believe she has changed. Think back on everything she has done. She betrayed us to Abu Abdullah. She lived with a woman who had a blacker heart than the devil himself. Some part, however small, of that darkness must remain within her." Thomas glanced at Jorge. "Yes, she tempts me, I admit. She has barely aged these last ten years. The scar that once ruined her face is healed, and I vividly recall how skilled she is with the body she so openly flaunts before me."

"You think too much," said Jorge. "Take her to your bed. Enjoy yourselves. It doesn't have to mean anything other than pleasure."

"I don't think about things in the same way as you do."

"Neither do I anymore, but perhaps you think too much the other way. With you it is always duty and doing what is right.

154

Sometimes a man has to fail, has to submit to his desires. The world won't end if you do."

Thomas might have argued, but at that moment, Helena came towards him, leaving Yves sitting alone, his expression that of an abandoned child. She trailed her fingers across his cheek.

"I am going to bed. Should it be mine or yours?"

Thomas looked up at her. "Mine, if that is what you want."

"It is what I have wanted for a long time now, you know it is." She leaned down and kissed his mouth, a long kiss rich with the promise of more. "Try not to be too long."

When she had gone, Thomas found Yves staring at him.

"I think I'll go to bed," said Jorge, "as you're getting me up again in a few hours."

"At least try to spend some of the time asleep."

"I'll see what Belia thinks of that when I get there."

After Jorge had gone, Thomas rose and walked across to Yves.

"You know what I have to do tomorrow, don't you?" He stood over the man, who remained sitting on the low wall.

"You ride in pursuit of my mother."

"You can stay here or you can come with us."

"Which do you want me to do?"

"It's not my decision. You don't have to make it now, you can let me know in the morning. I'm sure we can find another horse for you from somewhere."

"Are you and Helena lovers?"

"We have been, but not at the moment." *Well*, Thomas thought, *that situation is about to change, isn't it?*

"She is exquisite."

"Indeed she is."

"But she is not interested in me. She talked about you all the time. You are a fortunate man."

"Some might argue that is not the case, but I have had a

blessed life and a cursed one in equal measure. Sometimes both are needed to make a man what he is."

"My life has never been cursed. Perhaps that is why I have this feeling of..." Yves stood and waved a hand, searching for the right words "... Failure. Discontent. Of having my potential stifled. I have been too much in the shadow of my mother." Yves stood, a hardness in his eyes. "I wish I had known you sooner."

"I wish it too. Both our lives might have been different."

"Pa, Ami is crying and woke me up."

Thomas turned to see Will standing in the doorway.

"Where is she?"

"I'm here, Pa. I felt sad, but I'm not anymore." Amal came around Will. She had lost the pudginess of infancy and looked more like her mother with every passing day. Her dark hair shone, hanging loose almost to her waist.

Thomas beckoned them both to him. "I want you to meet someone very special." He offered his hand and Amal took it. Her eyes looked up at Yves, but Thomas read a doubt in them. She was wondering what was so special about this man.

"Do you know who this is?" Thomas asked, but it was Will who answered.

"His name is Yves, and he's French."

"That is his name, yes, but he is also something else."

Will glanced at Yves. "Lots of people have lots of names. *Morfar* is called Olaf here, but his northern name is *Hvirfla*."

"I know it is, though what it means, he would not tell me."

"It means whirling. Northern names describe the man or woman. *Morfar* has his because of the way he whirls his axe into battle."

"Then it describes him well." Thomas was aware of Yves watching the conversation without understanding a word of it, for they spoke in Arabic. Thomas switched to Castilian. "This man is Yves, but he is also your brother."

Will gave Yves a second look. He scanned him up and down, looked back at Thomas.

"He's tall, I suppose."

"Do I have two brothers?" asked Amal, her small hand tightening inside Thomas's.

"You do."

She looked up at Yves. "Am I meant to like him?"

"It would help."

"Can you fight?" Will asked Yves.

"I don't know."

"Then I don't expect you can. I can fight. *Morfar* says I fight almost as well as him and Pa. I can teach you if you want."

"Teach me?"

"How to fight." Will looked at Yves again. "You're too old to learn the axe, but a sword would suit you. And a knife. Every man needs to know how to use a knife as well as his hands and feet. In fact, anything at all. Usaden says a man must fight with every part of his body if he wants to survive, and I do."

"Want to survive, or fight?" asked Yves. Thomas could see he was amused.

"Both. You can't do one if you can't do the other. I will ask Usaden to teach you if you think I'm too young."

"Is Usaden the short man with dark skin? The African?"

"Don't let him hear you call him African," Thomas said. "He is Gomeres."

"Is that a land?"

"It is a following, a religion I sometimes think, but not a kind one. Usaden comes from the Maghreb, so he is African even if he would kill you for calling him that."

"Usaden is the best fighter in the world," said Will. "If he wants to kill someone they are already dead, but I will tell him you are my brother so there is no need to worry. Usaden likes me. He likes Pa and Ami and Jorge and Belia, too, so I expect he will learn to like you eventually. It's not necessary to be a good fighter for him to like you, but it helps."

"As would letting him train you," Thomas said. "If you stay here tomorrow, you can get to know your brother and sister better."

"I want to come with you," said Yves.

"Even if it is your mother we seek? You would be better to stay here. Make friends with Will and Amal."

Yves said nothing, his face taking on a stubborn stillness.

"Go find somewhere to sleep. There is probably a room or two unoccupied. I need to go with these two if they are to get any sleep tonight." He held his hand out and waited until Yves gripped it. Thomas offered a nod of recognition at some fresh bond between them, then took his children inside and lay down between them, comforted as always by their presence. Amal sat up and kissed his face. Will gave a nod of his own, believing himself too old for kisses now.

Thomas hoped Helena would forgive his absence.

CHAPTER NINETEEN

"What are you going to do when we capture Eleanor?" asked Jorge as he came to ride beside Thomas. They had passed beneath the Jaen gate out of Gharnatah barely a quarter hour before. Ahead lay rising ground with higher peaks beyond. Usaden rode a hundred paces ahead. Kin roamed even wider, dashing away, returning only to dash away again.

Thomas felt a weight lift from his shoulders. They were on a pursuit again, the three of them, and little else mattered for the moment.

"I expect I'll go back to Isabel."

"Is that what you want?"

Thomas glanced at Jorge. The man he saw differed in so many ways from the one he had met all those years ago as a boy and turned him into what had defined the rest of his life. Differed from the man of nine years before when they first worked together on the killings in the palace. Jorge had matured and gained a strength and surety to add to the grace he had always possessed.

"What I want is a peaceful life. I'm feeling old. I want to sit and watch my children grow into men and women. I want to see them marry and have children of their own."

"Gods, you're maudlin today, aren't you? Anyone would think you had eighty years, not ... how old are you?"

Thomas laughed. "I have fifty-one years."

"That isn't old."

"Some days it feels old." A cry from behind made Thomas turn in his saddle to see a grey stallion coming fast towards them. As it came closer, he saw Yves at ease on the beast.

Yves reined in and fell into place on the other side of Thomas, who stared at him.

"I couldn't find you before we left. I thought you had changed your mind."

"If my mother is guilty of what you accuse her of, I have to be there when she confesses her sins."

"We might be there a while, then. She is with other men. What will you do if it comes to a fight?"

"I can fight."

"If it comes to that, try to stay out of the way and safe. Leave the fighting to Usaden and me."

"And Jorge?"

"If he has to, but usually the two of us are enough." Thomas sat straighter in the saddle. Talk of fighting, and the fear of showing exhaustion in front of his son, made him feel better.

"Your dog is fast," said Yves. "I can scarce believe it is the same beast I saw Amal pulling the ears of last night." He glanced at Thomas. "I like your children ... Father."

Thomas scowled.

"Will looks like you, except in a year he will be taller. Do I look like you?"

"Don't ask me." Thomas looked at Jorge. "Does Yves look like me?"

Jorge leaned forwards so he could see him, though there was no need for it other than show.

"I'm afraid he does a little. I'm sorry, Yves, but Thomas has lured attractive women into his bed despite how he looks. Let's hope you can fight as well as him."

Thomas urged his horse ahead, leaving them to talk about him, and rode to fall in beside Usaden.

"Have you seen anything yet?"

"We are still on the busy roadway. Any spoor she left will have been long spoiled. What I can tell you is she and her party have not moved away from the road yet. It would be good if I had something of this woman's that Kin might be able to scent."

Thomas turned his horse and rode back.

"I don't suppose you have anything of your mother's on you, do you?"

"Only her money-bag. I brought it from the house knowing I might need coin for the journey."

Thomas laughed. "You need no coin. We won't be staying at inns or buying food. Kin and Usaden will feed us. I hope you like rabbit." He held his hand out, waiting. Eventually, Yves reached inside his jacket and drew out a dark blue velvet bag. When Yves' placed it in Thomas's hand, he felt the weight of coin within. He tugged at the drawstring and held the bag out. When Yves offered his hand, Thomas tipped the mix of coins into it before turning and riding back to Usaden.

He handed the empty bag across. "I don't know if it will be of any use. Yves has been carrying it close to his body since he left the city."

"Kin will tell the difference between their scents." Usaden sniffed the velvet and shrugged, making clear he could not. He lifted in his saddle and gave a piercing whistle. Kin, who was a black dot on a low ridge ahead, stopped, turned and ran back to them at full speed. He covered the ground between in mere moments. His long fur rippled in the wind, jaws wide so he looked as if he was laughing. Perhaps he was.

Usaden dismounted and held the velvet bag in his fist. He was not gentle when he rubbed it against Kin's snout, but the dog made no protest. When he stopped, he held the cloth directly over Kin's nose for a long time, then rose.

"Seek."

One word, but Kin knew what it meant. Thomas had acquired the dog from a dead farmer and his wife, acquired him a second time from their dead son when he pursued and killed Abbot Mandana, the man who had murdered Thomas's wife. Over the years since, Kin had become Thomas's, but now he belonged to Usaden as much as anyone. Or possibly Amal. Kin was nine parts vicious and ten parts loving, depending who he was with. Thomas made no pretence at understanding, only pleased Kin reserved the love for his family.

Kin ranged across the ground, nose lowered. Thomas felt a tension in his shoulders as he watched, expecting something, but Kin only ranged further afield. Thomas and Usaden urged their mounts on.

"If they stick to the roadway, he'll have trouble picking her scent out," said Thomas. "We should ride harder. They are bound to turn aside at some point. Unless they intend to ride to Jaen itself, but I doubt that."

"Why?"

"Because it's the obvious destination for people coming this way." He turned to look behind. "There has been little traffic, and I would expect it to be busy. Everyone is afraid of the Castilian army."

"We are here, are we not?" said Usaden.

"You are afraid of nothing, and I am a servant to the Queen of Castile." As he looked back, the sight of Yves reminded Thomas of another reason he had ridden to Usaden. "If it comes to a fight, ignore Yves. I suspect he is a poor swordsman and will be more trouble than he is worth. I'll try to protect him, but I'll tell Jorge to keep him back from any action."

"Will there be action? How many men did this woman meet?"

"Half a dozen, I was told."

"The action will be over fast, then. Do we keep her alive?"

"If possible."

"She was your woman once, was she not?" There was no hint of either curiosity or judgement in Usaden's voice, but Thomas wondered if he did not feel at least a little of both. It would be natural for the man to wonder. Except there was little natural about Usaden.

"Many years ago, and briefly again two years ago. You were there, you know that."

"She is also the one who came to the house when you were not there."

"She is."

Usaden gave a nod. "I cannot blame you for lying with her. She is handsome."

Thomas started to speak, stopped. He shook his head. He was curious, even if Usaden was not.

"Do you never want a woman?" he asked.

"I had two wives at home, but they died. When I feel the need, I visit Aamir and he finds me a companion for the night. He tells me I do not need to pay because I am a friend of yours, so I pay the woman and tell her to say nothing. Why is he so generous to your friends?"

"I saved the lives of two of his wives, but it was many years ago. If it was ever a debt he owed me, it is a debt long since paid. I have given up trying to make him take coin from me."

"He has the best women in Gharnatah."

"So I am told."

Usaden showed nothing, but Thomas believed he glimpsed some shadow of amusement beneath the surface. He thought he might be learning to read the man. Or more likely, Usaden was allowing himself to be read.

Ahead, Kin came to a halt off to the side of the main roadway.

"He has found her," said Usaden, as he urged his horse into a canter.

When Thomas reached them, Usaden was kneeling on one knee beside Kin, his fingers twisted in the dog's fur, just as Amal's had been the night before.

"They left the roadway here." Usaden pointed to a few vague marks in the dry earth that meant nothing to Thomas. If he looked at them long enough, they would mean even less than nothing, but he knew Usaden was right, as was Kin.

Thomas looked around. Jorge and Yves were approaching at a walk, neither riding hard. In the far distance, a cart climbed the slow rise from Gharnatah. In the other direction, a small party of soldiers was coming their way, but they were not those he was looking for. The hostler had told him Eleanor met with men in dark jackets, and these sported bright yellow coats. No doubt more recruits to Isabel's army, come from distant lands to witness her ultimate victory. Every noble, knight and squire for a thousand leagues wanted to say they had been here for the fall of Gharnatah.

"If they keep going in the same direction, they will end up nowhere."

"Everywhere is somewhere, Thomas."

"Not up there. It belongs to neither Gharnatah nor Castile, in part because neither of them wants it. It is high pasture land and rock. Dry and inhospitable, punctured here and there by villages, each of which speaks its own dialect. Some bastard mix of Arabic and what they have spoken for a thousand years."

"It sounds like a good place to hide."

"It is, if you are from there. If not, you stand out. Every man and woman for twenty leagues will recognise you as a stranger."

"Unless they have friends there."

Thomas looked at the marks in the dirt. "Can you tell how long since they passed?"

"A day, more or less. Did you say she left before noon yesterday?"

"I did."

"Then they are not riding hard or they would be moving away from us." Usaden looked around. "We can ride faster now Kin has their spoor. That son of yours might not fight, but he is a fine horseman. Even Jorge has improved. We can gain half a day on them if we push hard."

"Then let us push hard." Thomas swung into his saddle and pressed his knees into the flanks of his horse until it responded. It felt good to be flying across the ground with men he trusted. Some men, in any case.

As the day passed, the ground grew steeper and the track they followed twisted backwards and forwards in dizzying switchbacks. They were forced to slow, their horses skittering and slipping on the stony ground, but they pushed on. Kin ran ahead out of sight, then returned. The dog made no sound because he had been trained not to until his quarry was too close to escape.

Light was leaching from the sky as they crested a sharp ridge and stopped. Ahead lay a wide valley, the bottom flat and fertile where irrigation channels had been dug, dry and inhospitable where no water ran. Olives disappeared into the distance as far as the eye could see, interspersed with fields of wheat, stands of sugar-cane and mulberry. Sheep and goats grazed where crops would not grow. Across this flat valley, a small party of people moved.

"Is it them?" asked Usaden.

Thomas narrowed his eyes, but the figures were too distant to tell if one of them was a woman. What he could tell was the colour of their clothing, which was dark.

"More than likely."

"Then we follow and see where they go. They will either reach a destination or make camp for the night, and that will be our chance. Kin, to me."

The dog trotted over and lay down almost beneath the hoofs of Usaden's horse.

Tonight, Thomas thought.

He wondered what Yves would do when they captured his mother.

CHAPTER TWENTY

Thomas called a halt when they came to a clearing in the woods they had been riding through for the last half-hour. It had grown too dark to continue safely, and he was afraid they might stumble across the group they pursued. Usaden dismounted and walked away into the night, Kin at his side.

"Can we light a fire?" asked Yves.

"No fire." Thomas nodded at the dark sky. "A single candle can be seen over several leagues, and there is no moon tonight so a fire will show even more. Try to get some sleep. We start again as soon as there is enough light to see by."

Thomas unrolled the blanket he had brought and lay down beside Jorge, who already gave the impression he was lounging on the most comfortable bed in the world.

"Has Usaden gone off to kill someone?"

"I hope not. I expect he wants to see how close they are. Kin will smell them from a safe distance. They'll be back soon after we fall asleep."

"As long as that?" said Jorge. He glanced to where Yves was pacing around the small clearing. "I didn't think he would stay with us as long as this."

"Neither did I. I'm still trying to work out why he wanted to come. To capture his mother, or save her?"

"Which would you do?"

"If it was my mother, I would save her, but my mother wasn't a murderer."

"Do you think she still lives?"

"Eleanor?" Thomas wanted Jorge to stop asking questions so he could sleep. Yves had finally found a spot he considered suitable and sat with his back to the trunk of a tree. It seemed he had brought no blanket.

"Your mother."

"She died before I left Lemster. A pestilence came to the town and killed a quarter of those living there. My brother died, too."

"I am sorry."

"Don't be, it was a long time ago." Thomas rolled on his side away from Jorge, and after a while, he heard him begin to snore. He was still awake when Usaden returned. There was no sign of Kin. Thomas rose and walked across the clearing to Usaden, who was nothing more than a vague shape against the shadows all around.

"How far off are they?" There was no need to ask whether Usaden had found the group they pursued.

"Closer than I thought. If they rise late tomorrow, we could be on them before they are awake and end this thing fast."

"I want Eleanor alive."

Usaden nodded in the dark. "Agreed. But can I kill the others?"

"We don't even know who they are. They may be innocent."

"I will ask each before I run them through if you prefer. I will stand guard in case they get the same idea and come looking for us."

"Get some sleep. They don't even know we are here. Did you see any guards posted at their camp?"

"None, so you are probably right. They had a small fire, and

I saw it from a distance. They are on the edge of these woods. I saw the woman you seek. She was talking with two of the others. Everyone else was curled on the ground."

"Where's Kin?"

"He caught a scent of something and went off to catch it. He'll return soon enough."

"When he does, send him over to Yves. He didn't bring a blanket and Kin can keep him warm."

"He can have my blanket, I might sit up for a while." Usaden touched Thomas's shoulder. "Go to sleep, I will call you as soon as I see the first hint of dawn."

Thomas didn't think sleep would come, but it did. Usaden was as good as his word and shook him awake to discover his hair and beard wet with dew. He rose and went to relieve himself. When he came back, the others were all awake. Yves looked as if he had not slept at all, while Usaden, who had not, appeared the most rested of them.

By the time they reached the camp of those they pursued, the fire was cold and they were long gone.

"Are you sure they didn't see you?" Thomas asked Usaden. The man's expression was answer enough. "Then we follow."

It was almost noon before Thomas admitted to himself they had lost Eleanor and her companions. The land rose towards high hills with rocky peaks. The party they sought had been tracking along the base of those hills in the direction of a small town. A very small town. The soil below their horses' hoofs had changed to an almost white limestone, but the olives and sheep and goats remained, an unchanging constant here.

"Do you think that is where they have gone?" Thomas asked Usaden. "Or have they circled back and lost us?"

"I take it you missed their tracks?"

Thomas looked down. He was sure not even Usaden could read a track on the rough ground they were crossing.

"Kin can smell them, and there have been one or two indications they are travelling this way. We have not lost them. If they intend to go west or north, there are easier passages than this. I suspect they know we are following them by now. We can hardly hide our presence in country as open as this."

Thomas called across to Yves, who rode beside Jorge. "Do you know that town ahead?"

Yves shook his head. His face was pale and dark circles shadowed his eyes. Thomas wondered if he was sorry he had come.

They were a league from the small town when Usaden pulled his horse to a halt and swung to the ground. He knelt, his fingers tracing something in the dry dirt only he could see. Thomas dismounted and knelt beside him.

"They split up here. Look…" Usaden reached out to a fresh piece of dirt that looked no different to any other. "Three of them went on, the others rode north." He glanced up, his eyes tracking the looming mountains in that direction. "They must know of a pass we cannot see."

"Which group was Eleanor in?"

Usaden rose and walked a dozen paces, came back, walked in another direction, returned a second time.

"She and two men went on to the town. Her horse is of finer build and stands out. She should weigh less than the men, but the ground is too hard and I cannot read that in the tracks."

"She is carrying gold," Thomas said.

Usaden gave a nod. "That would explain it. Do we follow her?"

"We do."

"Do you not want me to find out where the others have gone?"

"No doubt they brought her this far and are returning to wherever they came from. It would be of interest to know who they are, but we can find that out from the two who stayed with her."

"She'll have gone to ground in that town somewhere."

After they started off again, Thomas went to ride beside

Jorge. Yves was further back, looking around as if concentration alone might reveal something.

"When we find Eleanor, I want you to stay close to Yves."

Jorge twisted in his saddle and looked back at the man.

"Do I have to? I know he's your son, but I can't say I particularly like him. He stinks of privilege."

"Perhaps he's trying to change, but I don't trust him, either, not yet. I can't help wondering why he wants to come with us, unless he means to help his mother when we find her. I don't want to hurt him, or her, if we can avoid it. Usaden and I will take care of the two men still with her. I want you to take care of Yves for me."

"Kill him?"

"Stop him killing himself, or trying to kill one of us. You can manage him, can't you?"

Jorge, who was still looking back at Yves, nodded. "Yes, I can manage him, if it comes to it. Will could manage him. Maybe even Amal."

Thomas laughed. "Not yet, but one day."

"She's a lot like Lubna, isn't she?" said Jorge.

"She is." Thomas didn't want the reminder of his dead wife, even if no day passed without her loss invading his thoughts. Besides, Jorge spoke the truth. Amal was growing more and more like her mother. Clever and brave and fearless. Perhaps because Thomas carried all her fear inside himself.

As they rode along the narrow main street—it appeared to be the only street—men and women sat in front of their houses watching them pass. Thomas dismounted, handed his reins to Jorge and approached one of the older men.

"What is the name of this place?"

"Agramadenos. Everyone knows that." The man's answer was hard for Thomas to understand. A coarse mix of Arabic, Castilian and some local dialect, each word cut short before reaching its natural end.

"Everyone except me. Have you seen other strangers pass this way today?"

"You mean the woman and the men? Fine figure of a woman, too. I hope she can manage both of them. They were big men." The man cackled at his own attempt at humour.

"How long since?"

"I was tending my trees, so before we stopped to eat. A while ago now." It seemed time was not a measured commodity here.

"Did you see in which direction they went?"

"Not me, but my son did." He inclined his head towards another man sitting on the far side of the roadway. He looked barely any younger, his face creased from a lifetime in the relentless sun of these high plains.

Thomas waited, but the man considered his answer complete.

"Should I ask him?"

"He doesn't like strangers."

Thomas felt in his jacket for a coin. He held it out so the man could see it. He wondered if he knew what it was. He didn't suppose money was much used here.

The man's eyes held to the dull gleam of silver. "Finca de Almadova. Follow this road half a league and you will see it on the right. You cannot miss it. There is nothing else out there for an hour's ride."

Thomas tossed the coin at him, expecting it to fall to the ground, but the man's hand came out fast and the coin disappeared.

The money loosened his tongue a little more. "The woman came here before, but there were more of them then. Another woman, too."

The finca came into sight as soon as they rode past the last of the houses. The eyes of the inhabitants tracked them the entire way through the town, but nobody else spoke.

The house was more recent than the town, perhaps only

two hundred years old rather than a thousand. A narrow terrace offered shade at the front. Half the building rose to two storeys, a tower at one end rising even higher. Tall trees offered more shade at the rear. A large stand of oleander stood to one side, their vibrant flowers reflecting the sunlight. Thomas thought them a strange choice of shrub to grow so close to a house because he knew every part of the plant capable of producing a virulent poison.

There was no sign of any occupants or their horses. Thomas and the others sat on the roadway and stared at the building.

"How do you want to do this?" asked Usaden.

"The simple way. You and I ride up and knock on the door."

"They will see us coming and have time to prepare."

"We are talking about the two of us. There is only so much preparation someone can do."

"That is true. And Jorge and the boy?"

"He has thirty-five years."

"But he's still a boy. You can see it in his eyes."

"They stay here for now. I've told Jorge to keep him under control."

Usaden laughed, but made no comment as he urged his horse up the slope. A narrow track showed where the others had come. Thomas knew Usaden could read it well enough to know how long ago, what weight the riders, and perhaps even what they had eaten to break their fast.

They tied the horses to a rail and Thomas hammered on the door. The sound fell like lead to the ground, any echo sucked away by the dry soil.

"Go around back and make sure nobody tries to escape."

Usaden nodded and darted away, Kin at his side.

Thomas hammered again, harder this time. He put his ear to the rough wood of the door and listened. He was still listening when the door opened so fast, he almost lost his balance.

Eleanor stood on the other side, her head tilted to one side in question.

"I wondered how long it would take you to get here. Come in, then." She looked past him. "And tell the others to come, too. I have made food enough for everyone. Is that my son with Jorge?"

"It is."

"Why did you let him come with you?"

"Because he asked. Are you going to tell me the truth this time?"

"I will, but only you, Thomas." She reached out and touched his wrist. "I owe you that much."

Thomas turned and waved his arms so Jorge and Yves knew to join them.

"Where are the men you arrived with?"

"Gone to meet with the others. They only came here to ensure my arrival. They took my horse with them so I would find it difficult to leave. They took my gold, too."

"Why were you brought here?" Thomas wanted to ask as much as he could before the others arrived, but knew they would be here before he had a chance.

"Come inside and I will put the food out, and then we can let them eat while you and I talk. I will tell you what you want to know, and then you can decide my fate. I am not—" But what she was not would have to wait as Jorge arrived.

Yves pushed past Thomas and embraced his mother. She kissed his cheek before pushing him away.

"Take Jorge inside, then go out back and tell the other one to come in, but the dog stays outside."

CHAPTER TWENTY-ONE

Yves stood close to his mother in a room at the rear of the house. Wide windows looked out over rocky ground that rose steeply. Thomas glanced at the array of food on the table, but ignored it despite his hunger. He noticed Usaden and Jorge did the same.

Eleanor saw their reluctance and laughed. She strode to the table.

"Do you think me stupid enough to poison you?" She took a slice of meat pie and handed it to Yves. "Eat this, my sweet, and show Thomas he has nothing to fear."

Yves looked at the offering, but made no move to raise it to his mouth.

Eleanor shook her head and took another slice. She bit into it, wiping crumbs from her chin.

"See?"

Usaden took a slice of the same pie, as did Jorge. Usaden walked to the rear door and tossed his piece to Kin, who caught it in mid-air, leaping high without seeming to move his legs. Usaden came back and took a second slice.

Eleanor stared at Thomas, waiting. He made no move and

she scowled. There was nothing left of the girl he had fallen in love with, however hard he searched for her.

"No matter, there is another table set next door, just for you and me. Come, we can talk there." She glanced at her son. "Yves, stay here."

Thomas followed her into the long corridor that stretched the length of the house, then into a smaller room. There was a table laid, chairs set, even plates, fine glasses and wine.

"I take it you don't intend to kill me, then?"

"If I did, you would already be dead. You might have been my first teacher, but I have learned much since. Including knowing my own mind. And you have been much on my mind of late."

Eleanor sat and reached for the leg of a bird coated with a rich sauce.

Thomas remained on his feet. The scent of the food made his stomach ache. He knew he could eat anything he wanted, but another smell underlay that of the food, sweet and smoky. It was familiar, but he couldn't place it. He assumed it was from the rich sauces that coated some of the dishes.

"As you have been on mine," he said.

"Oh, I think not in the same way. You have been hunting me down because you believe me guilty of a crime."

"Are you about to plead your innocence? It's a little late for that."

Eleanor met his gaze, her own softer than he expected.

"You must know I could have killed anyone I wanted. That strutting peacock in the palace on the hill, your queen, even you. It was you who first taught me about love, about herbs, about fungus. I did what I could because I hoped it would bring you to me."

"Which it has, but I am here to take you back for judgement. What is that smell?"

"It is only the food. Eat something. I need you to be strong, because I want your help."

Thomas laughed and shook his head. "Have you lost your wits?"

Eleanor's face showed no amusement. She looked afraid.

"I have been stupid. Love made me stupid. My love of you."

"You showed what manner of love we shared in Córdoba when you slept with Fernando."

"I was a fool. I wanted to hurt you, but ended up hurting myself. I could blame Castellana, but it would be a lie." Eleanor looked down at her hands, kept looking down as she continued. "I fled Castile to get away from my own feelings. Feelings about you. I never forgot you, but you were never in my mind often until we met again. I wanted to put distance between us, but it made no difference. You filled my head with thoughts of what I had lost."

"You lost nothing, because we had nothing."

"But we could have something, couldn't we?" Eleanor lifted her gaze to Thomas's, a hunger in hers that all the food on the table could not satiate.

"No." Thomas watched tears gather in her eyes and felt nothing. She had betrayed him. "If you truly care about me, tell me who sent you here."

"To this house?"

"To Castile. I assume it was not your idea to poison Isabel."

Eleanor attempted to control herself, and Thomas wondered whether her emotions were real or just another way of trying to influence him. Except he had learned his lesson where she was concerned. He trusted nothing she said and nothing she did.

"It was a commission, nothing more. It is what I have done for years. Take commissions."

"To kill people?"

"Sometimes. At other times, more subtlety is required."

"Who was this commission from? Who wants Isabel dead?"

"I will tell you soon, perhaps, when I am sure I can trust you." She moved her hand as if to reach for his, then stopped.

"Then we have only one thing left to talk about. What have you done with Baldomero de Pamplona and his wife?"

Eleanor offered a faint smile. "Patience, my love, patience. Soon you will learn everything."

"You were wild when I first knew you, but I never thought you evil."

"I do not consider myself evil, but after my husband died, I needed a source of income. The knowledge I had gained attracted a good price. The first time was almost an accident. I had taken a lover. He was not you, but a fine-looking young man all the same. He was married, but told me he would marry me if he was not. And then, when…" Eleanor hesitated, her gaze turning inward for a moment before she shook her head. "No matter the reason why, but I poisoned his wife. I made sure it was painless. I thought it was what he wanted, but he found out what I had done and threatened to expose me. So I had to get rid of him, too. I discovered I enjoyed the power."

Eleanor ate another of the small tarts. She poured wine into both glasses and drank half her own to show it was safe. Thomas sat across from her and pulled meat from the breast of a duck. The wine was excellent, rich and full-bodied.

"Why Isabel?"

"It was nothing personal. If I had known you lay with her, I might not have taken the commission, but it was a great deal of money, so I probably would have."

"I don't lie with her," Thomas said.

"Then you are a fool. Soon she will rule all these lands. Become her lover and you will have great power and wealth."

"I lust after neither power nor wealth."

"You always were an innocent about such things. I remember how you captured a hoard of gold and gave most of it away. It was how we met, was it not?"

"I recall it that way, yes. Who paid you?"

"The King of France."

Thomas hadn't expected an answer, and her response came as a surprise.

"Why?"

"Because France is a powerful nation and does not wish another powerful nation on its southern border. If Isabel wins this war, as she is going to, that is exactly what Spain will become. France has not long given England a bloody nose, but they still trouble her borders."

"I have always heard Charles is too affable for such underhand dealings."

"He is. It was his sister Anne and her husband the Duke of Bourbon who hatched this plan, but if anyone ever found me out, I was to blame the King." Eleanor smiled. "It is the truth, Thomas. You know I cannot lie to you. Are you really going to take me to Isabel now? Will she hang me, do you think?" She seemed untroubled at the prospect.

"As you said, you have killed no one yet. If I plead your case, she may do nothing more than exile you to your holdings in France."

Eleanor smiled again. "Which is where I intend to go. I have failed here. There is nothing to keep me in this land any longer."

"When can I see de Pamplona and his wife? I take it you had some kind of hold over the man to make him do as you wanted?"

"His wife was held hostage and he was told he would never see her again if he didn't use the tarts I prepared. It was a rare accident of luck I found out about him when I was in the Sultan's palace. Another when I heard the Queen wanted a Moorish cook. I had his wife kidnapped to ensure he placed the poison in front of Isabel." Eleanor shook her head. "Your Isabel."

"Would it have made a difference if you had known?"

"The money had already been paid and a service demanded. When I heard you served her, I reduced the dose."

"Theresa almost died."

"Except you were there. I knew you would be there. I also knew you would never rest until you searched out who was behind the poison. Clearly it was not de Pamplona. I thought you had uncovered me that first time you called. I was ready to confess, but you left again."

"Why would France act as you say? It has sent soldiers to stand beside those of Castile."

"It always pays to spread a wager over more than one outcome, especially when the stakes are as high as they are in this game."

"Game? We are talking of people's lives. What did you do with de Pamplona and his wife?"

"They were brought here until matters were settled. I intended to try again. That is no longer possible, which is why I intend to leave. I thank you for bringing my son with you. It saves me the journey south to fetch him."

"Are they here?"

"They were this morning. I have them locked safely away."

"I want to see them."

"I was hoping to seduce you first, one last time in memory of what we once had. Did you not enjoy our last encounter? I did."

"You were using me, nothing more."

"And would use you again. I am more skilled than when we were young, and sometimes that makes up for the excitement we had then." Eleanor stood. "Come on, if you must. I will introduce you to Baldomero de Pamplona and his wife. Then perhaps you can accompany me to my chamber. I am sure I can find something to enhance our experience."

Thomas followed her from the room. He could hear Jorge and Yves talking, but as he and Eleanor walked the length of the long corridor, their voices faded. The strange smell grew stronger as they approached a door set at the end. A heavy key was set in the lock and Eleanor turned it.

"Say hello, Thomas, I am sure they will be pleased to see you."

Eleanor swung the door open and Thomas stepped through before he was fully aware of the billowing smoke filling the room. As he turned back, the door slammed shut and the lock turned.

Thomas turned to the source of the smoke. A fire of logs burned in a wide grate, but the chimney was blocked so smoke billowed into the room. Baldomero de Pamplona and his wife sat in comfortable chairs set on either side of the fireplace. Both were dead, their faces almost black.

Thomas coughed, the smoke already affecting him. He went on hands and knees, trying to get beneath the densest layer, but knew at once it was not enough. He crawled to where sunlight streamed in to show where a window lay. He tried to kick the glass out, but an iron grill was bolted to the inside. He moved back to the fireplace, intending to tip de Pamplona's wife from her chair and use that, but the world spun away from him. His vision shrank to a small circle, and he knew he wouldn't make it.

Eleanor had confessed her sins, and now she had killed him.

CHAPTER TWENTY-TWO

When Thomas opened his eyes, he found a figure leaning over him, hand flat against his chest. Jorge sat back and let his breath go.

"Gods, but I thought we'd lost you."

"You know I'm a hard man to kill." Thomas rolled his head to one side to discover he was lying on pale soil in front of the house.

"Usaden says if Kin hadn't barked, you'd be dead."

Thomas tried to sit up and failed. His head ached and his stomach roiled. Saliva filled his mouth and he leaned to one side and vomited. Jorge rubbed his back like he was a child.

"Did she poison you?"

"She didn't have to. Usaden is right, another few moments and I would never have opened my eyes again."

"He did something I've never seen before," said Jorge. "He punched you hard on your chest, two or three times."

"Sometimes it works, most times not." Thomas let Jorge help him to his feet. "Where is she?"

"Usaden has them both locked in the room with the bodies. He doesn't trust Yves. Neither do I."

"I hope the fire is out."

"It is. He unblocked the chimney and smashed the glass. There is still a taint to the air, but they won't die, more's the pity."

"How did Kin know?"

"Eleanor came and told us you were talking with de Pamplona and his wife. I wanted to join you, but she told me you had asked to be alone with them. Kin had come in from outside. He went up to her and sniffed at her dress. She tried to kick him, but he was too fast. I think he smelled the smoke. How he knew it was killing you is another matter."

"She locked the door. How did you get in?" Thomas's head spun, but the ground had stopped moving under his feet. The remnant of smoke clinging to his clothes brought a fresh wave of nausea.

"Eleanor was foolish enough to leave the key in the lock. We dragged you out and brought you here to the fresh air."

"What is to stop them climbing through the window Usaden broke? Where is he—guarding them?"

"Usaden left the metal grill in place. Kin is watching over them for now." Jorge laughed. "He's lying on the floor and every time either of them moves towards the window, he gives that growl of his and they back off. Usaden's gone up into the tower. He thinks the men who accompanied Eleanor may still be close. No doubt they are out there waiting for a signal to come and finish us."

"Then they'll be waiting a long time. I want to see the bodies of Baldomero and his wife. Call Usaden down and take Eleanor and Yves to the room you were eating in, I'm sure you and Kin can guard them just as well there. And don't tell her I'm alive yet."

"She saw us drag you out," said Jorge.

"Did I look alive?"

"No, you didn't. I'll go fetch Usaden if you can stand on your own, but I'm not sure your dog will do what I tell him. Stay this side of the house if you don't want to be seen yet."

When Jorge had gone, Thomas walked to where the oleander stood and drew the branches aside. Deep within, out of sight, he found where several branches were sawn through. He leaned closer to see the cuts had been made some time ago. Which meant someone had planned their use before Eleanor came here. Which raised the question whether that someone was Eleanor herself or not. Thomas wondered if she had come to this place deliberately, or had she been brought? Were the men who accompanied her compatriots or only here to ensure she kept her side of whatever bargain had been made? Was the confession she offered the truth, or nothing more than another set of lies? He intended to ask her once he had examined de Pamplona and his wife. Thomas knew there was little point, but a sense of duty meant he could make no assumptions about how they had died.

When he saw Usaden descend from the tower and disappear inside, Thomas made his way to the side of the house and into the room. Water pooled in front of the fireplace where it had be used to extinguish the smouldering wood.

Thomas started with de Pamplona's wife. When he turned her head from side to side, it moved easily, which told him she had not been dead long. A quick examination showed no wounds, which told him the smoke had been the cause of her death. If he had come here as soon as they came to the house, perhaps both would still be alive, but he felt no guilt. How could he have known Eleanor would do this? Though he should have known she would do something. It was who she was. A killer. An assassin in a fine dress. Was Yves also involved? Thomas didn't want to believe it, but knew he could well be.

Baldomero de Pamplona was as recently dead as his wife, his lips as blue as hers. Thomas suspected their deaths had been relatively peaceful. They had been brought here and someone had closed the shutter in the chimney. Would they have fallen asleep, unaware they would never wake? He hoped so.

Thomas rose, ignoring a moment of dizziness. He would question Eleanor again, and this time she would tell him the truth. As he came from the room, Usaden appeared at the far end of the hallway. He saw Thomas and ran towards him.

"Men are coming. A dozen at least."

"The same ones we saw before?"

"They wear dark uniforms, so more than likely. What do you want to do with the woman and her son?"

"Bring them back in here. Lock the door and leave Kin to guard them again."

"You realise it will be you and me holding them off, don't you?"

"We've fought worse odds before. Besides, Jorge fights well these days."

"He does, but not enough for this. Perhaps he should guard the woman and her son and Kin come with us, he will be of more use. I found three bows inside, which might be useful if we have to retreat."

It was a good plan, and Thomas agreed with a nod. When it was arranged, he walked outside with Usaden. Both held a sword in one hand and a knife in the other. Kin paced ahead of them, his black and grey head turning from side to side as he sniffed at the air.

The party of men rode with no hurry along the roadway. Thomas narrowed his eyes. Yes, the same men, he was sure. Their uniform could mean they were no other. Each wore a soft cap tilted to one side, and each had a sword strapped to their saddle. Were they men of France or mercenaries from some other region? Thomas didn't know and didn't care. If he could keep one of them alive, he might get an answer to the question.

"Do we confront them here?" asked Usaden.

A dozen men against the two of them. It was possible, but not without danger.

"Did you say you found bows?"

"Three. I took them to the tower. I thought the extra height would help."

"Then that's where we go. We can hold them off between us."

"I prefer to fight a man a little closer, but it is the wiser option."

Usaden disappeared and Thomas followed, climbing a twisting staircase. They came out on a small platform surrounded on four sides by crenellated walls, against which three bows leaned. Two were short in the Moorish style. Usaden chose one and a quiver of arrows. The third was more than twice as long as the others, fashioned like those Thomas had trained with as a boy. He remembered he had been good, but that was long ago. He didn't even know if he could still draw such a bow, but chose it anyway.

When he looked through a narrow opening in the wall, he saw the band of men had turned off the roadway and were riding towards the house. Thomas considered shouting a warning, to at least offer them a chance to turn back. Usaden had no such intention. His first arrow missed its mark and buried itself in the pommel of the lead rider's saddle.

Thomas strung his bow, notched an arrow and drew. The pull of the bow fought him, but he knew more than strength was required. There was an art to using the power it held. He drew back further, stared at the man he wanted to hit rather than the arrow, and loosed. The arrow flew true to embed itself in the man's chest. He rode on for a moment, then tipped sideways and crashed to the ground. By then, Usaden had found his aim and took a second man in the throat.

The remaining men rode hard towards the house, but Thomas took another, as did Usaden, and then the last eight veered aside to crash through the edges of the oleander.

"We follow," Thomas said, knowing the bows were no use with the bulk of the house between them and the fleeing men, but Usaden was already gone and Thomas had to run to catch up with him.

Usaden had slung the bow over his shoulder and withdrawn his sword and dagger. When Thomas rounded the bushes, he was confronted by only five men. He glanced around, but couldn't see any others. He wondered if the show of force had come as a surprise and caused them to flee. He grinned. Whatever the reason, now it was only five against two and he liked those odds much better.

"Try to keep at least one alive," he said to Usaden. "I need to know who sent them and who they work for."

"I will try, but you know holding back does not come easily to me."

"Then take the three on the right and I'll keep one of mine alive."

Usaden gave a nod and ran at his first target. The man had only just started to unsheathe his sword when Usaden's took him in the chest. Usaden spun fast and opened the throat of another.

All at once, the rest ran. Thomas sprinted, threw himself at the slowest and brought him down. He cracked the hilt of his knife against the man's skull, then did it again when he remained conscious. The second time was the charm. Thomas rose to his feet and looked around. Usaden was nowhere in sight. No doubt he had gone in pursuit of the others. Except the others were not all the men who had come to the house. Eight survived their arrows, but only five had confronted them. None looked like the kind to run from a fight.

Thomas ran hard back to the house. When he entered the room Eleanor and Yves were being held, he was confronted by two men, an injured woman, and Yves who cowered in a corner.

Thomas ran the first man through before he even had time to turn. The second took a little longer to deal with, but not by much. Thomas went to Eleanor, who lay on her side. Blood pooled beneath her. Too much blood.

When Thomas rolled her onto her back and lifted her up, her eyes fluttered open and she tried to smile.

"I didn't think he would do it."

"Tell me who you are working for."

"I was betrayed. Men are all alike, even those closest to you." Her voice was a soft whisper. "All apart from you, Thomas. You were always different. You still are. I never…" She winced, and the breath left her lungs in a long sigh. Thomas stared into her eyes, waiting for them to lose their spark, but she rallied her strength from somewhere. "…never stopped loving you. Never. Goodnight." This time when her chest fell, it didn't rise again. Thomas lay her on the soiled boards and closed her eyes. As he rose, Yves pushed past him and went to his knees beside his mother. He lifted her, shook her, but to Thomas it looked like an act.

"She's gone. You need to dig a hole and bury her. Was she religious?"

"Of course she was. We attended church three times a week."

"It's not always the same thing. Where's Jorge?"

"He went after the third man."

Thomas had forgotten there was another man. He went to the door and listened, but heard nothing. He walked the length of the corridor, afraid of what he might find, but when he entered the large room at the far end, he found Jorge sitting in a chair, drinking a glass of wine. Kin was on the table helping himself to whatever he liked. There was more than enough even for a dog as large as him.

"Did you lose him?" Thomas asked. He picked up a small tart and bit into it to discover the contents sweet, a mix of apple and dates dotted with raisins. With the end of the fighting, his hunger was a ravening beast.

"I caught up with him outside."

"And?"

"He's dead—go check if you want to be sure, but I fear Usaden has done too good a job on me. I'm not sure I like it. I took no pleasure in killing the man, but he wouldn't yield."

"Sometimes there is no choice."

"Not around you, there isn't. The wine is very good, you should try some."

"We need to leave before any others come. Eleanor's dead, there's nothing to keep us here."

"I didn't see her struck, I was too busy chasing the other man."

"She was still alive when I reached her."

"Did she tell you anything useful, like who sent them?" Jorge refilled his glass, filled another for Thomas. Kin jumped from the table, having eaten his fill.

"Nothing important. I told Yves to dig a hole and bury her."

"He fought well, got a knife off one man and stuck him. It gave me the chance to come out here to finish it. Eleanor was different to how she was in Qurtuba, but I expect you have changed as well." Jorge drained his glass and refilled it once more.

Thomas wondered how drunk he was. Too drunk to ride?

Thomas thought for a moment. "Perhaps you're right. I don't believe I ever really knew her. She was wild, we both were, but her wildness always carried an edge of madness to it. I didn't see it, not then, because I was led by my cock instead of my head."

Jorge shrugged as if to say that was not always such a terrible thing.

Thomas took the glass of wine away from him and threw it on the floor.

"I'm going to find Usaden and see how many more he's killed. I knocked one of them out and want to question him. Then I'll help Yves dig his mother's grave. If you pass out, I'll leave you here."

Jorge said nothing.

When Thomas returned to the room, Eleanor's body lay where he had left it, but there was no sign of Yves. Thomas went outside to see if he was already digging her grave. Even after he had circled the house twice, he found no sign of him, only the bodies of the men he and Usaden had killed. Something would have to be done about them.

On the third pass, he noticed one of the horses was missing. He assumed the man he had knocked out had come round and taken it, but as he took one last look around, he found him half-hidden by the oleander. He was dead, his throat cut.

Thomas climbed the tower and shaded his eyes. He saw a single figure already half a league distant. It rode fast towards the hills, and Thomas cursed. He had underestimated his son. He was going in the same direction as the men they had followed for a day and a half.

Thomas glanced at Usaden. He had not heard him approach, but then he never did. The man was uncanny.

"Did you kill the man I knocked down?"

Usaden stared at him, shook his head. "You said you wanted him alive." Usaden followed Thomas's gaze. "Do you want me to follow him?"

"Let him go."

"I wouldn't kill him," said Usaden. "Not if you asked me not to."

"He won't come back now, he'll be scurrying for home if he knows what's good for him. We have other things to do." Thomas watched the diminishing figure. As it grew smaller, so did his attachment to both the man and his mother. There would be no grave dug for Eleanor. Any lingering feelings he might have had for her, she had destroyed by her actions.

Thomas turned back to Usaden. "See if Jorge is sober enough to help, we have bodies to drag inside and a house to burn."

CHAPTER TWENTY-THREE

The smoke began as little more than a faint haze beyond the hills, but as they rode closer, the sky turned almost black and roiling clouds rose into the air. Thomas sat astride the white stallion Eleanor had used because it was a better steed than the one he had arrived on, which was tethered behind.

"I see Fernando is trying to burn the world into submission again," said Jorge.

"Burning crops his own soldiers will need soon." Thomas looked to where Usaden rode point, Kin as ever running even further ahead. How the dog could cover so much ground and not exhaust himself was a mystery he had given up trying to solve.

"Are you heartbroken?" asked Jorge.

Thomas frowned. "I would rather he didn't ravage the land, but you can't expect anything else from the man."

"Not Fernando. Eleanor. You were with her when she took her last breath. What did you feel?"

"You talk too much about feelings."

"It is what I do. Were you relieved? Angry? I don't suppose you have even thought about how you felt."

"Will it change anything if I spend days lost in memory and

grief? I don't have the time to indulge myself. Isabel will want me as soon as we return."

"What if she asks you the same question?"

Thomas glanced at Jorge. "Why ever would she do that?"

"Because she cares about you."

"I hadn't planned on telling her. Do you think I should?"

"If only to put her mind at rest. De Pamplona administered the poison meant for her, but Eleanor was the mastermind behind the planning. She would have happily killed you and them. You know what that means, don't you? With them both dead, the threat against Isabel is over. She can concentrate on winning the war, and I believe the sooner she does so, the better. Then we can start rebuilding our lives. She will no doubt give you a position in the new Gharnatah. We can spend the rest of our days living in luxury in the palace."

"She won't offer me any position," Thomas said. "Even if she does, I am minded to turn her down. My job will be over when Gharnatah falls."

"Believe what you want, she won't let you go now."

As they came out through a pass, the land sloped away to the wide *vega*. When they had left three days before, it had been verdant with crops: mulberry, olive, sugar cane and rice growing beneath the sun while water channels irrigated every field. Now the land lay black as far as the eye could see and smoke stung Thomas's eyes and lungs. It reminded him of the billowing inferno of the house they had torched—the bodies of Eleanor, Baldomero and his wife, and the men he and Usaden had killed piled inside. He had watched it burn, and then ridden away without a second thought. It was a chapter of his life that had ended. The book closed.

He drew his tagelmust across his face, but it did little good. Soldiers and others with burning torches scoured the land, setting fire to any remaining crops. It was a vision from hell, the men's faces blackened with soot, their hands the same.

They rode into Santa Fe and returned the horses to the

stables. Thomas wondered if he should ask someone to take them back to Gharnatah, but decided there was little point. Everything that belonged to Gharnatah would soon belong to Castile.

As they approached the newly built quarters where Isabel was housed, Thomas knew he ought to bathe before seeing her.

Jorge leaned across and touched Thomas's arm. "Don't confront Isabel about the burning. You need time to reflect on what you have done and consider your next actions. Spend time with your children. Let them wash your soul clean before you decide."

"My soul is already clean, and she will expect me."

"Not everything revolves around you, Thomas. She will only expect you if she knows you are here. Our house is only half a league away."

Thomas stopped walking. He looked behind, but there was no sign of either Usaden or Kin. He suspected they were already on their way to the small farmhouse Isabel had assigned him. Jorge was right, he knew, but years of duty continued to bind his actions.

"Go to the house. Tell them I will be there by nightfall. Ask Belia to prepare a feast."

Jorge shook his head as he walked away. Thomas watched him go, then turned and entered Isabel's quarters to let her know she was safe. But as he strode along the corridor, a stocky figure emerged from a room and blocked his path. Fernando, King of Aragon and Castile. Another figure hovered just inside the shade within the door. Another of Fernando's conquests, flaunted here in the same building that housed his wife. Thomas could smell the smoke on the man, though he must have washed his face for it was clean and wore a scowl.

"I wondered when you would come skulking back. She doesn't want to see you."

"I have news for her and would rather she tell me the same, if it is true."

Fernando took a pace closer, always happy to invade others' space.

"Are you saying you doubt my word?"

"Not at all, Your Grace, but my news is for the Queen alone."

"Then try again tomorrow. She is with her advisors. That fool Columb has been here making threats."

"He needs your money too much to make threats."

"He needs someone's money. He claims both France and England will fund his crazed expedition. Well, let them pour their gold into the depths of the great western ocean, Castile and Aragon will be all the richer. Now, I have men to see." Fernando made no move, and Thomas knew he would not until he turned and left the building. He was about to do just that when the shadowed figure moved and Thomas experienced a shock of recognition. The woman was Salma, a sheet clutched against her naked body. She wanted him to see her, wanted him to see how close she was to the power in this land. Thomas glanced at Fernando to see a smirk on the man's face. It was all he could do not to punch him.

He was half way to his house when a familiar voice hailed him. He slowed and turned to see Christof Columb trotting towards him. Thomas had grown used to the man's ideas and no longer considered them those of a lunatic, as he first had. His own research led him to believe the man misguided, but not altogether wrong.

He came forwards with his rolling mariner's gait, a frown on his face.

"I thought it was you. I hear you work for the Queen now."

"Apparently so, but Fernando turned me away."

"As have I been, though not by the King himself. I have attempted to see her several times over the last week and each time has been the same. Can I buy you wine? I would like to talk."

"I'm on my way home, so come with me. Stay for dinner, though you will have to put up with my children's questions."

Columb gave a smile. "I like the questions of children. They ask them in a spirit of innocence rather than to trap a man."

As they approached the house set apart on rough ground that remained unmolested, too poor to grow crops on, Will walked down the track to greet them. Kin bounded from the house and ran past him and Columb came to a sudden halt.

Thomas laughed. "Fear not, he only eats rabbits and wicked men."

"What if he thinks I am a wicked man?"

"Then I will tell him otherwise."

Columb didn't look convinced, but started up again, veering away to avoid Kin as much as possible.

"Jorge said you were coming home today, Father, but I didn't believe him."

Thomas couldn't recall when Will had started calling him Father, only that it was recent. It felt like a distancing between them, but perhaps it was Will's way of letting him know he also felt that distance. The boy was growing into a man, his size and strength bringing that change early. Thomas knew he hadn't seen enough of his children the last year and determined that would end today.

———

It took a day and a half before Thomas realised his shoulders were no longer tense and his back had stopped aching. He put it down to a number of things. Usaden had not once asked him to train, Belia had massaged him after insisting he wash first, and Amal had spent most of her time either curled against him or kissing his face. Even Will had spent time with him, and Thomas found pleasure in seeing the changes in the boy— though how much longer he could continue to call him a boy was becoming hard to judge.

"I liked that sailor," said Will. They were walking through the hills north of the house, Kin ranging ahead in search of something to bring down and kill. Thomas had four plump rabbits slung on a leather thong over his shoulder. "Is he really planning to sail across the western ocean?"

"He is."

Will shook his head at the foolishness of the idea. Everyone knew the ocean was endless.

"When are you going back to Isabel?"

"Tomorrow most likely, and you should at least try to call her Queen Isabel."

"She told me I didn't need to. Nor Ami. I like her, and I know she likes you. It's a shame about Fernando or you could marry her. We wouldn't mind."

Thomas tried not to smile. "I think Fernando might well have something to say on the matter, and I would be a poor catch for a queen."

Will slowed to a halt and turned to face the wide plain. The fires had stopped smouldering, but the landscape remained blackened. Now and then a sudden gust of wind lifted the sooty remains to spiral them through the air.

"Can I come with you when you go?"

"Why?" Thomas found the smile harder to hide this time.

"I like her children. Even Juan and the mad one, though I think she might like me too much."

"You like one more than the others, don't you?" This time the smile came to the surface.

Will scowled. "We have become friends. She is the cleverest of them all, despite being the youngest. Juanna is a little crazy, and Maria quiet, but I like them both well enough."

Thomas wondered if the moment had come he had spoken of with Jorge. It was a strange place to have the conversation, but have it they would.

"You know there can be nothing but friendship between you and Isabel's daughters."

"Tell that to Juanna, not me, but I have no intention of marrying them, Father. I'm not a fool. We're friends, that is all. Like you and Isabel are friends."

Thomas wondered if Will was aware of what he had said and suspected perhaps he was. Already his son was growing too clever for him.

"Are you still going to work for her when Gharnatah falls?" Will asked.

"I expect so, if she asks. I need to talk to you about something. About you and Juanna and the other girls."

"If it's about sex, Jorge has already explained it to me. Probably explained more than I wanted to know, but at least now I know *all* about it. So don't worry, Father, I won't accost Juanna or anyone else." A fleeting smile touched Will's lips. "Not even if they beg me."

"You will find someone when the time is right." Thomas wondered when this talk had taken place between Jorge and Will. "You are a handsome man, and there will be girls out there who want to hold you close, so take care and choose well."

"Like you did with Ma?"

Thomas nodded. He took a breath, not sure he could answer because there came a sudden tightness in his chest, but he knew he had to.

"Yes, like I did with Ma." He glanced at Will, who continued to look out across the destruction Fernando had wrought. "You know Lubna wasn't your real mother, don't you?"

"Of course. Helena birthed me, but Ma was always Ma. Helena likes you too." Will shook his head at the strangeness of the concept of all these women liking his father. "She is different now, isn't she?"

"Yes, I believe she is."

"You can be with her if you want, me and Ami won't mind. We love Belia, but she's not a real Ma to us. We could grow to love Helena if we tried."

"You could, could you?"

"So, are you?"

"Am I what?"

"Going to be with Helena? You don't have to marry her, I don't think she expects that."

"Jorge did have a good talk with you, didn't he?"

Will gave a sharp nod. "He did." He turned and took a few paces up the slope before stopping again. "Who's that up there?"

Thomas turned. A lone rider was outlined against the sky where he stood on the ridge. Thomas narrowed his eyes, but couldn't make out any features.

"It looks like Yves," said Will. "My brother Yves." He looked at Thomas. "You have children all over the world, don't you? What would you do if I did the same? Not yet, of course, but I'm already feeling things I haven't before. Jorge explained those to me as well and told me what I could do if they get too strong. Why is Yves watching us?"

"Are you sure it's him?"

"Pretty sure, yes. He holds himself a bit like you, but not so upright. And he looks a little like you. Do I look like you?"

Thomas turned and looked at Will's face. He wasn't sure he did, and Helena still refused him any certainty.

"You look like Olaf," he said.

"Everyone says that, but I want to look like you as well." Will gave a tiny smile. "If you can get all these women to like you, then looking like you might not be so bad. Ami looks like Ma, doesn't she?"

"She does."

"It doesn't hurt as much as it used to, but some nights I still see the men attacking her in my dreams."

Thomas reached out and touched Will's shoulder. "It's good you remember her."

"I wish I had been as strong and fast as I am now because I would have killed them all and Ma would still be with us."

"You can't change what has passed. Remember her as she was, remember how much she loved you, and change what you can so she is proud of you, proud of both of you. Make her even more proud of you." Thomas found talking difficult again.

"I will if I can." Will didn't try to hide his tears and Thomas pulled the boy against him. He looked over his head at the figure on the ridge-line. If it was Yves, he remained there without moving. Thomas couldn't tell if he was watching them or not, but suspected he was.

Thomas kissed the top of Will's head. "All you can do is try your best. That is what she would want of you."

Later that night, after Yves had disappeared from the ridge, after Kin had caught three more rabbits and Belia had skinned and cooked two of them, after she and the children had gone to bed, Thomas sat beside Jorge with an almost empty flagon of wine between them and said, "Did I tell you Fernando has taken a new lover?"

"You didn't, but it comes as no surprise. Is it anyone I know? Is she beautiful?"

"It's Salma, so yes, she is beautiful."

Jorge hesitated, his wine glass halfway to his mouth.

"Koparsh's Salma? Can't say I blame him, but he plays a dangerous game, as does she."

"She was in his room when I tried to get in to see Isabel. She must know about her, Fernando was blatant in displaying her to me."

"That man is too much led by his cock."

"Speaking of which, how much did you tell Will about sex?"

"Everything a boy needs to know. I told him about love too, not just sex. I'm not as foolish as you might think me. It was what you wanted me to do, wasn't it?"

"It may have been, I forget."

"You forget nothing. He needs to know the consequences of what might happen. He is a handsome boy and will be an even

199

more handsome man before too long. Even if he looks a little like you."

"Does he? I don't see it."

"No, a father never does. It's time your children had a new mother in their lives."

Thomas smiled. "Will said the same thing."

"You could ask Theresa, I'm sure she would say yes."

"I'm not sure she would anymore."

"Helena then. I believe her changed, and she would say yes. I know who you want to ask, but that is a dream and nothing more."

"Perhaps there is someone else out there for me."

"And perhaps Gharnatah will win this war. Accept what you can't change, Thomas. You're growing older and deserve to see out what years remain to you with a woman who loves you. Or can at least put up with you. Women like that are few and far between."

"What will you do when Gharnatah falls?"

"Wait for you to ask me," said Jorge.

Thomas drained his glass and looked at Jorge. "Ask you what?"

"To stay at your side." Jorge laughed at Thomas's expression. "And remember, I still need Belia to have a daughter. I daren't ask anybody else."

CHAPTER TWENTY-FOUR

The following morning, Thomas made his way into Santa Fe. Will accompanied him, but as they approached Isabel's head-quarters, Prince Juan emerged and they went off together, friends just as Will was with Isabel's daughters. Well, perhaps not quite the same way. Thomas watched the pair stroll among the soldiers, his son towering over Juan, who was three years older. Thomas knew his son had been spending long hours walking among the gathered men, talking with them, working on his rapidly improving grasp of the Castilian language. Though some of the words he had picked up might cause eyebrows to rise in polite society.

Other than the two men guarding the main entrance, who nodded Thomas through without a word, there were no others inside. Thomas knew Isabel considered herself safe among the throng of her army, but he was less sure. He had mentioned it before and was sure he would mention it again with the same result. She would do as she saw fit. Which is why as he neared the room where he expected to find her, he was unsurprised to hear raised voices.

Thomas stopped and leaned against the wall. He glanced in both directions, but saw nobody. He felt no guilt at eavesdropping. He considered it part of his job to look out for her, even if the man she was arguing with was her husband. Thomas had briefly held a suspicion that Fernando might have been the instigator behind the attempt to poison Isabel before dismissing it as being over-fearful. Relations between the two had been strained, but, he hoped, not enough for him to want her dead. Not yet, anyway … though listening to their raised voices, he began to wonder.

So drawn by their argument was Thomas that he jumped when a hand touched his shoulder. He turned to discover Theresa, who offered the smile of a co-conspirator.

"They've been at each other's throats the last three days, ever since he returned. Where have you been?"

"According to Jorge, healing my soul."

"And did it work?"

"What do you think? Other than the arguments, how has she been?" Thomas kept his voice to a whisper and Theresa took his hand and led him away. The intimacy of the touch made him smile as he recalled Jorge's other instruction. Living with Theresa would not be such a bad choice, and the children liked her. She led him into a side room before releasing his hand and turning to him. Too close again, as always. She had bathed recently, and Thomas caught the scent of soap and perfume. Her red hair shone and her skin was unblemished, her eyes clear.

"What are they arguing about?"

"Could you not tell? You were standing there long enough."

"I think they had moved beyond the primary subject and on to general insults."

"Isabel disagrees with how he is conducting the war, and Fernando accuses her of being too soft on the Moors. He even mentioned you and said she should banish you from her presence. He claims you are a spy."

"He doesn't like me."

202

"Can you blame him? Isabel loves you more than she does him. No husband welcomes such a situation."

"Then he needs to stop bedding his lovers. No doubt you are aware he has taken a new one. He needs to be careful. Salma belongs to Koparsh."

"Everyone knows about Salma," said Theresa. "It's not as if Fernando even tries to hide his infidelities anymore. I suspect Koparsh is the one who put her up to the seduction, not that it would have been difficult. Fernando claims it is the duty of a king to spread his seed as widely as possible. It is a divine right."

"Then he's doing his duty with great vigour. How long do these arguments go on for? I need to speak with her."

"Sometimes they end quickly, other times they go on until her advisors call her."

"Am I not an advisor?" Thomas asked.

Theresa laughed, putting a hand to her mouth to stifle the sound. "If you say so. Nobody knows exactly what you are. Nobody dares even ask her. Do you not know yourself?"

"I do as she asks and am content with that."

"She listens to you more than anyone else, so even if those who advise her think otherwise, yes, you are her advisor. Her closest advisor." She smiled at his expression. "Now, I have a question for you and need an honest answer."

"That sounds serious." Thomas believed he knew what it would be. He also believed he knew his answer. They had waited too long, both of them.

Theresa stared into his eyes, her head tilted to one side, her expression unusually serious. She reached out and cupped his face in her palm and lifted on tiptoe, but was still too short. Thomas leaned down and kissed her mouth.

"I cannot wait for you forever," she said, "so I have made a decision. A hard decision. I have taken a lover." She continued to stare at him, her eyes moving as she searched for some reaction.

Thomas had closed his expression down. It was not the news he had expected, and the shock of it left him cast adrift.

"Am I allowed to know who?"

"Martin de Alarcón."

Thomas stared at her, his mind turning but gaining no traction.

"Why?"

"Because I like him, and he asked, and we have shared a bed before. He is a good and generous lover, but most of all, I cannot wait for you forever, Thomas." She put a finger against his lips as he started to speak. "No. It is too late. My mind is made up."

"Isn't Martin married?"

"He was. His wife died a year ago, did you not hear?"

He shook his head.

"I expect someone told you, but you did not consider it important enough to recall. It had been a marriage of convenience rather than love, and there were no children."

"Do you love him? Does he love you?"

Theresa raised a shoulder. "What is love, Thomas?"

"You need to ask Jorge, not me."

"I like Martin, and believe I will grow to love him."

"Is he going to ask you to marry him?"

"He cannot. Martin has a position to uphold, and marrying someone like me would never be sanctioned, but I do not expect him to. He will probably marry someone he does not love, but I will remain his mistress." She took a step closer. "I am sorry, Thomas. Sorry we did not indulge ourselves in the past." She stepped closer yet until her breasts touched his chest. "If you want to, perhaps we could indulge the once?" She looked around. "Here, in fact. I can lock the door like we should have done all those years ago."

"Thank you for the offer, but I cannot accept."

"No, I did not think you would. It was worth my trying, for I am sore curious how it would be between us. As I am sure are you. There must be something more to you than you show the world or Lubna would not have loved you as she did. Not to mention Isabel."

"You might have to ask Jorge again about all of that."

"Perhaps I will. Just so you know, I will stop teasing you from now on. It will no doubt make your life easier." She cocked her head to one side. "Can you hear them shouting anymore?"

Thomas listened. "No."

"Then go to Isabel." She lifted her face up for one last kiss, then giggled. "I am sorry, I said I would not do that again. Forgive me."

"There is nothing to forgive. Go and find your happiness."

———

"You are still too lax with your security," Thomas said.

"And it is a pleasure to see you, too, Thomas." Isabel's tone still carried a trace of the anger she had expressed to her husband. "Where have you been? I sent a message and that woman who lives with you told me she didn't know."

"I don't live with any woman."

"Belia? I am sure her name is Belia."

"She is Jorge's woman."

"But she lives with you both, does she not?"

"She does." Thomas knew he had to calm Isabel down, but there were things he needed to say that might serve only to make the situation worse. "Perhaps we can sit in the sun for a while and gaze across your troops."

"My husband will be out there somewhere, and I would as soon not have any reminder of what he has done." She glanced at Thomas, perhaps wondering how much he knew.

He tried to keep his expression neutral.

"As will my son and yours—they've gone off together."

"My girls talk about him all the time. I tell them it is not appropriate."

"Someone told me you talk about me all the time, is that also not appropriate? Besides, I have spoken to Will and told him to be less a friend to your daughters."

"You are my advisor, that is different. My children like Will, but he has grown so tall, so strong." Isabel's eyes flickered as they scanned Thomas. "So handsome. No wonder Catherine and the others moon after him. What is this Prince Arthur like?"

Thomas's head swirled with the sudden change of topic.

"I have no idea. He is a year younger than Catherine, so I know nothing of him. What do your spies tell you?"

"Spies? I have no spies."

"Then your friends in England. You have those, don't you?"

"I hear he is a studious boy with little liking for games of war and rumoured to be sickly. Perhaps I need to send you back to your homeland to cure him."

"Please, don't." Thomas was relieved when Isabel smiled.

"I may want to send you when Catherine goes to seal the marriage. I will need someone I trust with her."

"When will that be?"

Isabel waved a hand. "Likely not for several years, more if I can manage it. I do not want to send her away. She is more like me than any of my other children, and I know I should not say it, but I love her the most. Do you love one of your children more than the other, Thomas?"

He hesitated. It was not a question he had given any thought to, but it was a good question all the same.

"You do, don't you?" Isabel smiled, as if she had achieved some minor victory.

"Yes and no."

"What a very Thomas answer that is."

"I love them equally, but in different ways. Is that answer enough?"

"No. I love my children in different ways, but not equally. Explain."

"As you know, Will is strong and righteous. He cannot see an injustice he doesn't want to correct. Amal is clever and sweet and looks just like her mother. So I love them both, but differently."

Isabel reached out and touched his arm, a fleeting contact before she changed the subject to work.

"What bad news have you come to give me?"

"Good news, not bad. The man who poisoned Theresa— who tried to poison you—is dead. And the woman who put him up to it is also dead."

"Did you kill them both?" Isabel stared at Thomas, something bright in her eyes. "Your son is like you, for you also cannot see a wrong but want to right it. It is why I ... trust you so much."

Thomas heard her hesitation and wondered what she had intended to say. He had no idea ... or not one he wanted to consider.

"The woman behind the poisoning is someone you know. Eleanor, Countess d'Arreau. And no, I did not kill her, nor the cook de Pamplona, nor his wife who was an innocent in all of this." He thought it wise to omit any mention of those he had killed.

"Fernando's one-time lover, Eleanor?" She spat the words out. "He has poor choice in his paramours. Have you heard about his latest conquest?"

Thomas nodded. He watched her, observing the play of hurt passing beneath the surface, waiting for her to let it pass and return to matters of more importance.

"If you did not kill her, then who did?" asked Isabel.

"I still have to find that out. Eleanor claimed she was put up to the deed by someone in France. She told me they wanted you dead, though the reasons she gave made no sense, so I need to look deeper."

"What reasons?" Isabel asked, as if she cared neither one way nor another if he answered.

"Do you trust France?"

"I trust no country other than my own. I trust few people outside this room. Is that who was behind it? It would not surprise me. Not surprise me at all." Isabel waved a hand. "No matter, it is finished. So, what next?"

"It may not be ended, which is why I need to investigate further. In the meantime, you should have more guards, as I have told you before, and you need someone to taste all your food before you eat anything."

"And I have told you I will not do that. A queen cannot spend her life in fear. I am surrounded by the armies of Castile and Aragon, and I trust my staff. Even you. Did Theresa tell you about her and Martin?"

Once again, the sudden change of topic confused Thomas and he had to gather his thoughts.

"She did."

"And…?"

"And what?"

"You know what I mean, Thomas, don't pretend you do not. After your wife was killed, I was sure you and Theresa would form a pact. Why did you not?"

"Well, for part of the time I lived in Gharnatah, and now I serve you."

"But you have no intentions towards me, do you?"

Thomas tried to give a laugh. "You are the Queen of Castile and I am nobody."

"You are Thomas Berrington." Isabel smiled. "*Sir* Thomas Berrington." She laughed when he scowled. "If you believe France behind the attempt on my life, why do you need to investigate further? Have you spoken with Boabdil about our meeting?"

"Which would you like me to answer first? It may take some time to answer both to your satisfaction."

"Then I will send for food. It is almost noon, and I was awake before dawn."

"Doing what?"

"I am trying to decide if that is an impertinent question or not, but if it is, I forgive you because you know no better. And you have still not told me how you feel about Martin and Theresa."

"I am happy for them both," Thomas said.

"Indeed you are. Now, what would you like to eat? You can even taste everything for me if you wish, though it would distress me if you were to die doing so. I still have work for you to do. I want you to go to Boabdil later today and see if you can press him for a date for our talks. I also want you to find out what the Turks want by coming back here, other than to anger me."

"I will press Abu Abdullah as hard as I can. As for the Turks, Koparsh told me the last time we spoke that he is a seeker after experience. I suspect watching the end of Gharnatah is the experience he seeks this time. Should I start now?" Thomas rose, but Isabel waved him back into his seat.

"After we have eaten, and after you have told me what you really think about Theresa and Martin."

"Do you not have any difficult questions for me?"

Isabel laughed. "Tell me true what lies in your heart, Thomas, and perhaps I will tell you what lies in mine."

CHAPTER TWENTY-FIVE

Thomas found Will before he found the Turks. The gathered armies of the continent stretched over a league in all directions, and he was thinking he would fail in his attempt when he caught sight of his son. His long blond hair and height made him stand out from the mass of soldiers. Will was talking with a swarthy man whose face was marked by gunpowder. When he turned away and saw Thomas, he came loping across the ground with an effortless grace.

"What happened to Juan?"

"He thinks he enjoys talking to the men, but he soon grows bored. Did you see Isabel?"

"I think you should call her the Queen out here."

"Of course. But did you? Are you going home? Can I stay here if you are? I enjoy talking with the soldiers."

"How many speak Arabic?"

"None, but my Castilian is good enough, and I also have a little French. That man I was with is a French bombardier. He told me Fernando—sorry, the King—wants them to move their cannon closer to Gharnatah."

"Did he?" Thomas looked across the ranks, but the man had

disappeared. He would have liked to question him. "How would you feel if I started teaching you a little English?"

"That's where you're from, isn't it?"

"It is. And the Queen asked me something today that makes me think it would be good if both you and Amal spoke the language."

Will looked at him, and Thomas knew he did not need to explain why. His son might be big and strong, but he was also smart.

"If you want to, though there are men from England here. I am sure I can learn a little from them if you're busy."

"I won't be busy forever, and you don't need to speak it for a while yet. Perhaps ten years. But it's easier to learn when you're young, easier still for Amal." Thomas recalled the short time it took him to learn enough French to make himself understood, then the language of the south, and then Castilian. Arabic had been harder, but by then he was surrounded by it in the infirmary in Malaka.

"I have been teaching Ami Castilian," said Will. "I told her we're all going to need it before long."

"Good. Now, I need to find the Turks. Have you seen them? Last time they were here, they had an ornate tent and set themselves up beyond the edge of the camp."

"Haven't seen them," Will said, "but I'm sure someone has."

Thomas watched him run off and walked slowly after him. When he caught up, he discovered Will had lied about his Castilian. It was almost perfect. Better than his own.

"They're on the western fringe," Will said. "Do you want to go now?"

Thomas glanced at the sky. The day was barely half way through.

"When you go back to the house, tell them I'll be home in time for supper."

"I'd rather come with you."

Thomas considered the request, but only for a moment. He could see no danger, and even if private matters were discussed, he knew Will would never reveal them. He gave a nod and Will grinned.

It felt good to walk through the massed troops with his son at his side, even if Thomas had to take longer strides to keep up with him.

"What is England like? Will I like it?"

"I didn't much, but I suspect that's because of what happened to me there. That and my leaving."

"What happened?" asked Will.

"It's a long story best kept for an evening, if not two."

"Tonight?"

Thomas laughed. "How about I tell you my story in English?"

"That's not fair."

"I'll wait until you know enough to understand. I need to practise the tongue in any case, it's been too long since I spoke it, longer still since I spoke it well."

"Me and Ami will learn fast, then."

Thomas had no doubt of it.

It took them half an hour before a cluster of tents came into view, erected beyond a low rise in the ground which hid the gathered horde. The tents sat on a stretch of bare soil that, with no crops, had been spared the burning. Had he not known what lay on the far side of the rise, Thomas might think the spot idyllic. South, rounded hills rose. North, more jagged peaks reached to scratch at the sky. East, the great Sholayr mountain loomed, its peaks white with snow in a promise of the coming winter. West lay Castile and all the lands it had captured from the Moors over long centuries.

Thomas saw a figure emerge from the largest tent to stand waiting for them. He recognised Koparsh Hadryendo and raised a hand in greeting, which was returned.

"Do you know that man?" asked Will.

"He is the Ottoman emissary."

"What is an emissary?"

"Someone who comes to speak on behalf of his master."

Will thought for a moment. "Like you do for Isabel?"

"I don't speak for her, I work for her, nothing more."

Will gave no reply, and Thomas wondered whether he believed him.

"Welcome, Thomas Berrington. I see you have brought a man to protect you, but there is no need. I offer only the hand of friendship."

"You chose this spot well, and this is my son. His name is Will."

Koparsh's eyes were sharp on Will, judging him. "Is he the grandson of the Sultan's big general?"

"Where did you hear that?"

"When we were in the palace. I saw the man frequently, and I see the resemblance. What age is he?"

"He has ten years."

Koparsh laughed. "Now I know you lie, but I will not punish you for it. How old are you, boy?"

"Father speaks the truth, sir. He never lies."

"So I have heard. In that case, you are tall for your age. Are you as strong as your grandfather?"

"Not yet, but I will be when I am older. Usaden tells me so."

"Who is Usaden?"

Will glanced at Thomas, unsure whether to reveal any more, but he received a nod to tell him he could speak openly. There could be no harm in it.

It was some time before Thomas raised the matter he had come to discuss. By then, Salma had brought strong, dark coffee. Will stared at her with his mouth open for a long time, then went outside to talk with Koparsh's men. Only Thomas and Koparsh remained in the tent, the air hot beneath the relentless sun against its roof.

"Where have you been since we last spoke?" Thomas asked. He sipped at his coffee and nodded approval.

"I had matters my master wished me to deal with while I am here. We travelled north to discuss trade."

"What can Castile have that the Ottoman Empire lacks?"

"Who says we spoke with Castile? We lack the weapons that are being developed here. War is good for innovation, and this war has been fought over many years. The French make the finest cannon in the world, and I am interested in these new iron rods that spit fire."

"They kill as many who use them as the enemy."

"But they are getting better, are they not?"

"I trust in a bow if I want to kill a man at a distance." Thomas watched for any tell from Koparsh, but saw none.

"But you are English, and English archers are renowned the world over. We Turks are less skilled, but a crossbow is as powerful as an English bow, and almost as accurate. You have been a long time away from England, my friend. Can you still draw a longbow?"

"I did so only a few days ago and killed a man."

Still nothing showed. Thomas had come with a suspicion the Turks had been involved in some way in the attempt on Isabel's life, but if so, Koparsh was the most skilled liar he had ever seen. He knew he should have brought Jorge, except he would have been distracted by Salma, just as Will had been. He was unsure whether to mention her relationship with Fernando to Koparsh or not. He held it in reserve for now.

"Have you returned to talk more with the Queen?" Thomas asked.

"No, though if she wants to talk, I am more than happy. We are here to watch the end of al-Andalus and report back to my Sultan. Also to offer a haven to Abu Abdullah if he requests it. As a courtesy, one Sultan to another."

"Even if this one is a defeated Sultan while yours rules more lands than all the countries west of you?"

"I believe generosity is something to be admired."

"You offered men to Isabel the last time you were here. Does that offer still stand?"

"The few men I have with me would make little difference to the result, but if she wishes to avail herself of them, she is more than welcome. All she has to do is ask me to my face."

"I will pass your offer back to her, but no doubt you are right. How many other wars have you ridden to witness?"

"One or two. The world is changing, is it not? These days there are many small skirmishes, except for here. This might be the last great war ever fought. It is why all Christendom offers their help."

"You do not mind that they have?"

"We do not share your faith, but my belief is we share the same God under different names. How many men make up her army now?"

"You keep saying her army. What about Fernando?"

"We are honest men, Thomas, we both know who the army follows, and it is not that strutting fool. Oh, he can burn well enough. He is a devil in bed and a demon in battle, but the army does not love him like they love Queen Isabel. Tell me whether I speak false or not."

"It seems you have already made up your mind. It is not my place to change it."

"You have learned diplomacy, I see. Good."

"I assume you heard about Fernando's skill between the sheets from Salma. Do you not mind her infidelity?"

Koparsh stared at Thomas, amused. "It is not infidelity where none is expected. Salma is her own creature and makes her own decisions." He reached for his coffee, but was unusually clumsy. The cup fell to the floor, smashing. Koparsh uttered a loud curse and wiped at his foot.

"So she is not working on your behalf?" Thomas asked, leaning forward.

The sound of raised voices came from outside, and Thomas

recognised one as belonging to Will. He rose to his feet and walked to the entrance. Three of Koparsh's men held Will while a fourth stood in front of him with fists bunched.

CHAPTER TWENTY-SIX

"What is going on here?" Koparsh's voice was sharp.

His man took a step back and lowered his hands.

"The boy stole from me."

"I didn't, Pa. He says I did, but I took nothing."

"Show me what he stole." Koparsh strode to the small group.

Thomas glanced around, judging the number of Turks. Too many for him to take on alone. Had Koparsh erected his tent closer to the Castilian army, the argument would have brought others, men bored and looking for entertainment. As it was, Thomas and Will were the only interlopers.

A movement caught at the edge of his vision, and when he turned his head, he saw Salma standing in the tent's entrance. Her lips were parted, and her eyes on the developing situation showed a sharp brightness.

Will's accuser glanced at Koparsh for permission before taking four paces. He pushed his fingers into the pocket of Will's jacket. Thomas watched the movement and saw what the man did. He withdrew his hand and held the fist out to Koparsh.

Koparsh reached out and a small medallion fell, catching

the sunlight. Thomas stepped closer to see a silver moon on a chain. It was not the kind of ornament a soldier would wear, more like a token given by a wife. He glanced at Will, who shook his head but had the sense to keep his mouth shut.

"What is the punishment for theft in Castile?" Koparsh's voice was low. All trace of friendship from a moment before had drained away. "In my homeland it would be the taking of a hand at least. For something as valuable as this it might mean the taking of a life."

"Will is no thief," Thomas said. "Did you not see your man plant the trinket in his pocket?"

"I saw him withdraw what was already there. I am aware your son is not old enough to be punished, even if he was not your son. So how do you suggest we settle the matter?"

Thomas took a deep breath, fighting his own anger. It was out of place if they wanted to walk away with their lives.

"Your man has his trinket back, is that not enough?"

"Surely it is the act of theft that puts your son in the wrong. But what to do?" Koparsh looked at Thomas, at Will, and then at his man. He was short, wiry, with dark hair and beard. He looked as if he had been a soldier from birth. "Perhaps we can let Allah decide, if you agree to fight my man in place of your son."

"Why would I want to do that?"

"To stop me having to kill you both," said Koparsh.

"Are you willing to invoke Isabel's wrath? How would your master react to his emissary killing a man who advises the Queen of Castile?"

"My master would agree with me in this matter. He too is a believer in justice."

"Will stole nothing!" Thomas breathed slowly, fighting the tremble in his hands.

"I can fight him," said Will. His body had softened as the argument built, the opposite of Thomas's increasing tension. He didn't understand what Koparsh was trying to do, but recognised the danger. There were twenty men surrounding them and Thomas was unarmed. He had faced harsh odds before and triumphed, but on this soft afternoon all he saw was certain defeat.

"My son is ten years of age." Thomas directed his words at the man who had planted the medallion. "What honour is there in fighting a boy?"

"I can win this fight," said Will.

Thomas knew how Usaden had honed Will's natural talent, but how far would Koparsh push things here? To the death? He half believed Will could defeat the soldier, but did he want to watch his son take a life? Such an act would change him forever. One day such a thing would happen, but not now, not here. Yet he could see no solution. If he offered to fight in Will's place, he would have to kill the man, which he knew he could do. But what then? Would Koparsh allow them to walk away?

"What is this about?" He spoke softly, so only Koparsh heard him. "Have you been waiting for me to come so you can execute your plan to kill me? Was that a signal when you deliberately spilled your coffee and cursed?"

Koparsh said nothing. He watched Will, watched his man. He made a tiny gesture with his fingers, and those holding Will released him. Will shook his arms and took a pace towards Thomas.

"Stay there," Thomas said. He faced Koparsh, waiting.

"Blunted blades," said Koparsh. "First man bested. There will be no killing today, agreed?"

Thomas stared into the man's eyes, seeking a clue to show this was some manner of joke, but all he saw was disdain. Hatred would have been better. He turned and looked at Will, who was stretching as Usaden had taught him.

"Me and your man," Thomas said, with a nod.

"No. Your son. It is he who stole, it is he who must be punished."

Thomas knew they had little choice. Any alternative would see them both slain.

"What do you think, Will?"

"I can do this." No hint of doubt in his voice.

Thomas looked back at Koparsh and nodded. "First one to call a halt is the loser, agreed?"

"Agreed. If your son loses, you will make reparations for the insult. Say ten silver pieces."

Thomas walked to Will. A bare ten paces, but in that time he thought of his own father and how he had allowed a group of older men to beat Thomas senseless in the market square of his home town of Lemster. He claimed it would make a man of him. Well, it had made something of him. Angry, mostly. It had been the manner of justice favoured by John Berrington. The manner of justice favoured by Koparsh Hadryendo, too, it seemed. The man's veneer of civility had been cast aside to reveal a killer beneath the fine clothes.

Thomas reached Will and wrapped an arm around his shoulder, feeling the strength of muscle there, but still unsure of the result of the coming fight.

"He will come at you slowly. He wants to taunt you, so hit him hard and hit him fast. Remember everything Usaden has taught you."

"I can take him," said Will.

Someone pressed a blunted sword into Will's hand, another into his opponent's. Thomas didn't want to move away, but knew he had to. He glanced towards Salma, who had come closer. Her eyes held a strange, cold hunger as she stared at Will.

Thomas turned away, not wanting to see her.

"Don't be afraid to cry out if he hurts you," he said. "Most injuries I can fix. Don't make me have to work too hard to patch you up."

He stepped away without looking and bumped into a man. A circle had formed twenty paces across. In the centre stood

Will and the Turkish soldier, who swung his blade through the air, twisting it, tossing it to catch the hilt again. All very impressive.

"Let the fight begin!" Koparsh's voice rang out.

Will ran fast at the man, who took two paces backwards in surprise. He raised his blade to strike, but when it descended, Will was no longer where he had been, twisting away as fast as Kin could change direction.

Will ducked, brought his own blade down and smashed it against the man's extended forearm. There was a sharp crack as the bone snapped. The man screamed.

Thomas glanced at Koparsh, knowing this was the most dangerous moment. The man's face showed nothing. Neither anger nor pleasure nor relief.

Will did the right thing. He placed his sword on the ground and walked towards Thomas.

"I can fix his arm if you let me," Thomas said. "It is what I used to do."

"I heard you were a physician," said Koparsh, transformed once more into the soft-voiced diplomat. "It sounded like a bad break to me."

"But clean. Let me treat him and I guarantee he will fight again within two months."

"The war might be over in two months. Besides, if a boy can beat him so easily, I am not sure I want him in the ranks of my men."

"Will can beat any of your men," Thomas said. "He is the grandson of Olaf Torvaldsson. There is no disgrace in losing to him. It might even be worn as a badge of honour. The longer that arm goes without treatment, the worse it will be for him."

Koparsh gave a nod. "You, go with this man and let him fix your arm." He turned to Thomas. "Understand that this had to be done. Tell your son not to steal anything else of mine or I will come after you both myself. I am not so easily defeated."

Thomas made no reply. He took Will's arm and walked

away, aware all the time of those behind him. Only as they came close to the edge of Isabel's army did he start to relax. When he heard footsteps behind, he turned to see the injured man following, his arm gripped tight, face pale. When Thomas looked at Will, he saw he had closed down his expression. His gaze had turned inward, and Thomas knew they would have to talk about what had happened. Later, once he had set the soldier's bone and sent him back to his master. He knew there was no time now to visit Abu Abdullah, but determined to do so early the following day. If the talks took place, it might mean an end to this war he had believed would never end.

Thomas took the man to a small room and re-set the bone before binding it tight. He would normally have used poppy to dull the pain, but this time did not. He saw the man hold his mouth tight to stop himself from crying out, but his face was pale and sweat stood out on his brow.

"Did Koparsh plan all of this?" Thomas asked.

The man stared at him as if he failed to understand the words.

"Or was it Salma? It cannot have been your idea."

Still the man said nothing, and Thomas jerked on the wet bandages deliberately, pleased when the man cried out at last.

"Leave these on for a week, then come back so I can replace them. The bone will knit and you will fight again if Koparsh allows it." He recalled the man's words, the coldness of his judgement. "Do not concern yourself you have been bested by a boy. My son is no ordinary boy. Far from it."

The man stared at Thomas, then used his good arm to reach into his pocket. He drew out the medallion that had caused his defeat and held it out, swinging from his fingers on the fine chain.

"For your son. He fought well. This is his prize."

Later, as Thomas stood outside and watched the man descend the slope, Will came to join him.

"You did well," Thomas said. He held out his own hand. "For you. Your reward."

Will looked at the medallion. It was a thing of beauty, a thing of worth. He reached for it, lifted it to study it more closely.

"Did Koparsh give you this?" He looked up to meet Thomas's eyes. "I never stole it. That man put it in my pocket."

"I know he did, and now it is yours. Everything had been planned long before we went there. Why I don't know, but I intend to find out."

"We should have used sharper blades," said Will.

CHAPTER TWENTY-SEVEN

Ten days passed before Thomas dragged a grudging acceptance from Abu Abdullah to meet with Isabel and Fernando. With the King's return, the original plan to involve only Isabel on the Castilian side had been forced to change.

Now Thomas sat on the narrow terrace of his house and looked across at the gathered army. There were fewer men than two weeks earlier because a third had moved east and now camped almost at the walls of Gharnatah. The skirmishing continued, but it was only a pretence at war even as men died on both sides. Mostly those of Castile, Thomas heard. So many that Isabel had sent an order the invitations to combat must cease. Unlike most of Isabel's orders, it seemed this one was being ignored.

A man on horseback emerged from the throng and Thomas narrowed his eyes. He was expecting Martin de Alarcón, either today or tomorrow, so they could ride in search of a suitable location for the meeting between opposing leaders. As the figure approached, it shocked Thomas to recognise not Martin, but his own son, Yves. Apart from the brief sighting on the ridge the day Will fought the Turks, he had been absent since his mother's death at the farmhouse. Thomas assumed he had scurried back to his holdings in France. Or been killed by the same men who murdered his mother.

Thomas rose and went into the house to find Belia to see if there was any food left from their morning meal. He asked her to bring it to the terrace, then returned and watched his son close the final distance.

Yves dismounted and tied his horse to a rail. As he walked up to the house, Thomas examined his face. It was pale, and circles shadowed his eyes. He looked as if he had slept in his clothes the entire time since running away and found nowhere to wash. A conclusion confirmed as he came closer.

"I have sent for food, but you might like to bathe first."

"I was wrong," said Yves, ignoring Thomas's words. "My mother lied to me my entire life." Yves' head dropped and his shoulders shook.

Thomas took a step closer, unsure what to do, and then, as always in such situations, he asked himself what Jorge would do. He closed the gap between them and wrapped his arms around Yves, letting him sob against his shoulder.

"I don't know what to do, Father."

Thomas pushed Yves away and stared into his son's eyes, wondering if his manner was an act or not.

"There was a man at the farmhouse with his throat cut," he said. "Did you do that?"

Yves returned the stare, his own less certain. "What man?"

"I knocked him out, intending to question him. After you rode off, I found him dead, half hidden among the bushes. He was alive when I left him."

"It will have been one of the others. They were vicious. It would not surprise me if they killed one of their own if they thought he might talk."

"Perhaps. Why did you not keep riding north to France?"

"I was afraid to. It was always Mother in charge. I clung to her skirts when I was young and never lost the habit." Yves took a shuddering breath and pulled away. He wiped an arm across a face which reflected his pain. "Can I stay here until I know what I am going to do with my life?"

Thomas hesitated. He didn't know whether to believe Yves about the dead man, but he also didn't think him capable of cold-blooded murder. He was too weak, and he only needed to look at him to see he was a broken man. The question was, did he care enough to fix him?

"For a while. Let's see how it goes."

"Thank you, Father. Why is it your ten-year-old son is more of an adult than me, who is over twenty years his senior?"

"Will has been forged through many fires. It makes a boy grow up fast. Too fast, I sometimes think, but there is nothing to be done for it. You are grieving now, but believe me when I say it will pass. You will always mourn your mother, but the pain will grow less."

"Are there any days when you do not think of your dead wife?" asked Yves. "Jorge told me what happened."

"Not a single one, but I also remember her laughter, her beauty, and her sense of mischief."

"My mother had one of those."

"A sense of mischief? Yes, I know. How do you think you came into being?"

Yves shook his head. "I still struggle to think of someone else being my father rather than that old man I rarely saw. But I am pleased it is so, for you are a far better man than he ever was."

"Come and sit, Belia will bring food soon."

"I have barely eaten since I saw you. I stole some eggs from a farm, but that was all. I tried to return before, but could not make myself come further than the nearest ridge."

Belia came and laid plates of meat, fresh bread and sauces on the table. Another pot of coffee was brought and set down. Yves' gaze followed her as she left the room.

"Will and I thought we saw you. Tell me what happened. I believed you had ridden to join those men."

226

"I intended to hunt them down and kill them, but I am no tracker. I am fortunate I did not find them, because I am no fighter, either. Your man Usaden could have found them in an instant, could have killed them even faster. All I did was wander aimlessly through a land where I understood not a word spoken to me."

"Your Castilian is good," Thomas said. He watched Yves pile slices of lamb between two flatbreads and take an enormous bite. He waited while his son chewed and swallowed.

"I might have managed better if that is what they spoke, but you know it is not."

"Had you ever seen those men before? Or others dressed the same way? Did they ever visit your mother?"

Yves shook his head. "She kept much from me. Perhaps to shelter me, perhaps to hide her own guilt. She may have met them in the palace in Granada, for I was never invited there." Yves looked up, met Thomas's eyes. "Could the Sultan have sent them?"

"He has no love for Castile, but I doubt it. Why recruit your mother from France when there are a hundred assassins he could call on? No, it was not Abu Abdullah."

"She was his lover, did you know that?"

"I did."

"She has taken many lovers." Yves spoke the words without emotion. "Including you."

"Yes," Thomas said. "Including me. So why are you here?"

"I considered riding north to Arreau, but was unsure of what manner of welcome I might receive."

"You are the Count now."

"I suppose I am, but it was always Mother everyone obeyed. She could be harsh when she wanted. I expect you never saw that side of her."

"A little, in Qurtuba. She was a strong person."

"Not strong enough at the end. I should have fought, but I'm no soldier." Yves shook his head as he prepared a second round

227

of food the same as the first. He sipped at the strong coffee and pulled a face.

"I can send for tea if you prefer, or water."

"Have you no ale?"

"No ale, I'm afraid. How long before you turned back?"

"Five days."

"So what have you been doing since?"

"Hiding, most of the time. Then I returned, as you know because you saw me, and I saw you. I meant to come to you then, but feared you would turn me away after what had happened. Feared you would believe I had worked alongside Mother."

"Are you telling me you knew nothing of what she did?"

Yves stopped eating and met Thomas's gaze. "I knew she did bad things for money, but I didn't want to know what things. I don't think she wanted me to know, either. It was a coward's way to live, and I knew it."

"And this commission she took? What did you know of that?"

"A man came to visit her, but I only know because she told me. She had sent me away on some pretext, to visit a young countess in a nearby town. She did that now and again. I think she wanted to find me a wife, but this one was certainly not suitable."

"Not pretty enough?" Thomas asked.

"Not old enough. She had seven years, and her family were seeking an arrangement with money in mind. Mother always let it be known she had money, even if she lacked a husband."

"I don't understand—why did she never marry again?"

"Because of you."

Thomas stared at Yves. "Me?"

"She never forgot the father of her child. She would talk to me constantly about you, though she never mentioned your name until we met you again in Córdoba."

"She had a strange way of showing it in that case. Falling into bed with Fernando."

"Mother had … strong desires. She took many lovers, but none of them lasted."

A sense of dread settled through Thomas. "Did she kill them?"

Yves shook his head. "Of course she didn't. Although … yes, some perhaps. I don't know. I have already told you she sheltered me from much. I know now it is no way to raise a son, but it was all I ever knew."

"When I met you both in Qurtuba, was that part of the plot to harm Isabel?"

"No, we went out of curiosity, nothing more. The commission to kill the Queen was agreed only half a year ago."

"Did you always know what she did?"

"I cannot remember a time when I did not."

"She killed to order, didn't she?"

Yves gave a nod. "She was an assassin. When I first discovered it, I was afraid, then as time passed, I grew proud of her. She showed me her work, the herbs and roots and minerals she used. She tried to teach me each of their uses, but I do not believe you passed your intelligence down to me, Father."

"Call me by my name, Yves. It is strange when you call me Father. I set a seed in Eleanor's belly, that doesn't make me your father. Call me Thomas."

"I will try, but forgive me if I slip up." Yves gave a shy smile.

"I need to know something." Thomas waited, but Yves busied himself with his food. "Is the threat against Isabel over now with the death of your mother?"

"It is." Yves spoke curtly, still arranging the food on his plate to his satisfaction, though what satisfaction there could be in it, Thomas failed to grasp.

"I need to be sure," he said.

"And I will tell you everything I know, what little there is, but my head is swimming with fatigue and I am not sure I will make any sense. Can I sleep and we will talk again later?"

"I may be gone later. Tell me the important part now, and then you can tell me your entire story if I am still here. Do you know if Eleanor was the only assassin recruited?"

"As far as I know, yes."

"To kill Isabel and Fernando?"

Yves frowned. "No, Queen Isabel and the Sultan Muhammed. Cut off the heads from both sides, Mother was told. They want them both dead. No doubt her employer would be happy if Fernando died, but he was not mentioned."

"Is that what she was doing in Gharnatah, looking for a chance to poison Abu Abdullah?"

"It was, but Mother has always loved luxury and the company of powerful men."

"She made no attempt on Isabel directly. Did she do the same with Abu Abdullah?"

"She gave him a tincture over several days and he drank it because they were lovers. She told him it would make a stallion of him, which I believe it did, even though it was slowly killing him. Then you came to talk with him and Mother stopped, because she knew you would see the signs. If you had not come, the man would be dead by now."

"So why did she send de Pamplona to poison Isabel rather than do it herself?"

"Because of what happened in Córdoba between you and her, between her and Fernando. She could not return to Isabel's court, so she had to send someone else. I did not know she would kill de Pamplona and his wife."

"Was it you and her seen talking with him the morning he disappeared?"

"Not me, but it was most likely Mother. She was gone from the house when I woke and did not return until later that night. Who the man was, I have no idea." Yves stared into Thomas's eyes. "I am homeless, Father."

"No, you are not."

After Yves had gone, Thomas stared into space, seeing nothing as Yves' words ran through his mind. He didn't know how much he believed. How much made sense. Could Yves truly be as ignorant of what Eleanor had done as he claimed? Or was he only trying to protect himself? What Thomas was sure of was Yves had not the heart to do what Eleanor had done. The man was weak. He was a disappointment to Thomas. Was it possible to change him, or was it too late for that? Yves had thirty-five years. His personality was fully formed. Men, particularly men of that age, did not change unless it was forced on them.

Perhaps he was not beyond saving. Losing his mother, losing his place in the world, might be enough to change him. The question was, would it be an improvement or not?

CHAPTER TWENTY-EIGHT

Thomas and Martin de Alarcón reined in their horses as they approached Gharnatah and watched as two men fought to the death in front of the eastern gate. Two hundred paces away, Fernando sat on his horse beside his constant companion, Perez de Pulgar, watching the bout. Behind them, Koparsh Hadryendo and Salma sat astride their own mounts.

"I thought Isabel had put a stop to all this," Thomas said.

"She issued an instruction, but Fernando countermanded it. He likes the tilts."

"These are no tilts. These men fight with swords and knives, and they fight to the death."

"There is some jousting, but he considers it all chivalrous. Man on man." Martin glanced at Thomas. "Sometimes he takes part in the contests himself."

"Then it's a pity he survives, is all I can say."

"He is not so bad," said Martin. "Fernando is a good war general, and that is what Castile needs at the moment. Isabel is the heart and head of the country, but Fernando is its strong right arm. They are a good match, despite you wishing it otherwise."

Thomas looked at Martin, ignoring the clash of blades ahead of them.

"How do you enjoy sharing Theresa's bed?"

"Very much. She is highly skilled and adventurous. Sometimes I wonder if she is not too adventurous for me." Martin gave a low laugh. "She confessed I was her second choice. You are a fool, Thomas Berrington."

"Try not to break her heart when you leave her for a duchess. And try not to take as many mistresses as Fernando is doing. One of whom is sitting over there in full view."

"You will not change him now, and I will not leave Theresa even if I marry a duchess. There is a glut of noble ladies at the moment who are only too willing to accept a man with a mistress. Their previous husbands had an unpleasant habit of getting themselves killed or captured. I am coming with you today to seek the freedom of two such. There will need to be an exchange, but we have plenty of their nobles locked up. I believe you know one of them, Faris al-Rashid?"

Thomas laughed. "He is captured by Castile? That is sweet news."

"Two months since. I am surprised nobody mentioned it to you, for he constantly asks for you to be told in the belief you will have him freed. He claims a friendship between you."

"Then he claims wrong. He tried to kill me only a few years ago. He is a snake. If it was up to me, he would rot in his cell until hell freezes over."

"So, not friends then." Martin smiled as he urged his horse into a slow walk. Ahead, men dragged a body across the ground. "I think your side won that contest. You Moors fight well, I give you that."

"Do you consider me a Moor?"

"I am making my mind up on that. I know the Queen does not, so I expect the rest of us will have to follow her example."

The victor mounted a horse lacking a saddle and rode hard for Gharnatah's open gate. On the way, he showed his horsemanship by whipping his legs from side to side to bounce from the ground.

Thomas and Martin left their horses at an inn and walked up the steep slope to the palace. Before they reached the outer gate, Martin said his goodbyes and Thomas continued alone.

Abu Abdullah was expecting him and Thomas was brought directly to a courtyard half in shade where palms rose to sway their tops in sunlight. Birds nested among the fronds, dropping as many dates as they consumed. Thomas studied the Sultan as he walked towards him, recalling what Yves had told him the day before.

"I heard you have been unwell, Malik, but you appear to be in fine health now."

Abu Abdullah spread his arms. "I had a little pain some time ago, it is true, but it has gone now. I have no need of your services today, surgeon."

"I am pleased to hear it." Thomas considered it unwise to make any mention of Eleanor's death, or her attempt to poison the Sultan.

"Has that woman sent you?"

"She has, Malik. She also sent me with an offer, but the terms have changed."

"Then you can scurry back and tell her I refuse."

"You have not heard what they are yet. It is only one minor change. The King wishes to be included."

Abu Abdullah looked off into the distance to where men were tending dark-leaved shrubs.

"I saw how he burned our crops."

"I believe he considers them his crops now."

"Then he is even more of a fool than I took him for. What does he think his army is going to eat?"

"They bring supplies from Qurtuba and Malaka constantly."

"Some of which my troops destroy. There was food all around them and they destroyed it."

"Are people growing hungry, Malik?"

Abu Abdullah waved a hand as if it was no concern of his what happened to the people. Thomas was sure there would be enough food in the palace. He thought he might even call on Bazzu before he left to confirm the fact. It would be useful for Isabel to know.

The Sultan rose from where he was sitting, a half-foot shorter than Thomas. He was no doubt used to everyone tall in the palace bending their knees to offer him the advantage. Thomas had done the same at one time, but no longer felt the need.

"Walk with me while we discuss your mistress's demands. See if you can persuade me to agree to this meeting."

Abu Abdullah led the way to a viewpoint where the armies of Castile stained the land as far as the eye could see. Cooking fires spiralled smoke into the air to hang in a grey layer. Abu Abdullah's mouth tightened into a line of distaste.

"Look at them, they are not even civilised. How can I negotiate with such unbelievers?"

"I think Isabel is a believer, only in a different God."

"They have no manners. They never wash. Their food is disgusting. They take only one wife at a time and allow them to argue with their husbands. And *they* are going to win this war?"

"Isabel is not unreasonable," Thomas said. "She will strike a deal. Gharnatah will be spared, the palace too. She will allow you to leave with your life and a portion of your wealth. Perhaps the negotiations can decide what that portion should be. Agree to the talks, Malik. It is the only way the city can survive." Thomas hesitated, then risked the truth. "Fernando has ordered the French cannon closer to your walls and is preparing their use. I saw what the siege of Malaka did to that city. You do not want to repeat the mistake of thinking you can win the fight that is coming."

Abu Abdullah paced the dusty ground. To either side, guards stood at a discreet distance, unmoving, aware their

Sultan could see them. Finally, he stopped and turned to Thomas.

"Arrange it, then." He turned to leave, then stopped. "Whatever happened to that French Countess? When I lay with her, she revealed to me you and she were once lovers."

"It is true, Malik, but it was long ago. I believe she returned to France. Her son too." Thomas knew Abu Abdullah was trying to get a reaction, but refused to satisfy the man.

"Your son. She told me that as well."

"It seems she told you a great deal, Malik."

"Yes, she did. No matter, she was a pleasant diversion, and at least now she knows how it feels to lie with a real man. Go to your Queen and tell her I agree. Arrange it before my people grow ever more hungry and ungrateful. Arrange it before the traitors—and yes, I know who she talks with— sell my soul for a piece of silver."

———

"Where is it you conduct your other negotiations?" Thomas asked Isabel. "The ones Abu Abdullah is meant to know nothing about? He does, by the way."

They sat on a terrace that looked north, away from the devastation wrought by her husband. Jagged peaks thrust towards an almost clear sky, marred only by a single strange circular cloud that seemed always to hover above the ridge. Thomas had only ever seen such clouds here in the south of Spain.

"You are asking the wrong person," said Isabel. "They are my husband's idea, not mine. It is his people who negotiate, but they are getting nowhere. Has Boabdil agreed to meet with both of us?"

"In a neutral location. He doesn't like Fernando's involvement, but I think he can live with it. I promised him you would allow him to leave the city with at least enough wealth to let him live well. Not as well as he does in the palace, but well enough."

Isabel suppressed a smile. "I am not sure it was in your power to make such an offer, but I will take it under consideration. If it was up to me, it would be agreed, but you know it is not. Fernando will have his say."

"He was watching the fighting when Martin and I passed. I went to Olaf after visiting Abu Abdullah and asked if he could do anything to stop it."

"I suspect I know what his answer was."

"And I suspect you are right. If it was up to him, there would be no skirmishes. Olaf believes a war is fought army to army. He has given orders, but Gharnatah is not the place it was. Men no longer obey orders, even his."

"When was the last time you obeyed an order, Thomas?"

"I went to Abu Abdullah for you, didn't I?"

"And you also went off in pursuit of your woman, the poisoner, without consulting me."

"Am I meant to sit here waiting for your next order?"

"Do I not employ you?"

"Is it employment when I receive no wage?"

Isabel frowned. "Do you need money, Thomas? I assumed someone else would take care of all that. I will arrange it. How much do you want?"

"I need nothing, Isabel. What I need is my independence. I am happy to serve you in any way you wish, but I have to know I can be my own man when I need to be. When do you want this meeting arranged? Abu Abdullah said soon."

"Then let it be soon. Is there hunger among the people on the streets?"

"A little, but the walls of the city are porous and supplies filter through from the north and the Alpujarras."

"I did not hear you say that, and if I did not hear it, I cannot pass the news on to my husband. He would find where these supplies come from and raze the fields to smoking stubble. If he can find time between bedding his new paramour." If Isabel was bitter about her husband's lover, it did not sound in her voice.

"Perhaps he is right to burn them."

"He is wrong, but I do not tell him that. Neither do I tell him I know who he lies with. When Gharnatah falls, it will need a supply of food. This land is rich and well-irrigated. I pray it will recover from his ravages."

"Will you live in the palace?" The air was warm, the atmosphere between them relaxed despite her mention of Fernando's infidelity. Thomas knew that soon, someone would bring wine and small plates of food. He could grow used to such ease, aware he was not the man he had once been. The hunger to cure the world had leached from him, and he was still waiting to discover what might replace it. Perhaps to continue serving this woman.

"I would love to. You have been there today, tell me what it is like."

"Again?"

"Yes, again. Or do you have something better to do?"

"I have to find a neutral place for your meeting. Somewhere safe. Somewhere that belongs to neither Castile nor al-Andalus, and I think I know of somewhere. I visited the great library in Gharnatah to search their records. Do you know they have over three million books held there?"

"I did not. Did you find what you were looking for?"

"I did."

"Good, so you have no need to rush off again. Tell me about the inner chambers. Is it true there is water everywhere? Fountains?"

"No fountains, but there is water. It is a form of worship. The water is still, the better to reflect the glory of heaven."

"And the writing on the walls? Are there truly no depictions of people or animals?"

"It is not the will of Allah." Thomas laughed. "Though there are lions holding up a bowl of water in one courtyard."

Isabel clapped her hands together in delight. "I would so love to see that."

"Soon you will walk the corridors of the palace and see it all for yourself."

"Will you walk with me and explain everything?"

"Do I not serve you?"

"I am trying to make my mind up whether you do."

Thomas raised his eyes and looked into Isabel's, the atmosphere between them precarious, teetering on the edge of something he could not define.

"You know I do. I am your man, Isabel, yours to my core. I would die for you."

"I pray it never comes to that." She took a breath, let it go. "I am tired of this talk of war. Tell me what I am to do about Columb."

That again, Thomas thought, but he told her what she must do, and Isabel listened to his words, asking sharp questions that showed her understanding. Then wine arrived, together with plates of food, and shortly after, Theresa and Martin de Alarcón arrived, but Fernando was nowhere to be seen and Isabel made no mention of his name, or where he might be, or who he might be with … as if she no longer cared.

CHAPTER TWENTY-NINE

On a warm morning when thunderclouds massed to the south, Thomas watched Martin de Alarcón ride up the slope towards his house and walked down to greet him. He knew the man had moved into Theresa's quarters in the house she shared with Isabel and the other courtiers. He looked content as he dismounted, as well he should.

"We are going to get wet," said Martin as he gripped Thomas's arm.

"It is only rain, and I expect we have both been wet before."

"More than once. Are you ready? Who rides with us, or is it only you and me?"

"Jorge and Usaden, if that is acceptable to you?"

"It is. I like Jorge. I like Usaden, too, even if I do not understand a word he says. He needs to learn to speak Castilian for when we win this war."

"I suspect when that happens, Usaden will return to where he came from. Wherever that is." Thomas glanced back at the house. Will stood on the terrace, his face showing nothing, but he was dressed for riding and carried weapons. "One other as well, if you agree. My son."

Martin looked towards the terrace.

"He is tall now, isn't he?"

"He is. And fast."

"His face still carries the softness of youth. What age is he, thirteen, fourteen?"

"He has ten years," Thomas said.

"Ten years?" Martin shook his head. "You have no idea who or what we might meet. A ten-year-old boy has no place riding with us."

"Then I will tell him to stay well back, but I think you are wrong. I would wager Will against any grown man. Only recently he fought one of the Turks and defeated him."

"Then the man must have let him." Martin's eyes returned to Will, a judgement in them.

"I might have said the same had I not witnessed it, and if so, why did he let Will break his arm?"

"He broke the arm of a Turk? They are outstanding fighters, I have seen them at the tilts."

"He did. I fixed the arm, so in a month, he may be back at the tilts."

Martin shrugged. "Don't blame me if he gets killed. He is your responsibility to look after if we find trouble. Not that I expect any. But then I have no idea where you intend to take us."

"North," Thomas said. "We were there recently and it is good country for our purposes. It belongs to neither Castile nor Gharnatah, and I believe I know somewhere that suits our needs."

"Then let us ride, but tell your son to keep up."

Thomas thought briefly of his other son, who still lay in bed even at this time of the day. It should be an annoyance, but was not. He knew Yves needed time to recover, to come to terms with the loss of his mother. Thomas was happy to allow him all the time he needed, and a place of safety while he searched for his new role in the world. He doubted it would be as a member of Thomas's family, but at least the opportunity lay there if he wanted it.

————

Noon had come and gone before they rode through a narrow pass and the town of al-Loraya appeared below, sitting in a wide valley. They were some distance east of where Eleanor had died, but the valley was the same one, Thomas was sure. It cut through a fold of mountains that protected it from the outside world. Thomas had visited the town once, many years before, and remembered it had a fort perched on a bluff of pale rock. He had not known it was owned by Faris al-Rashid at the time, a fact he had only discovered in the great library.

"Is that the place?" asked Martin de Alarcón.

"It's a possibility, nothing more."

Martin leaned forward to look left, then right.

"Is it Moorish?"

"Notionally, but this land belongs to neither side. I suspect that's why its current owner wants it."

"Are you sure the place is suitable?"

"The people here are peaceable enough if left alone. I think they will find a sultan and a queen more of an amusement than a reason to attack."

"I still do not know why Isabel is so set on this meeting."

"She wants to take Gharnatah with as little loss of life and property as possible."

They started down the slope on a twisting track, their horses' hoofs dislodging rocks that clattered away down the steep hillside.

"The palace is an obsession for her. I could understand why if she had seen it, for it is a wonder of the world, but all she has are second-hand accounts and rumour. Has she questioned you about it?"

"She has. I assume she's asked you as well?"

"Sometimes she talks of it more than the matters I discuss with Boabdil." Martin gave a laugh. "Not that there is ever much news from him."

"Do you still have a hold over him?" Thomas knew Martin had spent almost a year with the man after his capture eight years earlier during a foolish raid. Rumour had it Abu Abdullah was now Martin's pawn.

"He appears to have found a little courage from somewhere of late."

"He knows the end is inevitable. Perhaps he welcomes not having to fight anymore."

"We can only hope that is true."

It was an hour before they approached the town. The buildings cast valleys of deep shadow as the sun lowered.

"If what you say is true," said Martin, "this could be the perfect place." He lifted in his saddle and looked around before nodding at the ramparts that loomed above them. "From up there, a single man could see attackers approaching from leagues away. Is it as secure as it appears from this side?"

"There is a single roadway that climbs from within the town, but it has three gates protecting it, the last of which is almost impregnable if any attacker makes it that far."

Men, women and children stopped what they were doing to watch the strangers pass, the sound of the horses' hoofs loud in the narrow streets. Thomas led the way, trying to recall the twists and turns that would lead to the roadway and the castle. He made a few wrong turns, but found the right place, eventually.

"Do you know who owns this place?" asked Martin.

"How did your negotiations with Abu Abdullah go?" Thomas smiled. "Did you agree to an exchange of nobles?"

Martin frowned. "We did."

"Was Faris al-Rashid among their number?"

"He was not. I put his name forward, thinking Boabdil would jump at the chance to free him, but he waved it away."

"He fears Faris wants to oust him, and I suspect he isn't wrong. Though the time for such is long past. When the man last visited this place, I don't know, but the records show he bought it over ten years ago."

Martin laughed. "That would be a fine justice, would it not, to hold the negotiations here?"

"Perhaps you can get the property signed over to you when Gharnatah falls."

Martin looked at the ramparts. "It is a dour place. I am not sure Theresa would approve."

"But your duchess might," Thomas said, which only made Martin laugh even harder.

———

The lower of the three gates was closed when they reached it, and Thomas took Martin back into the town to find someone who might offer them admittance. He expected at least a brief resistance, but one man sent them to a second who sent them to a third who was the holder of the keys to the fort. He was middle-aged and as thin as a stick, but when he walked alongside them, Thomas was sure he could keep up his steady pace all day long if need be.

"How long have you been the key-holder?" he asked the man.

"Since my father passed the duty on to me, and his father before him. Who lay before that, I do not know."

"Have you ever met the owner?"

"Saw him once, from a distance. Sour-faced, he looked."

"That would be Faris," said Thomas, and the man nodded.

"I am content to grant you admittance, for there is little inside to steal. Even if there was, the entire town would see you carrying it away. What purpose do you have, sirs?"

"That we cannot say," said Martin, "only that it is a matter of high politics."

The man gave a rough laugh that came out as a cough. "We hold little with politics here, high or otherwise. When it comes to politics, I see little honour in it. How is the war going out in the world?"

"You do at least know of that?" said Martin.

"Strangers passing through, like yourselves."

"Have there been any recently?" Thomas asked.

"Only the Turks."

Thomas slowed and looked at the man, who went on at his steady pace so he had to catch him up. They were almost back to where they had left the others.

"What Turks?"

"They came…" the man looked off into space "…two months since. They, like you, wanted to see inside. People do, now and again, but other than yourselves and the Turks, there has been nobody for some time. They asked if it was for sale."

"Is it?"

"It is not my place to know. I hold the keys. I let strangers look around because I see no harm in it. Other than that, sale or not is the business of better men than me."

Thomas doubted those he referred to were his better. He liked the man. He was carved from this land, as stubborn and uncomplicated as it was.

The man used the largest key to turn a heavy lock, then handed the rest to Thomas.

"I will not accompany you. My wife will have a meal on the table going cold and want to know where I have been. Do you remember my house?"

Thomas gave a nod. "I will return these to you when we are done." He glanced at the sky. "Would we be allowed to stay the night within its walls?"

"I expect so … for a price."

Thomas glanced at Martin. "Did you bring coin?"

Martin shook his head.

"I can arrange for something to be sent," Thomas said.

"I don't want that kind of payment. High politics, you said?"

"Which we cannot discuss."

"I would like to meet the Queen," said the man. "Queen Isabel. I hear she is beautiful. And kind."

"She is both," Thomas said. "She can also be stern."

"That is a good thing. If these high politics involve the Queen, then I would like her to acknowledge me the once. That would be enough. I ask for no more."

Thomas looked at Martin, who shrugged. Neither could see any harm in the request, but whether Isabel would agree was another matter. At least they could ask.

"One condition," said Martin, who waited for the man to acknowledge him. "No word can spread we have ever been here."

"Nobody has been here," said the man. "Not since the Turks. If anyone asks, that is what I will tell them." He turned and walked away down the cobbled road at the same pace he had climbed it. Steady. Relentless.

———

"It's perfect for your purpose," Thomas said. He and Isabel sat once more on the terrace that looked across the army. He smiled. "It is owned by a Moor you hold captive. Large and easy to defend. And neither side lays claim to the surrounding land."

"Why not?"

"Why not what?"

"I thought I laid claim to all lands south of Alcalá de Henares. Why not this land?"

"Do you lay claim to the mountain-tops, the beds of all lakes and rivers, the lands nobody else wants?"

"They must all belong to someone."

"Then perhaps this land does belong to Castile, but it has

never been fought over, and I doubt it ever will be. Do you want your meeting with Abu Abdullah to go ahead or not?"

"Go to him and present our case," said Isabel. "Does Martin agree with you about the suitability of this … what is it, a house, a fort, a castle?"

"A fort, I suppose. It sits on a rock pinnacle with sheer cliffs on three sides and a heavily guarded roadway on the fourth. It is neither too big nor too small. Abu Abdullah will bring men of his own, as will you, but we can insist only the negotiating parties enter the fort. Martin and myself will be with you and I will ask for Olaf to be present for the other side, a man you can trust."

"And Fernando will be with us, do not forget that."

"Have you raised the matter with him?"

"When an agreement is reached. There is no need to concern him until then. He is not one to fuss over details."

"If you say so."

"I do." She offered the shadow of a smile as if to soften her words. "I have another task for you in the morning."

"Name it."

"I want you to dress in your best fighting clothes. I intend to walk amongst my troops to raise their spirits. I also intend to talk to them to see if I can stop these stupid challenges. They will solve nothing, and both sides are losing valuable men. Will you do this?"

"You and I?" Thomas said. "What about Fernando?"

"He tells me he intends to burn more lands south of the city. I was not even aware there was anything left to burn, but he claims the Moors are stealing crops there."

"I expect they consider the crops are theirs."

"Then they are wrong."

"In case you don't know, I possess no fighting clothes, let alone a best set."

Isabel gave a smile. "In that you are wrong, Sir Thomas. I

have had several outfits made for you. Theresa has taken them to your house. She may still be there if you hurry."

"Theresa is with Martin now."

"I know." Isabel rose and smoothed her dress, her body stiff within its constraints. "But she still talks of you with a longing, and Martin will marry someone else soon."

"A duchess?" Thomas asked.

"I believe so, once I find one pretty enough, young enough, and willing enough. I will need to find a dukedom for Martin, but there are several free."

"Martin is a man any woman would want," Thomas said.

"Perhaps not all women."

CHAPTER THIRTY

"You look nice, Pa, where you going?" It was morning and Amal stood in the doorway, feet planted firmly. Yves stood beside her, also in bare feet, his hand holding his sister's in his. The two had become inseparable in the short time he had been living in the house. Their closeness seemed to be doing him good.

It took Thomas a moment to realise Amal had spoken Castilian. He glanced down at himself in the new clothes Theresa had brought for him and smiled. The only concession to the old Thomas was his dark tagelmust, which hung down on either side almost to his knees.

"Isabel wants me."

Amal laughed. "Is'bel always wants you."

"Indeed she does. Where's Will?"

"Out with Kin. Can I come with you?"

"Not today, my sweet, but soon."

Amal nodded and gave a smile. She was far too sweet-natured sometimes, and Thomas hoped he was not raising her wrong. Perhaps he was over-protective after losing Lubna. He knelt and kissed Amal's face and gave her a hug, touched Yves' shoulder.

"See you later, Pa." They went off to find Jahan so Amal could play mother with him. Perhaps Yves played father to them both.

Thomas smiled at the thought as he walked through the gathered army until he stood outside the royal building, aware of a few people watching as he passed. His new clothes were comfortable, but of far finer cut than he was used to, and he wondered if this was how it would be in the future. Women choosing his clothes for him.

He felt a tap on his shoulder and turned to find Theresa.

"She wants you to go inside so you can come out together."

"Why?"

"How am I supposed to know that?" She gave the end of his tagelmust a tug. "And what are you doing with this?"

"I had to wear something that made me feel like myself."

Thomas followed her to a small chamber where three women were about to leave. Isabel stood in the middle of the room. Pale leggings clung to her slim legs, her feet encased in soft leather. A short skirt of silvered chain-mail fell to her knees. Her upper body was encased in mail, bright in a shaft of sunlight through the window. She wore an open helmet, her hair covered.

"Well?" she asked. "Will I pass muster?" Her eyes tracked Thomas, something brittle in them as she examined him. "You look good."

"And you look magnificent."

Isabel giggled. "I believe I do. Give me your arm a moment until I am sure I can walk in all this iron."

He went to her side and allowed her to lean against him as they made for the doorway. She released her hold before they came to the outside door.

"I think I can manage, but stay close." She slowed, stopped and took a deep breath. The rings of her mail made a soft sound as they slid one against another.

Outside, a man held the reins of a tall Arabian stallion, but Isabel waved a hand in dismissal.

"I think we should walk, like my soldiers do, to show my humility."

Thomas stayed close as they descended the steps, but Isabel managed them without any problem. As they passed among the men, every face turned their way, but Thomas knew all eyes were on Isabel. At least his new clothes made him look as if he belonged at her side, and he straightened his back.

Isabel stopped and turned to a young man.

"Where are you from, young sir?"

The youth stared at her with his mouth open, but Isabel was patient.

"M-malaga, Your Grace."

"And before that?" She would know the men here from Malaga were recent incomers to that city since its fall four years before.

"Ronda, Your Grace." The youth controlled his voice this time.

"Is your father with you?"

"He is, Your Grace, over there." He pointed to a short man dressed in the uniform of a pikeman.

"Has he served me man and boy like you are doing?"

The youth nodded over and over, having difficulty knowing when to stop.

"I thank you for your service, both of you." She touched the youth on his shoulder and moved on.

Thomas looked back to see the youth's father go to him and nod in approval of his actions. They watched Isabel as she moved away, and Thomas knew every man here would sacrifice himself in her service if it came to the need of it. *As would I*, he thought, surprised to discover how he felt, wondering when the change had come about. He recognised it as some kind of turning point.

Isabel stopped to speak with another man, this one older, a

grey beard covering half his face. Thomas held back a dozen paces, feeling himself relax. There was no danger here, only unquestioning loyalty and, yes, love. These men feared and respected Fernando, but they loved Isabel. She was aware of the fact, which is why she walked among them, sharing a word here, a touch there. She changed the lives of those she cast her gaze on, from grizzled warriors to the young boys and girls who carried water and food.

The sun rose higher and Thomas began to sweat, but Isabel appeared untroubled despite her chain-mail weighing far more than his clothes. Noon came and went before they reached the edge of the camp and she stopped, staring across the narrow strip of land that separated Castile from what remained of al-Andalus. The white walls of Gharnatah glittered. The palace perched atop its red hill seemed to strain to reach the sky.

"Soon the city will be mine," said Isabel, her voice so soft only Thomas heard.

He stood at her side, wondering what people made of the two of them together, of this interloper beside their Queen.

"And the palace."

She glanced at him. "You know it well, do you not?"

"Every chamber and passage. It will be my pleasure to introduce you to its wonders."

"My thanks. I like your new clothes. Are you always going to dress this way from now on if I ask it?"

"Ask, or demand?"

"Ask," she said. "I will never demand anything of you, Thomas. Surely you know that. I have not demanded you remove that silly scarf you always wear, have I?"

He considered silence the wisest option.

Isabel took a deep breath and let it go. "Oh, to be an ordinary woman and be able to walk through those gates unrecognised. You could show me where you live, where you eat, the streets you inhabit."

"One day, perhaps," Thomas said.

She smiled. "Yes, one day soon, I pray."

"They would recognise you dressed as you are now, but dressed as a woman in ordinary clothes? Those within the walls of Gharnatah would have no idea who you are. Most would not even recognise Abu Abdullah if he walked past them."

"Could we do it, Thomas?"

"I should not have spoken of it. You could, but there is one chance in a thousand someone might recognise you."

"Shall we return? Eat with me once I get out of these weapons of torture. Perhaps I can dress as an ordinary woman for you."

A clash of metal on metal made Thomas turn, and he felt a wash of fear run through him. A small band of Moors had seen Isabel and were fighting their way on horseback through the disorganised ranks on the edge of the Castilian army.

"You have to leave, now." He clutched her arm and dragged her away, but already the fighting was growing closer. Thomas looked around, a panic rising in him. He raised his voice at the men nearest him. "You, form a wall in front of your Queen. Do it now!"

Men ran towards them. Pikemen, archers and swordsmen. Then a dozen men on horseback thundered their way in the direction of the band of Moors, who were now only a hundred paces away. Thomas watched one man hit by an arrow and go down, then four surrounded him and he fell to the ground and his horse fled its master. Thomas recognised the uniform of the horsemen. They were Koparsh's Turks, riding to save Isabel.

"Stay here. Don't move an inch."

Thomas ran as hard as he could in pursuit of the masterless horse. It had stopped and was tugging at a patch of grass spared Fernando's burning. He took the reins and pulled himself into the saddle, then bullied the horse back to Isabel. As he reached her, he offered his arm and she grasped it. He pulled her up to sit in front of him, then slid down from behind her.

"Ride!" He slapped the rump of the horse hard and it took off, Isabel clinging to its mane.

When he turned, the Moors were retreating. Their prize had escaped, and they would not throw their lives away for nothing. Isabel's men cheered as if they had won a glorious victory, but Thomas knew they had been lucky. All of them.

———

Thomas found Isabel in a subdued mood. She had changed into a simple dress beneath a long robe open at the front. She sat on a plain chair and stared through the window at Gharnatah. She looked up as Thomas entered the room, but offered no smile. Thomas remained dressed in his fine new clothes, but now they were blood-stained.

"You were away a long time. Did you not want to see me after what I caused to happen?" Isabel held up a hand as he started to speak. "I know, I was wrong. My vanity cost men their lives and others were injured."

"Which is where I have been. I did what I could for the injured men and believe they will recover to fight again."

"What happened? It was all so fast I could scarce tell."

"A Moorish raiding party saw you and fought their way through your soldiers." Thomas held a hand up as Isabel opened her mouth to speak. "There is no blame on your men. If there is any blame, it is mine. I should not have allowed you to get so close to Gharnatah."

"It is not your fault, Thomas. I wanted to see the palace. It calls to me. Come, sit here." She tapped the arm of a chair set beside hers. "Where did you find the horse? Was it one of theirs?"

"The Turks came." Thomas sat, aware that once again they were alone together. It was an increasingly common state of affairs between them. "They lost one of their men and his horse ran off. I managed to catch it."

"You put yourself in danger."

"I did what needed to be done to save you."

She reached out and touched his arm before withdrawing her hand.

"I must thank the Turks. I will send a message to their leader."

"Koparsh. Koparsh Hadryendo. They have set up their camp to the west."

"How many are there? Can I trust them, do you think?"

"They came to your rescue today, so I would say yes."

"He is exceedingly handsome, is he not?"

"Is he?"

Isabel gave a tiny laugh. "Are you jealous, Thomas? You know there is no need to be. Perhaps I can invite them to eat with us here. Offer them a meal they might enjoy. All except that woman, of course."

Thomas smiled. "As long as you choose your cook better than the last time."

"That was not my doing and you know it. The man…" Isabel stared off into space and Thomas waited for whatever thought had distracted her to come to fruition. "I asked for someone who knew Moorish food, but who selected him, I do not know."

"You are safe now, and Theresa is recovered. Once Ghar-natah falls, I will look to set up more protection for you."

Isabel smiled. "My Thomas, always looking out for me. I want to talk to you about something else. What shall I do with you once Granada is mine?"

"Do with me?"

Isabel's eyes captured his, but if some message lay behind them, it was not one he could read.

"You know the city better than any man in my employ, and

it makes sense to have you involved in its running when we take it."

"I was hoping to live a quiet life in my house on the Albayzin, to return to treating patients and turn my back on politics. I am not cut out for them."

"Which is why I want you to do it. Those who seek high position do so for their own advantage. You do not, which is why it must be you." Her eyes tracked his face, perhaps looking for some sign he might agree to her request. "Five years, Thomas. Give me five years to create a system to run the city peaceably. I will allow those living there to remain, provided they swear allegiance to Castile."

"And their God?"

"I need to think on that, but it may be possible to allow them to follow their false God, within limits."

"Spare the great mosque. Convert the others, knock them down, but leave one place of worship standing they can use. Can I recruit my own staff? Men I trust?"

"Are you accepting my offer?"

"I am thinking on it."

"Then think on it while you go into the city. I have decided to go ahead with this meeting with Boabdil. Go to him and tell him that. Tell him where it will be held—and yes, the place you suggested is acceptable. I asked Martin and he agrees with you it is safe. So make the arrangements."

"He will want to bring his own troops, which cannot be allowed, but I am sure he will agree otherwise."

"Both of us must be allowed to take men. How many, Thomas?"

"Sixty to a hundred makes sense. Enough to offer a threat, but not enough to put either side off. Will Fernando agree?"

"I am minded to arrange the meeting when he is on one of his expeditions. He has some idea about attacking Almeria, or perhaps he wants to recruit Boabdil's uncle to our cause."

Thomas watched Isabel. "You are treading on dangerous ground if you go ahead without Fernando."

"Not if I succeed, and I will. I will not allow Granada to be destroyed like Malaga and Ronda were. Too many lives have been lost already, on both sides. This is a chance to stop the killing and start rebuilding the whole of Spain as the leading power in the world. When Catherine marries King Henry's son…" she waved a hand, "…oh, not for a decade yet, but when it happens, I will have built this land into a force to be reckoned with. And with England alongside us, we can rule the world."

"And when Catherine's husband is King?" Thomas rose and left Isabel to consider the implications of that.

CHAPTER THIRTY-ONE

Thomas took Will and Amal to visit Olaf and Fatima, but after he left them a reluctance made him pause at the foot of the Albayzin. He stopped to eat a meal at one of the inns set around Hattabin square. He ate slowly, sipping at a single cup of wine while the light around him grew soft with the setting sun. Eventually he rose, but instead of climbing the cobbled alleys to his house, he went to Aamir's bathhouse and cleansed himself.

Finally he could think of no further excuse other than to return to his accommodation among the Castilian forces, so he let his feet guide him while his thoughts lay elsewhere. When he pushed at the courtyard door, he found it locked and hammered on the dark wood. For a moment, he wondered if Helena had abandoned the house, grown tired of waiting for him to decide. The last time he saw her, he had told her the house was hers. Perhaps she had sold it and a new owner not yet taken up residence.

When he heard the bolt thrown, he pushed the tangle of thoughts from his mind.

"I wondered when you might return." Helena stood in the doorway, not blocking it, but neither offering a welcome. Her eyes scanned him from head to foot. "I see you are dressing better at last."

"Isabel's doing," Thomas said.

Helena leaned to the side to look past him. "Is it only you?"

"I took Will and Amal to stay with Olaf and Fatima. I can fetch them if you want."

"No, let my father enjoy them while he can. You are enough. I assume you want to come in?" She remained in the middle of the doorway. The light from the courtyard behind cast her face in shadow. Thomas recalled when she had always wanted to hide her face, but did not recall her doing it so much of late. "Do you want food? There is not much here, and I have already eaten."

"As have I."

"Why are you here, Thomas?"

"Can I not come to my own house?"

Helena stared at him, her face without expression. "As long as you do not expect me to leave."

"I don't."

Helena stepped aside and Thomas brushed past, her scent filling his senses, the warmth of her body touching his. He almost turned to her then, but a sudden doubt gave him pause. She was different tonight. Less teasing. He wondered if he had expected to arrive and have her throw herself at him. He knew he was being stupid, or desperate, or something. He should have spoken with Jorge before coming, but it was too late now.

"I think there is still some wine in your workshop."

"Yes, please."

"You know where it is." Helena turned away and went into the house, leaving Thomas alone. He raised a hand and pushed fingers through his hair.

That could have gone better, he thought.

He found several bottles of wine set on their sides and took one he recalled as being good. Some bottles were better than others, some only good for mixing with poppy or hashish to ease pain. When he returned to the courtyard, Helena had placed two fine glasses side by side on the table and taken a seat. She set a second chair beside hers and Thomas took it. He poured wine for them both and drained half his glass in one swallow.

"Has Isabel grown tired of you and thrown you out?"

"Not yet, strange as the idea might seem."

"You are a good man. She is fortunate to have you at her side." Helena leaned closer.

His eyes tracked her face. Not even the faintest blemish showed a scar had ever marred her beauty. Not that the scar had ever made a difference to him, but he knew the despair she had felt when her life had been savagely changed. Torn from the heart of the harem to live with a cold man who didn't welcome her presence. Even when Thomas took her into his bed, it was not love that drew them together. He didn't know if it was love that brought him here tonight. No, not love, he was sure, but something that might be deeper. Companionship. Knowledge of each other. So much had changed since Helena first came to live with him. She too had changed since he freed her from Abu Abdullah's captivity. Thomas hoped the changes happening all around him might slow when Gharnatah fell, but feared they would not.

The air was cool and he saw Helena shiver. The year was slipping towards its end and snow crept further down the face of the Sholayr to mark the passage of the days.

"You should go inside."

"I would, but you are out here." She reached out a hand and Thomas took it, holding it within both of his.

"Shall I make up a bed for you?"

"I would prefer to share yours, if you will have me."

"Everything within these walls is yours, Thomas. I want you to share my bed. I have ever since I came to know what a good man you are." She leaned closer and kissed him, her lips soft. "I have not always been good to you, and for that I apologise." She cocked her head to one side. "Is this for one night only, or more?"

"More, I hope."

"As do I."

Helena smiled and rose to her feet, her hand still in his.

"Come and warm me up, Thomas. Let us see if we can remember how we once fitted together to make our beautiful son."

As she pulled her hand from his and walked towards the house, Thomas watched her go, aware of what she had just revealed to him, of what she had confirmed. Will was his son. His true son. He rose and followed her, something breaking loose in his chest as if the last piece of ice had melted from his heart.

––––––

Thomas came awake slowly from a deep place, deeper than he had slept in a long time.

"Can you not wait until morning?" he said as he opened his eyes to discover Helena leaning over him.

"Something is going on in the city." She shook him again, even though he was starting to sit up.

Thomas slipped from the bed and padded to the small window. He opened it, but heard nothing … and then he did. Distantly, coming from below. The sound of shouting, and then a sharp crack as someone fired a musket. He turned from the window and started to dress, then stopped.

"Are my own clothes still here?"

"In the other room, there was not space for them here as well as mine."

Thomas went through and pulled back a curtain. Everything he once wore hung from hooks and he dressed quickly. When he came out, a still naked Helena blocked his way.

"Stay, Thomas, this is not your responsibility."

"I am only going to see what is happening. Go back to bed, I will return soon." He gripped her shoulders and kissed her mouth, recalling the long kisses, and more, they had shared only a few hours before. The remembrance of them almost made him change his mind. He eased Helena to one side and descended the narrow staircase.

In the alley, the sound of fighting was louder and he smelled burning. The noise came from below and he ran across the cobbles. Other men emerged from doorways, but by the time they called out to ask what was happening, Thomas was already past. He emerged into al-Hattabin square to find a throng milling about. He stopped a man who seemed to be trying to organise some of the others.

"What's going on?"

"Castile has sent a force into the city and they are attacking the great mosque. I am trying to get enough men together to drive them back, but most here are too old, or too afraid." He looked at Thomas and frowned. "You are Thomas Berrington, are you not? I hear you can fight. Help me."

"We will need more than the two of us. Where are the palace's men?"

"Still abed, or scared."

"If Olaf hears this noise, he will bring them down, but it takes time to gather a force. They will descend on the other side of the square, so gather anyone willing to fight and wait there."

"What are you going to do?"

"Find out what is happening."

Thomas strode across the square in the direction of the noise. As he entered the wide road leading to the mosque, people moved past in the opposite direction. Some ran, others walked more slowly, looking behind for pursuers.

Thomas grabbed a man. "Where are they?"

"There is an army led by a madman. He is trying to climb the wall of the mosque."

"Is anyone fighting them?"

The man pulled from Thomas's grip and ran off, leaving him unsure what to do next. He advanced cautiously, stopping at each corner to check he wasn't about to walk into an ambush. As he entered the wide square surrounding the great mosque, he saw the attackers. They were surprisingly few, less than a score, and they had stopped making so much noise. Thomas recognised the man who appeared to be in charge as Perez de Pulgar, one of those who Isabel had spoken with only the day before, but he knew this was not her doing. The man took a large wooden panel from one of the others and dragged it to the mosque.

Thomas moved closer, sure he could defend himself if need be, hoping the leader might recognise him in turn. Three men of Gharnatah rushed from a side street and attacked those on the left flank, but one was killed almost at once and the others retreated.

De Pulgar approached the wide door of the mosque and knelt before it.

Thomas was confused. The man appeared to be praying to Allah. Which was impossible.

He crept closer to hear the last of the words spoken. De Pulgar was claiming the mosque as a Christian church, dedicating it to the blessed Virgin. He rose to his feet and picked up the wooden board, drew his dagger and nailed the board to the door of the mosque before turning away.

Thomas thought it was all over and the attackers would retreat, but after milling around for a moment, de Pulgar started directly towards where Thomas stood in a doorway. He could hear de Pulgar passing orders to his men. They were to search out anyone, man, woman or child, and make an example of them. Only Moors lived here, he said. They all deserved to die.

As the small group approached the doorway where Thomas

hid, one of them saw him and gave a loud cry. The others stopped and turned.

Thomas hesitated, then tried to open the door behind him, but it was locked. He stepped into the roadway. When the man who had first seen him attacked, Thomas feinted one way, then brought him down with a fearsome blow. He knelt and took the man's sword. By the time he rose, the others had organised themselves and stood in a semi-circle in front of him.

"I know you," said de Pulgar. "You were with the Queen yesterday."

"And I know you. What are you doing here?"

"God's work." The man glanced at his felled companion. "Join us, sir, for we have more work to do tonight. You can replace the man you killed."

"He has lost his wits, nothing more. And I would advise you to leave as fast as you can. There are few of you, and word will have reached the palace by now."

"We are none of us cowards."

"Then you will die brave men, for there is no other choice unless you leave."

De Pulgar spat on the ground and shook his head. "I never liked you, Berrington." He waved a hand at his men. "Kill him."

Thomas struck first, but his blade was deflected. He was stepping back, preparing to tackle however many he could, when there came a bellow of rage and Olaf Torvaldsson appeared at the head of the street.

"Two men to kill, then," said de Pulgar. "And the bigger, the better."

As Olaf approached, more men poured into the roadway behind him, a hundred, then two. They came silently, dark eyes catching what little light came from burning lamps set in the walls. By the time Olaf reached Thomas, all the attackers had fled.

"Why is it when there is trouble, you are always the first to find it?" Olaf watched as his men streamed after the retreating attackers. "Are those men mad to think they can come into this city and fight?"

Thomas approached the mosque to see what was nailed there. He grabbed a torch from a niche and held it up so he could read the words burned into the wooden board.

Ave Maria. Writ large and gilded with yellow paint. It was the ultimate insult.

Olaf strode to the door and reached up. His first attempt did nothing, but his second brought the wooden board down. He laid it on the ground and raised his foot, then stopped to pick it up again.

"They will pay for this with their blood," he said.

CHAPTER THIRTY-TWO

Thomas walked up the dark hillside beside Olaf. He had decided not to return to his own house. The chaotic attack by de Pulgar had unsettled him, and he wanted to lie between his children and take comfort in their presence. Already the hours he had spent with Helena seemed dreamlike.

"It was lucky you arrived when you did," he said as they approached Olaf's door. "I don't know what would have become of me if you had not. De Pulgar would be happy to see me dead. He was the leader of the attack, by the way." Thomas didn't know if Olaf was familiar with the man.

"I know of him," said Olaf. "He has a reputation which tonight he reinforced." Olaf looked down at the banner still held in his hand as though it weighed no more than a twig. "Something will have to be done, and done soon. I cannot leave this insult to lie."

"Take care. I suspect he came to deface the mosque in order to incite the rage of the city. He hopes it will force any retaliation to be done in haste."

"It has to be soon. Tomorrow if I can work out a plan. How did you know of the attack? Did you hear about it before you came here?"

"Do you not think I would have warned you if I had? I knew no more than you. Helena woke me and I came to find out what the noise was all about."

"Helena woke you?" said Olaf.

"Yes."

Olaf looked across the barracks square to where two soldiers stood on watch.

"It is good you and she are reconciled." He turned to Thomas. "Is it permanent?"

"It may be. I hope so."

"Why now and not before?"

"I expect I am ready now, and she has changed. You and Jorge told me that and I didn't believe it, but now I have seen the change for myself."

"That is good, Thomas. Your children need a mother."

"She confirmed something else to me tonight I have never been certain of before. She told me Will is both my son and hers."

"Will has always been your son."

"Did she tell you?"

"I only have to look at him to see he is yours. Can you not see it yourself?"

"Perhaps I haven't allowed myself to see it because she withheld the certainty from me." Thomas looked at Olaf. He could also see him in Will. "Do you think this change in her will last?"

"Jorge is a better man to ask, you will get more sense from him than me. But remember, do not think about it too much. You do that more than is good for a man. If she changes, she changes. In the meantime, she will prove a pleasant companion for you and a distraction from the responsibilities Isabel places on you."

"She has sent me to meet Abu Abdullah in the morning," Thomas shook his head. "Today, I suppose. To discuss the details of a meeting where the city's surrender will be the only topic."

Olaf smiled. "I heard rumours of such."

"Will you accept a surrender?"

"It is not up to me whether or not to accept. I do as ordered. If the Sultan tells me to fight, I will fight. If he tells me not to, I will find something else to do."

"If the meeting goes ahead, I want you there. Isabel has agreed a small force from either side to ensure mutual safety. She knows you and trusts your honour."

"Who will be on the other side? Fernando? I do not trust his."

Thomas took a breath and decided he had gone too far to hold anything back. He knew Olaf would never utter a word of their conversation to anyone.

"Fernando doesn't agree with her, but will go along with her plan for now. Perhaps he wants her to fail so he can save the day. Or raze Gharnatah to the ground. Which is why she must succeed."

"She plays a dangerous game."

"She does, but it is an essential one. She admires Gharnatah and doesn't want to see it destroyed. You were with us in Malaka and saw what happened there. This city's end has to be different."

"What of Abu Abdullah?"

"She will offer him something. I suggested the Alpujarras, he can't cause too much trouble over there."

"Fernando will want him dead."

"And Isabel does not."

Olaf stared at Thomas. "Who will be the victor between them?"

"Isabel. I walked with her yesterday and saw the awe she instils in her soldiers. The army respects Fernando, but they love Isabel. Though she can be harsh when she needs to be. Stubborn too. She always gets what she wants."

"At one time I thought it might be you she wanted." Olaf gave a shake of his head at such a strange idea, then clapped

Thomas on the shoulder. "I am glad that two of the women you loved have been my daughters. Come and see if you can sleep for a while. We all need to be sharp come morning."

"I have to go back to her before noon."

"Helena?"

"Isabel."

Olaf glanced at the sky, but there was no hint to show the new day was near.

"Then come and sleep while you can. I will wake you when I rise if you are not already up. Amal and Will are in the small room so you will have to share the space with them."

"It is what I intended."

Olaf gave a nod of approval.

Thomas removed his cloak and lay on the bedding arranged on the stone floor. Amal continued to sleep when he slid between them, but Will rolled over and opened his eyes.

"Where did you go?"

"To our house."

"Why didn't you take us?"

"There was something I needed to find out."

"Did you?"

"I think so."

"Good." Will closed his eyes.

Thomas stared at his son. Helena's revelation changed everything. It had ripped away the scab of uncertainty he had carried for too long and left him at ease, at least for tonight. He stared at Will's face, searching for features that confirmed her words, but he was no good at such arts. Others said Will resembled him, but he had always dismissed their words. Now he would have to listen more closely.

———

When Thomas returned to his other house beyond the Castilian camp to leave his children, Jorge insisted on coming with him when he went to see Isabel.

"You can't come inside with me," Thomas said.

"I have no intention of doing so. I will talk with the soldiers while you are busy doing whatever it is you two do with your time. Something boring, no doubt."

"I'm sure you would consider it so."

As they walked side by side down the shallow slope, a thought occurred to Thomas.

"Why on earth do you want to talk to the soldiers?"

"They are always the ones who know what's happening."

"Be careful, then. De Pulgar attacked the mosque in Gharnatah last night, and I suspect word has spread by now. No doubt the entire army is full of a false sense of achievement."

"He reached as far as the mosque?"

"I saw him with my own eyes. And he saw me."

"He is Fernando's man. I am amazed you are still alive, but you are always a constant surprise to me."

Thomas suppressed a smile. "I spent the night in my house."

"I should have come with you, then. I like that house. When Castile destroys it, ask Britto to build you another the same. Or you can come and live with me and Belia in Da'ud's old house."

"I spent the night with Helena."

Jorge stopped walking so abruptly, Thomas was a dozen paces beyond him before he realised he was alone and turned back.

"You what?" Jorge shook his head. "About time is all I can say. Was she as good as you remember?"

Thomas wondered whether or not to lie, but was aware something had broken loose inside. Now he soared like an eagle above all the concerns that had once seemed to constrain his life and decisions.

He smiled. "Better."

"Damn, Thomas, in that case, I'm surprised you're still alive. When did you decide?"

"Only when I went there. Or perhaps long ago. I don't know, only that when I saw her, the decision was already made."

"Was she glad to see you? Did you make her scream in ecstasy?"

"She was glad to see me, but the rest is none of your business."

"Ah well, I expect if I explain a few techniques to you, she might scream one day. Is this reconciliation permanent?"

"I believe so. If I want it to be."

Jorge shook his head again and started to walk. They split up outside the white-walled building Isabel used and Thomas entered, expecting her to be with her advisers, but he saw Theresa who told him Isabel was free and eating a midday meal in the courtyard.

She looked up when Thomas entered and smiled a greeting before turning back to a sparse plate holding fruit, berries and nuts.

"I hope someone tasted all of those before you started to eat." Thomas pulled out a chair and sat beside her. Too close, but Isabel made no protest. Instead, she picked up a dark mulberry and offered it to him. Thomas took it into his mouth, the sharp sweetness delicious.

Isabel widened her eyes. "Oh no! Now we might both die." She gave a small laugh. "Your friend Belia picked these and gave them to Theresa. I think the two are becoming good friends. I like it that your family and mine are forging ever closer bonds. Belia said I should send my children to play with your children and hers." She looked into Thomas's eyes. "How is such possible when he is a eunuch?"

"They must have had help from someone."

"Mm."

271

Thomas accepted another sweet offering, then wiped his mouth.

"I assume you know about the attack last night?"

"Fernando took great delight in calling it a magnificent victory. He told me he wanted to take part in the raid himself, but I told him he could not."

"Have you heard what they did?"

"A fast attack into the city to show they could, and then they escaped. Most of them."

"I was there," Thomas said. "It was a well-planned assault intended to spit in the eye of their God. They nailed a banner to the door of the great mosque."

Isabel stared at Thomas, the food in front of her forgotten.

"Nobody told me that. Whose idea was it? What did they do?"

"They nailed a sign saying 'Ave Maria' to the mosque door with a knife. I saw Perez de Pulgar do it with my own eyes. Then he saw me. If Olaf Torvaldsson hadn't arrived, I believe de Pulgar would have killed me."

"Ave Maria?" said Isabel. "Is that such a great insult?"

"How would you react if the Moors nailed an inverted cross to the door of the church here? Or to the cathedrals of Córdoba or Sevilla? The only thing that might have been worse is if they had nailed a pig's head to the door." Thomas let his breath go, trying to release a sudden anger but only partially succeeding. "I should not tell you this, Isabel, but I will because I am your man now." *Like it or not*, he thought. "There will be retaliation, most likely today. You might want to warn Fernando and de Pulgar. When the attack comes, it will be vicious. You have insulted their God. What would you do if they insulted yours?"

"It was not at my order, but you are right. Retribution would have to be taken. Why are you telling me this? Do you not consider Granada to be your city?"

"It is, but I have a higher mistress. I told you, I serve you now, like it or not." This time he could not withhold the words. "I made a choice and will serve you as long as you ask."

Isabel reached out and took his hand. "I need you, Thomas. I need your intelligence, your wisdom, and your knowledge. I need your skill. You saved Theresa when nobody else could. You saved Catherine and Juan. You will save others around me, I know you will. One day, when this war is over, you and I will have a conversation and I will ask what it is you want. You will tell me how you wish to spend the rest of your life and, if you ask it, I will release you. But until then, you are mine. Agreed?"

"Agreed."

Isabel giggled as she released his hand. "Do you know, I almost kissed you then? What if someone saw us?"

"Then it is good you controlled yourself, Your Grace."

Isabel reached out and patted his face, pretending it was a slap.

"Now, you will come with me while I go to berate my husband. I will not tell him who told me of this coming attack, but he will know anyway. I suspect you will have more men to heal before the sun sets on this day."

CHAPTER THIRTY-THREE

They found Fernando on the edge of the camp, together with Perez de Pulgar. The two men sat on stallions, watching as a cohort of Moorish soldiers gathered beyond the walls of Gharnatah. As Isabel approached, de Pulgar twisted in his saddle, then leaned close to whisper into Fernando's ear. Whatever he said must have been amusing, because both of them laughed.

"This may not be a good idea," Thomas said. "It looks to me like a battle is in the making. You should go back to where you are safe."

"I have never turned away from conflict and I will not do so today. I will speak to my husband and de Pulgar both."

Thomas glanced around. "Whatever you want to say might be better done in private."

"I will take care to lower my voice, but what I have to say must be said here and now before more lives are lost in another pointless show of male pride."

Thomas wondered if Isabel's female pride might be just as dangerous, if not more so, but considered it wise to omit mention of the fact.

Beside Fernando, Isabel stopped, a tiny figure who did not even reach his thigh where he sat astride his horse.

"I need to talk to you. Both of you."

"Can you not see we are busy?" Fernando barely glanced in her direction.

"No, you are not. You are strutting peacocks, both of you. Either we have this conversation here and I shout up at you so everyone can hear and I get a sore neck, or you come down and we walk a little distance so nobody but you will ever know what I have to say."

Fernando gave an exaggerated sigh, but Thomas saw he was beaten. He slid from the saddle, making Isabel take several steps back to avoid being crushed beneath him. She looked at de Pulgar, who followed the example of his master.

Isabel glanced around. The bulk of Castile's troops stood thirty or more paces distant, but several nobles had gathered around the King. When Isabel glanced in Thomas's direction, he nodded his head at a small rise where boulders were stacked to form some kind of enclosure. No doubt it was where night-watchmen settled for the night. Isabel nodded and strode in that direction. Thomas caught her up, but she did not look at him. They reached the enclosure and turned, waiting.

Fernando and de Pulgar remained where they were, talking between themselves. Isabel said nothing, but her body was tense, and Thomas could see she was holding her anger in check.

"When they come, do not shout at them. Yours must be the voice of reason."

"When has my husband ever listened to reason? Ah, see, they have ignored me long enough to make a point and now they deign to honour us with their presence."

Fernando arrived first. De Pulgar came ten paces behind and stayed the same distance when they stopped walking.

"What is this about, my love?"

"My love?" Isabel's voice was too loud and she made an attempt to control herself. "Do you know what that man has done?"

"Struck a righteous blow for all of Christendom." Fernando glanced at Thomas. "Is it appropriate that he be here?"

"I trust Thomas implicitly. He stays."

Fernando shrugged, as if he cared not whether Thomas stayed or went. Despite what Isabel said, Thomas moved away and went to stand beside de Pulgar.

"Was it your idea or Fernando's?" he asked.

"Fernando, is it? I call him King, or Sire, or Your Grace. What right do you have to use his name?"

"The right of a common man," Thomas said.

"Does he know you lie with his wife?" said de Pulgar. "Everyone else does, so no doubt one day he will have to kill you. If I do not do it first. I would have done so last night if that mad Northman had not come to spoil our fun."

"Do you even know how great an insult you made to them?"

"They are heathens. Whatever insult they think I gave means nothing to me or the King. See, I call him correct. You would be minded to do the same."

"Men will die today because of what you have done. Do you not care about their lives at all?"

"As long as you are one of them, I will consider my work done." De Pulgar turned and walked away to one side, careful to keep his distance to Fernando the same.

Thomas watched him go. The man took a dozen paces, then stopped, not wanting to be far from his master, but wanting to distance himself from Thomas, who turned away to watch Isabel and Fernando. Both their faces were stark with restrained anger. Isabel was doing most of the talking, but if she believed Fernando would buckle under her onslaught, there was little sign.

Thomas wondered if she had made the wrong decision. Wondered if he should have been more forceful in opposing her, but it was too late now.

How long the argument would have gone on became irrelevant as a great cry rose from the gathered soldiers. Thomas turned to see a single figure ride out from the army of Gharnatah. At first, he thought it might be Olaf himself, then saw it was not. Instead, another Moorish warrior came towards the Castilian line. Thomas recognised him as Abu Abdullah's younger brother, Tarfe, regarded as equal parts insolence and bravery. He rode a dazzling Arabian stallion back and forth in front of the Castilian line while threatening them with a lance. Such was his confidence that nobody thought to challenge the man until he turned one last time and somebody called out, pointing.

Thomas saw a stained board being dragged behind Tarfe's horse, the same one de Pulgar had nailed to the door of the mosque the night before. Now it was covered in ashes and manure. Thomas was still staring at the display when Fernando came past, deliberately knocking him to the ground. De Pulgar followed, aiming a kick at Thomas. A moment later, Isabel knelt beside him.

"Are you all right, Thomas?"

"They need to hit me harder than that if they mean me to stay down. What did you say to him?"

"I told him I can never sanction such an insult again. Never! How can I broker a peace when he spits in the eye of the city?" She offered a hand to help him up. "I also told him he is not to see that Turkish woman again."

Even though he didn't need the help, Thomas took her hand as he rose. Let the soldiers see. Most already believed them lovers, let them have evidence for their unfounded suspicions. It was a petty move designed to enrage Fernando even further, but Thomas smiled all the same. Small victories.

"What did he say about that? About Salma, that is?"

Isabel scowled. "He tried to tell me it is ended. She has another conquest now. He expected me to believe him. Does he think me a fool?"

"I think he considers everyone other than himself a fool."

Thomas knew his words were dangerous, but he and Isabel shared too much now to withhold the opinion.

A disturbance made them turn to see Fernando shouting at the front rank of nobles, demanding someone challenge Tarfe. Most hung back, finding something interesting to look at elsewhere. Then one young warrior jostled his horse through the ranks until he dismounted to stand before the King.

Tarfe had stopped displaying the soiled sign and waited to see what was going to happen. He had risked everything on the insult. If he had guessed wrong he would die at the hands of a hundred men. But it appeared he had guessed right. His challenge had been accepted.

The young knight mounted his horse again and walked it towards Tarfe. Isabel ran to intercept him and reached up. He lowered his lance and she tied her lace kerchief to it.

Thomas stayed where he was, aware someone was about to die, but which of them it would be, he didn't know. Olaf had told him Tarfe was a skilled warrior, but headstrong. The evidence of that judgement was in front of them.

The two men faced each other. There was little point in conversation or insults because neither would understand the other. Instead, some kind of agreement was made without the need for words and they turned and trotted away to put distance between themselves.

A joust it was to be. To begin with, anyway.

Fernando waved a hand. A trumpeter gave a loud blast and the two men started for each other. The thunder of their horses was loud for a moment before it was drowned out by the cries of the Castilian army.

"What is this all about?"

Thomas turned to find Koparsh Hadryendo standing beside him, Salma a few paces back with the other Turks beyond her. Thomas wondered who her new lover might be, not that it was any concern of his.

"Did you hear what happened last night?" he asked.

"Something about an insult to Allah, but Gharnatah is not my city." Koparsh narrowed his eyes. "I take it that thing being dragged behind the horse is the item in dispute?"

Thomas shook his head at the stupidity of Tarfe for not cutting the sign loose. It would slow him and make manoeuvring more difficult.

Even above the shouts of the soldiers, the clash of lance on armour cut through the noise, but both men rode on, still seated.

They slowed and turned. When they met a second time, it was the Castilian knight who came off the worse. Thomas saw Tarfe shift at the last moment. The tip of his lance shattered into a hundred shards, but it landed true. The knight tumbled backwards and hit the ground hard.

Had Tarfe followed through in that moment, the result would have been different, but he wanted to show off, riding backwards and forwards with the board still dragging behind. Only when the Castilian knight rose to his feet did he approach and dismount as they drew swords.

Both antagonists fought well, but slowly the young knight began to gain the ascendancy. To Thomas, it was clear Tarfe was the more aggressive, but the knight more skilled.

The two men clashed, pressed chest to chest. Tarfe drew a long dagger and tried to plunge it into the knight's belly, but he twisted away just in time. He swung around, his sword a blur. Before Tarfe could defend himself, the sharp blade sliced into his neck.

Tarfe stood a moment longer, but he was already dead. His head lolled at an angle, barely connected. When he fell to his knees, and then his front, the young knight took Tarfe's knife and used it to complete what his sword had begun.

He turned to the Castilian army and held Tarfe's head high, greeted by a tremendous cheer. Then he turned and did the same to the gathered Moors, whose cry was one of rage.

The young knight tossed Tarfe's head to the ground, picked

up the soiled board and carried it back, holding it aloft so everyone could see the words. Thomas looked at Isabel, but if she felt any sense of victory, her face did not reflect it. Unlike Fernando, who strode to the man and embraced him.

When Thomas saw Isabel approach the pair, he moved to join her, afraid Fernando might hurt her. No doubt he believed this victory justified the actions of himself and de Pulgar.

"You have started a war with your actions!" Isabel shouted at Fernando, unable to control herself any longer.

Thomas reached out to take her arm, then stopped, knowing he could do no such thing, not here in front of everyone. He had to be the loyal servant, not the master.

"No, I have stopped a war. We start the war only when I am ready. But this man," Fernando slapped the young knight's shoulder, "has shown the skill of Castile. We should do the same. Challenge their general, that big Northman. Him against this man."

"I fear I cannot fight again so soon, Your Grace," said the knight.

"Then someone else. Perez, you are ready for the challenge, are you not?"

"The big general?" De Pulgar appeared less confident than his master.

Fernando laughed. "Perhaps I should order Thomas here to fight him. He claims to be a skilled swordsman. He even claims he can best me, but in that he is wrong."

Thomas said nothing. He was sure none of the gathered men would face Olaf. Not unless they were insane.

Which, it appeared, one was. A man with no loyalty to either side.

Koparsh Hadryendo approached Fernando.

"I will challenge the man. I met him when I was in Gharnatah and believe he has a weakness."

"Olaf has no weaknesses," Thomas said.

"I watched him practise with his men. He favours the axe,

that was clear to see, but he is less skilled with a sword. I will challenge him, man to man, with swords."

"Olaf will still kill you," Thomas said.

"I think not."

Thomas only shook his head.

"I would like to see that fight," said Fernando, "but fear I cannot allow it. You are our guest. Besides, how could I explain your death to your Sultan?" He looked around. "Who else is brave enough?"

Another man approached. He was tall, almost as tall as Olaf himself, almost as broad across the shoulders. When he spoke, his Castilian was guttural, and Thomas heard the accent of Germania in his words.

"I fear no man, Your Grace. I will challenge him."

Fernando looked the man up and down. "You will fight with a sword? I have seen you before, but forget your name."

"I am Arnulf Hanmman, Your Grace, and sword or axe, all weapons are the same to me."

"And the stakes?" Thomas asked, knowing it was not his place to speak, but doing so anyway.

"No stakes. Only honour. We will offer the General an opportunity to avenge the loss of his man. If he wins, I will allow Isabel her pointless meeting with Boabdil. You and she can attend, for I want nothing to do with it. Wars are won through might, not words."

"And if Olaf loses?"

"It gives me permission to start my siege. The cannon will sound and walls will fall. What say you, Berrington? Will you walk out there and talk to the father of your dead wife?" Fernando spat out the final words in a deliberate attempt to anger Thomas.

"What if he says no?"

"He will not. Torvaldsson is a proud man. Too proud to turn away from proving himself the better warrior."

Thomas looked at Arnulf Hanmman. He was big. He was strong. But Olaf was unbeatable. The man would die.

"I will talk to him." Thomas glanced at Isabel. "And when Olaf wins the fight, that is the end of it. Agreed?"

Fernando shrugged, his attention already on the coming conflict.

"Agreed. And when my man wins?"

"Agreed," Thomas said, glancing at Isabel. "With your permission, Your Grace?"

Isabel stared at her husband, her anger still simmering, still barely under control.

"You will keep your word if I allow this? I can have my meeting with Boabdil, and Olaf can walk from the field?"

"Do whatever you like. And so will I." Fernando glanced towards Salma. Any relationship or love that had once lain between him and Isabel had turned to dust. Destroyed by Fernando himself.

As Thomas moved away, a blond-haired figure came running towards him. It was Will.

"Let me come with you," he said, clutching at Thomas's hand, fear showing in his eyes.

"You know Olaf cannot be defeated," Thomas said.

"I do, but I want to stand behind him when he fights. You and me, Pa. We have to let them see which side we stand for."

Thomas looked beyond his son to where Jorge stood. At least he had left Amal behind with Belia. She was too young to witness this madness. Usaden stood at a distance, Kin beside him. Thomas nodded at him and they loped across the ground to join him.

"Then let us stand with your *morfar*. Let us stand for Gharnatah." He gave one last glance in the direction of Isabel, whose face showed only despair, and wondered if he had just destroyed any chance of continuing to serve her.

CHAPTER THIRTY-FOUR

Thomas's doubts started when they were half way between the two armies. Four men and a dog. Even Kin felt it, sticking close to his side. Five tiny figures in a vast landscape. He was sure many on both sides would be more than happy to kill him and all those with him. And then, as if sensing his uncertainty, Olaf walked out to greet them. He clapped each of them on the shoulder, then knelt to stroke Kin, a sight Thomas had never seen before.

"I used to have a dog much like yours when I was a boy," he said as he rose. "Did the Queen send you?"

"Fernando. He sent me with a message. He wants another challenge. You and one of their men. The victor wins the day."

"That does not seem like much of an offer," said Olaf. "If they promised to end the war, I might consider it, but win the day? What exactly does that mean?"

"He also said if you are the victor, he will not stand in the way of the meeting between Isabel and Abu Abdullah. That may be a way to end the war, though it will put you out of a job."

"I am thinking I am getting too old for this job, anyway."

Thomas knew whatever age Olaf had, twenty years or a

hundred, he was a match for any man.

"I can go back and tell them you refuse."

"And look like a coward?"

"So you agree?"

"I agree. Besides, I have to punish them for what they did to Tarfe. I am going to have to tell Abu Abdullah his brother is dead." Olaf narrowed his eyes as he gazed across the space between the two armies. "Who is this man they send against me?"

"His name is Arnulf Hanmman, and he is big. As big as you, I'd say, and of Germania."

"They fight well there, but they are not true Northmen. Weapons?"

"Swords, I'm afraid."

"No matter. I can take his head just as well with a sword as an axe. It would be a fitting response. Am I correct in believing the fight is to the death?"

"To the death," Thomas said.

"Then let us get it done." Olaf glanced at Will. "Are you sure you want him to watch?"

"What would you do if he was your son?"

"He would watch. Will fights well enough, but he needs to know how a fight ends."

"I'm not afraid," said Will.

Olaf touched the boy's head. "Then you should be. Watch and learn. Learn to be afraid, because I am. Fear keeps you alive longer than the lack of it." He glanced at Thomas. "Is there to be some manner of protocol?"

"I assume Fernando will want to appear chivalrous. Are you content with that?"

"I approve of chivalry. There is less of it than when I first became a warrior, and we are the worse for its lack. Stay here, I will go back and tell my men they are not to avenge me if I die. I will tell them if that happens, they are to follow your orders."

Thomas shook his head. "You know they hate me."

"True. But they also respect you. You have saved the lives of many and they do not forget that."

Thomas watched Olaf stride away, a rock, a mountain, and yet still a man, and all men are mortal. When he turned, Fernando and de Pulgar were bringing their champion across. Koparsh Hadryendo was with them, together with Salma, and Thomas thought what was about to happen would be no sight for a woman to witness—except Salma was no ordinary woman. The thought made him wonder yet again what manner of person she was. As she came, all men turned to watch her. When she passed close to Thomas, her exotic scent touched him, and her sensual lips offered a smile, as if sending a message. When she was gone, he searched for Isabel, but she was nowhere to be seen. He looked to the low rise where he had stood beside her, but it was empty.

As Olaf returned, both armies drew closer until only a narrow strip of ground lay between them, allowing the men to stare into the eyes of their enemies. Thomas knew they would be sizing each other up for the coming battle.

"Who is your second?" Fernando asked Olaf.

"Thomas Berrington."

Fernando frowned at Thomas. "Is that allowed? You serve my wife, not this man."

"Olaf and I have been friends a long time, as well you know ... Your Grace." Thomas saw Fernando catch the hesitation which turned the honorific into an insult.

"Are you content with Thomas being second for Olaf Torvaldsson?" Fernando spoke to de Pulgar, who was clearly the second of their man.

"They can do whatever they want, the result will be the same." De Pulgar possessed a disdainful manner Thomas had witnessed in many of the Castilian nobles. They believed they ruled the world. Perhaps soon they would, and the world would be the worse for it.

Fernando turned back to Olaf. "To the death?"

The big Northman nodded. "To the death." He had not yet so much as glanced at his opponent, who stood passive, long arms hanging loose.

"Swords, not axes," said Fernando. "And no shields."

"And a knife," said Olaf.

Fernando appeared to think about it for a moment, but it was a reasonable request and eventually he nodded agreement.

"Let us drink a toast, then. To a fair fight and a just result." Fernando held his hand out and de Pulgar placed a bottle into it. Salma came with two cups and handed one to each of the combatants. Thomas wondered why she was so close to the action, but knew she was a woman of strange desires. Perhaps the wine was a gift from Koparsh. Perhaps Salma wanted Hanmman to believe she would also be a gift if he triumphed.

Let the man believe it if he wishes, Thomas thought, for it would never happen. More than likely she was there because Fernando wished to flaunt her strange beauty to the world. No doubt it was another reason Isabel had fled the fighting grounds.

Fernando poured wine into each cup, then drank from the bottle. Red wine dribbled down his beard. The two combatants drained their cups. Thomas wondered at Olaf drinking wine, but knew he had gained a taste for the illicit liquor over the years.

"May God shine his light on this field of combat."

Fernando stepped back and all at once, Olaf and Arnulf Hanmman were enclosed within a circle of men. On the edges, Moor and Castilian mingled. Wagers were set, most placed on their own man. Olaf stripped out of his shirt, his pale skin almost dazzling in the sunlight. Arnulf grinned and followed his example. Both their bodies displayed scars—badges of honour all watchers would recognise.

The conflict began slowly. Arnulf circled Olaf, who stood rooted to the spot. He did not even move his feet when Arnulf went behind him, only turning his head, then turning it fast the other way to pick him up again. Arnulf swung a few lazy strikes to test Olaf's response, each met with a disdainful parry.

Will took Thomas's hand and he looked down to see his son's eyes on his *morfar*. His face was paler than normal, expression set hard. Beyond him, Usaden stood, relaxed as always, but his body swayed in sympathy with the movements of the two men.

It was several minutes before Arnulf made a serious attack. He came in hard, light flashing from both sword and knife. Olaf raised his own sword and caught the blade. He let it slide along until it met his pommel, then struck out with the knife. He caught Arnulf on the arm and blood flowed. It was a shallow cut which would not slow the man, but he stepped away, shaking his head at the suddenness of the strike. Some watchers would also be surprised, but Thomas was not. He had seen Olaf fight before and the man was invincible.

Olaf shook his own head and raised a hand to wipe sweat from his brow.

He stepped forward and attacked. Thomas narrowed his eyes, watching the way Olaf worked. His attack was fast, but it was not meant to end the fight. Not yet. He was testing his opponent, searching out any weaknesses, any strengths. Thomas looked down at Will, whose mouth hung open in admiration. He had never seen Olaf fight, not this closely, but Thomas was sure he would do so again. They all would. With a sense of dread, he suspected it would not be long until he watched Will fight in the same way. It was in the boy's nature, inherited from Olaf, but also inherited from Thomas. There had been times when he had fought with abandon, and for no reason at all.

When Olaf's attack ended, Arnulf was breathing hard, Olaf hardly at all. Thomas glanced across the gathered men and saw some were trying to change their wagers.

"He could have finished him then," said Will.

"He could, but Olaf wants to put on a show for these people.

He wants them to see the strength of Gharnatah."

"He should have killed him. *Morfar* and Usaden always tell me: no mercy."

Arnulf came at Olaf before he had fully recovered. He was fast and strong and forced Olaf back several paces, which surprised Thomas. Arnulf swung a heavy blow which Olaf caught on his blade, then twisted to dislodge the sword from Arnulf's grip. It flew through the air and fell to the ground.

Olaf stepped back.

"Pick it up," he said in Castilian.

Arnulf walked to his sword, his eyes on Olaf the entire time, no doubt expecting some manner of trick, but Olaf allowed him to recover his blade. Thomas saw him shake his head. Olaf raised a hand to his eyes and wiped across them. He glanced at the sun, as if it was too bright.

While he was distracted, Arnulf came at him.

Olaf stepped back, but something was wrong. His balance, usually so sure, had deserted him. Thomas saw him sway and almost fall. He struck out, but this time it was Arnulf who almost sent Olaf's sword spinning.

Olaf stepped back again, then came forwards. As he did so, his feet caught in the dust. He raised his sword high and brought it down, but it was short of its target. As his arm descended, Arnulf dropped his knife and set two hands on the hilt of his sword. He used the grip to swing the blade hard in a wild side-stroke.

For Thomas, the world slowed. He watched the coming contact and knew what was about to happen, but could do nothing to prevent it. At the last moment, Olaf saw the danger and raised his sword arm. He blocked the blow to his neck that would have removed his head, only for the rising blade to slice clean through his arm.

Olaf's sword dropped to the ground, his detached hand still clutching the hilt.

A great noise rose from the watchers, half gasp, half cheer.

Thomas took a step closer, then stopped. He wanted to call a halt to the combat. Something was wrong with Olaf. Something more than the loss of his hand. The man was sick. Or poisoned. Thomas glanced around, searching for Koparsh and Salma, but if they were here, they were lost among the throng.

Arnulf looked down at Olaf's sword and grinned. He raised both arms above his head in triumph, then came in to finish what he had started. He gripped his sword with both hands again and ran at Olaf.

It was only later that Thomas worked out what happened next.

Olaf stumbled and fell backwards as Arnulf's sword swept through the air where his head had been a moment before. He went to one knee, then thrust himself up with all the strength left to him. His left hand rose, clutching the knife, and before Arnulf could recover from what he had intended as a killing blow, Olaf thrust the blade into his chest.

Arnulf grunted.

Olaf stepped away, leaving the knife embedded in his opponent.

Arnulf gripped the hilt.

"No," Thomas said under his breath, but only Will heard him.

Arnulf pulled the knife free. As he did so, a jet of dark blood erupted from the wound and he stared at it before crashing onto his back. His eyes stared at the sky, sightless.

This time, Thomas moved. He went to Olaf and grasped the bloodied stump of his arm.

"I declare Gharnatah the victor!" he cried at the top of his voice. He knew this was the most dangerous moment. He turned to search out Fernando, wondering what his reaction would be. The King's face was dark with anger, but it was clear he could not change the rules, not now, not in front of his own men and the army of Gharnatah.

Fernando met Thomas's eyes and he knew the impossible

had happened. The man hated him even more than he already had.

Beside him, Olaf went to his knees and threw up on the dry ground.

Fernando turned away and pushed through his men.

"I want my hand," said Olaf. "Can you stitch it back on, Thomas?"

"I cannot. But we will take it with us. I would not want someone to steal it away and boast over it."

"I'll take it, Pa." Will had joined them. He knelt and freed Olaf's sword from the grip his hand still had on it, then took both sword and hand in his and stood tall.

Someone came and dragged the body of Arnulf Hanmman away. Thomas hoped Fernando would at least honour him with a Christian burial. He put an arm beneath Olaf and urged him to his feet. He came slowly, his head drooping.

"They did something to me, Thomas," he said. "They drugged me. The wine they gave us."

"I saw you both drink it, Fernando too. Perhaps you are sick."

"I am never sick. I felt as if I had drunk ten bottles of wine, not one mouthful. They meant me dead. Fernando wanted me dead."

"But you are not. Can you walk?"

"I don't know. You fixed me before, fix me again."

"I cannot grow you a new hand, but I can stop you bleeding to death." Thomas held a vice-like grip on Olaf's wrist, but knew the moment he relaxed it, the blood would flow again. He looked around and waved to no one, to anyone. "Is there a cart somewhere? Find me a cart and bring it."

He urged Olaf forwards. Jorge and Usaden supported him on the other side, and then someone brought a cart and they laid Olaf on its bed. Usaden, Jorge and Will drew the cart while Thomas knelt in the back beside the father of his dead bride and fought to keep him alive.

CHAPTER THIRTY-FIVE

It was a week before Thomas knew Olaf would live. The wound had been cleaned and he had picked out the tiny slivers of shattered bone embedded in the flesh. He cauterised the wound before washing the stump and wrapping it in a clean bandage, an action he had repeated three times a day since. Now he sat with Olaf, who had endured all the pain without showing anything.

"I need to ask you something," said Olaf.

"I think I know what it is. Will you ever be able to fight again?"

"Not exactly, I know I can still fight. Northmen are trained to use either hand equally. I can use a sword, a knife, especially the axe with my left hand or right. What I want to know is can you do anything with this stump that will let me hold something?"

"It may be possible, but I would have to remove some bone. It's too sharp as it is now, too close to the end."

"Explain."

"Hold your arm out."

When Olaf did as requested, Thomas unwound the bandage and discarded it. He would burn it later and apply fresh. He touched the healing end of Olaf's wound with the tip of his finger.

"It would have been better had you asked me a week ago, but no matter, I can still do it at the expense of more pain."

"I see why my men love you so much," said Olaf.

Thomas shook his head. "See here? This is bone. Your flesh is starting to knit, but it will be many more weeks until it heals completely. When it does, this bone is going to be too close to the surface. Every time you try to use a weapon—and yes, I think I can do something that will let you hold a knife, possibly a sword, but—"

"And an axe?" asked Olaf.

"Perhaps. I have seen you use one, Will as well, and neither of you grip the handle. You let it swing on a leather thong tied to your wrist."

"Of course we do not grip it, that would be stupid. An axe has a mind of its own, and that mind connects to its master's. I only have to think where my blade should fly and it obeys. It is the same with Will. He is better than me with a sword, and will be better than me with an axe before he is fully grown. It is as the world should be. Our children should always exceed us."

Thomas smiled. "I had hoped Will might want to learn something of my work, but I think he prefers to fight."

"When he is older, perhaps. He will soon be a man, and a man needs to fight when he must. You can fight, Thomas, I have stood beside you, so do not pretend to me you cannot."

"I don't mind, not really. Amal is interested in what I do. She wants to know everything. She reminds me so much of her mother."

"As she does me. I look at her and see Lubna at the same age. It is as if she has returned to us." Olaf raised his eyes to meet Thomas's. "Tell me what you have to do."

"There will be pain. A great deal of pain. I can help with that, but only a little."

"I am used to pain."

"I will have to open your arm and saw a section of bone away, then close the wound and wrap your flesh around the end. If I do it right, you will have a good pad of muscle we can strap some kind of mechanism to. I have already given the idea some thought. We will need someone skilled in wood, but Britto has that, and someone skilled in metal, and that is Jorge's brother, Daniel."

"Will I be able to fight again?"

"Yes." Thomas considered it wise not to add 'if you live' to his answer. Carrying out the procedure was not without risk. He knew he could control the bleeding, knew he could make a clean cut of the bone, but as always when a man was opened up, there was a risk of infection. If that happened, Olaf could lose the entire arm, even his life.

"Then do it. Do it today. Now. The sooner it is done, the sooner I will heal and the sooner I can fight. Gharnatah will need me before the year is out."

"That is too soon."

"I cannot stop the passage of the days, and you know I am right. Call Belia and do what you have to do today."

———

It was another five days before Thomas knew the operation had been a success, ten before Olaf tested the healing flesh and pronounced it good. Jorge and Belia had moved down the hill to Da'ud's house, so there was space for Olaf and Fatima to stay with Thomas and his children. When he had asked Belia about Yves, she told him he had wanted to stay at the house in Santa Fe.

"Alone?" Thomas had asked.

Belia offered a rare smile. "I believe he may have found a distraction."

"A woman? Good."

Now, Thomas sat in front of Olaf.

"Is there any pain?" He examined the stump, four inches shorter than it had been, and knew he had done excellent work.

"There is pain, but less than there was, and it will be less again in a week, even less in a month. I need to fight by then. Can you make me that thing you said you would?"

"I have already told Britto what I need and he says he will bring it later today. Once we fit it, we can attach the ironwork. That will not be so pretty. When I return to Qurtuba next, I will get Daniel to create something more elegant."

Olaf laughed. "Elegant? For me? Whatever you have will suit."

"Daniel's work will let you fight better."

"Then that is what you must do." Olaf turned his head as Amal came into the courtyard. She came to him and leaned close to look at the raw flesh that was still healing.

She raised her eyes and met her *morfar's,* and he nodded. Amal reached out and touched the red skin. Olaf allowed her to prod him until she was satisfied. Thomas watched her with pride. Yes, exactly like her mother. As she grew, Thomas had feared that closeness, both in looks and nature, would only bring him grief. Instead, it did the opposite. She would never be Lubna, but she would always carry her mother within her.

"Martin de Alarcón called last night," Thomas said.

"Has he been talking with Abu Abdullah again?"

"I don't believe so. He came with a message from Isabel. She asks if you are healed yet, and if so, she wants me back at her side."

"Is that wise? You saw how Fernando was. He hates you even more than he did before, and I did not think such was even possible."

"Martin told me he and Isabel barely see each other these days. They have not done so for close to a year. He likes to ride out and destroy things, attack small towns that can put up no resistance, and seduce women like Salma. Though he also told me she is no longer his lover. I believe I will be safe enough at Isabel's side."

Olaf glanced at Amal, then met Thomas's eyes.

"Only at her side?"

"Despite what everyone believes about us, yes. I am with Helena now, you know I am."

"I know you have shared her bed these last weeks while you fixed me, but is that the same thing? Do you love her?"

"People overvalue love. There is friendship between us now."

"I believe she loves you," said Olaf.

"And I believe she believes it, but it is only because I freed her from Abu Abdullah. I am content with that, and so is she. We will see what happens as time passes. Perhaps it will turn into love." He reached out and picked Amal up and set her on his lap. "What do you think, Ami? Would you like Helena to be your new Ma?"

"She is very pretty," said Amal, as if that was reason enough.

Thomas smiled. "She is. Is that good?"

"I want to be pretty one day. Can she show me how, Pa?"

Thomas kissed the top of her head. "You are already more than pretty. You are beautiful."

Amal made a dismissive sound, and both Thomas and Olaf laughed.

———

Thomas and Jorge, together with Belia, the three children, Usaden and Kin, left Gharnatah the following morning. Thomas had asked Helena if she wanted to accompany him. He had grown used to lying beside her at night and knew would miss her companionship even more than the sex, but she said she would stay to care for her father. She would move to the hill until he was fully recovered.

"And after that?" Thomas asked.

"Let us see when the time comes."

Thomas left the others to return to their house when they reached Santa Fe and went directly to the building Isabel had made her headquarters. He felt a nervousness when he thought of meeting Fernando, wondered what manner of reception he might receive. As he passed through the gathered troops, he stopped to ask questions, relieved to discover the King had ridden out only that morning. There were rumours of a band of Moors harassing a small town to the south which Castile now considered theirs. Thomas walked faster after receiving the news, eager to see Isabel. He was aware he had missed her presence. Missed their conversations.

Approaching the building, he saw a familiar figure and ran across to Theresa, who turned to him.

"What did you do with those fine clothes Isabel bought you?"

For a moment, Thomas didn't understand what she was talking about, then it came to him. He had worn the second outfit barely a day before he got Olaf's blood all over it. They were hanging somewhere in his house in Gharnatah, unless Belia had considered them too soiled to save and burned them. Perhaps she had done so in the same fire they used to burn Olaf's hand. Thomas had been busy saving the man's life, but Will told him he had done it.

"I got Olaf's blood all over them."

She looked him up and down, a spark of amusement in her eyes.

"So you come to the Queen of Castile dressed as a desert nomad?"

"I have told you before, these are comfortable and practical." It pleased Thomas when Theresa smiled. Some unrequited spark remained between them, though he knew Martin de Alarcón was the better man for her. "They are also easier to remove in a hurry if need be."

Theresa laughed. "You only say that now because I am

spoken for. One day, perhaps I will not be, and then we will see."

"I am also spoken for," Thomas said, barely knowing where the words came from. "Is Isabel in residence?"

"She is, and she will be pleased to see you. How is the big general?"

"Recovering."

"Fernando found it hard to let you take him away, but I heard him telling de Pulgar that to do anything else would set the men against him."

"I thought he might have tried, even so."

They entered the building, the air immediately cooling. It was a little after noon and the heat was growing. The year was passing, but had not yet fully let go of summer.

"Who is she?" asked Theresa. "Your new conquest."

"Hardly new."

Theresa slowed and turned to him. "I have to leave you here, but you will find Isabel in her offices. She will eat soon and I expect she will ask you to share her meal. When you say not new, do you mean that concubine you used to live with? What is her name?"

"Helena."

"I thought you hated her."

"I did."

Theresa shook her head. "I thought I almost understood you, Thomas Berrington, but I see I was wrong."

"She has changed."

"So have you. I may see you later, you need to hear all the news of what has happened while you were away."

"Come to the house and eat with us."

"Is that a ploy? Will you want to show me all the rooms when I arrive?"

"The children will be pleased to see you. Is there a great deal of news?"

"Perhaps I will come. And yes, much news, but we do not

have enough time now. Later." She rose on tiptoe and kissed his cheek.

After she left, Thomas stayed where he was for a moment, wondering why he had acted as he had. Was Theresa an itch he still needed to scratch? He did not believe so. If not, why had he flirted with her? Perhaps it was only a habit he found hard to break.

When he entered Isabel's office, she was leaning over papers on her desk, the fingers of her right hand stained with ink. She looked up, then rose at once. She came rapidly on small steps to stand in front of him.

"You are back, Sir Thomas. Good. There is much to talk of and much to arrange. You will eat with me?"

"I hear Fernando has ridden out."

"He has. Which means we will not be disturbed. How is Olaf?"

"His hand will never grow back, but he is half-mended already and will soon be as formidable as he was before."

"With only one hand?"

"Olaf claims he fights just as well with the other, and arrangements are being made."

"Good. I assumed you would return today after I sent Martin with the message, so I have arranged a treat for us both. Moorish cuisine."

Thomas smiled as they walked along the corridor to the terrace.

"Are you sure that is wise after the last time?"

"I have eaten spiced food since and look, I am still here, still breathing."

They reached the terrace where a table was set. It afforded a view of al-Hamra, and Thomas knew Isabel ate here most days so she could gaze on its splendour. The pale walls rose sheer from the rock face. The battlements spread across the hillside and beyond, the magnificent dome of the palace mosque showed where Abu Abdullah prayed every morning, noon and night.

"I am glad to hear it. You look well, Isabel."

"No 'Your Grace' today, Thomas?"

"I will if you wish it."

"You know my wish on the matter." Isabel touched his arm, leaving her fingers there a moment. "Come, sit and tell me what you have been doing."

"Theresa tells me there is a great deal of news I have missed."

"The principal item is the meeting with the Sultan. Martin has been hard at work, and I believe it is going to happen soon. We have decided on the location you suggested." Isabel smiled. "I can always rely on my Thomas, can I not?"

"You know you can."

Four servants emerged with covered trays which they set on the table. Isabel took a seat on one side. The only other chair was set opposite her. One servant leaned close to Isabel and pointed out what all the dishes were before leaving. It was becoming a common occurrence, the two of them alone together. One Thomas still found a little shocking. What the servants thought, he dare not even consider. Perhaps Isabel's and his actions, their obvious friendship, sparked the rumours that caused half the army to believe they were lovers.

I have too many lovers, both requited and unrequited, Thomas thought.

"Apparently this is the star of the dishes," said Isabel, pushing a plate of rice mixed with vegetables and some pale meat. The scent of the spices were strong and Thomas felt his stomach grumble. They had left his house on the Albayzin without breaking their fast. "Pour wine and I will put a little out for us both."

Thomas poured pale, cold wine into two glasses as Isabel spooned the mixture onto their plates. He raised his glass.

"To a successful conclusion."

Isabel raised her own and they drank.

"What would you consider a success, Thomas?" Isabel took a small mouthful of the food and closed her eyes. "Oh my goodness, this is exquisite. Try some."

"What I consider a success and what you might will no doubt differ."

"An end to this war I believed might never end?" Isabel took another bite of the spiced dish, washed it down with more wine. A flush coloured her cheeks.

"Yes, that. But it could end with you acknowledging al-Andalus and allowing it to continue in peace. Abu Abdullah would agree, and it would show you in a magnanimous light."

"That I cannot do. You know I cannot."

"I was afraid you would say that." Thomas looked down at his plate before trying the dish Isabel sang the praises of. She was right. He could not remember when he had ever tasted anything so fine. The spicing was layered, shifting from one level to another as he chewed, remaining long after he swallowed. "So if not peace, then an end with dignity. Do you know what Abu Abdullah will demand yet?"

"That is the purpose of our meeting. I will not attempt to humiliate him. Do you know what he might accept?" She fanned her face with a hand. "I believe I might melt."

"It is delicious. Who prepared it? Did you send to Gharnatah again? If so, I hope you chose better this time."

Isabel giggled. Thomas tried to recall if it was the first time he had ever heard her do so.

"No doubt you are aware of my husband's lover. Or should I say ex-lover?"

Thomas frowned, wondering at both the admission and the reason for it.

"I think the whole of Castile does," he said.

"When their affair ended, she went to Theresa and said she wanted to talk to me. She came to apologise for hurting me."

"That doesn't sound like Salma."

"She was sweet. She told me her master forced her to seduce Fernando. Not that it would have taken much effort, for she is exquisite."

"She is."

"She likes you, she told me, but not as much as she likes your son."

"She likes Will?"

"Your other son, the Count. You may not know it, but she has been living with him in your house for the last two weeks. She claims to be smitten."

"With Yves?" Thomas thought back to what Belia had told him and knew he should have taken more notice. Not that it was any of his business who Yves slept with. He was a grown man.

"Do not sound so surprised. He is your son, and I know several women who are smitten with you."

Thomas said nothing. He loaded his spoon with more of the delicious dish, but did not raise it. He was confused as he thought back over their conversation.

"Are you saying Salma cooked this meal?"

"I am. Salma and your son. Is it not exquisite?"

Thomas looked at the food he was about to put into his mouth and set it down.

"Salma was there when Olaf was injured," Thomas said. "It was she who handed the cups to each of them when Olaf was poisoned. It is why he lost his hand. Where is she now?"

Thomas started to rise, but a wave of dizziness ran through him and he gripped the edge of the table. His lips, which had burned with the spice, no longer did so. They were numb, and it was harder to draw air into his lungs. When he looked at Isabel, the flush that had a moment before coloured her cheeks was gone. She was deathly pale, trying to draw breath, but it seemed she could not.

Thomas rose and ran to the edge of the terrace. He thrust two fingers into the back of his throat until he retched and brought up the food he had eaten. When he turned, intending to do the same for Isabel, she had tipped from her chair and was lying on her back with one arm splayed out. Her chest was no longer rising and falling.

Thomas shouted at the top of his voice, "Help! Help the Queen!" And when the first servant ran in, "Go find Theresa. Fetch her. Fetch her now!"

CHAPTER THIRTY-SIX

Thomas rolled Isabel on her side and stuck his fingers down her throat, but she didn't react. He cursed and tried again, then knew there was only one chance. He had used the technique before when nothing else would work, but had only ever had success once.

He put Isabel on her back again, then leaned over her. He laid a hand flat on her chest, searching for a heartbeat and finding one, faint, but at least it continued to beat. He leaned close and gripped Isabel's chin and nose, placed his mouth over hers and breathed into her. He felt her chest rise as he sat up. He took five deep breaths, then repeated the process. He was still doing so when Theresa came in.

"Thomas, what are you doing?"

"I am breathing for her. Help me."

He was relieved when Theresa made no protest.

"Watch what I am doing." He showed her several times. His own head spun, but he thought it was only because of having to breathe too fast to fill his lungs. The poison that paralysed Isabel no doubt still flowed through his blood, but he had eaten less, and ejected what remained in his stomach.

After a dozen breaths into Isabel, he sat up and looked at Theresa.

"Do you think you can do this?"

"I think so." She leaned forward as he had done and took a deep breath.

"Don't use too much force, it requires only a little. Keep your hand flat on her chest. Count to twenty after you breathe into her, then press down to force the air from her lungs. Then repeat. Over and over."

He watched as Theresa copied what he had done, pleased she had taken in everything he had said.

After a while, Theresa stopped and he took over again.

"Should we not move her to a bed?"

"The harder the surface beneath her, the better." Thomas glanced up, aware three servants were watching. "But privacy would be good. I would like to loosen her clothes so her chest moves more easily. These skirts you wear have too much whalebone in them. I'm surprised you can breathe at all."

"She dresses to impress."

"Exactly."

Thomas breathed again for Isabel.

"We can take her to my room," said Theresa. "It is nearby and we can close the door. Is it safe to move her?"

"How long to carry her there between us?" Thomas shook his head. "No, I can carry her, it will be quicker. How far?"

"It is…" Theresa stopped to think "…only fifty paces, perhaps sixty."

A minute at most. Less if he ran.

"Get the servants to clear a way, I don't want anyone slowing us down. And tell them to leave everything here exactly as it is. Nothing is to be moved. Then have them send a message to Fernando, if anyone can find him. He needs to know what has happened. Then send another message to Belia to come, I need her help."

"Will she live?"

"I don't know. Go tell the servants what to do."

Thomas turned back to his task, barely aware how much time passed before Theresa returned.

"Now?" he asked, and she nodded.

He breathed into Isabel three more times, then scooped her into his arms.

"Go. Show me the way."

He ran after Theresa, almost losing his footing as he turned into the corridor. It seemed over sixty steps, but he knew it was only panic that made it feel that way. Theresa crashed through a door and Thomas followed. There was a narrow bed, a table, a chair and a space on the floor where Thomas laid Isabel. Once more, he leaned close and breathed into her mouth. When he laid his hand on her chest, he felt no heartbeat and a sense of despair flooded him. Then he moved his hand and found it. Slower now, almost normal. He breathed again, again, then glanced across to where Theresa stood with her back to the closed door.

"She needs to get out of this dress and any corsets she is wearing. If I stand outside, can you do it?"

"I can, but not breathe for her as well. Stay. I will tell no one."

"Get a blanket, then. I will close my eyes and breathe for her while you do it. Do you have a knife?"

"A knife?"

"It will be quicker to cut her clothing off than undo all these ties. Do you have one?"

Theresa went to her bed and reached beneath the thin mattress. When she drew her hand out, it held a slim stiletto. It looked sharp.

"Perfect," Thomas said.

He breathed into Isabel. Breathed again. He closed his eyes, aware of Theresa moving around him. The next time, when he placed his hand on Isabel's chest to expel the air from her lungs, he felt only bare skin. He tried not to think of what he was doing to the Queen of Castile.

"She is covered again now," said Theresa, close to his ear. "Let me take over. Sit on the bed."

Thomas nodded. His fear had debilitated him. Perhaps that and the little poison he had also ingested. Isabel had eaten more. Much more. He watched Theresa work and tried to think of what poison could act so fast and paralyse the breath as it had done. He came up with nothing, which is why he had sent for Belia.

"You sent those messages, didn't you?" he asked Theresa, as he went to relieve her.

"Both of them, yes." She brushed hair back where it had fallen across her face. "How long do we keep doing this?"

"Until she wakes, or dies."

Theresa stared at him. "How long can we keep doing it? Surely she must grow weaker not breathing for herself."

"Her heart beats strongly, so I believe we can keep her alive for a few hours yet. Once Belia gets here, I will know more. Go to the terrace and check that the servants have touched nothing, as I asked."

Theresa rose and left the room, closing the door behind her. For a moment, a wave of unreality washed over Thomas. He was in the room alone with a near-naked Isabel. Then he breathed into her again, losing his doubts in the work of keeping her alive. He was still doing so when Theresa returned, Belia behind her.

"Look who I found when I went on your errand. The table is exactly as you left it."

Thomas sat up. "Good. Take over here for me." He took Belia's arm. "Come with me, I need your knowledge."

She said nothing, only gave a nod of acceptance. Thomas led the way back to the terrace.

"We both ate the same dish. This one." He pushed the small plate of spiced food with his finger. "Isabel ate more than me, which is why we must breathe for her. Can you tell me what it is, and whether there is an antidote?"

Belia leaned over the dish and sniffed deeply. "I smell only spice, nothing else. Did it taste strange?"

"It is so heavily spiced, it was impossible to tell."

"No doubt they used that to mask whatever the poison is. How did it make you feel?"

"When my lips went numb, I realised something was wrong. I made myself sick and brought most of it back up, washed my mouth out well and drank more water to dilute anything left. I couldn't make Isabel sick. She was unconscious by then and had stopped breathing."

Belia picked up the spoon Thomas had used and took a mouthful of the food. She held it in her mouth a long time, moving it around, then spat it out on the floor.

"I taste spice, nothing else." She shook her head, took another spoonful and this time swallowed. She walked to the edge of the terrace and stared out towards al-Hamra before glancing back at Thomas. "How long before you felt the effects?"

"It was soon."

She nodded and turned away again.

Thomas waited.

A minute passed, then another. A sense of urgency thrummed through his body. He should be with Isabel, keeping her alive. Then Belia leaned over the edge of the terrace and did as he had, making herself empty her stomach. She came back to the table and washed her mouth out, spat, then swallowed a cup of clean water.

"Some kind of mushroom. I cannot think of anything else that has the same effect. There are a few I know of, but which one is it?"

"Does it matter?"

"Of course it matters." She closed her hand around Thomas's wrist. "We should go back to the Queen. There are

307

three I can think of that grow in these lands that may be the cause, but one of them has no cure if someone has eaten too much. Do you know who did this?"

Thomas thought about it as they made their way back. Inside the small room, Theresa continued to breathe for Isabel. Thomas touched her shoulder and knelt to take over, and Theresa sat on the bed. Her face was pale from the effort of breathing for two. As Thomas worked, he considered Belia's question.

When he rose, Theresa came back and took his place once more. He sat where she had, on the bed. Belia came and sat beside him. When she took his hand in hers, it gave some small comfort.

"The Turkish woman," he said. "Isabel wanted Moorish food, spiced food. She told me Salma had prepared some dishes and given instructions for others. Salma handed cups to Olaf and the man he killed in the arranged fight. No doubt she had tainted one of them. I realised it later, but we were all in Gharnatah. If I had returned sooner, Salma would not have poisoned Isabel. This is my fault."

"Do not blame yourself, Thomas. Jorge does not like her, and Jorge likes everyone—especially beautiful women. She may be one of the most beautiful I have ever seen, but Jorge is never wrong about people." She looked to where Theresa knelt over the Queen. "You should go back to the house. Get Jorge and Usaden and your dog and go after her. You might discover what she used. If it is not what I fear, then I can make something up."

"Shouldn't you do that, anyway? If it is one of the others, then will it do any harm?"

"It may. Better that I know first. I can help Theresa, I have seen what you are doing." She gave a soft shake of her head. "Isabel is fortunate you were here. Nobody else could do what you have done for her. Where did you learn such a thing?"

"I don't know, it was a long time ago. It may have been from an old man I met in the high northern mountains when I was young, or I may have read it in a book."

"You read more books than anyone I have ever known."

Thomas laughed, the comfort of Belia's closeness bringing a sense of hope.

"I read more than Jorge, that is true. Isabel told me Salma is no longer thc lover of her husband, but is now with Yves. They have been living together in our house while we were in Gharnatah."

"Well, they are not living there now. There was a woman's scent in Yves' room, but all their clothes had gone. Find the woman and the Queen may wake the sooner."

"I know that, but I cannot leave her, can you not see that?"

"I can." Belia squeezed his hand. "In that case, I should go. I can make up some potions that may work."

"You said they could do harm if they are the wrong ones."

"That is true, but if what Isabel has ingested is the other, then there is no cure. How long can you breathe for her, Thomas?"

Forever, if need be.

"Go then, and hurry."

The door crashed open as Belia rose.

Fernando stepped into the room. Perez de Pulgar stood behind him, together with a short priest Thomas recognised as Isabel's confessor, Hernando de Talavera.

Fernando took in the scene in front of him.

"You are a dead man, Thomas Berrington. And Theresa, stop kissing my wife. What manner of deviancy is this?"

"Isabel is poisoned," Thomas said. "She cannot breathe for herself, so we are doing it for her until she recovers."

"She is naked!"

"Because her chest needs to rise and fall the easier."

Fernando glanced at Belia and scowled.

"Why have you brought that witch with you? What were the three of you going to do to my wife?"

"This blasphemy must stop," said de Talavera, his voice soft. "If Queen Isabel is meant to die, she must be allowed to depart in peace. I will take her confession as she is, but we should take her out of this hellish place."

"Take her out and she dies." Thomas put himself between the three interlopers and Isabel. "Belia, go do what we talked about."

As Belia pushed past Fernando, he grasped her wrist.

"Do you want the Queen to die?" Thomas spoke to Fernando, but his eyes tracked the other two. De Pulgar, he saw, had his doubts. The priest would be too set in his mind to accept what they were doing. Thomas knew he had to take a risk. "Give me an hour, Your Grace. Go find the Turks, Koparsh and his concubine, for they are behind this act. Bring them here so we can question them."

"Are you giving me orders now? Do you think being my wife's lover has elevated you so high?"

"You talk nonsense and you know it. It is your lover who has done this. Bring the Turks here, you will be good at that, and I will be good at what I do. One hour. If she has not recovered by then, the priest can have her."

Fernando stared into Thomas's eyes and he knew there would be a reckoning, but he also saw something that surprised him. Fernando cared about his wife. There had been a moment when Thomas wondered if he would let her die so he could rule Castile and Aragon alone. Now he saw he was wrong. Fernando wanted Isabel to live.

"If she dies, so do you." Fernando turned away. De Pulgar followed, but the priest remained.

"I must pray for her."

Thomas looked around. "Take that chair then, but don't get in our way."

Belia rubbed her wrist where Fernando had gripped her, then turned without a word and ran from the room.

The allotted time had almost passed before Thomas felt

Isabel's chest hitch. Behind him, the priest's soft words sang like music in his ears, hypnotic, somehow soothing if he didn't listen to the words.

Thomas laid his palm on Isabel's chest, fearing the movement had been her heart struggling, but it continued to beat strongly. Then he felt the movement again. Isabel was trying to breathe for herself.

"Theresa, help me roll her onto her side. I think she might be waking."

Theresa knelt behind Isabel and offered support for her. Thomas re-arranged the loose blanket so it covered her. He leaned close and put his ear against her mouth. Was that the faintest breath he could feel or not? If so, it was too faint to be sure.

He rolled her onto her back again and breathed into her.

"Blasphemy," said the priest, without rising from his seat. "If God has seen fit for her body to stop, then we must allow her to ascend to Him without interference. Only Our Lord and His Son have the power over life and death."

Thomas turned, still on his knees, as Theresa took over breathing into Isabel.

"Has a physician never healed you, priest? Has anyone ever removed a rotten tooth to ease your pain?"

The priest met Thomas's gaze without flinching.

"Where do you draw the line?" Thomas asked. "I have saved men in battle who would have died, but they lived to fight again, to do God's work in this war."

"You favour the wrong side. I know you, Thomas Berrington. You are a snake suckling against the Queen's breast. You will burn in eternal hellfire for what you are doing."

"Good. I prefer the heat. Now start your prayers again. Who knows, they might even do some good."

"Thomas!"

Theresa's cry made him spin around, a fear running

through him that Isabel had lost her battle. Instead, her eyes were open and she coughed.

"What...?" It was all she could summon at first. She sucked in her cheeks. "My mouth is drier than the great desert." She sat up, then clutched at the blanket when it slipped. She stared hard at Thomas. "And what have you done with my clothes?"

CHAPTER THIRTY-SEVEN

When Belia returned with Jorge, she carried a small bag from within which Thomas heard the soft chink of glass bottles. Theresa had gone with Isabel to her own room. Thomas sat on the terrace, which was now cleared of food and the floor washed. He rose when his two closest friends entered.

"Is she dead?" asked Belia.

"She woke a quarter hour ago. She may not need your potions, though I would like you to talk to her to satisfy yourself."

"I brought tonics in any case. Is she still in the same room as before?"

"Gone back to her own. Wait here, I will find someone to show you the way. I don't know it myself, only where her office is, though I expect it can't be far from there." Thomas knew he was making little sense, aware of how tired he was. Only a few hours had passed while Isabel clung between life and death, but it felt as if it had been days. He went out to the corridor and sent a message with a guard that one of the Queen's ladies-in-waiting was to be fetched. As the man turned away, Thomas called out, "Do you know if the King has returned?"

"He rode out after noon, but I have not heard if he is back. I understood he might be away several days."

It was clear the man had heard nothing of what had happened and Thomas waved him away. When he returned to the terrace, he caught Jorge embracing Belia.

"Let her loose, I have a job for you. Usaden as well. Is he at the house?"

"Watching over the children," said Jorge.

"Usaden?" Thomas shook his head. He could think of better people to provide child care. No doubt the man would be teaching Amal how to kill an attacker. Thomas smiled. Perhaps he was the right man after all.

"What's so funny?" asked Jorge.

"Nothing. I'm exhausted and my mind constantly slips into flights of fancy. I know who poisoned Isabel."

"Belia said something about the Turks."

"It was Salma, and if she is involved, then so is Koparsh. Even my son. But why? Were they sent here to kill Isabel? Eleanor said it was the French wanted her dead. Why would she lie when she was intending to kill me? Fernando has ridden out to find them, but hasn't returned yet."

"If Salma has done as you claim, and I have no reason to doubt you, they will have fled. It also explains her seduction of Yves, but now we may never find either of them."

"The Turks were here three weeks ago when Olaf lost his hand. Theresa told me Salma had seduced my son and was living in our house with him. She handed out the cups before the fight, and I believe the one she gave Olaf had poison smeared inside it. Not that I can ever prove it now. She had been bedding Fernando, and at first I thought it might involve him, but I saw how devastated he was when he saw Isabel. Salma was still here this morning when she cooked for Isabel, so she can't have gone far."

"You need to ask Usaden, he seems to know everything from his wanderings."

"I can't leave here in case Isabel relapses. I will feel better once Belia has seen her."

The sound of rapid footsteps made Thomas turn to see Theresa come onto the terrace.

"I didn't ask for you, one of her maids would have done."

Theresa frowned, knowing nothing of his message. "Isabel sent me to fetch you. Both of you as you are also here, Belia." She glanced at Jorge. "Perhaps not you, though she is dressed again now."

Jorge raised an eyebrow, but made no comment. Possibly a first for him.

"Go to the house and talk to Usaden," Thomas said. "Ask him to go out and see what he can discover. I'll return later if I can. If not, come back here and we can talk."

Jorge gave a nod and left. Thomas fell into step between Theresa and Belia as they made their way through the corridors of what the soldiers were calling a palace, though poor excuse it was for one.

When they entered Isabel's chamber, she was sitting up in bed, heavy drapes gathered above her. Thomas went and felt her neck, but she swatted his hand away.

"Why do you always do that? It is becoming annoying. Tell me what you have found out."

Poison had not improved her temper, but Thomas understood her impatience.

"Did Theresa tell you what happened?"

"Did you really breathe for me?"

"Theresa and Belia did most of the work."

Isabel ran a hand across her mouth. "My lips are sore and my chest aches. If you kiss all your women this way, no wonder you are still a single man."

Thomas smiled. "I will try to be more gentle next time." It pleased him when Isabel suppressed a smile. It was another small sign of her recovery.

Belia came forward and he stepped to one side, drew Theresa away so they could whisper together.

"Has she been sick?"

Theresa shook her head.

"Complained of any pain, other than her mouth and chest?"

"She tells me her belly aches, and her bones. Is that the poison?"

"More than likely." Thomas glanced to where Belia was talking softly with Isabel. She was also touching her, which now appeared to be allowed. He watched as Belia drew a corked bottle from her bag and set it on a table beside the bed. She searched through the bag and drew out two more before straightening.

"I need something to dilute these with. Wine if there is any, clean water if you can find none. And a cup or glass. I have everything else."

Theresa left the room and Belia came across to Thomas.

"I believe she will recover, but I am going to make a tonic which will help. I will also add something to counter any lingering effects of the poison. She was lucky she ate no more than she did, or I suspect it would be a corpse lying on that bed."

Theresa returned with a bottle of dark wine, the cork already pulled. Belia took it and returned to Isabel. Theresa stood close beside Thomas and her hand sought his.

"You saved her, Thomas." She squeezed his fingers. "If not for you, she would be dead." Her words mirrored Belia's.

"We were lucky I knew how to help, that is all." He watched Belia, recognising her skill, her gentleness. "You also played your part, and played it well. Thank you." He leaned across to kiss her cheek.

"Be careful, I am a taken woman now."

"Which I know well. I like Martin. I like him a lot."

"As do I. But you know I could have been yours. All you

ever had to do was ask, but I came to realise you never would. I had to move on."

"Why?"

"Because I could not wait for you forever."

"No—why did you want me in the first place? I'm no great catch, and as Jorge always tells me, I am not a handsome man."

Theresa cupped his face in her palm. "When has handsome ever meant anything, Thomas? Besides, he is wrong. You are handsome, and the cleverest, kindest, most loyal man I have ever known. That is what a good woman looks for."

Thomas smiled. "What about a bad woman?"

Theresa returned the smile. "I can be bad if that is what you want." The smile turned to a laugh. "What am I saying? My head spins from what we have done this day. Do not listen to me until I have slept."

This time, Thomas kissed her mouth.

"Stop that!" said Belia as she approached.

Thomas looked beyond her to see Isabel had fallen into a doze.

"What else is in that tonic?" he asked.

"She will sleep until tomorrow and her body will heal itself." She looked at Theresa. "Can you stay with her?"

"Of course."

"Then I will stay as well. One of us to watch while the other sleeps. We wake each other when we feel ourselves doze. Thomas, go to the house and tell Jorge I will be back tomorrow." Belia shook her head. "At least I hope I will be back tomorrow."

"If anything happens, send for me. I should stay, but to do so will only anger Fernando the more." He kissed Belia on the cheek, then did the same for Theresa.

"Catch the woman who did this," said Belia as he turned away.

———

When Thomas reached the house, it was to discover only Will and Amal present.

"Where's Jorge?"

"Gone with Usaden." Will sat on the floor, playing a game of dice with Amal. She liked to count the faces to make her favourite numbers. Seven was one of them, nine another.

"Gone where? And why did they leave you both alone?"

"Jorge was going to stay, but I told him I was old enough to look after Ami." Will glanced up. "I am, aren't I?"

Thomas watched his children, a deep love for them welling through him.

"As long as you don't teach her to fight."

"Usaden does that better than me. I want to help. I can help you more if you let me."

Thomas touched the top of Will's head. "I know you can." He folded himself down to sit beside them, touched Amal's cheek and she smiled, her eyes still on the dice. "You still haven't told me where they have gone."

"Your friend Theresa told Jorge what happened to Isabel, and that the Turks had something to do with it. They have gone to find them. I would have gone as well if I wasn't needed here to look after Ami and Jahan."

"The Turks are hard men," Thomas said.

"I beat one before, remember? *Morfar* says I'm as good as any man he has ever seen, apart from three."

"And I expect one of them is him, isn't it?"

Will smiled. "And another Usaden, but I don't mind him being better than me. Is he going to stay with us when Isabel wins the war?"

"I haven't asked, but I would like him to. Who is the third man?"

Will laughed. "Do you need to ask?"

"I do. It might be Fernando, but I don't think so. Perhaps it's one of the Turks. Which one? Koparsh?"

"*Morfar* says it's you, Pa. You fight better than almost anyone. Apart from him and Usaden."

"He's wrong. Once, perhaps, I was that good, but I'm old now and my bones ache. I'm not as fast as I was."

"He says you are still good enough."

"Then that's all right, isn't it?" Thomas rose to his feet. The talk of the ache in his bones reminded him of how uncomfortable he was sitting on hard floors. He was pleased at what Olaf had said, even though he knew he was wrong. Good enough, yes. Thomas knew he would have to be good enough for what was coming. "If I go looking for Jorge, can you stay with Amal?"

"I can go find him for you if you like. They left the best horse behind in case you needed it." Will glanced up at his father. "You look tired. Is Isabel going to be all right?"

"I think so. I hope so. Belia and Theresa are staying with her." He looked towards the window, beyond which the day was fading in a glow of orange light. "And yes, I am tired. I might try to sleep, but send Jorge to me when he returns."

"Can we sleep with you tonight, Pa?" asked Amal. She threw the dice and laughed when they showed a six and a three. Thomas knew about her favourite numbers. He also knew she liked certain combinations that made them up, and six and three was one of those—one number half the other.

————

When a hand shook his shoulder, Thomas came awake slowly. In the light of the candle burning beside the bed, he saw Jorge's handsome face looking down at him.

"What time is it?"

"Late, but Will told me to wake you as soon as we got back."

Thomas glanced to his side. Amal continued to sleep, flat on her back with her arms spread. Jahan was in his cot at the foot of the bed. Will had been beside Amal earlier, but was gone now, no doubt back to his own bed with a complaint his sister wriggled too much and kept him awake, though it was clear who did the wriggling. Thomas sat up, rose and dressed in the clothes he had taken off the evening before.

Usaden was waiting on the small terrace, looking out over the burning campfires of the army a quarter mile away. He didn't turn when Thomas and Jorge approached.

"Tell me what you found," Thomas said.

"First tell me about Isabel," said Jorge. "Is she recovering?"

"She is. Now it's your turn."

Jorge shook his head. "The Turks broke camp the day after Olaf was injured, according to the men we spoke with, but Salma remained behind. With Fernando at first, but not for long. She set her sights on Yves and moved in here, though she has been visiting where Isabel lives often. People there appear to like her, including the head cook. It was she who suggested Salma cook for Isabel."

"I was a fool not to send a message telling Isabel to beware of her. She is also the reason Olaf lost his hand, except that was not her plan. The Turks wanted him dead. So where is she now? And where are the others?"

"The woman and your son travelled north," said Usaden, without turning. Had he not spoken, someone watching might have taken him for a statue. "I assume to join Koparsh and the rest of their band."

"I decided we should return when we hadn't found them by dark," said Jorge. "Usaden wanted to go on, but I made him come back with me."

"He is afraid of the dark," said Usaden. "Kin and I could have followed their spoor on our own. Jorge is a grown man, I am sure he could have found his own way back."

Thomas glanced at Jorge, who shrugged, knowing Usaden meant nothing by his comment.

"Do you remember that house where your lover died?" asked Usaden.

"She wasn't my lover," Thomas said. "Not anymore. And how could I ever forget it?"

"I believe they were headed in that direction. They may turn off, but they followed the same pass as before, so it makes sense their destination lies in that valley."

"Or beyond it," said Jorge, and Thomas knew they had discussed the matter before they arrived at the house. "Pass over the next ridge, as Yves did after Eleanor died, and you open up the whole of Spain."

Thomas pulled two chairs across and sat after offering the other to Jorge. He knew there was no point asking if Usaden wanted one.

"Do you think they are running for home?" He shook his head. "No. Three weeks ago they left, is what you said." He waited until Jorge nodded. "Isabel was poisoned yesterday. Salma prepared the tainted food. Is it the reason they left her here? Did you ask if anyone else had seen them recently?"

"I agree her purpose was to kill Isabel," said Jorge. "And she seduced your son to use him as an accomplice. That cook said they were together in her kitchen."

"I need to find out if Isabel knew Salma was cooking for her." Thomas shook his head. "It makes no sense she would allow her to do such a thing after she seduced Fernando."

"Isabel knows full well what her husband is like. Knows she cannot change him. I suspect she bears his conquests no ill-will, for they have little choice but to submit to the majesty that is King Fernando of Aragon and Castile. The rumours I hear claim he has bedded over half her ladies-in-waiting. You can ask Isabel why she let Salma cook for her when you see her in the morning. Unless she is dead by then."

"She is getting better. Belia and Theresa are looking after her. You are right—Isabel must know how Salma came to be there to prepare the food." Thomas clenched his fists. "Salma is the one we need to find, and Yves if he is still with her. Koparsh left her here for one purpose only. To kill Isabel."

"Do you think Fernando knew what she was going to do?"

Thomas turned to look at the sky. Was that the faintest glimmer of the coming dawn in the east?

"That thought occurred to me, but no, I don't believe he did, and he already hates me enough. I can't ask him such a question. I need to talk with Isabel's kitchen staff and find out when Salma arrived, and when she left. Her trail will be fresh and we can use the bedding she slept in with Yves for Kin to track her. That perfume of hers is unmistakable."

Usaden finally turned to face them. "I will go and do that. Your son's bedroom stinks of her. Jorge can stay here, Kin and I can track a lone woman. Or the two of them if Yves is still with her and has not been disposed of now his use is over."

"I want her brought back here. I have questions. Do you promise not to kill her?"

"If I can manage it, but I suspect the Turks will not be so far from where we are now. She will have gone back to them." Usaden shook his head. "They may even kill her themselves now she has failed."

"Except they don't know she has failed. Nobody does." Thomas rose, a fresh urgency filling him. "Yes, Usaden, go seek them out. I will talk with the kitchen staff and see what I can find out."

CHAPTER THIRTY-EIGHT

Thomas saw a slim figure standing in the doorway as he approached Isabel's quarters. Jorge also saw her and ran ahead to embrace Belia. Thomas walked at a slower pace, allowing them a moment together.

"Are you waiting for me?" Thomas asked when Jorge released her.

"You cannot go in. Fernando and that sour priest are with her."

"Has she worsened?"

"On the contrary. She is more herself than normal, but ask Theresa, who knows her better than me. Isabel and Fernando are arguing, so I thought it wise to wait out here for you." She smiled. "I knew you would come before it was full light."

"What are they arguing about?"

"The war, and you."

"Me?"

"Do not look so surprised, Thomas. I know how the Queen feels about you. Jorge tried to explain it to me and I did not believe him, but I talked with Theresa in the night and she said the same thing. You and Isabel are more like man and wife than she is with that man."

"*That* man?"

"I left when the shouting grew too loud. I did not want to remain in the room any longer, but Theresa stayed. To protect the Queen, I think. Isabel told me she would meet you in the usual place."

"The usual place? Is that what she said?"

"It is. I assume you know where she means?"

"I might. Are you going back to the house with Jorge?"

"I should stay with her. I would like to give her another dose of tonic, and be there if you need assistance."

"I don't suppose you know if the kitchens are open yet, do you?"

"How would I know that?"

"How long do you think they will be arguing?"

"I do not know that either, but if asked to guess, I would say not too much longer. A storm that violent cannot last. Are you going to show me where we should wait?"

"You can come with me. I want to find out what the cooks know about the food they served us."

Thomas led them deeper into the building. He had no idea where the kitchens were, but his nose led them in the right direction. The room was set at the back with a wide doorway thrown open to let the cool air of dawn in. A dozen women worked, all bustle and skill, each knowing their role. Maria de Henares, the cook Thomas had spoken with after Theresa fell ill, came across as they entered.

"Tell him we are working as fast as we can," she said as Thomas approached.

"Tell who?"

"The King. He has asked me to prepare special food. Something plain. And fish. How am I supposed to get fish at this time of the day? I sent someone to the river, but have no idea if they will catch anything. Are you not with them?"

"Fernando asked this?"

"He is the King, is he not? What is it you want? I can probably find a girl to make you something to break your fast, but it will not be fancy."

"I need to ask you about the meal prepared for the Queen yesterday."

"If you can talk while I work. I have no time to stand and indulge in idle chatter."

"You know what happened, don't you?" Thomas watched as Jorge strolled away to talk with some others. Belia held back a moment, then joined him.

"I heard the Queen was taken ill, but it was nothing I made, I can promise you. Is she recovered?"

"I will know that when I am finished here. Go back to your work, we can talk as you do. Was it you prepared the spiced dishes?" Thomas accompanied her to a well-worn table where bowls, flour, vegetables and meat lay scattered on various plates. As they moved further into the room, the heat grew, making sweat break out on his skin.

"Not the spiced ones, no. I do not approve of spice, I believe I have told you that before. It is bad for the system. No doubt it is that which caused the Queen to fall ill, you mark my words."

"I will try to remember them," Thomas said. "So who prepared those?"

"The Frenchman."

Thomas stared at the woman as she tipped a lump of dough from a bowl, scattered the surface with flour and began to knead it. That had not been the answer he expected.

"What Frenchman? I heard there was a woman here, a Turk, very beautiful."

"There was, but it was the man who did most of the work. I had no idea the French knew spices, but he claimed to do so."

There was only one person who could be the Frenchman. Yves and Salma had been setting up home together while everyone was in Gharnatah. Had they been doing more than sleeping together? Plotting, perhaps?

Thomas realised he had been a fool. He should have pressed Yves harder about his involvement in Eleanor's work.

"Who appointed them?"

"I believe it was the Queen herself who asked them to cook for her. That was the story they told me, in any case."

"Did you not check?"

"I heard the Turkish woman has become close to both King and Queen. Someone like me does not question the word of their masters."

"But Isabel did not tell you directly."

"Why would she do that? I told you, the woman spends time here and the man is also familiar. I tasted their dishes, of course. They were good, if you like food that burns your mouth so you can barely taste anything else."

"Did they act like a couple?"

The cook continued to knead the dough, tendons standing out in her arms.

"They did. I caught them kissing once. I don't hold with kissing in a kitchen. It is not hygienic."

"No, I expect not. There was a rice dish mixed with meat, raisins, mushrooms and vegetables. Who prepared that?"

"I did."

Thomas stared at the woman. "I thought you did not hold with spices, and that dish was heavily spiced."

"They told me they had not enough time to prepare everything, so they gave me instructions and I followed them. But I could not tell if it was correct. The woman did that and approved my work."

Thomas was even more confused. "Salma tasted the dish?"

"That was her name. Now you say it, I recall the man calling her by it. And yes, she did. She said it needed more spice and added that herself at the last moment."

"I don't suppose you heard her call him by name, did you?"

The woman looked into space for a moment before shaking her head.

"Not as I recall. Is it important?"

"It might be. Why did you allow two people you don't know access to your kitchen after what happened when Baldomero came here?"

"I heard what he did, even though I still cannot believe it. I also heard he was dead, so there was no reason to suspect someone else would try to poison the Queen."

"You told me before you know Bazzu. So do I, and when I spoke with her, she didn't recall your name."

"That is because it was different then, before I married. I assure you, she knows me. Do you suspect I am involved in some manner, sir?"

"That is what I am trying to find out. Did anyone else taste the dish?"

"Only the woman. Salma. It is a pleasant name, is it not? Heathen, though, no doubt."

"No doubt. Did the man with her taste any food?"

"Some, but not that dish."

A servant entered and said the King was ready to eat. The woman shooed Thomas away and turned back to her work. Thomas drifted through the kitchen, watching the industry going on, impressed at how everyone knew their role and carried it out without need for instruction. He met Jorge and Belia at the door and they went into the long corridor that ran the length of the building from front to back. Here the walls were unadorned. Closer to the front, tapestries hung as well as portraits of Isabel, Fernando and their children. And horses. Fernando liked pictures of horses, preferably with armed warriors mounted on their backs.

"The head cook prepared the poisoned dish, but did not try it," Thomas said, his steps slowing. "She said Salma did, and added extra spice at the very end. I suspect that spice contained the poison she used."

"I heard a man accompanied her. You know who he was, don't you?"

"Yves."

"Two of the cooks heard them speaking and she used his name. His mother was involved in the first attempt on Isabel's life, and now he's involved in this one."

"Yes, he is." Thomas felt a sense of despair. He had discovered a grown son only to find out he was a killer, just like his mother. "If Yves is guilty then he must be punished, but I have grown to like him. I need more proof before I am convinced of his guilt. I am confused."

"Is that meant to be news?"

"Theresa was poisoned when Baldomero came from Gharnatah. The head cook allowed two more strangers to cook for Isabel. Why would she do such a thing after Theresa nearly died?"

"Everyone we spoke with told us it was Isabel who sent them."

"But did they hear her speak those words themselves, or was it only what Yves and Salma told them?"

"Several of the girls told me Salma has become a familiar figure among Isabel's court. They all know about her and Fernando, but I believe half of them have tumbled with him in the past. He has both a reputation and a position. It is difficult for anyone he sets his sights on to say no. Even the head cook, I heard. I believe it was she who told the others that Isabel had sent Salma and Yves to cook for her."

They had walked half the length of the corridor when Theresa appeared from a side room.

"There you are. She wants you."

"On the terrace? Is Fernando there?"

"He is, but she is in a smaller room. She wants to speak with you in private. I am sorry, Jorge, but she insisted on Thomas only."

Jorge turned to Thomas. "We will return to the house. Is there anything either of us can do before you arrive?"

"Not yet, let me think on matters first. See if you can find out if Salma was seen around this place, and who with."

After he was gone Theresa said, "I can tell you about Salma. She befriended several of Isabel's ladies-in-waiting. She even befriended me. I liked her. And your son visited with her frequently. I think some ladies took a liking to him. He is a Count, a man with a position, so of course they liked him."

"Did they ever visit Isabel?" Thomas wondered how he could have been so stupid as to accept Yves' story.

"Not that I heard, and I hear everything to do with her."

They walked side by side along the corridor. Raised voices came from outside, but Thomas ignored them. No doubt men arguing, as they always did. The lack of any plan to attack Gharnatah did not sit well with the gathered troops. They wanted action, whether or not it was the right kind.

Isabel wanted him. That was his only concern.

"I was not aware you even knew who Yves was."

"He came to the palace in Córdoba last year with his mother, didn't he? Isabel should never have allowed them access then, it has only caused trouble ever since. And now this. If he is responsible for what happened, I will kill him with my own hands." She gave a small laugh at her show of anger. "Perhaps better I get Martin to kill him for me."

"You would have him kill my son?" Thomas felt pulled in a dozen directions, at the mercy of tides of loyalty and family.

"Forget I said anything. She is in here." Theresa stopped outside a closed door. "She said for you to go straight in. The servants will bring food for you both. After it has been tasted."

"At last," Thomas said. "She should have done as I asked at the start and none of this would ever have happened."

"I agree, so do not berate me, tell her." Theresa turned and walked away. Thomas might have watched her go at one time, but now he opened the door and entered the room.

It was smaller than he had expected. Isabel sat at a table that took up a full third of the space. There were two chairs set on opposite sides and Thomas took his.

"I hear you are having your food tasted."

"Before you say anything, yes, you were right."

"Who is doing it?"

"Captured prisoners. They are kept in a stockade nearby—but not so near we can smell them. They are made to eat everything before I do. I believe the system will work, though it has not been tried before."

"Moorish prisoners?"

"Of course Moorish prisoners." Isabel met his eyes, a sharpness in hers. "At least they are used to spiced food."

Thomas knew trying to argue with her was pointless. She was only doing what he had asked. And who did he expect would be chosen? The role was meant for those who were dispensable.

"I assume it was not you who sent Salma to the kitchens to cook spiced food for you?"

Isabel frowned. "I did not, though I have seen her around for some time now. In the company of your son, which told me she must have changed. Better him than my husband." She shook her head. "I cannot banish all the women he has ever slept with, or I would have no staff left to serve me. Even Theresa."

Thomas stared at her. "I never heard that before."

"It should not surprise you. It was a long time ago, shortly after you cured Juan. Theresa is pretty, though sometimes he does not even need them to be that. It was only the once, she told me, and left her unsatisfied." Isabel looked as if she was about to add something, but stopped herself.

Thomas gazed into space, connections forming in his mind only to be discarded. Salma and Yves. Was it as simple as that? How far back was their relationship formed—only in recent weeks, or much earlier? Eleanor had lied about her commission coming from the French King. Did that mean it came from Koparsh? Had Yves and Salma known each other all this time?

He opened his mouth to ask once more about the head cook, but before he could do so, the door opened and two women brought in food. They laid it on the table and started to back out.

"Has it been tasted?" asked Isabel.

One woman bowed. "It has, Your Grace. All of it. An hour since, so we heated it up again for you."

When they had gone, Isabel said, "Reheated food. Is this what my life has come to?"

"At least you have a life."

"Thanks to you." She suppressed a smile as she picked out a few morsels. "And next time you put your lips on mine as I lie naked before you, I hope you make sure I am awake first."

Thomas stared at her, unsure if she had made a joke or not until she gave a tiny laugh.

"Eat, and tell me how you intend to find whoever tried to steal my life." She sighed. "If I lay dead now, I know not what would happen to this war. Fernando is too harsh. He would punish the city even though its gates stand open. He does not understand there is a different way, but you do. Find them, Thomas, but you also need to arrange this meeting with Boabdil. I am filled with a new energy and must use it before it leaves me."

"I will ask Belia to send you more of her tonic."

"Do that. And there is one more task I have for you."

"Ask it."

Isabel stared at him. "I need you to find somewhere remote, but close to the city. I must stare on the palace. It calls to me. You know it does. I would set my eyes on its wonder, and you will find me somewhere from where to do so. Go do what you are good at, but return here shortly after noon and you will show me where we can watch from."

Thomas stared at her until she waved her fingers.

"You can go now. This food is perfectly safe. You will not need to put your mouth on mine again."

CHAPTER THIRTY-NINE

"What is in that tonic you give her?" Thomas watched as Belia mixed herbs together. She ground them with a pestle and mortar, then tipped them into boiling water. "Is that more you are making? She asked for more."

"She will. It raises the spirits of a woman in a wondrous way."

Thomas stared at Belia, her black hair, eyes almost as dark. He had joined his body with hers, but believed he barely knew her.

"She wants me to find somewhere she can observe al-Hamra from."

Belia laughed. She picked out three pale leaves and cut them into small pieces.

"Your house on the Albayzin offers a fine view of the palace."

"Why didn't I think of that? The Queen of Castile walking through the Albayzin."

"Its people would no doubt rise up and follow her, for they have no love for Abu Abdullah."

"I still think not. Isabel is different today, is that the tonic?"

"Possibly. She came close to death. She would have died if

not for you. That can change a person, but most likely it is the tonic. What else does she have for you to do?"

"Nothing much. Only to conclude arrangements for a meeting with Abu Abdullah, find this wondrous place I have no idea where to look for, and catch those who tried to kill her. I have a mind to talk to the cook again."

"Do you think it involves the cook?"

"I intend to confront her until she tells me the truth. It's possible Koparsh paid her to let Salma and Yves cook for Isabel, and she doesn't want to admit it. If there is truth in that, it also explains why Baldomero was used."

Belia glanced at Thomas, her expression stern, but he knew that meant nothing.

"You do not have to do everything yourself. Use your friends. Send Jorge to talk to the cook. Send Usaden to track down Salma. Set me to making this tonic for Isabel."

Over in one corner, Jahan, lying in his wicker cot, began to complain. Belia glanced across and gave a sigh.

"He is hungry all the time these days. Here, finish cutting the leaves as fine as you can, then steep them in the mixture. Let it boil while you count to three hundred, then filter the liquor into that jar."

"Will it be finished then?"

"Almost. Do you think you can manage a task as complex as that?"

"I will do my best. You need to feed Jahan solid food. You cannot keep him at your breast until he is a grown man."

"Jorge never complains."

"Jorge wouldn't, would he?"

Thomas turned back to the task set before him. He had seen Belia feed Jahan often enough to feel no discomfort at the sight, but he had a job to do. He finished cutting the leaves, set them in the hot water and counted.

Jorge came into the room.

"Usaden has found what you need."

Thomas held a hand up, his lips moving as he reached ninety.

"He is counting for me," said Belia. "Do not disturb him."

"Counting? Are you sure he can count?"

"I am doing it as well in case some foolish person should come and distract him."

"Should I stand at the door to prevent such a thing?" asked Jorge.

"Are there any foolish people left out there?" Belia lifted Jahan from her breast, uncovered the other and set him to suckle there.

Thomas reached three hundred. He pressed fine muslin into the wide neck of the bottle Belia had set for the purpose and used tongs to pour the dark liquor into it. When the beaker was empty, he set it aside, but not before he sniffed the dark mess remaining. He recognised some scents, but not all.

"There is honey on the shelf," said Belia. "Pour a little in, but not too much. Just enough to take the bitterness away."

"How will I know how much that is?"

"Taste, Thomas. It is what any good apothecary does, the same as a cook. Otherwise, how are we to know when our work is done?" Jahan had gone back to sleep and Belia laid him in his cot before covering herself.

"Can't you do it? You're finished now, aren't you?"

"I am trying to teach you something."

"But not the recipe."

"Perhaps I will reveal that secret to you when you have set a girl in my belly. I trust you have not forgotten that is one more duty you must carry out?"

"Jorge never allows me to." Thomas found the honey and used a small spoon to add a tiny amount to the mixture. Once it had dissolved, he used the same spoon to taste the warm liquor and pulled a face. Too bitter.

He added two more spoonfuls and tried again. Better.

"How much of this does Isabel take?"

"Theresa knows, but about as much as you have taken now."

"I assume it is not poison."

"I need to keep you alive, remember?"

Thomas passed the bottle to Belia before turning to Jorge.

"All right, what has Usaden found out? Has he found Salma or Yves? I suspect if he finds one, he will find the other."

"He says he has the perfect place for your tryst with Isabel."

"Tryst? What are you talking about?"

"The way Usaden explained it to me, you asked him to find somewhere safe where you and she could steal away to be alone together."

"What else did he say? You know there is something else."

Jorge waved a hand in dismissal. "He might have mentioned it must be within sight of al-Hamra."

An hour later, Thomas stood beside Usaden looking at a small farmhouse while Kin chased rabbits that ran from beneath one side of the wall, where they had made a burrow beneath the abandoned building.

The walls were solid, rising two floors, but half the roof had caved in. At some time in the recent past, a fire had been set and allowed to burn.

"What is it like inside? Safe?"

"Take a look. I will stay here in case anyone comes."

Thomas looked around. The house sat closer to Gharnatah's walls than the Castilian army, and a stand of trees that had escaped Fernando's firestorms offered cover almost the entire way there.

"Who is going to come?"

"Would you prefer I am not ready if they do? The door on this side is sound, but the further one is not."

Usaden turned to survey the approach. Thomas knew when he was dismissed and entered the building. The lower floor took up the entire space. A narrow set of stairs led to a hole in the ceiling, and Thomas tested each tread as he ascended. Upstairs comprised of two bedrooms by the look of the furnishings, not that there was much left of them, though one bed was intact. It stood in the room Thomas knew was perfect for Isabel's purpose. A window in the eastern wall had fallen out, together with some of the surrounding stone. The opening framed the palace sitting on top of its red hill. Thomas felt he could reach out to touch its walls. Yes, this was the place.

He turned and descended the stairs and went outside to thank Usaden, who shrugged. All he had done was what was asked of him. No thanks were needed.

———

"I do not think she is well enough for this madness." Theresa blocked Thomas's way, her arms crossed. He could have brushed past her, but didn't.

"It's been almost a week, and Belia's tonic has worked a miracle."

"I still think it too dangerous. I have told her so, but she refuses to listen to me. She is obsessed with that damned palace." Theresa stared into Thomas's eyes and he wondered what this was really about. "I should come with you."

"Then you would also be in danger. Not that there is going to be any danger. None at all."

"Is that Thomas?" Isabel's voice sounded from the room Theresa was trying to stop him entering. "Send him in, I am ready." Her voice was bright with excitement and an edge of mischief.

Theresa leaned close and whispered into Thomas's ear, "If you let any harm come to her, I will ensure you die a slow and painful death."

Thomas grinned and kissed her cheek. As he turned away, Theresa held out her hand. Gripped in it was a linen sack containing something weighty.

"You will need this. Isabel asked for food for the journey."

"Who made it?"

"I did."

Thomas took the sack, then brushed past her into the room. He wondered if Belia's tonic was having an effect on him too. He felt as if he hadn't a care in the world, and in that he knew he was wrong.

Isabel stood ready, but if he hadn't heard her voice, he may not have recognised her. She was dressed as a boy, dark hose, brown shoes, white linen shirt and brown vest. Her lustrous hair was tied up and forced beneath a cap. She gave a little curtsy.

"Will I pass as an ordinary person, Thomas?"

"I believe you will. Even so, I have worked out a route that avoids us being seen."

Isabel came across and took his hand. "This will be our secret, yes?"

"Yes."

"If Fernando discovers what we are about to do, he will be angry. Even more angry than he usually is. Did Theresa threaten to have you hung by your heels should anything happen to me?"

"Worse."

"Good." Isabel released his hand and made for the door.

When Thomas followed, he found Theresa no longer standing guard. The long corridor was deserted, as arranged, and they headed for the rear door. Outside, a breeze from the north tempered the heat of the day. Thomas pulled his tagelmust around his face to hide it before stopping. Everyone knew who he was by the way he dressed, but if anyone saw them, with luck they might consider the figure beside him to be his son. Except if they knew Will, it would be obvious Isabel was far too slight, and despite her clothes, she still walked like a woman. Fortunately, they saw only a few people, and none of them showed any interest.

Thomas pointed to the tree-line and they made their way

337

towards it. Once they were beneath the wood's cover, the air cooled even further.

"Is it far?" asked Isabel. Her hand came out and sought his and Thomas allowed the touch, aware of something different between them. Perhaps her brush with death had changed her. Escaping death had a habit of changing people. Sometimes for the better, more often for the worse. He was still unsure about the new Isabel. She was softer and looked younger, her manner also that of a girl rather than a grown woman with a host of responsibilities.

They stayed in the wood for some time, Isabel's hand in his the whole time. Birds sang, and now and again some animal crashed away through the undergrowth, but Thomas never saw what it was. He knew there were ibex, boar and even lynx nearby, but he feared none of them.

Isabel stopped when they came out and she saw the farmhouse and, beyond it, the rising walls of al-Hamra.

She turned to him. "This is the place?"

"It is."

"Oh, Thomas, it is perfect. Thank you." She squeezed his fingers.

Thomas looked around to discover they were not alone. Usaden sat on the hillside, his knees drawn up. Kin lay on his side at his feet. Thomas gave a nod and Usaden nodded back.

Thomas drew Isabel forward and they closed the narrow gap to the farmhouse.

"We need to climb the stairs," he said. "I tested them and they will take our weight, but I will go first, you come up after."

Isabel looked around, unimpressed with the state of repair of the building.

"Are you sure the walls are sound?"

"Sound enough, and there is nowhere better."

"Then let us go." She released his hand, but he offered it again when she followed him.

As they rose into the upper room and Isabel turned to the

338

broken window, she gasped, her eyes wide. The afternoon sun painted the walls of al-Hamra in a soft light. It might have been only a hundred paces away rather than five times that.

"It is truly a wonder," said Isabel.

"Sit on the bed." Thomas led the way. "You can gaze on the palace as much as you like from there. I moved it so your view is unbroken."

"You will sit with me?"

"It would not be seemly, Your Grace."

She slapped his chest.

"Who will ever know?" She walked to the bed and sat after examining the covers. They were clean. Thomas had seen to that. She gazed across at the palace. "Do you think they can see us as well as we can see them?"

"The sun is behind this house, so the room is in shadow. Nobody can see anything within it from that direction."

"Was that your man I saw on the hillside with your dog?"

"It was."

"Will he say anything?"

"Usaden?"

Isabel laughed, raising a hand to cover her mouth. She looked around.

"Perhaps we can repair this house and come here together. It could be our secret place. We can have assignations."

Thomas went to the bed and placed a hand on her brow, wondering if she had a fever, but it was cool to his touch. Isabel turned her head so his palm ran across her cheek and he withdrew it quickly.

"Sit beside me." It was an order, but one Thomas was content to follow. He ensured there was a seemly space between them when he sat.

"What is that? And that?" Isabel pointed, and Thomas explained about everything she asked. She wanted to know who the people on the ramparts were and he told her. She wanted to know how many rooms and he said he had no idea, but soon she could count them for herself. She wanted to know how many people lived in the palace, how many in the city, and he lied to her, unsure if the information might not be used against it.

Without being aware of either of them moving, Thomas felt the slightness of her against his flank. When he turned, she was no longer looking out at the palace, but up at him, her eyes wide, sharp with some emotion he dared not even try to understand, only that he was sure she would see the same need in his own. This place, this moment, was outside of time. They were cut loose from all ties and responsibilities.

"Oh, Thomas," she said, and when Isabel lifted her face, Thomas lowered his head and kissed her. She clung against him, gripping his shoulders as she pulled him back onto the bed.

CHAPTER FORTY

Thomas was unaware he had fallen asleep until a hand shook his shoulder. He opened his eyes to find Isabel leaning over him. Her hair hung free, fine strands stroking his face to enclose them both in a golden tunnel.

"Men are coming."

He rolled off the bed and went to the window. He saw no one between Gharnatah and the house, but when he leaned out and looked north, half a dozen men on horseback were riding fast towards the house.

"How did you see them?" He turned to Isabel, who still sat on the bed.

"I told her."

Thomas spun around. Usaden stood at the head of the stairs, as still as he always was. Thomas wondered how much he might have seen, knowing whatever it was didn't matter because he would never speak of it. He saw Isabel glance at Usaden and a flush coloured her cheeks, showing she shared his thoughts.

"Only six men?" Thomas said.

"Agreed, but I think they are Turks. They are outstanding fighters. Do you have a weapon?"

Thomas patted his hip. "A knife, nothing more."

"Then it is fortunate I thought to bring another sword."

"Are they coming for Isabel?"

"Well, they do not want me. I know you have made enough enemies to make you their target, but I would judge it the Queen they are after."

"Theresa is going to kill me," Thomas said under his breath.

"Only if the Turks do not. How do you want to do this? We could stay here and fight as they climb the stairs, but I would rather do it outside. Leave her here, it is as safe as anywhere else."

"And if they kill us both?" Thomas leaned out again, feeling the stone he gripped move beneath his touch. This whole adventure had been a bad idea.

"She is no more at risk here than outside. Less so."

Isabel rose and came across the room.

"Go, Thomas, fight them. I will find somewhere to hide. Under the bed if I have to. Besides, they will not kill you, nor Usaden. I know you both. You cannot be killed."

Thomas wished he believed her. He pressed his knife into her hand, not knowing if she even knew how to use it. He thought of stealing a last kiss, aware that was what it might be, but did not want to do so in front of Usaden. But when he turned away, Usaden had gone, and Isabel grasped his wrist.

"This will always be our magical day, Thomas. Thank you, my love." She raised her face to his, and then Thomas followed Usaden down the stairs.

As he stepped through the rear door, Usaden thrust a sword into his hand. Kin was already running towards the approaching men, who were close now. At this distance, Thomas saw Usaden was right, they were the Turks, but he couldn't see Koparsh among their number. How did they know where he and Isabel were, and how did they know they would be unprotected? Except they were not.

Kin reached the lead horse and snapped at its ankles. For a

moment, Thomas feared the horse would trample the dog, but Kin was too fast, too agile. He inflicted no damage, but he made the horses lose their stride. In one case so badly, a rider was thrown clear.

Five men now. The odds had improved.

"Over there," said Usaden, showing where he had been sitting with his back to a low cliff. "Better we have height."

Thomas ran after him, knowing he could not keep up and not trying. When he glanced back, the men had changed direction and were heading to cut them off. Except Usaden was too fast. He turned to confront the first man, ducking a wild swing of the rider's sword.

Thomas discovered himself separated from Usaden by the five men. He glanced back at the farmhouse, relieved to see nobody had gone to it. The Turks had formed an outward facing circle. Three men confronted Thomas, two Usaden. They had marked him as the smaller and so less dangerous. It was a mistake that had seen men killed before, and today was no different.

Usaden attacked at an impossible speed at the same moment Kin returned to the battle, once more snapping and snarling beneath the horses. The dog leapt and sank his teeth into the thigh of one man, who flailed out with his sword, but Kin was already gone.

Thomas ran at the man on his right, ducked his sword and plunged his own blade into his belly. The man swung again, but there was no force to the blow and he clung to the reins as his horse cantered away. The other man dismounted, knowing Thomas would be easier to fight on the ground. In most circumstances, it would have been the right decision, but the man had forgotten about Kin. The dog streaked in and caught his sword wrist. Kin shook his head, snarling as blood spattered from his lips. Thomas almost felt sorry for the man until he remembered why he had come.

When he looked up, he saw Usaden had killed two of the

men, but the third had fled. Already he was two hundred paces away, his body laid almost flat against his horse as he urged it to greater speed. Thomas stepped close to the man Kin had by the wrist and ran him through without a moment's regret.

"Shall I follow him?" asked Usaden, his hand on the reins of one of the horses.

"We both will, once I check that Isabel's safe."

"Take her back. Take two of their horses, then come and find me."

"I can never track you. Go, follow and return to tell me where he goes."

"Do you want me to kill him if I catch him?"

Thomas looked at the farmhouse, something working its way to the top of his mind. He glanced around. Four men littered the ground. A fifth was fleeing.

"If you catch him, bring him back. I assume you can do that?"

"I would rather kill him."

"And I would rather question him to find out why they came. Nobody knew I was going to bring Isabel here."

"Somebody must have." Usaden swung into the saddle. Normally he rode without one, but Thomas knew he could ride anything. "All right, I will bring him back to you. If I catch him, which grows less likely the longer we talk. I can always kill him after you have asked your questions. Kin, come!" Usaden urged the horse into a gallop.

Thomas turned back to the farmhouse, then ran. There had been six men. One was missing. He ran harder.

He found Isabel sitting on the bed, and at first he thought his fears without foundation. Then he saw the blood.

He pushed her down and patted her body, but found no wound, despite the blood that soaked her front. Then he saw his knife discarded on the covers.

"Where is he?"

Isabel stared into space, and Thomas shook her hard.

"Where is the man?"

Isabel blinked as she regained her wits.

"He fell through the window."

Thomas rose and went across to it. When he looked down, he saw a body. From the amount of blood pooled around it, the man had to be dead.

"Who knew you were coming here?"

"Only Theresa."

"Theresa would never betray you, but somebody has. The Turks knew you were here. They have tried to take your life before, and this time they risked a direct attack. Would Theresa have told anyone? Martin, perhaps?"

"Martin would not betray me either. Perhaps they followed you the first time you came here."

Thomas thought about her words before shaking his head.

"Usaden was with me, he would have known if we were being watched. He has uncanny senses."

When Thomas looked up, tears streaked Isabel's cheeks.

"This was the happiest day of my life, and now the memory of it will be forever tainted." She picked the knife up and Thomas reached out and took it from her, knowing she spoke the truth. It was one more turning point. Had the attack not come, their lives might have shifted on their axes. But the attack had come and Isabel had taken a life. Almost certainly for the first time.

"There are horses outside. I have to get you back."

"Can I come to your house? I do not want to return to the real world yet." She stared at him until Thomas nodded, though exactly why he did so, he couldn't say.

"The children will be pleased to see you."

"Who were they?" She looked through the window at the now deserted landscape, her eyes drawn to the palace. "Where are the others?"

"I'm convinced Koparsh sent them. Now they're all dead but one, and Usaden is after him."

"Then I feel sorry for him. Will he kill him?"

"I hope not. I asked him to bring him back so I can find out why they came. Find out who told them you would be here. This is no coincidence. They knew it would only be the two of us. We were lucky Usaden was out there."

"I must reward him. He saved us both."

Thomas wondered if that was true or not, but suspected it was. He had fought such odds before, but he had been younger then.

"He expects no reward."

"That does not mean he deserves none. He is your friend, is he not? Your good friend?"

"He is. Not like Jorge, but we are close in a different way."

"He deals in death, as do you." She lifted a hand to still his lips before he could speak. "I know you do, Thomas. It is why I feel safe with you. Safer than I do with my husband." Her chest hitched and a tear ran down her cheek. "Today was—"

This time it was Thomas's turn to still her words. "You must never speak of it again, and neither will I. This day did not happen. We stepped outside the world for a few hours, that is all. Nothing happened."

"But—"

"Nothing happened." Thomas took one last look around, knowing they would never again return to this place. He saw the blood-stained bed, the trail of blood across the floor where the man had tried to flee, and the linen sack of food Theresa had given him. They had not touched the contents, and as Thomas stared at it, he knew who had betrayed them.

"Did you ask your cook to prepare this for you?" He picked the sack up. "Did you ask her for enough food for two?"

"I did not do it myself, but I asked Theresa to do so for me."

"Did she tell her what it was for?"

"I asked only for food I could carry, nothing that would spoil."

Thomas threw the sack through the window with a curse at his own stupidity.

———

Jorge looked at Thomas and tilted his head in that way he had, which was barely a movement but carried a thousand questions. Thomas ignored them all. Let him spin his own flights of fancy.

"Isabel!" Will rose to his feet and came across to hug the Queen of Castile, then stopped when he saw the blood-stains on her dress. She went to one knee to greet Amal, looking at Thomas over his daughter's shoulder.

"You are the most fortunate of men," she said as she rose. "And who is this?"

Belia had entered with Jahan on her hip, one side of her robe barely covering her breast.

"This is Jorge's son, Your Grace," said Belia. "His name is Jahan. It means the world in my language, because he is the world to me and Jorge both."

"I would ask to hold him, but I fear I am in no state."

Belia crossed the room until she was close to Isabel and held Jahan out to Jorge. There were times Thomas looked at the boy and almost forget how he had come into this world. If he thought of it at all, he considered Jahan looked most like Belia, and even a little like Jorge. Which he considered fortunate. Except Isabel was a clever woman.

"He is Jorge's son, you said?" she asked.

"He is."

Isabel reached out and stroked Jahan's cheek, tickled his belly, which finally raised a laugh from him.

"Can he walk yet?"

"A little if you hold his hand, but he enjoys being carried more. Like his father."

Isabel looked at Jorge, who only smiled.

Belia held her hand out, waiting until Isabel took it.

"Come with me, I will show you where you can wash, and then I will find you one of my robes. I will burn those clothes you wear." She glanced at Thomas for confirmation, and he nodded.

When they were gone, Will came to stand next to Thomas.

"Is Cat coming, and Juan?"

"Juan is with his father, but we could send for Catherine and the others. I'll ask Isabel when she comes back."

Thomas tried to work out when Usaden was likely to return, and when he did, if he would have a prisoner with him. He knew he should question Isabel's head cook. But he also knew this day was already unlike any other he had ever experienced, so gave a nod. Tomorrow would be soon enough. Thomas knew he needed to wash, but perhaps he should wait until Isabel was clothed once more.

———

Jorge stood beside Thomas on the narrow terrace as they watched Will stride down the slope in the direction of the Castilian camp. He had a message from Isabel to her children saying those who wanted to come could accompany him back to Thomas's house. He also had a message for Martin de Alarcón to take the head cook into custody. Thomas had watched Isabel write her note in his study in her neat hand. There had been no message for her husband. Thomas whispered his message for Martin into Will's ear so no one else could hear.

Now Jorge held Jahan's hand to help him stand, while Jahan also gripped Amal's in his other. Isabel had gone to the kitchen with Belia, who promised to show her how to add spice to food to improve the taste.

"So, did you?" asked Jorge.

"I killed a man, if that's what you're asking, so I should probably wash before we eat."

"It is a shame Isabel has already washed or you could ask her to join you."

They watched Will disappear into the throng of the camp.

"Nothing happened," Thomas said, wondering if he said it enough times, it would make it real.

"She knows Jahan is your son," said Jorge. "I saw it in her eyes when she looked at me."

"Then that is another thing you are wrong about today. Jahan is your son. Yours and Belia's. I have my two children, and you have your one."

"And a girl—don't forget you promised me a girl."

"Not today, please."

"Helena told me you always took some time to recover, even with her."

"I am an old man."

"And bad-tempered."

"Would you have me any other way?"

Jorge smiled. "I recognise the impossible when it is standing in front of me." He turned his head to look at Thomas. "Be careful. You are walking across burning coals, and I would not have you burst into flames. Is Usaden really chasing down a man? What happened?"

So Thomas told him. Not everything, but he told Jorge of the attack, of the six men, and that they were Turks. He told him of his suspicions of the cook. He knew he should be asking questions, but all of that could wait until the morning. Today was a day for friendship. And love.

CHAPTER FORTY-ONE

Thomas woke alone to darkness. He rolled his head to one side to see a shape barely distinguishable from the shadows. Usaden. Thomas sat up and sparked a flint until the wick of the lamp on the table beside him flared.

"Did you catch him?"

"I did."

"Is he alive?"

"He is in the small room at the back of the house. The one with a lock. Jorge is watching over him."

"Are you sure Jorge is the right man for the job?"

"He might have picked up one or two injuries. Enough to slow him down." Usaden looked around in the pale light. "I half expected the Queen to be with you."

"She returned to her duties hours ago." Thomas swung his legs from the bed and walked past Usaden to get his robe.

"You can stay where you are, he is not going anywhere. Better to let him think things over before you talk to him, not that I expect he is going to tell you any more than he did me."

Hence the injuries.

"Is Jorge happy to guard him until morning?"

"I will do it, he can return to his bed."

"You need to sleep too."

"I can sleep tomorrow. Go back to bed, Thomas, I only wanted to let you know he is here."

After Usaden left, Thomas tried to find sleep again, but it evaded him. He rose and dressed, went onto the terrace and stared to the east. He believed there was a faint hint of the coming dawn. Kin got up from where he was sleeping and padded to his side, claws clicking against the tiles. Thomas dropped his hand and scratched behind the dog's ears and Kin twisted his head until Thomas's fingers found the spot he liked best. The contact comforted both of them.

Thomas wondered how his life could have changed so much in ten years. From a solitary existence to this. A family, friends, a dog and a place at the side of the most powerful woman in the world. He felt no different within himself, but knew he must have changed. How could he not? He had loved and lost and loved again. He had fathered children and lost a child. He had saved men and killed men. Fortunately, the former outweighed the latter. The land he loved was about to undergo a cataclysmic change. Could he accept that as well? He smiled, knowing he had to. Knowing he was a part of it all, that he would play a role in whatever happened. Here, balanced on the edge of that change, he felt that if he stepped to one side, the balance would tip one way, step the other and it would tip again, but which was the right way was unclear. Only that he would do what he had always done. What was right. What was just.

He turned and went to question the Turk.

———

"Where was he going when you caught him?" Thomas, Usaden and Jorge sat at the table where everyone had recently eaten their midday meal. Belia was with the children in another room. Will was watching over their captive.

"North. Heading for that wide valley we went to."

"Is that where Koparsh and the others are, do you think?"

"It is possible. I considered letting him go on to make sure, but decided to bring him back. Would it be useful to know where they are, or not?"

"I don't know."

"There were many of them, and they fight well. Even those we killed fought well. Just not well enough to come up against the two of us. How many did Koparsh have?"

"There were forty when he was here, so less than that now, but he may have more we know nothing about."

"Too many for the three of us," said Usaden.

"I can't let their attempt on Isabel's life go unpunished. Salma prepared the food she ate and Yves helped her." Thomas shook his head. "My son tried to assassinate Isabel. I sent a message to Martin to arrest the head cook. I suspect Koparsh recruited her. It would explain almost everything. Someone inside the palace, someone preparing Isabel's food."

"The prisoner said nothing about a cook," said Usaden.

"He barely said anything at all," Thomas said. "That doesn't mean the cook's not involved."

"Don't forget Eleanor," said Jorge. "Yves admitted she came to kill Isabel. He will have worked alongside his mother just as he worked alongside Salma. Has it always been the Turks, do you think? Right from the start?"

"I don't know, but we're going to find out and end it." Thomas looked up as Belia came into the room and sat at the table. "What was in that tonic you made for Isabel?"

Belia gave a smile in reply.

"Who is with the children?"

"Nobody. They are on the terrace. Amal is playing with Jahan. It does them good not to have someone fussing over them all the time."

Thomas wanted to argue, but knew he had abandoned his children often enough into Belia's care not to deserve much say in how they were raised. He wondered if that would change when Gharnatah fell. Wondered what plan Isabel might have for him. He should ask her, he supposed, but was not sure he wanted to know her answer.

"Do you intend to tell Isabel we have captured one of her attackers?" asked Jorge.

"Not yet." He looked at each of them. "There would be only the three of us, and that is not enough." He had no reason to explain what for.

"Did he tell you nothing at all?" asked Belia.

"Nothing of any use, not even his name. He pretended he didn't understand Castilian, French or Arabic, but he must know the latter if he's one of Koparsh's men."

"We could always allow him to escape," said Usaden.

"We have only just captured him. He might weaken, given time."

"Do you believe that?"

"I am trying to."

"Let him think we made a mistake and he escaped through his own efforts. I will follow, find out where he goes. I will watch how many there are, and then come back and we decide what action to take. I am sure after the attempts on the Queen's life, she could find you some men to accompany us."

"You know you don't have the time for this now, Thomas," said Jorge. "A message came from Isabel that she needs you again."

"What message?"

"When you were interrogating the prisoner."

"And when were you going to tell me?"

"I am telling you now. Usaden's plan is sound. He finds out where Koparsh and his troops are and comes back here. Once we know more, how many they are, we can decide the next step. I agree we must punish those who tried to kill Isabel, but what if one of those is your own son? Can you watch him hang?"

Thomas thought of his own father and wondered if he would have watched him hang when he was thirteen years of age and accused of murder. He suspected he might have, but knew he was not the same as his father. He wanted to believe Yves innocent in all of this, but the evidence showed otherwise.

"Did Isabel say what she wanted me for?"

"Only that she wanted you."

Thomas watched Jorge suppress a smile and offered a scowl in return.

"Who is going to let the man escape?"

"It would make sense if it was Will. No doubt the man considers him a child he can overpower."

"Too dangerous," Thomas said. "Besides, if he's one of Koparsh's men, he might have seen Will defeat one of his compatriots."

"I will do it," said Jorge. "No doubt the Turk considers me weak and I will pretend to be so. I'll take him outside to relieve himself and let myself be distracted."

"Will he believe you so stupid?"

"I can make him believe," said Jorge.

———

Thomas took Will, Amal and Jahan with him when he responded to Isabel's summons. She had, after all, said their children ought to see more of each other, and he wanted them away from the house in case there was trouble. Belia decided to stay, but sent a fresh bottle of tonic for Isabel with a warning it would be the last.

Thomas searched out Theresa to leave the children with and also ask if Martin had done as requested.

"Did you think he would not? He searched high and low, but the cook is gone. Fled, if your suspicions are true. He questioned the kitchen staff, questioned them hard, he told me, and discovered a little that confirms your suspicions. Apparently she came into some small wealth recently and several of the girls told him she was often absent. It was her idea to use Baldomero. She sent no message to Gharnatah."

Thomas stared into space for a moment, working through what she had said.

"I wonder if she knew Baldomero was going to die. If she did, she has a stony heart and disguised her nature from both me and Jorge. It's unlike him not to see through to the core of a woman."

"She deceived us all," said Theresa.

"Isabel told me she asked you to have food prepared yesterday. Did you go to Maria for that?"

"Who else would I go to?"

"Did you tell her what it was for?"

"Only that the Queen wanted food she could carry easily. I said nothing about where she was going. Do you think me stupid?"

"No, but I'm trying to work out how those men knew where we would be."

"I will leave such clever speculation to you."

Thomas knew he had upset Theresa with his suspicions, but pushed on.

"Baldomero is dead. Eleanor is dead. I expect the cook is also dead by now. See if Martin will conduct another search, but tell him this time he is looking for a body."

"He will think you don't trust him to do his job," said Theresa, "but I will ask."

Thomas found Isabel sitting behind the desk in her office. He wondered whether she ever did anything else and believed she might not. She liked to know everything, and at the moment there was a great deal to know.

She glanced up when Thomas knocked against the side of the door and waved him inside before picking up a sheet of paper. It was as if the day before had never happened.

"Here, tell me what this says. It is a note from Boabdil

written in Arabic. I do not want my translators to know what it says before I do. Besides, you are better than them."

"I should hope so, I have been using little else for over thirty years." He glanced at the note. "He has agreed to the meeting, but it must be soon, within days if possible."

Isabel held her hand out until Thomas passed the note back. She stared at the flowing script as if concentration alone could impart some meaning.

"Does he say why so soon?"

"He doesn't. But we both know the reason. The last time I visited the city, there was an atmosphere on the streets. The people are likely to rise against him, and if they find out he is in talks with Castile, it might be all the trigger needed. He wants an agreement before that happens. He wants an offer of safety for himself and his family."

"Which he will get in return for the keys of the city." Isabel set the note down and stared at Thomas. "I want no more blood spilled than necessary." She pursed her lips. "Sooner is good. I am not sure how much longer I can hold Fernando back from launching an all-out attack. The men grow anxious and discipline is breaking down. There are small fights all the time, and some end in death. We fight amongst ourselves instead of against the enemy."

"It is the same in Gharnatah. It happened in Ronda and Malaka too."

"Does he say how many men we can take?"

"He does not."

"I will need to know. I want you to go and discuss the details with him. I assume he will talk to you?"

"It depends on his mood."

"Am I better sending Martin?"

"No, I will do it. Abu Abdullah hates Martin because he still has a hold over him. He hates me, too, but not in the same way."

"Nobody could hate you, Thomas."

He laughed. "Oh, I think you are wrong in that. There are plenty who do. Perhaps all except you."

She looked into his eyes, her own unreadable.

Thomas reached into his robe and drew out a small phial.

"Belia gave me this for you. She says it is the last. The tonic cannot be used indefinitely."

"In that case, return it to her. I will stop today. Perhaps I should have stopped before yesterday. Did Usaden catch the man who escaped?"

"He lost him." Thomas considered it wise to omit mention of the man's capture, questioning and subsequent release. He doubted Isabel would understand his logic. He was no longer sure he understood it himself, only that it might lead to some resolution. There were too many questions unanswered. No doubt too many questions he didn't even know needed to be asked.

"I thought Usaden was an expert tracker," said Isabel. "And he had your dog with him, did he not?"

"He did, but sometimes even being the best is not good enough."

"So I am learning." Isabel pushed a strand of pale red hair back into place from where it hung across her cheek. "Am I safe now, Thomas? Can I eat or not?" There was a fragile tension in her that made him want to reach out and embrace her, but knew he could never again do so. In that moment, it felt like an ultimate loss.

He pushed his own emotions aside, as he had always done.

"It appears your cook brought both Baldomero and Salma into her kitchen. I believe she was recruited by Koparsh, or sent by him. How long ago did you say she came here? A year and a half? If this attempt on you has been that long in the planning, it is cunning indeed. Martin has put extra men to guard all entrances of this building, so yes, you are safe for now. I will question everyone in the kitchens, everyone in this building if you ask me. Where there is one traitor, there may be more."

"I cannot believe that, Thomas. The sooner Granada falls to me, the sooner I will be safe. There will be no reason to take my life then, will there?" She stared at Thomas, waiting for an answer.

"I do not know, only that I will be close beside you and lay my life down for you if need be."

Isabel stared at him, emotions playing across her face and through her body. Thomas thought of all he knew of her that he did not know two days before. He watched as she put her own feelings aside and returned to business. It was as if a box had been locked and set in a drawer away from sight.

"I will have to tell Fernando about this meeting with Boabdil, and no doubt he will want to come."

Thomas tried to follow her example, but it came hard to him. No doubt he had less practice than the Queen of Castile.

"If he sees an agreement reached, it may hold him back from an attack. You will have men with you, and Koparsh has only two score."

"So we need to take more." Isabel stared into Thomas's eyes a long time, a fragility clinging to her, and he wondered if she might crumble under the pressure on her. Then she blinked and became her old self. "Columb was here again today and got past everyone to confront me directly, so perhaps I am not as safe as you claim."

"Except he is no cook." Thomas was relieved to see a smile touch Isabel's lips. "What did he want?"

"He says he needs a decision within a week, or he is setting sail for England."

"It is winter in England. He will turn around and come straight back."

"Do not make light of it. When you return from talking with Boabdil, find Columb and see what I need to offer to prevent his defection."

"Do you intend to fund his voyage?"

"I do."

"Can I tell him as much?"

Isabel stared off to one side, her eyes tracking empty space as she thought of her answer.

"Yes, tell him I will fund him, but only after Granada falls. That must happen first. Everything else has to wait. Can you do that?"

"I can. You know I am yours to direct as you wish." He watched Isabel fight a smile that threatened to show on her lips. Lips he had kissed only the day before, but knew he would never kiss again, which was only proper. The knowledge firmed another decision he had to make. Perhaps he could fit in a visit to his house on the Albayzin to see if Helena was there. She might tempt him to stay overnight, but he doubted he had the time. There was too much to do and he wanted to know if Usaden's plan had worked.

CHAPTER FORTY-TWO

"Is the big general coming?" Isabel asked. She and Thomas were once more in her office as the day drew to a close. Three days had passed since she had sent him to Gharnatah. More time than either Isabel or Abu Abdullah wanted, but finally the negotiations were agreed. Each side would take fifty armed soldiers. Isabel and Fernando were both to attend, and Abu Abdullah was bringing his mother. This last almost caused Thomas to abandon the talks. Aixa was a spiteful creature who dominated her son completely. She would be hard to control, but at least something was happening.

"He is," Thomas said. "Abu Abdullah insists Olaf be present, but the troops from both sides are to stay outside the fort."

"Can he still fight with only one hand?"

Thomas suppressed a laugh. "I expect Olaf could fight with no hands, but yes, he can. He claims he is no less a warrior for it, and—" He cut himself short.

"And what, Thomas?"

He considered whether to lie, then decided the truth would do no harm.

"I have had a device made for him. It attaches to the stump of his arm so he can hold a second weapon. A knife. An axe.

Even a sword. Though he will need to decide which before he uses it."

"You made this?"

"I had it made. A friend of mine shaped the wood, and a smith created the metalwork."

Isabel shook her head. "I suspect Fernando will not be pleased. I think he was hoping Olaf would no longer be a threat."

"If the talks succeed, nobody will be a threat."

"Did you speak with Columb?"

"I did."

"And persuaded him to stay until … I don't know when, but the turn of the year at least? It is not so long now, is it? He owes me that much."

"Yes, I persuaded him. We got drunk together with Jorge and talked of distant lands."

"Am I sending men to their deaths?"

"There is a risk in every new venture, but I believe this one may succeed. Who can tell when a man sets sail into the great ocean?"

"Indeed, who can tell? You will come here again tomorrow in time for us all to leave together. I want you to ride beside myself and Fernando. I need people to see where your place is. Where you belong."

"Your men of God will not like it."

"Which is why I am planning not to take many of them. Our numbers are limited and I want only those I trust, and those who have proven their worth. Did you bring your children again?" When Thomas nodded, Isabel said, "I worry that Catherine likes your son too much. Not to mention the older girls, who are possibly the more dangerous. But I will not prevent their meeting if you give me your promise."

"My promise of what?"

"That you will explain to him they are princesses and there can be nothing but friendship between them. I asked

Theresa to speak with some of my daughters to explain the same."

"What did they think of that?"

"They were not pleased, but they are sensible girls, with older heads than their years, and they know their responsibilities. Catherine need know nothing of that conversation yet. Her love for Will is innocent still."

"I have already spoken with Will and he also understands. They are young yet, let them enjoy their friendship while they can. Soon enough they will have more responsibility than they might wish."

"When your son is of an age, I will arrange a suitable match."

"I would prefer he makes his own choice."

"As you wish, but remember my offer. You are to be at my side for a long time yet, I pray. I can find a place for all of you."

"Even Jorge?"

"All of you." Isabel suppressed a smile. "Though what I might find for him could prove a problem."

When Thomas turned to leave, Isabel rose from behind the desk and came to him. She took both his hands in hers and stared up at his face.

"You will be beside me, won't you, Thomas?"

"Until you tell me otherwise. I am your man now, to do with as you wish."

Isabel released her hold and he went in search of his children. He found them all together, even Juan who now usually considered himself too old to mix with the younger ones. He was a prince of Castile and that responsibility seemed to place a heavy weight on him. He was pleased to see Thomas, even if they now grasped each other's arms rather than hug as they once had. It had been many years since Thomas broke the boy's leg to reset it and now he walked with barely any limp at all.

As they approached the house, Will carrying Jahan, Thomas carrying Amal, who said she was a princess now and princesses did not have to walk, Kin came bounding down the slope. Which meant Usaden had returned.

Thomas picked up his pace, knowing Will would have no trouble keeping up.

———

"He led me to the valley beyond the one where your woman died."

"She wasn't my woman," Thomas said.

Usaden didn't look convinced. "One of your women, then."

They sat once more around the table, as they so often did. This time, Will was with them, leaning forward to listen intently.

"How many?" Thomas asked.

"I counted eighty-three, but there may be more. They are in an old fort two days north of here and I could not get inside without being seen."

"So not the twenty Koparsh claims. Did you see him or Salma?"

"They rode out together on the second day to a nearby town. Salma bought something, but I could not see what it was, then they rode back." Usaden raised his eyes to meet Thomas's. "There was a third person with them. Your son, Yves."

Thomas cursed. "Did he look as if he was a captive?"

"He had the chance to ride away from them, but did not."

"Love," said Jorge and Thomas nodded.

"So he is involved with them and everything he told me is a lie." Thomas didn't want to consider the implications, though he knew he would have to soon enough. "I can't think about any of this right now. Isabel is preparing to ride out to meet with Abu Abdullah. If the talks go well, it means the end of the war before the turn of the year, possibly sooner." Thomas pinched between his eyes with finger and thumb, but the tension there only grew. "She wants me with her." He

363

looked at Usaden. "Is there anything you can do while I am away?"

"Nothing, because I will be close to you. I will not let you ride into danger if I am not nearby. I know the Queen will not sanction my presence, but I will never be far away and I will be watching. Like I did the last time."

"What about you?" Thomas asked Jorge. "Isabel tells me I can bring anyone I want and I want you with me. I value your expertise with people. I'm also interested to see how Abu Abdullah behaves when he sees both of us there."

"Of course I will come."

"It is settled then, if Belia agrees to care for the children once more. I will make it up to you both. I would send Theresa to help, but Isabel has requested she also come."

"I will stay," said Belia, "and you know how you can make it up to me."

Thomas nodded. A daughter for Jorge. Not such an arduous debt to pay.

"Pa?" said Will.

"You will help Belia."

"I want to come with you."

Thomas stared at his son. Taller than Usaden, though Usaden was not a tall man, Will was also broader across the shoulders.

"Let him come," said Jorge. "He needs to learn skills other than how to fight. It will do him good."

"Please, Pa?"

"If you allow him," said Belia, "I will take Amal and Jahan back to our house in Gharnatah. I want to do some work there and Helena will be company. They will be as safe there as they are here. I assume your dog will be with Usaden. When you return, come back there if you can."

Thomas looked around the table at each of them. Jorge at ease. Will tense. Usaden standing with Kin at his feet. Amal playing with Jahan on the floor, her profile exactly like that of her mother. Belia, as mysterious to him as ever, even after what they had shared.

"Yes, you can come," he said to Will, hoping he would have no reason to regret the decision.

———

They rode out from Santa Fe at dawn. Fifty soldiers accompanied them as agreed, plus another twenty hangers-on, who included Thomas, Jorge and Will. There were Fernando and Juan, who was turning into a man at fourteen years of age. He was being groomed for power and Thomas believed he would make a good King. He was harder than he had once been, but that was to be expected, and the core of him remained. As well as Isabel's close retinue, there was Catherine, who was also being groomed for her future role as a queen. There were men of God and men of power. These made up the bulk of their twenty and Thomas hoped they would not interfere too much.

He expected Abu Abdullah to come with a similar number in addition to his fifty protectors, one of whom would be Olaf. Thomas knew Will would be glad to see him, but didn't know if he could. The soldiers were to remain at a distance to ensure the good behaviour of the other side and to offer protection. From what danger was a question nobody had thought to ask.

The afternoon was fading before they reached al-Loraya. The gold light of a lowering sun bathed the walls of the fort on its rocky outcrop, giving it a more welcome air than it deserved. Abu Abdullah and his troops had appeared a few hours earlier. They maintained a distance of a mile, which shrank as they neared the town. Now the soldiers had been left behind and only those involved in the negotiations advanced, the distance between their smaller groups shrinking as the streets forced them closer.

Thomas rode beside Martin de Alarcón, the first chance he had had to speak with him in almost a week.

"Did you ever find any trace of that cook?" he asked.

"Fled," said Martin. "Her house was empty, clothes missing. The neighbours said they saw her leaving two days after Isabel was taken ill."

"Not taken ill—poisoned."

"After Isabel was poisoned, then, but gone she is. I suspect she ran as soon as you finished talking to her."

"I half expected you to find a body."

Ahead, Isabel and Fernando had slowed as they approached the foot of the slope that would lead to the fort.

"As did I," said Martin. "If she has any sense, she won't stop running until she reaches France or Italia."

"I still don't think Koparsh will let her live. She knows too much and I would dearly love to know what it is."

"You know he is guilty, as is his concubine. Is that not enough?"

Thomas wondered if Martin omitted Yves' name on purpose.

Isabel walked her mount back to Thomas and Martin.

"Go talk to Boabdil," she said to Thomas. "Tell him what you and I discussed."

"Shall I go as well, Your Grace?" asked Martin.

"Only Thomas. And perhaps Jorge. Take your son as well if you wish." She turned in her saddle to see where Will was, smiled when she saw him riding beside Catherine. "Perhaps not."

"I will go alone," Thomas said. He turned his horse and encouraged it into a canter.

He saw Abu Abdullah send a man out to meet him, but it was not an attempt to discourage him. Thomas drew up in front of the Sultan who had once threatened to kill him.

"There are quarters arranged in the town for your people," Thomas said, "but you and anyone you choose have rooms in the fort. Queen Isabel has invited you to eat with her tonight if you will honour her with your presence."

Abu Abdullah laughed. "I hear she has a reputation for eating poisoned food, so perhaps it is not a sensible idea."

"Everything will be tasted and I have uncovered the culprits in that matter."

"Will you be there?"

"I will."

"And the eunuch? I see him over there, together with your son. Who is that he rides beside? Does he have a young lover already?"

"That is the Queen's daughter, Catherine. They are friends."

"She is the one promised to England?"

"You are well informed, Malik."

"Knowledge is power, is it not? I believe it might even have been you who first said that to me."

"It is possible, though I have said many things, not all of them sensible. Shall I say you will join her?"

Abu Abdullah stared at Thomas for a long time before offering a nod.

"Tell her it will be my honour to accept, though I may arrange for my own food."

"The food will be good, Malik. Isabel likes spice as much as a Moor, though there will be other dishes of a blander nature. And meat. A great deal of meat."

"Perhaps she and I can talk and we will settle this matter today, then we can all go home and sleep in our own beds."

"Yes, perhaps we can."

"Will the King be there?"

"He will."

"I hear it is she who decides. Is that right, Thomas?"

"Do you expect me to give an honest answer, Malik?"

Abu Abdullah laughed. "Your refusal is answer enough. Tell her it will be my pleasure."

Thomas nodded to Aixa, who had watched the conversation in silence, a sour expression on her face. He wondered if she grieved for Tarfe, her youngest son, but doubted it. Grief would require her to possess a heart. He knew she would be at the meal, which might be a problem if she contributed to the discussion. Thomas would ask Jorge to sit close to her. Theresa also.

As he rode back, he played different scenarios through his head before deciding to ask Isabel to arrange the seating so that those of Castile and Gharnatah were mixed together. He recognised language might be an issue, but knew Abu Abdullah had some Castilian, as did almost everyone who once spoke only Arabic. It was the sensible thing to do.

CHAPTER FORTY-THREE

The solution had been Jorge's idea, and when Thomas went to Isabel with it, she agreed at once. Thomas was concerned Fernando might attempt to dominate Isabel if they sat together and he wanted Abu Abdullah close to her so they could talk without being overheard.

"Cushions," Jorge said as they stood waiting for Isabel to finish talking with the key-holder of the fort, who was achieving his ambition to meet the Queen of Castile. A small price to pay for what he had offered them access to.

"What?" Thomas was distracted as he tried to come up with a solution to the problem.

"How does Abu Abdullah like to eat? The same way as all Moors, which is to sit on a cushion with a low table. I have seen Isabel do the same on occasion. Even you can manage it, though not without a great deal of complaint."

Thomas grinned and kissed Jorge on the cheek.

"Always with a promise and never the delivery," he said, as Thomas moved away.

Now they sat on cushions and Thomas had tried not to complain. Abu Abdullah sat to his right, Isabel beyond him. On Thomas's other side sat Jorge, with Aixa beyond him—far enough from the low conversation that he hoped Jorge could control her if she attempted to interrupt.

They had invited Fernando to join them, but he said he preferred to sit on a chair like a civilised man. A low table had been found and set in one corner. They had obtained piles of silk cushions from the residents of the town, and a dozen people sat picking at the spiced dishes arrayed across the table. In deference to Abu Abdullah, there was no wine. Instead, a variety of teas, juices and coffee was available.

Thomas made no pretence at not listening to their conversation, conducted primarily in Castilian Spanish. Every now and again, Abu Abdullah would ask for help in communicating a concept he lacked the words for. It was an interesting challenge, making Thomas aware there were some ideas that had no equivalent in the other language, on both sides. Despite the occasional stumble, slow progress was being made.

Isabel was dressed in fine Moorish robes. Gold threads ran through the silk and her head was covered. She showed no ill-effects from her brush with death, and Abu Abdullah was charmed. He also cast occasional glances in Theresa's direction. She had dressed herself in the same manner, but without covering her head. She looked stunning, as beautiful as Thomas had ever seen her, and he experienced a brief pang of loss before deciding what had happened was entirely his own fault.

"Thomas, where is Tablatee?" asked Isabel. "Do you know the town?"

"It is south of Gharnatah, Your Grace, and straddles the road south to Salobreña." He had heard Abu Abdullah's demand and knew this fact important.

"Then no, you cannot claim the town," she said to Abu Abdullah, a smile on her face to soften the words as she reached out to touch his wrist with her fingers. Thomas thought of all the times she had done the same to him and wondered if it was for the same reason—using the power a woman possesses over a man to persuade him to an action he might not want to take. Isabel leaned around to look at Thomas. "Tell me a suitable town. The Sultan has agreed terms, though they will need to be confirmed tomorrow by our people. He demands a swathe of lands as his own in the Alpujarras. You know them well, I believe. What can we offer?" She spoke quickly and Thomas knew it was deliberate so that Abu Abdullah could not follow her words.

"He needs to go east, much further east." He said the words in English, aware Isabel would understand. He saw her smile. "There is a township called Laujar de Andarax in your language. It would be suitable, together with the surrounding lands."

Despite not understanding the words, Abu Abdullah heard the name of the town and shook his head.

"No, it is too isolated. Am I not a king equal to you as a queen?"

"But you are shortly to be a defeated king, Malik." Isabel used the honorific deliberately. "I am generous in making this offer. If you refuse, I will have no choice but to unleash my husband. Your city will be destroyed and your life forfeit."

Thomas was aware he had never witnessed this side of Isabel before and it took his breath away. She was magnificent. He saw Abu Abdullah cowed by her majesty and power.

"Perhaps you will allow me to come up with a proposal, Malik? Your Grace?"

Abu Abdullah looked at him. There was fear in his eyes.

"You?"

Thomas leaned out so he could meet Isabel's gaze.

"And Olaf Torvaldsson?" He waited until she nodded before turning back to the Sultan. "Myself and Olaf, Malik. Together with anyone you would want to add, but remember for each person on one side, there will have to be another added for balance. A small group can decide more easily."

"Just so long as the Alarcón is not involved." Abu Abdullah

turned back to Isabel. "Now, about a date and the other arrangements."

It was late before Thomas found a glass of wine. He felt he deserved one. At least one. He sipped at it as he sat at the big table on a real chair, grateful for the comfort. His back ached from sitting on the cushions. Most of those who had attended the meal were gone, so it surprised him when someone pulled a chair out and sat next to him. He was even more surprised to discover that someone was Abu Abdullah.

"Is that wine?" the Sultan asked, reverting to his native Arabic.

"It is. Do you want some?"

"It is against the Qur'an."

"I am aware of that, but you know I do not follow your religion."

"Perhaps one goblet, in consideration of what we have achieved."

Thomas reached out and found a clean glass and poured the wine.

"I have drunk it before, on occasions that demanded it. She is glorious, is she not?" Abu Abdullah's eyes were on Isabel, who stood talking with Theresa and Jorge. Fernando had disappeared an hour before, no doubt to start the serious drinking with his cronies.

"She can be less intimidating to those who know her."

"Those like you, Thomas? Is it true you share her bed? What is she like? Looking at her now, I imagine she would be a disappointment, but if she is as she was earlier, then you are a lucky man. Which is it?"

"If I am ever fortunate enough to find out, I will come and tell you."

Abu Abdullah scowled. "Then you will have to come to Laujar de Andarax. I should have held out for better."

"You are fortunate to get that much. If I had not intervened,

I know she intended to give you nothing. She would have demanded you leave the entire peninsula of Spain."

"Do not expect my gratitude."

"Why would I do that?"

"I hear you have taken Helena back into your bed, as well as Isabel."

"Only Helena, but yes. You changed her."

"No need to thank me."

"I wasn't, though it is true she has changed for the better."

"Some women need breaking before they can be rebuilt."

Thomas had forgotten how much he hated this man, but knew he had to hold his true feelings in check. He noted that Abu Abdullah had finished his goblet of wine, so went to find another bottle and poured more for both of them.

"Who is the red-haired woman with the Queen?"

"Theresa."

"She is also wonderful."

"All those concubines in the harem and you lust after her?"

Abu Abdullah turned to Thomas. "Is she not beautiful?"

"She is. Is it the red hair and pale skin you find so attractive? You must have concubines like that. Helena's sisters are still members of the harem, are they not?"

"They are, but they are too familiar to me now." Abu Abdullah rose. He looked down at the wine left in his glass and shook his head. "I may speak with them and see if I can persuade her to visit me later. Perhaps she too lusts after the exotic."

Thomas watched the man walk away and wished he had killed him when he had the chance. It was too late now.

———

Thomas knew sleep would elude him, so he climbed stone stairs to emerge onto the ramparts of the fort. A full moon seemed pinned to the crags of the mountain tops, its light painting them silver. Uncountable stars sparked the sky to the east, and the town and surrounding land lay quiet. Somewhere out there, Usaden would be awake, Kin at his side, both of them keeping watch. Tonight felt like both a start and an end, but to what, Thomas was unsure. Only that change was becoming normal in his life, for good or ill.

He leaned on the battlements and gazed without thought, not wanting thought, and slowly his mind stilled until he believed he might sleep. He turned at the sound of footsteps, surprised to see Isabel approach. She still wore the Moorish robes, which clung to her body to reveal more than her usual dresses.

"I wondered where you had gone, Thomas. I wanted to say goodnight."

"Where is Fernando?"

"Still with his friends, still drinking. I expect they will do so until dawn and then sleep tomorrow away. I believe we have an agreement with Boabdil, do we not?" She stopped beside him and reached for his hand.

"It seems you do, but I have known him go back on his word a hundred times before. He listens to astrologers and believes in omens. All it takes is for a crow's shadow to cross him and he will renege on his promises."

Isabel tightened her fingers through his. "Then we must ensure matters progress at speed. Give him no time to change his mind." She stepped away, her hand releasing his only slowly. "Goodnight, Thomas, sleep well. Tomorrow will be a busy day."

Thomas watched her walk to the narrow doorway and disappear, then turned back to the mountains. He was wide awake again. He wrapped his cloak around himself and waited for dawn, while his mind fought to find some kind of equilibrium. He was still leaning on the stone battlements as the sky lightened. There had been a shadow at the foot of the hills all night, which he had assumed was woodland. As the light grew, he saw it for what it really was. An army. A large army.

He turned and ran down the steps three at a time.

Fernando was slumped in a chair. Other men lay on the floor or crouched in corners. Thomas shook the King's arm until he came awake with a scowl.

"What do you want? Are you going to fight me again?"

"There are men outside. I think it's the Turks."

Fernando made a sound of dismissal. "They were a score, no more."

"They are no longer a score. I estimate two hundred, at least."

Fernando tried to stand, but staggered, and Thomas gripped his arm to steady him. He looked around the room.

"Where's Martin?"

"In Theresa's arms, if he has any sense."

Fernando put a hand to his head. For a moment, Thomas thought he was about to throw up, but he made an effort and the moment passed. No doubt it would return.

"Go fetch him and find out what is happening," said Fernando. "I need to know if they are here for us, or only passing through."

Thomas thought it too much of a coincidence, but the idea was worth pursuing.

After two false attempts, he found Martin de Alarcón in bed with Theresa and told him the news. It took little time for him to dress. They picked up horses from the yard before descending the twisting roadway and riding out through the town.

"Go to your men, I will talk to Olaf." Only after Martin had ridden away did Thomas realise what he had said. He had placed himself on the side of the Moors, not Castile. He shook the idea away for examination another time.

Olaf had already seen the gathered men by the time

Thomas dismounted. The big general stood with his arms crossed, staring across the mile of open ground between them.

"Who are they?" he asked as Thomas stood beside him.

"I think it's Koparsh Hadryendo."

"I thought he had no more than two score with him."

"Clearly not."

"Do you think they are looking for a fight?"

"Fernando is hoping they are passing through on their way home."

Olaf gave a snort to show what he thought of the idea.

"I sent Martin to talk to the Castilian soldiers while I came to you."

"Good. I agree."

"You don't know what I'm going to suggest."

"That we combine our forces to repel them. That means a hundred against…" Olaf surveyed the army which was gathering itself, putting out fires, mounting horses "…two hundred? Perhaps more."

"Not bad odds," Thomas said, and Olaf looked at him.

"Normally, I would agree, if it was my men and you and that Gomeres, but we are talking of men who were enemies yesterday and will be enemies again tomorrow. Who will lead?"

"You are the Sultan's general and they have nobody like you with them. Martin is their most senior man, but he has nothing like your experience."

"What about the King? He is an outstanding leader of men, I have been told."

"When he is sober, which is not today. Besides, no doubt that is what Koparsh wants, so he can kill Fernando. Better he stay away from this fight."

"Will his men follow me, do as I order?"

"If Martin puts himself at their head, yes. He has already agreed it."

"And you will fight beside me?"

"Have I not always done so?" Thomas slapped Olaf's

shoulder and the big man's lips thinned in what might have been a smile.

Olaf looked up at the sky, blue now, a few clouds hovering over the distant peaks.

"It is as good a day to die as any." He looked at the ground between them and the approaching army. "We should join our forces now before they reach us. The Queen and King and Sultan must try to make their escape as best they can. We cannot offer them any guard."

"In that case, they are better off staying where they are. The fort is impregnable unless Koparsh has artillery, and I doubt that. I judge we have less than half an hour before they gather themselves to attack. We need to have a plan before then."

"Shield wall," said Olaf. "We stand and resist. We keep discipline and let them throw themselves against us. Will the Spanish understand the concept?"

"They fight battles too, but it might be best to put your men in the vanguard and let the Spanish protect the flanks."

"I am glad you are here, Thomas, your mind works faster than mine. Let us fight." Olaf grinned. This is what he did. Kill men in service of his master, even if it was a master he no longer respected.

CHAPTER FORTY-FOUR

It was chaos. Despite the planning, despite the organisation, all battles are chaos. It comes down to man against man, sword and axe and pike against an enemy you can barely see. At least there were no cannon or muskets, but the Turks were harsh fighters and threw themselves with wild abandon against Olaf's rushed shield wall.

It held … just. The Castilian troops suffered more on the flanks, but they fought well enough. Men died, but as the battle continued, Thomas saw more Turk than Moor or Castilian dead. Slowly, the tables turned.

Then he saw the group who had held back from the fighting, the group where Koparsh sat, Salma at his side—but no sign of Yves—turn and ride away. For a brief moment, Thomas wondered where his son might be, then the thought was torn from him as a man attacked and Thomas ran him through with his sword.

Olaf roared, "We have them, Thomas!" He swung his axe and buried the blade into a man's chest, jerked it free. His new hand worked well.

Thomas turned to see where Koparsh would flee to, but instead of riding away, he urged his men towards the small town. Thomas stepped back, stepped back again, only then aware of blood on his face and hands and clothes. He sheathed his sword and ran as hard as he could. As he cleared the rear of the combined soldiers, he saw a slim figure approach, going even faster than he was, then Kin darted ahead of Usaden and leapt at Thomas. He bounced off his chest and rolled as he landed, only to run on ahead, mouth wide and tongue lolling.

"Isabel!" Thomas gasped out the word. "Koparsh is going for Isabel."

"Then we had better save her again," said Usaden, as if this was only a morning stroll.

"He can't get in. Gates are closed." Thomas hoped the gates were closed, but as they reached the town, he discovered them standing open. The body of a man lay slumped to one side, and as they passed, Thomas saw it was the holder of the keys. He wondered what Koparsh had promised for his betrayal. Not death, that was certain.

As they entered the inner courtyard, they found two score of men. Koparsh stood at the rear, directing them, Salma at his side. They had arrived just as Isabel and Fernando were making their escape. Will and Jorge stood in the wide entrance to the inner chambers of the fort, protecting Catherine, Juan and Theresa. Abu Abdullah cowered to one side. He held a sword in his hand, but the tip dragged on the ground.

Four men confronted Fernando where he stood to protect his wife and children, a sword in his hand. Under normal circumstances, Thomas might expect him to triumph even against four, but he could see how pale his face was. He wondered if the man could even see straight after what he had drunk the night before. But he was brave and doing what he could.

Thomas touched Usaden's shoulder and he went running to the side. Koparsh Hadryendo turned his head at the movement, but appeared to consider him no great danger. He gave an order and another ten men joined the four, changing the odds from small to impossible. Thomas took a breath and drew his sword. He glanced at Koparsh, considering whether he should attack him first to draw his men back in defence, but knew he was only one man. Instead, he followed Usaden, who was already attacking the flank of the Turks. Thomas took the other side, running a man through before edging towards Isabel. He took up position beside Fernando, who offered a nod, and then Usaden was on the other side. Three against fourteen. Still too many men. Then Koparsh sent the rest in and Thomas knew they were all dead. He stepped back and gripped Isabel's wrist, raised his voice to be heard above the clash of swords.

"When I release you, you must run. There is space around the edge and I will keep them away from you. Take your children and run as fast as you can. There are horses outside. Take them and ride. Ride for your lives."

"And you?"

"I will fight beside your husband."

She stared into his eyes for a moment before turning away. She gathered Theresa to her, then Will, Juan and Catherine. Will looked at Thomas, fear in his eyes, but his face was set firm and he put a hand to his waist where he carried the sword he had insisted on bringing. He stood between Isabel and the fighting men, and Thomas shook his head, but Will shook his own in return. He was too young for this, but the fight was here.

Thomas searched for Jorge and found him emerging from the fort with a sword in his hand. He caught his eyes and nodded at Isabel, and Jorge understood. Protect the Queen at all costs.

Thomas turned away and threw himself back into the melee, striking a man about to run Fernando through. The King gave a grunt of acknowledgement before having to defend himself again.

Thomas waved at Usaden, who darted across to join him,

and they fought back to back as Isabel and the others ran. It took a moment before anyone noticed, then Koparsh raised an arm and gave a great shout. His men turned from attacking Fernando and ran after the fleeing Queen.

Isabel was almost at the open gates when she was caught. Thomas broke away and sprinted towards her, deflecting blows without even thinking, all his attention on Isabel. Then he saw Will draw his sword and stand in front of her. He was the tallest of Isabel's group other than Jorge, and the strongest, but he was only ten years old. Olaf Torvaldsson's grandson he might be, but he was not Olaf. Not yet. But the fight had come to him, ready or not. A boy and a eunuch against the Turks.

Thomas yelled and Will ignored him, as no doubt Usaden had taught him.

One of the Turks laughed and ran at Isabel. Jorge placed himself in front of her. He looked dangerous, which Thomas hoped would help.

Will stepped into the path of the attacker and raised his sword. A second man came and swung down at him and Will twisted, ducked and struck out. The man screamed and fell. Will turned again and thrust his sword through the back of the other man just as he raised his own sword to strike down at Jorge. Then Thomas was there and put himself beside his son to confront the others who were coming at them. He bumped into a figure and turned to discover Jorge. His face was set hard, his sword already bloodied.

"Run!" Thomas shouted at Isabel. He pushed her and she began to move.

Usaden arrived, then Kin, his jaws stained with the blood of men. The five of them faced a group six times their number, but Thomas saw Isabel reach the gates and pass through, and knew he had done his duty.

When he glanced at Will, there were tears streaming from his son's eyes, but his jaw was set, and when the next attack came, he held firm.

It would have ended badly, Thomas knew, a tale of courage against impossible odds told around firesides, if Martin de Alarcón and Olaf had not appeared ahead of a mixed group of soldiers. Olaf's axe dripped blood onto the stones, his naked chest and face streaked with the same. Thomas ran at the men in front of him, who had also seen the reinforcements and were falling back. Thomas left them to run and looked around for Koparsh, but he was gone.

Olaf and Martin advanced on the remaining men, fearsome, ruthless, leaving none standing.

Thomas turned back, searching for Will. He found him on one knee, head down. He put his arms around him and felt the boy sob as he grasped him in return. Thomas kissed his head and held him while the impact of what he had done coursed through his son like a fire. Thomas remembered the first time he had killed, and what it had been like. Not at the time, but later. He had relived the act over and over in his mind until he had to put it aside, knowing if he let it remain, it would drive him mad.

"Pa…" Will raised his face and Thomas kissed his tears.

"It's all right. You did what you had to do."

Will nodded. "I know, Pa, but … but it brought it all back…"

Thomas frowned, not sure he understood.

"I couldn't save Ma, but I'm older now and stronger. I saved Isabel, didn't I?"

"You did. She will make you a knight or something."

"I don't need honours," said Will, and Thomas stared into his eyes and saw he meant it, saw how much like him Will was, despite the fact one day he would tower over him.

"Want them or not, you will get them, so smile when she does and pretend to be pleased."

Will looked around. "I killed three men, Pa." Tears filled his eyes again.

"So did I. They were three men who would have killed you without a second thought."

"You killed more, I saw you did. I want to fight like you one day."

"Better you never have to."

"*Morfar* says that to me, but sometimes you have to fight, don't you? If we hadn't fought today, Isabel would be dead. And Cat and Juan. And you and me and Jorge. All of us would be dead." He glanced beyond Thomas. "Perhaps not Usaden."

"No, perhaps not Usaden, or Kin." Thomas wiped fresh tears from his son's face with his thumb and pulled him to his feet. "You won't believe me now, but I hope you will later. What you did today is going to change you. Let it make you better, not worse. Grow, be brave, protect those you love. That is all there is in this life, so do it as well as you can." Thomas smiled as a sudden memory came to him, wondering what had summoned it. He spoke the words a girl he had once loved left him in a message when he was only a little older than Will. "And don't take any shit from anybody."

"I'll try, Pa." Will embraced him, then pulled away. He firmed his shoulders and walked away, breaking Thomas's heart.

———

"As soon as Koparsh realised Isabel had escaped, he withdrew his men and ran." Olaf Torvaldsson sat on a rock while men, Moorish and Castilian alike, tracked across the battlefield. Some administered mercy to those who would linger in agony with no chance of living. Others dragged those already dead to a pile where the bodies would be burned later that day. The Turks wore fine fighting clothes which were stripped from them.

"How many injured?" Thomas asked.

"Less than a dozen. Most have no need of your services, but I would like you to look at the others. Unless you have plans. You can still catch up with Isabel if you ride hard."

383

"I intend to track Koparsh down and end this once and for all. What his argument is with Isabel, I do not understand, but it's clear he wants her dead. She won't be safe until we deal with him. That woman of his as well." He tried not to think of his son. His other son. The grown man. But he knew Yves might have to stand before Isabel's judgement. If he lived.

"You have no argument from me on that, but there were still over a hundred who rode from here today. Who rides with you, Thomas?"

"Jorge and Usaden." Thomas smiled. "And my dog."

"And me if you will have me."

"Abu Abdullah will expect you back."

"And Isabel will expect you, but this is more important. Did the talks go well?"

"They had barely started. They were meant to sign off on the details today, but yes, it went well enough. They have reached an agreement."

"Does that mean I will need to seek a new master soon?"

"It does."

Olaf gave a nod. "Good. I am growing tired of being tied to a sultan I do not respect." He looked beyond Thomas. "Will is quiet. I expected him to come to me, but he is sitting with your dog."

"He killed men today. Three, he claims, but I suspect it was more. He fought like a mixture of you, me and Usaden. He has to come to terms with what he has become. You know how it is. There is a before and an after, and nobody crosses that divide unchanged. When was your first time?"

"I was younger even than Will. Men attacked my village. They killed my father, but I fought and killed one of them. I was big even then, and strong. They were renegades who thought we were easy pickings. I tracked them down, every last one, and took their lives." Olaf stared into Thomas's eyes. "Yes, it changed me, but not so much. I had already decided to be a warrior. A Northman decides at eight years of age. I had picked up the axe, so knew I would kill one day. And you, Thomas?"

"I took the life of my father, but that was only to spare him further suffering. He was crushed under his dead horse and there was no chance he would survive. It felt bad, but not as bad as taking the life of a stranger. That came later, though not so much later. I had thirteen years."

"A little older than me, then. Do you want me to talk to him? Northern blood runs in Will's veins, too."

"Perhaps, but not yet. He needs to come to terms with what he has done. Then I will talk to him, and I would like you to do so as well." Thomas laughed, no humour in the sound. "Jorge has already had the other conversation with him."

"Women?" said Olaf. "I saw him with the princess. She stares at him like he is some kind of idol."

Thomas pushed fingers through his hair. "There are too many lessons to learn as we grow up, aren't there?"

"There are, but every one is another you do not have to study a second time, not if you learn it well." Olaf stood. He massaged the stump of his right wrist, the prosthesis discarded on the ground at his feet. "It aches, but that is to be expected. I could fight well enough today, almost as well as I used to, and I am sure with practice, I will be just as good."

"There may be no more fighting," Thomas said.

"I hope you are wrong about that. How many men do you want me to bring?"

"How many can you spare?"

"I am coming, so all of them if you want."

Thomas looked across to where Martin de Alarcón was talking with one of his captains.

"It's not a case of how many, they will still be three times our number if we take everybody, your men and Martin's. A lot of the men went to protect Abu Abdullah and Isabel on their journey home. Better we take a small group of the best. We can't fight them directly, but Koparsh has to be punished, as does Salma."

"You would kill a woman?"

"This one, yes."

"You should ask Usaden to do it."

"You know I would never do that."

"Then I will bring ten of my best. Go talk to Martin and ask him the same. It should be equal numbers from both sides if he agrees. Twenty can move fast without being seen. We find out where they are and decide then. If there are too many, we send men back for reinforcements while we stay to watch."

"I think Usaden already knows where they are going. If we travel fast, we can get there before them. We each ride a horse, send those who are left back, but we take the best." Thomas waited until Olaf nodded. "Then let us get this done before they get further away from us."

CHAPTER FORTY-FIVE

They made camp in a clearing among dense woods. Everyone was cold because there would be no fire that night and the year was sinking to its end. Snow that had clung to the high peaks a month before now crept lower each day.

As the sky lightened, Thomas gave up on any pretence at sleep and went to join Usaden on the edge of the tree-line.

"Is that it?" he asked, and Usaden nodded.

"Doesn't look easy to get into."

The structure was perched atop almost sheer cliffs on the side facing them. Stone built walls rose three levels to a tiled roof. This was no castle, not even a fort, but it was secure. And small.

"His men must be camped somewhere nearby," Thomas said. "There isn't enough room for more than a score in there."

"Which is to our advantage. I will find out where the others are and come back with the information."

Thomas watched Usaden walk into the open. He wondered if anyone in the distant house was watching. Kin trotted at his side, then stopped and turned back. When Thomas looked around, he saw Will standing at a distance. He approached now, the dog running to him and Will stroked his head. Thomas hadn't wanted Will with them, but he had insisted. He remained troubled, and Thomas gave in because he didn't want him examining his thoughts too closely alone.

"Where is Usaden going?" Will asked.

"To find out where Koparsh's army are."

"Why are they here, Pa?"

"You saw why. Koparsh wants Isabel dead. Fernando and Abu Abdullah too, if he can manage it, but Isabel most of all. With all three gone, it would leave the country in chaos, and the Turks are greedy for conquest. A foothold here would give them access to France and Italy, as well as North Africa."

"You know about all this stuff, don't you?"

"I think about it. How much I know is another matter."

"I'm not as clever as you," Will said. "Ami is, but not me."

"You're not stupid, either."

"I've been thinking about what happened. About what I did. I'm glad I killed those men. I would do it again to protect Isabel or Cat."

Thomas suppressed a smile. "And the King?"

Will shrugged.

Thomas touched his son's shoulder and Will leaned against him, wrapping powerful arms around Thomas's waist. Will's acceptance was one thing, the reality would take longer to settle through him, to become a part of the man he would grow into. A man to be proud of, Thomas was sure. And then he saw something and pushed the boy away.

"Go back into the woods, there are men coming."

"I'm not afraid, Pa, we will fight them."

"Then fetch Olaf and the others." Thomas pushed at Will again. "Do as I say. Do it now!" He waited until Will dropped his head and ran for the trees, Kin at his side.

When Thomas turned back, he saw a dozen men climbing towards him. He drew his sword in one hand, knife in the other, and waited.

They stopped twenty paces away, their own hands holding no weapons, so Thomas put his away.

"What do you want?" He used Arabic, assuming they were Koparsh's men.

One of them came closer, but only by a few paces.

"We have been told to find a man called Berrington. Do you know him?"

"Did Koparsh send you?"

"Who sent us is not your business. Do you know the man? He is tall, with long hair and pale skin, and dresses like a Moor even though he is not one." The man looked Thomas up and down and smiled. "You are the Berrington."

Thomas said nothing.

The man came closer still until he stood face to face with Thomas. The others stayed where they were. There were too many and Thomas was too tired. He held his arms out from his sides. At least this way, he would get to stand face to face with those he sought.

Men gripped his wrists and pulled them behind his back, and he felt the burn as a rope was jerked too tight. They looped another around his neck. One of them tugged at the rope and Thomas followed him, wondering how long they would allow him to live. At least until he saw Koparsh. What the future held after that was something he could not foresee.

————

Someone placed a hood over Thomas's head, presumably so he had no idea how to find his way back to wherever he was taken in the house. Despite the stuffiness and questionable cleanliness of the hood, he took it as a good sign until he cracked his head hard on a stone lintel and his captors laughed. When they removed the hood, blood ran down his face.

Koparsh Hadryendo sat in front of him in a chair with a high back and gilded arms, designed to look as much like a throne as could be found in these parts. Salma stood at his side, her unearthly beauty turned loathsome in Thomas's eyes.

"I am sorry my men injured you," said Koparsh. "Would you like me to have someone bathe your wound? I am sure Salma will oblige."

She stared at Thomas, a sultry heat emanating from her.

"Does she still beguile my son?"

Koparsh turned his head to Salma. "Is Yves still beguiled?"

"I believe he is." She stared at Thomas. "He is a wonderful lover. Are you a wonderful lover, Thomas Berrington? Should I compare you one to the other? Perhaps both at the same time?"

"Did he accompany you willingly when you made the attempt on Isabel's life?"

"More than willingly. He even helped in preparing the poisons. He has knowledge his mother passed down to him. He misses her very much. I can never replace her, but I have other compensations. The Queen should be dead. I know she should. Was keeping her alive your doing?"

"Theresa and Belia helped. I believe you know them both."

"This is most pleasant," said Koparsh, "but we have more serious matters to discuss. We are about to eat our morning meal and you are welcome to join us."

"So she can poison me?"

"Would you do that to a guest, Salma?"

"You know I would, if asked. Are you asking?"

"I need Thomas alive." Koparsh raised a hand to the man standing beside Thomas. "Remove the ropes. He cannot escape and cannot eat with his hands tied."

Thomas rubbed at his wrists and neck, aware the rope had left a weal on his flesh. Koparsh rose and offered an arm to Salma, who placed her hand on it. Thomas wondered how long they would allow Yves to remain alive once their plotting ended. And end it would, either with their deaths or his. But for now, he wanted to know why they were here.

Koparsh turned and walked away with Salma at his side.

Thomas watched them go, then glanced at the men beside him. He judged he could disarm them and use their weapons to attack Koparsh and Salma, but was sure there would be others close at hand.

He followed the pair into a fine room decorated with ornate tapestries. A large window offered a view across the surrounding plain, which was coming alive with the rising sun. Koparsh had already taken a chair at the head of the table with Salma to his right. A third chair was set opposite her. Nobody else was present.

Thomas took the empty chair and waited for them to choose from the bread, fruit, nuts and meat laid out. His stomach rumbled loudly and Salma smiled.

"Eat, Thomas. It is all good, I promise."

Still he waited and her smile grew. She reached out and took a spoonful of rice mixed with fruit, identical to the dish served to Isabel. Salma slid the spoon into her mouth. Thomas waited until she swallowed, then spooned some of the mix onto the plate set before him.

"Why?" he asked, looking at Koparsh.

"Do we want Queen Isabel dead?" Koparsh raised a shoulder. "It is nothing personal, merely politics."

"Merely?"

"I would not expect you to understand. Your Queen wants Islam expelled from Iberia. She fights a holy war as well as one of conquest. She has no wish to subjugate, only to cleanse this land of those she regards as vermin."

"Abu Abdullah sent a request to your Emperor for help, which was dismissed."

"It was seen to be dismissed, but why do you think he sent me?"

"And only two hundred armed men? How can you defeat Isabel or Abu Abdullah with only two hundred?"

"Who is to say I do not have more?"

"You would need twenty thousand and you cannot hide that

391

many. Not even in this abandoned country."

"I need no thousands when I have Salma. She possesses many esoteric skills, as you have already witnessed."

Thomas put down the spoon of food he was about to put in his mouth and Koparsh laughed.

"She has already promised the food is not poisoned."

"It would not be the first time she has lied to me." He looked directly at Salma. "What hold do you have over my son?"

Salma smiled as she ate another mouthful. "Oh, I think you know the answer to that without me having to explain it to you."

Thomas turned back to Koparsh. "Does your master wish to see a resurgence of Islam in Spain? You know even without Castile that will never happen."

"My master would see both sides destroyed. I come to seed confusion and destruction. It is what I have done for him before and will no doubt do so again once I am finished here. The Ottoman Empire has ambitions. Why stop at a continent when there is a world waiting?"

"Except you have failed. Isabel and Abu Abdullah both live, and soon this war will be over and you will have to scuttle back to where you came from. If I do not kill you first."

Koparsh laughed. "You speak brave words for a captive man, even one as difficult to kill as you are proving to be."

"There are only the three of us here at the moment," Thomas said.

Koparsh stared at him, amusement still on his face. Then he clapped his hands together twice. Within moments, a dozen men swarmed into the room. Koparsh continued to stare at Thomas, all humour leaching from him. He waved a hand to dismiss the men.

"Those you speak of remain alive, but that omission can soon be remedied. Do you think I do not have people placed close to them? People in senior positions? People close to all of them?"

"I know about the cook," Thomas said. "Have you disposed of her yet?"

Koparsh ignored the question, which Thomas considered answer enough.

"This thing I do is not something planned over months, but years. My master takes the long view and his eyes are on Spain. He has watched its growing strength, its victories and defeats, the former outweighing the latter, and he grows concerned. His ships and army await only my word and they will sail for these shores. Once Spain is ours, how long before the rest of the continent falls? Even your homeland."

A chill ran through Thomas. Was Koparsh doing no more than boasting, or were there people close to Isabel working for him? He thought of how easy it would be to slip a knife between her ribs and wondered why poison had been chosen instead. He thought of Eleanor's claim the French had commissioned her and knew it was a lie. He thought of Yves' claim to have been seduced away from the light and wondered at the truth of it.

"What do you want?" he asked.

"Want? I want you to die, together with your mistress and her husband and that strutting peacock in Gharnatah."

"So why am I still alive? There must be some negotiation to be made. Even you must admit the possibility you will fail. What will persuade you to leave? To give up your quest?"

"Failure is not an option."

Thomas sensed some shadow of fear in this man he had always considered did not know the emotion. His master would not forgive failure. Koparsh had come very close to that and knew it.

"When do you intend to kill me?"

"Not here, not now. That would be uncivilised. Tomorrow, perhaps. Or perhaps not. I am minded to keep you with me until events play out to their inevitable end. That would be a more worthy punishment for your annoyance to me, to watch your beloved lands razed and built again in a new form." Koparsh smiled. "I have a place for you tonight and Salma says she would like to join you. All you need do is ask, or even if you do not. She is a woman who seeks new experiences, like you, and she can be most entertaining. Even more so than your concubine, I suspect."

"I want to see my son."

"That can also be arranged." Koparsh clapped his hands again, but this time only a single man appeared, as if everything had been choreographed. "Bring him in."

The man disappeared. Thomas waited until he heard footsteps approach, then turned, but instead of Yves coming into view, he gasped as Will was led in, his hands tied as Thomas's had been.

CHAPTER FORTY-SIX

"What happened?" Thomas sat beside Will, their legs drawn up, backs against the cold stone wall. They had been taken to a small unfurnished room at the top of the highest part of the building and locked in. When Thomas looked through the single unglazed window, considering an escape, he saw a sheer drop of eighty feet onto rocks and decided against any attempt.

"I should have done as you told me and gone back for *Morfar*," said Will. "I thought … I don't know what I thought, maybe I could attack them and free you. There were not so many and I know you have fought worse odds before, but they caught me. A second group came out of the woods and took me."

"Sometimes saving yourself to fight another day is the right choice."

"Are we going to fight another day, Pa?" Will's voice hitched. "They're going to kill us, aren't they? I don't want to die. I've barely lived and now I'm never going to find out about any of that stuff Jorge told me."

Thomas pulled Will against him and kissed the top of his head.

"We're not going to die."

Will melted against him. The boy's arms circled his waist, holding tight to the father who had always offered protection. Thomas stared into space, wondering how he could make good on that promise now.

Time passed slowly and the air grew hot, the sun baking the tiles above their heads. Will fell into a doze. Thomas's eyes grew heavy and he fought to stay awake. He needed to be ready when Koparsh sent his men. He hadn't believed him when he said they would live. Why would he make such a mistake when he had made few so far? Thomas knew he might not triumph, but he would not die without taking at least some of them with him.

The sound of the door opening woke him and he rose fast. Will was a little slower, but within moments, he stood at his side. Then Thomas laughed.

"How did you get in here?" He glanced at the dagger in Usaden's hand, the tip of which dripped blood.

"Are you going to stand there all day, or do you want to escape?"

"Escape, if it's all the same to you."

Usaden shrugged.

"Where are the others?"

"Waiting for you. When neither of you returned, Olaf guessed you must have been killed or captured. I voted for killed, but Olaf said captured. So I came to find out if I was right or wrong." For a moment, Usaden almost smiled. "I am pleased to see I was wrong, but you owe me a silver coin."

"For freeing us it should be gold."

"For the wager Olaf and I made over whether you were alive or dead."

"How do we get out? Do we have to fight?"

"These steps lead down to a door, which is the way I came in. Some fool forgot to lock it."

"Or someone opened it for you. Is Jorge with you?"

"Possibly. I told him to stay outside. Are we going to stand here talking or should we leave while we can?"

"Leave," said Will, going to Usaden and embracing him.

Thomas drew the door shut behind him as he left the room. As he descended the steps, he passed four men slumped in various positions, all of them dead. They would have stood little chance against Usaden. Outside, Jorge embraced Thomas, and then knelt to throw the lock on the door, another small addition to their safety. Added together, one by one, they might make a difference.

"Who else?" Thomas asked as they moved away. He felt vulnerable in the bright light, but Usaden led them to a shallow defile where they ducked down to take advantage of what little cover it offered.

"Olaf and your friend Martin."

"And the others?"

"Olaf sent them back. He said it will be only us. The same as when we went after Mandana."

"We took an army with us that time."

"Almost the same, then. We talked it through while we were waiting for you to come back, assuming you had been captured, not killed. Olaf says, and I agree, they will send men out to find us. As Mandana did, remember? And we killed them and sent the bodies back. We pick them off one by one."

"And if they send their entire force?"

"I spent my time after leaving you searching for any sign of them and found none. There are a hundred camped a few miles south, but only that. We are few and they are many. They will never catch us."

"I hope you're right."

The defile ended, then scattered boulders sat at intervals and they made their way from one to another until they reached the tree-line. Olaf sat with his back to a cork oak while Martin de Alarcón stood in the shade.

"I am glad to see you are not dead, Thomas," said Olaf,

rising to his feet. "Even more glad to see you, Will. It is not like either of you to get caught."

"Koparsh will come after us soon. Why did you send your men away?"

"If we had kept them much longer, Abu Abdullah or Fernando would wonder what we are up to."

"Koparsh has hundreds of men."

Olaf raised a shoulder. "Usaden told me, but how many are in that house? It does not look big enough to hold hundreds."

"There are others close."

"But not close enough. So again, how many in the house? Martin rode out this morning and saw the men Usaden found, but no larger force is hidden anywhere. We both think he's sent them away. To what purpose concerns us both."

"I would like to know in which direction they have gone," said Martin.

"They are not enough to bother either Castile or Gharnatah," Thomas said. "And their leader is here, not with them." He looked back at Olaf. "I don't know how many in the house, only those I saw and those Usaden killed."

Olaf smiled. "I am glad he is on our side. So we do not know what we may be up against?"

"We wait and see," Thomas said. "Unless you have something better to do? I don't intend to abandon my son."

"Will is here," said Olaf.

"My other son. Yves." Thomas wondered if he still lived. Koparsh had been ruthless in disposing of those who served him and failed. Baldomero. Eleanor. The cook. All killed except for Salma. Had Yves also been disposed of? Thomas knew he had to work on the assumption he still lived.

Olaf walked to the edge of the trees and stared across the wide plain to where the house sat perched on a jumble of crags in the distance. Nothing moved on the open ground between.

Without saying a word, Usaden ran down the slope. After a

moment, Kin rose from where he was lying and chased after him.

"Where is he going now?" asked Martin.

"Who knows?" Thomas said.

"This Yves," said Martin. "Is he the one I met in Córdoba the year before last? The son of the French Countess? He is your son? I heard word that was possible, but did not know whether to believe it. I also heard his mother was screwing the King."

"It's complicated," Thomas said.

"It sounds as if it is. So is he captive, or a willing accomplice?"

"That I don't know, but would like to. You saw the Salma woman when Koparsh was in Santa Fe, didn't you?"

Martin nodded. "She was in Fernando's quarters in the weeks before the attempt on the Queen. I can see how a man could be swayed by someone like her, but she is a dangerous companion, is she not?"

"It was she who almost killed Isabel. Why she didn't kill Fernando when she had the chance, I don't understand, unless to do so would have shown her hand too soon."

"Theresa told me all about her, and what she did."

"I keep forgetting you two are lovers."

"As do I, but it makes the remembrance all the more pleasant. Do we wait? I dislike doing nothing."

"We wait," said Olaf. "Those we seek are in that house. They will have to come out sometime, and when they do, we make a judgement once we know their numbers and where they are headed."

"Where they go is no matter," Thomas said. "We must punish them." He stared at the barren land, the brown grass and occasional stunted tree. The air shimmered as the sun rose higher and baked the ground.

"If they are less than a score, we attack directly," said Olaf. "Yes?"

Thomas thought of the manner of fight that might be and nodded.

"Agreed, but I want Will safe before we launch an attack."

"I stay." Will had listened to the conversation without comment until that moment.

"You have done well so far," Thomas said, "but this will be hard killing. It's no place for a boy."

"You can't make me go."

"Let him stay," said Olaf. "He speaks the truth, you cannot make him leave, and we cannot spare a man to tie him to a horse and carry him back. You know how stubborn he is, he will only return as soon as he is left on his own. Besides, he is ready."

"He is ten years old," Thomas said.

"And the grandson of Olaf Torvaldsson. You saw how he fought in Al-Loraya. Do not tell me he is not ready."

Thomas took Olaf's arm and led him a short distance away.

"Killing those men hurt him in a place beyond my skills to heal."

"He will learn to heal himself if he is the man I believe him to be. The first time is hard, it always is, but it gets easier. You of all men must know it does."

"I don't want him to be like you and me. He is better than either of us."

"I chose to be a warrior," said Olaf. "Did you? No, you have told me you did not, but when the time came, you accepted what you could not turn away from. Will has to do the same, you know he does."

"This war is about to end. There will be less need to fight when it does."

Olaf laughed. "Let him stay, I will make sure nobody kills my *sonson*."

Thomas shook his head. "Don't you mean *dotterson*?"

"You have known me too long, Thomas, if you recognise that much of my language. No, I mean what I say." Olaf clapped

Thomas on the shoulder, almost sending him to his knees. "I consider you my son now, so Will is my *sonson*."

———

They sat and waited as the sun rose to its zenith and moved beyond. Flies swarmed until Thomas wrapped his tagelmust around his face so only his eyes showed. In the distance, something moved. A single man, a single dog. They came up the slope at a run and Usaden folded his legs to sit amongst them.

"Koparsh's army went north. I could not catch up with them, but the sign was clear enough. I would say they left almost as soon as they arrived from the battle. He has sent them away for certain."

"But we still don't know how many in the house," Thomas said.

"Four less than there were," said Usaden. "I can go back tonight and find out."

"Let them come to us, but we can't stay here much longer. We're going to need water soon, and food. But agreed, we wait. If they haven't shown themselves by nightfall, we find somewhere. There must be a town around here."

"We passed one four hours before we got here," said Martin. "It wasn't much of a town, but it will do."

"It lay south," Thomas said. "When they leave, I expect them to go north after their men. We should—"

The rattle of hoofs brought him to his feet. For a moment, he thought Koparsh had avoided them and was about to launch an attack, then he saw a single rider racing down the slope.

"Will!" Thomas yelled, but his son continued to ride hard.

"He rides well," said Martin.

"What does he think he's doing?"

"He is clever," said Usaden. "He is doing what we should have done. We have been too passive. Will is going to draw them out."

"Or get himself killed."

"No, he is not. Look, it is working."

Will had covered a quarter of the distance to the house when men emerged. They swarmed in confusion, dots barely bigger than the flies that swarmed around Thomas, then they recovered their wits and mounted horses.

"Turn back," Thomas whispered, but Will went on, directly towards the men.

Usaden ran back into the trees in search of a horse, and after a moment, the others followed, but Thomas feared they were already too late. He was slow tightening his saddle, but saw Usaden didn't bother with one and was first away, him and the horse becoming one. Thomas finally mounted and followed, fearing they were too few. Far too few.

Will came within two hundred paces of the lead riders before he swerved hard, almost bringing his horse to its knees. He urged it to a fresh effort and rode back in the direction of the five of them, who were closing the gap.

Olaf raised an arm. "Slow down, we wait for him here."

Thomas rose from the saddle and shaded his eyes. How many? Too many.

"I count twenty-nine," said Martin.

"As do I," said Jorge.

"I don't see Koparsh or Salma," Thomas said.

Usaden rode ahead before returning.

"They are not there, I am sure."

Will was halfway back to them when Thomas looked around at where they were.

"We should make a stand on that rise." He pointed to where a cluster of rocks formed a mound. They would make it harder for the attackers to approach. Olaf nodded and urged his horse in that direction before dismounting.

"We form a circle facing out," he said. "Backs as close together as we can get. Thomas, Will comes between you and me, agreed?"

"Agreed."

They climbed through the rocks and made ready. Will pulled his horse to a halt and slid from the saddle and Kin came up the low slope at his side. Thomas made room and they waited.

The riders came hard and fast, spreading out as they approached, but not slowing.

"They are going to break their horses' legs," said Martin.

"It will make it all the easier to kill them." Already the cold was flooding into Thomas, making the world sharp around him. He laid a hand on Will's shoulder, as much for his own comfort as to offer any, and was pleased to feel only firm muscle and no tremor. They might live to see the sun set.

CHAPTER FORTY-SEVEN

The riders came closer, almost on them as the thunder of hooves shook the ground beneath Thomas's feet, and then the front ranks parted. They flowed around the mound of rocks without slowing, to merge again once past. Thomas turned to see if they intended to attack from both sides, but the riders kept going. The dust of their passage slowly settled around the small group on the knoll. Several minutes passed. Only then did Thomas allow himself to hope.

"Koparsh wasn't among them," said Jorge. "Nor Salma or Yves."

"What are they doing?" asked Olaf. "There were enough to kill us all. Why did they not even try?"

"We would have taken half their number," Thomas said. "Koparsh knew that. He has seen how we fight. He wants to keep as many of his men alive as he can." Thomas watched the distant riders as they moved away. "They're going north to join their companions."

"Leaving Koparsh alone," said Usaden.

Thomas turned back. The house was closer now, close enough to see any movement around it, but there was none.

"I don't understand. Why would they send their soldiers away?"

"Do not question our good fortune." Olaf picked his way down the slope. Usaden passed him, leaping from stone to stone with ease.

They re-mounted their horses and headed towards the house. Thomas's unease remained and he kept turning to look back to where Koparsh's men had disappeared, but the land lay quiet.

Thomas dismounted and left his horse to wander in search of grass. He glanced at Usaden.

"You and me?"

Usaden nodded.

"Stay here and keep an eye on Will," Thomas said to Olaf. "Don't let him follow until I call you inside. This could be a trap."

"In which case we should all go," said Olaf.

"We know the lie of the land inside, you don't. If you hear a fight, then come in after us, but stay with Will, promise me."

They got as far as the heavy oak door before being halted. It was locked.

"Jorge," Thomas called, waving him over. "We need you."

He waited as Jorge knelt and used a sliver of metal to free the lock. Thomas recalled the first time Jorge had demonstrated his ability to open doors that were not meant to be opened. It had been many years before and come as a surprise. How had a palace eunuch learned such a thing? He tried to recall if Jorge had ever offered an explanation, but could not. If he had, Thomas had forgotten it, or more likely not listened hard enough. He knew he did that more than he should.

Jorge rose and pushed the door open with a grin.

"You can thank me later."

Usaden was first in, Thomas close behind. Jorge followed despite being told to stay outside. They stood in a loose triangle, each of them listening. There was nothing. The air felt stale, the house abandoned.

"Split up," Thomas said. "Search every room and corridor. Call out if you find anyone."

Usaden went right, Jorge left. Thomas climbed the stone steps, which he knew eventually led to the small room where he and Will had been held prisoner. He went slowly, checking every passage and room that led off the steps, but each was abandoned. The room they had eaten in still had the table sitting square in the middle, the remains of a meal scattered across it. The tapestries had been cut down and piled on the floor. He almost missed what they covered before he caught sight of a foot emerging from beneath their folds. He knelt to lift the heavy material from the body beneath until Yves emerged. He lay on his side, eyes closed.

"In here!" Thomas called out, an unexpected emotion rising through him. He had lost the woman he once loved, and now a son he barely knew, all in the space of a few weeks.

Then Yves drew a breath and coughed.

Thomas rolled him to his back and tore open his shirt. He lay a hand on Yves' chest, felt a steady heartbeat. He opened his son's mouth and ran his fingers around inside, examined them for any trace of food he might have eaten, but there was nothing.

Jorge entered the room and knelt beside him.

"Is he dead?"

"Alive, for the moment."

"Why did they leave him?"

"Perhaps he is meant to be dead."

"I don't understand. A knife to the heart would have been more sure."

"This is Salma's doing. She can't help herself, she has to show her power, her skill."

"So he's poisoned?"

"I don't know!" Thomas was sharper than intended, but he

was afraid Yves was going to die. He wondered why he cared as much as he did. He had only just started to know the man, and what he had found out had not endeared him. But he was his flesh and blood. Thomas would fight to keep him alive if he could.

He stood as Usaden came into the room.

"Anything?"

"Abandoned. Beds slept in and unmade. Food on the table uneaten. Is that your son? Did they kill him?" No inflection in his voice.

"They intended to, but failed. Go back to the others, tell them there's nobody left here. You and Kin are our best trackers, so go see if you can find out where Koparsh and Salma went."

"What are you going to do?" asked Jorge.

Thomas walked to the table without replying. He leaned over and studied the food that was left. Was one of these dishes tainted, and if so, had Yves eaten some of it? Thomas had no way of knowing. He used the tip of a knife to separate ingredients, but was no wiser for having done so.

He turned as Jorge came to stand beside him.

"We can't stay much longer, this might be a trap to lure us in. We should carry him down, tie him to a horse and take him with us."

"I will not allow them to escape punishment," Thomas said, "but I stay until he wakes or he dies. Go tell the others to leave. If anyone is watching, they will think we have all gone. Ride south."

"You know I can't leave you on your own," said Jorge. "How would you manage without me?"

Thomas didn't consider an answer necessary. He tossed down the plate he had been examining and returned to where Yves lay. Jorge had moved him to be more comfortable and now he lay across the piled tapestries. Thomas wondered why they had bothered to tear them down to hide Yves. If Salma had given him enough poison to kill him, there would have been no need to hide his body.

"Come help me."

"See?" said Jorge as he came across. "I knew you would need me. Aren't you glad you didn't send me away now?"

Between them, they dragged Yves from the tapestries and Thomas began to pull them out one by one. He examined the first and second, but there was no secret hidden between the folds. It was only as he turned the last one over he found what he had not until then known he was searching for. A small ceramic bottle, dark blue with a wooden stopper. He picked it up, pulled the stopper out and sniffed. Poppy, a familiar scent, together with hashish and perhaps some spirit. Apples … no, cherries. A powerful scent of cherries.

He took the bottle to the table and emptied food from a plate, went back and pulled one tapestry up and used a corner to clean the plate. Then he poured the contents of the bottle onto it.

He leaned over and sniffed hard again.

Yes, sour cherries, the bitter inner kernel of the stones, the smell unmistakable. He cursed.

"What's wrong?" Jorge was at his side once more and Thomas allowed himself to take some small comfort from his presence.

"They made him drink what was in this bottle and he's been poisoned. Do you know where the kitchens are?"

"As a matter of fact, I do, I searched them when we split up. They are one floor down and at the end of the corridor."

"Stay with Yves," Thomas said. "If he starts to wake, he might throw up. Put him on his side and keep him there."

"You offer me all the most pleasant jobs, don't you?"

"Just hope he only vomits," Thomas said as he walked to the door.

He found the kitchen easily enough and looked around for what he knew must be there. As in the room above, this one was abandoned. One pot remained on a hook over a recent fire. It had dried out and a strong smell of burning tainted the air. Thomas used a rag to remove the pot and peered inside. He nodded, his suspicion confirmed. It had been used to distil down whatever mixture Salma had created. He looked around, convinced broken cherry stones would be here somewhere, but saw none. Instead, he found larger stones and the pale green flesh of plums. He cursed. The kernels of four cherry stones contained enough poison to kill a man. A single plum stone had the same effect. There were at least a dozen scattered across the floor.

Thomas filled a jug with water and ran back upstairs.

"I think he moved a little," said Jorge, sitting cross-legged beside Yves. He had piled the tapestries together to form a makeshift bed.

"Sit him up." Thomas knelt beside him, and as Jorge supported Yves from behind, Thomas forced water into him. Yves choked and most came out, but Thomas tried again, emptying half the jug before Yves' chest heaved. Thomas rolled away as his son brought up the contents of his stomach.

"There are times I wonder why I'm still your friend," said Jorge, but he continued to wrap his arms around Yves as he vomited again.

"You would only grow bored if not for me," Thomas said.

When he was sure Yves had brought everything up, he came closer and used the tapestry to wipe his mouth and face. He felt his neck, relieved his pulse continued steady.

"Keep him like this for a moment." Thomas rose and went to the table and looked at the remnant of poison that had been in the small bottle. He judged Yves had drunk only half of it, but had Salma distilled the poison from all the plum stones or not? Half the bottle would still be too much if she had used them all.

He heard a deep cough from behind and spun around.

Yves' eyes were open, but unfocused.

Thomas went and grasped him beneath his arms.

"Get him to his feet, we need to walk him around. I'll try to get more water into him in a while, but I want him awake first."

They supported Yves between them, his feet slack as they dragged him around the room. Slowly, hesitant at first, Yves attempted to takes steps. As time passed, he became more confident. Thomas tried to release his hold, but immediately Yves swayed and he grasped him again.

"He lives, I see," said Usaden as he returned to the room. Thomas thought he detected a note of surprise in his voice, which was a first.

"I know you…" Yves' voice was slurred. Thomas thought he must be referring to Usaden, but when he turned, Yves was staring at him.

"I am your father," he said.

"I knew I had seen you somewhere before. I thought you were dead."

Thomas wondered if he was thinking of the Count d'Arreau, who had stolen the seventeen-year-old Eleanor from him. Then Yves said, "Salma told me you were dead before she gave me my tonic."

"Your tonic?"

"She has made me drink it for weeks." Yves rubbed at his head. "It makes me feel strange, but she says it is good for me." He gave a sly smile. "It makes a ram out of me. Though Salma can do that without the need of any tonic."

"She drugged you?" Thomas experienced a wave of relief. Yves had not turned into a killer. Salma had drugged him to bend him to her will. He saw how it was possible. She was mesmeric, and achingly beautiful.

"It was to make me strong," said Yves. His wits were returning, and when Thomas released his hold, Yves stayed on his feet. "Except the one she gave me today was different. She said it was special and she would return for me and we would spend the rest of the day in each other's arms. She told me to drink it all."

"But you didn't, did you?"

"I told you…" Yves frowned, "…Father?"

Thomas nodded. "Yes, I am your father."

"Thomas… Thomas Barrington…"

"Berrington."

"It tasted strange, not what she usually gave me, so I didn't drink it all. When she left, I hid the bottle in the tapestries we pulled down."

"She left? While you were still awake?"

"I told you, she said she was coming back to pleasure me to within an inch of my life." Yves looked around. "Is she waiting for me somewhere?"

"Salma tried to kill you. If I hadn't found you, she would have succeeded. She has kept you drugged ever since…" Thomas realised he didn't know how Yves had fallen in with the Turks. "How did she seduce you?"

The sly smile came again. "How do you think? Any man would lie with her, even you. Is she here?"

"She has fled." Thomas turned to Usaden, who nodded.

"South. Ten horses, one with a slighter rider than the others."

"Why south?"

"I assume you do not expect me to know the answer to that?"

"Koparsh's men went north."

"Then perhaps they have unfinished business with Isabel."

CHAPTER FORTY-EIGHT

Thomas rode hard beside Martin de Alarcón. He had sent Yves ahead with the others and told them to return to his house in Gharnatah. He would join them when he could, but they would be safer there. They had all agreed apart from Jorge, who said he would fetch Belia first and take the children to Da'ud's old house.

Now, as the day drew to an end, Thomas and Martin raced along a narrow pathway between bored troops who stood to watch the passage of these madmen. Thomas leapt from the saddle and left his horse for someone else to care for. He ran into Isabel's quarters only to collide with Theresa.

"Where is she?" He gripped her shoulders too tightly and saw her wince.

"Where she always is, working in her office, and she wants to see you." Theresa looked past him and her face softened when she saw Martin. Thomas released her and strode past.

Isabel looked up, her hair once more coming loose from its pins to drift across her face.

"Where have you been? I have work for you. There is much to arrange and little time. Two weeks, Thomas, that is all that remains before we make Castile whole."

"I have been chasing down the woman who tried to kill you. Would you rather I not bother?"

Isabel stared at him and Thomas wondered if he had gone too far. He wasn't sure whether he cared anymore. His life had unravelled thread by thread. He wondered if, when the process concluded, there would be anything left of him, or merely an empty shell where a man had once stood.

Then Isabel rose and came around the table. She stood in front of him and took both his hands in hers. Thomas almost kissed her. He wondered what she would have done if he had. The threads drew taut once more, cutting into him. Duty. Honour. Friendship. Love … Revenge.

"I still have all my food tasted, Thomas. I have made myself eat less and drink only wine that has not been opened."

"You will fade to a wraith."

"Only until we conclude matters. I assume you are talking about the Turkish woman and your son?"

"I believe she forced my son to act as he did. Salma had a hold over him. She drugged him."

"You are sure?"

"I think I am. I will know more when he recovers and I can question him. I have sent him to my house in Gharnatah with the others. Koparsh and Salma have come south. No doubt to achieve what they could not before and steal your life. Koparsh admitted as much to me when I was his captive—that you were the reason he came to Castile. The Ottomans want Spain as part of their empire."

Isabel reached up and laid a finger on Thomas's lips.

"Stop, you are saying too much and I do not understand it all. You need to tell me everything, but not now. When did you last sleep?"

Thomas shook his head. "I don't know. Two days ago, perhaps three."

"Then sleep now. Theresa will find you somewhere, but stay within these walls. There are ten thousand men outside and

Koparsh has no chance of reaching me. No chance at all. Believe that and sleep. You can explain everything tomorrow. Eat first—it is not me who looks like a wraith, but you."

"Where is Fernando?"

"He is here somewhere, why?"

Thomas realised he had no idea why he had asked. He shook his head.

"It doesn't matter." Then it came to him. "He was friendly with Koparsh, wasn't he?"

Isabel frowned. "Him and that woman both. I have told him he must act as a true king now. After…" she reached out a hand as if trying to pluck some truth from the air "…after Granada falls, he can do as he wishes."

Thomas stared at her. "And you?"

"Will also do as I wish." She squeezed his hand. "Now go, eat, sleep, lie in bed as long as you want tomorrow, and then we will talk about many things."

Thomas was in a daze as he walked along the corridor. He wondered if Theresa could find him somewhere to bathe. His body stank of sweat and blood and death.

As he approached the outer door, an altercation started up as the guards tried to prevent someone entering and Thomas broke into a run. He expected to find Koparsh or Salma, but instead, Usaden stood there, allowing two guards to restrain him.

He met Thomas's eyes and made some slight movement. All at once, he was no longer held.

"Olaf sent me. Koparsh and Salma were seen entering Gharnatah mid-afternoon. Olaf is making enquiries to find out where they went once they were inside the walls."

Thomas shook his head hard, trying to dismiss the sense of unreality that clung to him.

"I brought a horse for you," said Usaden as he turned away.

They left the horses at the foot of the Albayzin and climbed cobbled alleys in the last light of the day. One or two people called out to Thomas, asking where he had been, telling him they were glad he had returned.

"Who is at the house?" Thomas asked.

"Only Helena, Yves and Will. I told them to bar all the doors. Jorge said he was going to spend the night in Da'ud's old house. He is keeping Amal and Jahan with him, and Belia. Olaf went home." Usaden glanced at Thomas. "It is over. You know it is. We will track them down tomorrow and kill them."

"I have a better plan."

"There is no better plan than to kill them."

"I want to send Koparsh back with a message to his master."

"I doubt there is one a sultan will listen to."

"A message he cannot steal this land. Yes, Salma can die, kill her yourself if you want."

"I take no pleasure in death, Thomas. I know what you think of me, but I regret every life I have ever taken."

"Not as much as you would regret losing your own."

"I see we understand each other. I suspect we are not so different under the skin."

"Perhaps not. Does that make us friends?"

"We could be, I suppose."

Thomas thought he caught the faintest of smiles from Usaden.

"At least my dog likes you," he said.

"Kin likes everyone, unless he is trying to tear their throat out."

They came out on the level path that led to Thomas's house. To their right, the palace loomed over the city, its myriad windows illuminated.

"Isabel will live there soon," Thomas said.

"And you?"

"I have a fine house this side of the Hadarro, why would I want to live in a palace?"

"With a queen? Many men would be envious of your position."

"I am not many men."

"No, indeed you are not."

They entered the narrow passage leading to the courtyard. As they did so, Thomas wondered why the door had not been barred as Usaden had ordered.

Once inside the courtyard, Thomas stopped dead in his tracks, trying to take in the scene that lay before him.

Helena stood beneath the terrace, held in the grip of Koparsh Hadryendo. Will stood in front of them, a sword in one hand and an axe in the other. He looked so much like Olaf that Thomas's sense of unreality deepened.

Two men lay dead on the flagstones and there was blood on Will's weapons. His son glanced up and saw Thomas. He gave a single nod, his face set hard. The cold was in him, Thomas could tell, driving all his demons away to leave his mind calm.

Salma stood behind a kneeling Yves, a slim knife held to his throat which had already drawn blood. Her eyes met Thomas's and she smiled.

"I should have taken more care and done it this way before. Pride is a poor companion for an assassin."

Koparsh pulled Helena tighter against himself, his knife also at her throat.

"Which of them shall I kill first, Pa?" Will asked.

Thomas heard the certainty in his voice and wondered for a moment what he had created. Him and Olaf and Usaden. Had they done too good a job with Will and turned him into a killing machine?

"I will take the woman," said Usaden softly beside Thomas. "You go for the man. Will has done enough here tonight."

Thomas gave a slow nod. "On three."

"Fuck three," said Usaden and launched himself at Salma.

Her hand moved, but before it could draw more blood, Yves reared up fast and pushed back against her. She toppled and cracked her head against the low stone wall that bounded the terrace.

Thomas saw no more as he ran hard. He pushed Will aside, then threw himself at Koparsh and Helena. He crashed into them, all three tumbling to the ground. Helena screamed, trying to squirm away but getting tangled between them.

Thomas grasped Koparsh's wrist to keep the knife away from Helena, but he knew he was too late. Koparsh's blade had already opened her cheek, the unblemished one. The wound was even deeper than that which had brought her to his house many years before.

He heard Salma scream and ignored the sound.

He glimpsed Will dancing from side to side, readying himself to strike as soon as he could distinguish between the three bodies writhing together.

Thomas felt a pain in his shoulder and realised Koparsh had released Helena and struck out with a second knife. He ignored the wound and kicked out, landing a lucky blow to send the knife clattering away. Koparsh was strong, far stronger than Thomas, and he knew he was fading. Too little sleep. Too little food. Too much fear.

Then Helena fell against him. Her arm rose, descended. Thomas saw the discarded knife in her hand. So did Koparsh. He raised his hand to deflect it, but the knife slid through his palm to emerge from the other side. Thomas took his chance. He leapt into the air, then came down with all his force to drive his knees into Koparsh's belly. The man gasped and splayed out, unconscious.

"No!" Thomas reached out and gripped Helena's wrist as she withdrew the knife and attempted to thrust it into Koparsh's chest. "I want him alive." He breathed deep, his lungs ragged. "Your face…" His fingers reached out, wanting to take away her pain. "I will fix you again."

She smiled, the gesture ragged and blood-streaked.

"I know you will, my love."

"He stuck you, Pa." Will stood over Koparsh. "Can I kill him?"

"No." Thomas tried to rise to his feet and failed, managed on the second attempt by hanging on to Will's strength. "But there is something you can help me with, if you are willing."

"Anything, Pa."

Thomas staggered and Will reached out to keep him upright. Over on the far side of the terrace, Yves sat on the low wall. Salma lay with arms thrown wide. Her throat was cut, blood soaking the surrounding slabs.

Thomas walked to his workshop and picked up a stool. He brought it back, cracked it on the flagstones to break the legs, then set the seat beneath Koparsh's arm, halfway between wrist and elbow.

"Give me your axe," he said to Will.

"I will do it. I have killed two already, I can kill another."

"Give me your axe," Thomas said again, and eventually Will gave in and held it out.

Thomas couldn't use it as Will and Olaf did, swinging free from a leather thong secured at the wrist. It made the weapon one with them, a feat he could never emulate, but he had no need of their skill. He gripped the handle of the axe and kicked his toe against Koparsh, who was recovering.

"Usaden, is she dead?" Thomas asked without turning.

"She could not be more dead."

"And Yves?"

"He looks like he might throw up, but otherwise unharmed. He did well. He moved faster than I thought possible."

"Come hold Koparsh's arm for me." He glanced at Will. "You hold the other."

Thomas waited until they did as asked, then waited some more until Koparsh was almost fully recovered. As he regained his wits, he spat at Thomas.

"You would not dare. If you kill me, my master will not rest until I am avenged."

"And who will tell him it was me?"

"There is always someone. You can never sleep safe."

Thomas laughed. "Ah, if only I could sleep. Confess and I may spare you."

"So the Queen can take my head instead? No, do your worst."

"You have my word I will not kill you, but I need to know the truth. Tell me and you can return to Turkey, or whatever land you come from."

Still held by Usaden and Will, Koparsh stared up at Thomas. His eyes dropped to take in the axe, the bloodstained blade.

"You will let me walk away from your house alive?"

"You have my word."

"Everything I heard about you said your word could be trusted, but—"

"What have you to lose? Don't tell me and you die here. Tell me and you may have a chance. Your decision."

Thomas waited, watching the man. His head swam with exhaustion, but he knew he had to hold on a little longer. Helena's face needed repairing, Salma's body needed to be disposed of, and Yves had questions to answer of his own.

"Ask, then," said Koparsh.

"Eleanor claimed the French recruited her to kill Isabel. Is that true?"

"No, I recruited her. The French have nothing to do with any of this. It was a tale we agreed she should tell so nobody would know it was my master who wanted the Queen dead. Your lover was known as the most skilled assassin in the western lands. Somewhere in her home, she claimed to have a list of all those whose lives she had taken. So many, she had to make extra space for their names."

Thomas didn't care about the others.

"Did you have her killed?"

"I did, because she failed me. Those who fail me suffer the

419

consequences." Koparsh glanced beyond Thomas. "Even Salma, it seems."

"And Baldomero and his wife?"

"Collateral damage, nothing more. As you would be if you were not so difficult to kill." Koparsh smiled, his strength returning. "There is still time to remedy that mistake." He glanced beyond Thomas once more.

"I have a message for your Sultan," Thomas said.

"What message? Tell me then, before you die."

"This." Thomas brought the axe down hard. Koparsh screamed, high and sharp. Thomas pushed at the detached arm with his foot and kicked it away. Blood poured from the stump to pool on the flagstones.

"Will, kneel on his arm to slow the bleeding, I don't want him to die."

His son did as asked.

Koparsh continued to shout and Thomas was tempted to kill him, but knew he could not. Instead, he leaned close and put his mouth to his ear.

"Go back to your master and tell him to leave this land alone. It is not for sale. It is not for conquest. He will take his eyes away from the west and settle for what he has. Do you understand?"

Koparsh nodded, reaching over to grasp his arm.

"Keep him where he is." Thomas walked into the workshop and found a cloth and distilled alcohol. He searched in drawers until he found needle and gut, and went back out.

Koparsh screamed even louder when Thomas cauterised the wound with coals from the fire as he stitched it closed. He did not tidy the end of the stump as he had for Olaf. The sharp bone would grate painfully when the wound healed, a constant reminder of Koparsh's failure.

When he was finished, he allowed the man to his feet. Koparsh glared at Thomas without speaking, glanced at Salma's body, then turned and left.

"You should have killed him," said Usaden. "I can follow and do it for you."

"I need him to carry a message." Thomas glanced at Will, reached out and pulled the boy against him. He rolled his shoulder, testing it. The wound Koparsh had inflicted was not serious and there was more important work for him to do. He glanced at Yves, who sat on the flagstones.

"You were a fool to fall in with them," he said.

Yves looked up. He stood tall, different now, as though killing Salma had turned him into something he had not been before.

"Who are you to call me fool?" Even his voice was more confident. "You are the fool," he sneered, "Father."

Thomas ignored the taunt.

"What are you going to do now?"

"Whatever I want. It is none of your business. I am a grown man of thirty-one years and will make my own decisions. My mother tried to control me and I know you want to do the same. I will not stand for it anymore. Not from you. Not from anyone." He glanced down at Salma, his face expressionless. "As she discovered."

Thomas turned away, then stopped. He needed to attend to Helena as soon as possible. The longer he left her wound, the less perfect the repair would be, but something in Yves' words had stuck in his mind. He had said he was a man of thirty-one. Thomas thought back a long way, counted forward. His son should be thirty-five. Not thirty-one.

When he looked at Yves again, Thomas saw the realisation of what had been said in anger come to him and his sneer return.

"Did you really think I was your son? *Your* son? You are an even bigger fool than I thought you."

Thomas continued to stare, trying to make sense of everything Eleanor had told him, everything he had believed until this moment.

421

Why had she lied about such a thing?

"Who, then? That old man?"

"Of course not. I doubt he could even get it up, and if he could, he wouldn't know what to do with it. Another came. Young, like you. Handsome, unlike you. A travelling minstrel, Mother told me. Except he stopped travelling for a while. I think I remember him, but cannot be sure. He was there, and then he was not. It is what men like him do. What you did."

He was there, and then he was not. Thomas recalled Eleanor's confession to him. The lover she had killed after poisoning his wife. Another lie, but perhaps one with a grain of truth to it.

"Eleanor carried my child when I was torn from her," he said.

"That may be true, though it was only many years later she admitted it to me. When she recognised you in Córdoba, she asked me to pretend to be your son."

"So who is that child, if it's not you? Where are they now?"

Yves smiled. "Oh, I am sure you would like to know the answer to that question, but I have no inclination to give it."

"You will, eventually." Thomas turned to Usaden. "Hold him until I finish."

Usaden gave a nod and moved forward, as sure as ever. And then the impossible happened.

The knife Salma had held at Yves' throat appeared in his hand and he struck out, lightning fast. All at once, blood bloomed on Usaden's chest. He coughed and stopped, then went to his knees.

Before Thomas could react, Yves turned and ran through the door to the alley.

CHAPTER FORTY-NINE

The year was drawing to a close and Thomas knew that soon, he would have to return to Isabel. He tried to ignore his reluctance and pretend it was nothing more than weariness. Some was that, but weeks had passed and still he remained in his house on the Albayzin. Jorge lived with Belia and Jahan in their new house, and life had settled into a peaceful rhythm.

Thomas treated Helena's face every day with a lotion Belia made for her and already the flesh had knitted together. It formed a raised red welt down the side of her face, but Helena made no complaint.

Usaden healed slowly, but had started to train with Will again. He owed even more to Thomas now, because nobody else could have saved his life after Yves struck out. Even Thomas had been unsure he could do so, but the thought of losing the man had been too much to bear, so he had exceeded even the skill he already possessed. They had talked of how Yves had struck him. Nobody ever struck Usaden and he claimed they had all underestimated the man who was no longer Thomas's son. He wondered often what had happened to the child Eleanor had carried, a thought that scratched at his mind. Had the child died? Did it live? Did it still live? He knew, one day, he would have to find the answer to the question. But it was something for the future. If he had one.

———

"Your face will heal," Thomas said to Helena one night as they lay in bed together. "I know you may not believe me now, but it will heal."

"I did not believe you when first you fixed me, but you were right. I cannot see the scar on my other cheek anymore, however hard I look. This wound is deeper, but I do not mind so long as you continue to lie beside me." She kissed his mouth, half-lying across him. "Will you always lie with me, Thomas? You haven't touched me since that man gave me this. It is my face he damaged, not anywhere else."

"I don't want to hurt you."

"You would not. You know I have ways and means."

"Soon." Thomas stared at the perfection of her body, touched the narrow valley along her back.

"The sooner the better." She kissed him again and turned away. "I love you, Thomas Berrington."

He reached out and snuffed the candle and lay for a long time, listening to the sounds of the city that came muffled through the glazed window.

In the morning there were visitors, Martin de Alarcón and Theresa. Helena set two more places at the table in the courtyard where they could all gaze across at al-Hamra.

"I expect Isabel has sent you, hasn't she?" Thomas asked.

"She wants to know if you are all right," said Theresa. Martin stood chatting to Jorge and Belia, who had arrived only moments after them. "She said you were not all right the last time she saw you."

"That was weeks ago. I have slept since, and as you can see, I am eating."

"She is grateful for what you did. 'Trust Thomas to sort it

out,' she said." Theresa smiled. "She wants you to go to her today. There are arrangements to be made."

"When is it to be?" Thomas did not need to be told what manner of arrangements. The time had come and he had no clear idea of how he felt about it, only that he knew whatever he felt would stop nothing. Like everything else he had done, he would have to accept it as best he could. The fall of his beloved Gharnatah.

"The day after tomorrow. The first day of a new year. The first day of fourteen hundred and ninety-two." Theresa covered her mouth with a hand as she laughed. "And she says you have to do something about Columb. She has never encountered anyone so single-minded or persistent. Other than you. She says she cannot think about him a moment longer."

"I will return with you and Martin."

Theresa smiled at him. "He has asked me to marry him."

"I thought he was looking for a duchess."

"Am I not better than a duchess, Thomas?" She shook her head. "Oh, but it would have been nice to have seduced you the once."

"My apologies."

Theresa looked past him to where Helena was laughing at something Jorge had said.

"What happened to her face?"

"Koparsh Hadryendo. I took his arm off and sent him back to his master with a message that Spain cannot be touched."

"And the woman?"

"Dead."

"Martin found the cook you were looking for."

"Also dead?"

Theresa nodded. "And your son, Yves? Has he also been punished?"

"He is gone. One day I may tell you about Yves, but not this day. This is a day for friendship, not betrayal. I am pleased about you and Martin. Without him, none of this would have happened.

The war would still go on, but now it ends the day after tomorrow." Thomas could scarcely believe it. "What will Isabel do then?"

"What she has always done. Her duty."

"And you will be at her side?"

"As always. As will you, Thomas. I know she wants you with her. She needs you now more than ever. You know this city and its people. The war might end, but the peace is not yet won. She will demand you help her forge a just peace."

Thomas drew a breath and held it deep before releasing the air from his lungs. The weeks since he had returned felt like a dream, nothing more. Duty called. It felt like a return to normality.

———

A cold wind tugged at Thomas's robe as he stood beside Isabel's white stallion. She sat astride it like a man, as she always did, her silver armour bright in the thin sunshine. It had rained overnight and the ground underfoot was sticky with mud.

Abu Abdullah stood with head bent beneath the open eastern gate of Gharnatah. His mother Aixa stood to one side, a scattering of nobles and officials also present. But it was the Sultan who mattered here.

The time had come. It could be put off no longer.

Abu Abdullah raised his head as if with a great effort and stepped forward.

"You majesties, I present you with the key to this city, which has served me good and well. Take care of it and its people, for I no longer can." He held out his hand, which held a large, ornate key. Thomas knew it would open nothing and was only for show, but the symbolism mattered.

Isabel made to urge her horse closer, but Fernando cut her off, riding to loom over Abu Abdullah, who reached up and handed the key to him. Without looking at it, Fernando held the key out, waiting. Juan stepped close and took it. He carried it back and handed it to his mother, who passed it on to someone else. The key did not matter. The moment did.

"Help me, Thomas," Isabel said.

He offered his cupped hand as she dismounted, touched her slim back to steady her. When he looked beyond her, Fernando's eyes were on him and they blazed with hatred.

Isabel picked her way across the slippery ground until she stood before Abu Abdullah, a slight figure, but the stronger of them.

"I give my promise, Malik, that we will do as you ask." She afforded him one final small honour as he bowed his head. Protocol demanded he should kneel, but they had made an arrangement so as not to demean him further.

Thomas looked beyond the gathering, his eyes searching until he found the people who mattered most to him in the world. Will stood tall, Amal perched on his shoulders. Jorge had one arm around Belia while the other held Jahan on his hip. He saw Thomas find them and nodded. Helena stood beside them.

And then Thomas saw two other figures and smiled. Usaden stood apart from everyone, unarmed as were all but those of Castile. Beside him stood Kin, alert, eyes on everything.

There was one other Thomas sought, but failed to find. Olaf Torvaldsson had chosen not to attend this surrender.

Isabel turned away and it was as if the earth gave a great sigh. Thomas met Abu Abdullah's eyes and saw defeat in them. When he looked at Aixa, he found only hatred of him and those who had humiliated this great city.

There were others Thomas knew from the many years he had lived within Gharnatah's walls. Friends and neighbours, soldiers he had healed who had never thanked him, but the lack never concerned him, only that he had done his duty. As he knew he would continue to do his duty.

"I need you with me tomorrow, Thomas," Isabel said. "I am allowing Boabdil until the end of today to say his goodbyes and gather whatever he needs. Tomorrow, I enter the palace and I want you to show me everything."

"Then I will need Jorge with me," Thomas said, "for he knows it far better than I do."

"Bring him then, but not when we enter. That will be Fernando and myself, with you behind us. I want the world to see the trust I place in you. Ask Jorge to join us later. You are right, who better than a eunuch to know a palace?" She gave a shake of her head, as far as the armour would allow. "I forget he is a eunuch these days. A eunuch who can father children. Truly it is a time of miracles." She gave a wicked smile. "Perhaps I should have him made a saint. I am sure Cardinal de Borja would oblige me."

"Saint Jorge?" Thomas shook his head. "I think not."

———

It was gone noon when Thomas once more stood beside Isabel. This time, the ceremony was almost as symbolic as the sham that had occurred that morning. Abu Abdullah was mounted this time, while Isabel sat on her own steed and waited for him to approach.

Fernando was at her side, and as the party of Moors approached, he urged his horse to stand between his wife and Abu Abdullah.

"You are to ride directly to Laujar de Andarax. You are not to detour. You are not to make any attempt to contact your army, do you understand?"

It was one final insult, but Abu Abdullah nodded while his mother scowled. Aixa was a handsome woman, but the expression made her ugly.

428

"Martin will accompany you to ensure you do as the King asks," said Isabel.

Abu Abdullah stared at her. "I do not want the Alarcón. Can you not send Thomas in his place?"

"Thomas has other duties to perform."

"Which are not until tomorrow, I hear. I will not have the Alarcón." He met her eyes, unflinching until Isabel turned to Thomas.

"Are you willing to go? Only until the city is no longer in sight. Fernando is sending men, but they have been told to stay at a distance."

"I will go if you ask it." Thomas didn't want to, but was aware of Abu Abdullah's reasons.

Their small party followed a winding track up a steep incline, the air growing colder the higher they went until at last they reached a narrow pass and stopped.

Abu Abdullah dismounted and walked back to look down at the city he had ruled and lost. Gharnatah sat among glittering waterways, its pale walls catching the lowering rays of the sun. A year ago, the *vega* surrounding the city had been verdant and rich with crops. Now it lay blackened and spoiled. Men worked to recover the riches that once grew there. Perhaps in another year, they would restore a little of its former glory.

Thomas stayed back as Aixa stood next to her son.

He saw Abu Abdullah's chest hitch as he wiped tears from his face.

"Gone," he said. "All of it gone. God is great!"

"You do well to weep like a woman," said Aixa, scorn making her voice harsh, "for what you failed to defend like a man." As she turned away, she caught sight of Thomas and stopped. "As for you, traitor, you can go now you have witnessed this last humiliation."

———

It was growing dark as Thomas climbed the slope of the Albayzin to his house. Jorge greeted him as he entered, wrapping his arms around him.

"You almost looked like you belonged there today, my friend. Belia has made us all a fine meal and Olaf has brought Fatima across. They are inside with Will and Amal." Jorge held Thomas's shoulders and stared into his eyes.

Thomas expected more words, but was instead shocked when he saw tears in Jorge's eyes. He pulled the man against him, knowing tears streaked his own cheeks.

"What is to become of us?" he asked.

"You are to be rich and showered with honours, and I will be your loyal companion. However, do not expect any work from me because I am going to be far too busy looking after at least six children."

Thomas laughed and pushed Jorge away. "Six?"

"At least six."

"And how do you expect that miracle to happen?"

"I have a friend," said Jorge. "At least, I hope I still have a friend, if he does not consider himself too important to help me."

"I will ask when I see him," Thomas said. "Now, I need to get out of these pompous clothes and dress in something I can breathe in."

"She will expect you to wear them again in the morning."

"The morning is a long way off yet." Thomas embraced Jorge once more, then dragged him inside, both of them laughing.

———

It was late afternoon before Thomas and Jorge escaped from Isabel and Theresa, who together with at least a dozen other women wanted to see every inch of the palace. Thomas had stood beside Isabel as she stared for long minutes at the bowl of crystal clear water held aloft by six lions. Her hand had briefly reached out and her fingers stroked the back of his hand. Then Jorge had shown them the harem, the narrow chambers where the eunuchs slept, and the baths. There were cries of delight and shock at the hot water, the spouts, the deep pools. Some women, Theresa included, wanted to try them at once, so they sent Thomas and Jorge away.

As they descended the slope, Thomas said he wanted to walk the city for a while to clear his head. Jorge said he would return to his new home.

Thomas made his way towards the southern gate which gave out on to the banks of the Genil River. There were shade trees and the soft music of the water always eased his mind. He was staring into a pool where small fish swam when a figure passed him with his head down.

"Hey!" Thomas called out and ran to catch up with Christof Columb. He recalled Theresa's words, that the man had been insistent of late and Isabel had grown tired of his pleas for funding.

Columb stopped and turned back. "Thomas. I was told you were with the Queen."

"I was, but I escaped. Where are you off to?"

"That is a good question and one to which I have no simple answer. Perhaps I will keep on walking until I reach the sea and find a ship to take me away from Castile."

"What is wrong?"

"I went to the palace to make one last plea and was sent away. I was told she was too busy and could not see me. When I pressed my case, they forcibly ejected me. I have had enough, Thomas. You have always been kind to me and listened even when I know you did not believe in my dream, but you have changed your mind, have you not?"

"You are both right and wrong, but more right than wrong."

Columb frowned. "The King of England has sent a message to say he will speak with me. I am minded to travel there. It is where you are from, is it not? Do you know the King?"

Thomas laughed. "Why would I know the King of England? I was a boy of thirteen years when I left there."

"But you are Sir Thomas."

"A joke, and a bad one at that."

"And you are a friend to Queen Isabel. I was hoping you might give me an introduction to him. King…"

"Henry," Thomas said, unsure if he spoke the truth or not. England was far away and news took a long time to reach this far south. "And it was you he sent a message to." He put a hand on Columb's shoulder. "Come with me, I will make sure Isabel sees you. I will support you in what you ask."

Columb smiled. "You will do that for me?"

"And for Castile. If you are right, then you will bring great riches to this country, and if I am right, there will be unknown lands to explore. Come, we will go to her now. She was in a good mood when I left. Let us pray she remains so."

CHAPTER FIFTY

Thomas was lying in bed when a knock came at the door.

"Ignore it," said Helena, pulling him back down. She was all silk and heat and need.

The knock came again and Thomas rolled away.

"What!"

The door opened and Will put his head into the room.

"There is someone to see you, Pa."

"Who is it?"

Will smiled. "She said you would know her."

"Belia?"

"No, not Belia."

"Tell whoever it is I'll be down as soon as I'm finished here."

"Shall I tell her what you and Ma are doing?"

Thomas threw his boot at Will, who laughed as he ducked away.

"He called me Ma," said Helena, lying naked on top of the covers. "I think it is the first time he has ever done so."

"Well, you are his mother. It's not so unusual, is it?" Thomas began searching for his clothes and pulling them on.

"Can we continue where we left off this afternoon?" Helena asked.

"What do you think?"

"I think I would like to." She reached out and touched Thomas's flank. "I would like to very much. Go find out who it is and I will join you soon."

"I expect it's Theresa come with some fresh demand from Isabel."

He hesitated at the door as he bent to pick up the boot he had thrown at Will. He looked at Helena and felt an unfamiliar emotion swell within him. The last few weeks, he had been thinking of asking her to marry him. He didn't mind if she said no, as long as she continued to share his life, but he felt he owed it to her to ask. Except not now.

When he entered the courtyard, it was to see Will sitting at the table next to Catherine. Their heads touched as he pointed something out to her in an open book. Thomas hoped it was not one of his medical tomes which showed how bodies worked inside. Or even worse, the one from the east he had shown to Jorge.

Isabel stood with her back to him, dressed in plain clothes, staring up at al-Hamra. She turned as he approached and offered a warm smile.

"It must draw you to look at it all the time, Thomas. It is almost more magnificent from here than it is inside."

Thomas reached out and put a hand on her brow.

"Are you here because you are unwell, Your Grace?"

She slapped her hand against his chest and laughed.

"I wanted to see where you lived. Your house. Your family."

"You know my family, you always have."

"Except it is different now." She glanced away as Helena came into the courtyard. "I hear she was scarred when Koparsh attacked you. Such a pity."

"Can you see the scar on her other cheek?" he asked.

"There is no scar on her other cheek."

"Not anymore. When she first came to me ten years ago, it was as ugly as the one you see now. In a year, this scar will

434

also fade. In ten more years, nobody will ever know it was there."

"It is what you do best, Thomas, is it not? Heal people. Cure the sick. Like you cured Juan's leg. He barely limps these days, only when he is tired."

"He is growing into a fine young man."

"Yes, he is, thanks to you. And Catherine into a fine young woman, also thanks to you. How can I ever repay you?"

"There is no need. I am yours to command, you know I am."

Isabel laughed. "Then I command you to show me your house. I want to see where you work. Is it inside?"

"Over there." Thomas nodded to the workshop that sat at the end of the terrace.

Isabel turned to her daughter and his son.

"Will, go outside and tell the men there they can leave. I will send for them…" She glanced at Thomas. "How long may I stay?"

"As long as you wish, you know you can."

"If only that were true. Tell them I will send a message when I want to return to the palace."

When Will came back, Thomas led Isabel into his workshop.

She stood looking around at the shelves, the row upon row of books, the scarred workbench and narrow cot.

"Do you sleep here?"

"I have in the past, but now I sleep on a bed indoors. I have grown civilised and old and need my comforts."

"As do we all."

Thomas was aware of a tension between them after what had happened in the farmhouse. A sense of unfinished business lay between them, the tension drawn tighter because they both knew it could never be resolved.

"I was thinking of asking Helena to marry me," he said. "I might need your permission and a dispensation from the church."

"Is she not a follower of another God?"

"Not anymore, as well you know. We are all converts now. She is Lubna's sister and I have a mind marriage to a dead wife's sister is not sanctioned by your church."

Isabel waved a hand. "Have you asked her yet?"

"Not yet."

"Then I will talk to someone and arrange it. You should marry in the new Cathedral."

"I would rather it be somewhere less grand."

"In the palace, then, yes? Theresa can be your maid of honour."

"I think Belia will want that honour, but Theresa will be invited to the night of henna."

"The night of henna?"

"The bride and her female friends celebrate the coming marriage and paint their hands and feet with dye, as they did for Lubna when we were in Sevilla."

"Will I be invited?" asked Isabel.

Thomas stared at her. "Do you want to be?"

"I think I do."

"Then I will ask, but the answer will be yes." He shook his head and laughed. "The Queen of Castile with henna on her feet and hands. What is the world coming to?"

"I may not go quite that far. And I apologise, this is your life and I must try not to manage it for you." She moved away, the threads joining them only growing more taut as she did so. Thomas stared at her slimness, the pale red hair now loose about her shoulders, and ached for something he knew he could never possess. It would be easier to be married. One more barrier against the need. He should resign his position, but knew he could never do so, not as long as she needed him. And need him Isabel did, he was aware of that. Fernando was already seeking new battles and spoke of taking an army to Naples.

She pointed at a bottle on a shelf. "What is that, Thomas?"

All business again, the ties knotted and tucked away for the moment.

"Distillation of poppy. I use it to stop pain if I have to use a knife. I used it with Helena the first time she was injured, but she came to rely on it too much. This time less so. The years have changed her, as they have us all."

Isabel pointed again. "And this?"

And so it went on, the two of them standing shoulder to shoulder in the warmth of his workshop. Eventually, she reached out and took his hand.

"Catherine wants to know if she can visit Will now and again."

"You should ask Will, not me."

"She is doing that now."

"It might be better if we stopped them," Thomas said.

"I had the same thought, but we both know, and I am sure they also both know, that it is a friendship of youth and nothing more."

"Like we are friends?" Thomas asked.

"Yes." Isabel looked into his eyes before shaking her head. "No. Are we not more than friends? I think perhaps we are. We think in the same way. We are curious in the same way. We are diligent and loyal."

"Except you are the Queen of Castile and I am nobody."

"I will make you somebody. There are dukedoms going spare at the moment. Where would you like?" She laughed and clapped her hands together. "Or I could create a new one. Sir Thomas Berrington, Duke of Granada."

He pulled a face. "I would prefer to remain a nobody."

"You can never be that."

"But I can try."

Isabel stood close to him now, her face tilted up.

Thomas thought of all the times Jorge had tried to explain love to him. That it was infinite. That one man could love many women, one woman many men. That love had no boundaries. Love was limitless. For the first time, he thought he might be starting to understand what he meant.

"I have made many wrong decisions in my life," said Isabel, "but you are not one of them. I have a hard decision to make now."

"I understand." Thomas knew what she was about to say. He was too close to her and she had a position to maintain.

She stared into his eyes for a long time, her own tracking backwards and forwards, as if seeking something.

She drew a breath and let it go.

"Marry Helena, Thomas. Marry her and have more children, and give Jorge more, but I want you to continue to serve me. Marry so I am not constantly tempted." She came up on tiptoe and Thomas leaned down to kiss her. It was a lover's kiss. Their last, they both knew, so they made it worth the while.

"You will serve at my side until my daughter comes of an age and has to leave me to cross the sea to England. When that time comes, I want a man at her side I can trust. A man I know will lay down his life for her if need be. A strong man."

Thomas laughed. "And where are you going to find such a paragon?"

Isabel slapped him softly on the cheek and turned away.

"Now, show me the rest of your house. All of it. And then have Belia and Helena cook us spiced food, for I miss it so. I want to spend the entire day with your family, for this house is outside of time and space. It will be my refuge, for a few hours at least."

"For as long as you need it," Thomas said. "Forever and always."

HISTORICAL NOTE

Many of the events leading to the surrender of Granada on 2 January 1492 are well documented. The forces of Castile, together with those who came from other countries to witness and take part in the defeat of Islam in Europe, are historical fact. Most of the events surrounding battles, skirmishes and negotiations recounted in *A Tear for the Dead* are as accurate as my research allows. However, I have altered some of the timings to more readily accommodate the pacing of a novel. Sometimes history moves exceedingly slow.

It is known that during the last years, when Abu Abdullah, Muhammed XII, saw the way the conflict was heading, he sought help from other Islamic nations. These included Egypt as well as the Ottoman Empire, both of which refused to offer any aid. In my telling of this last battle, I have inserted a fictional character acting on behalf of the Ottoman Turks (and a nod of thanks to my son for the name of Koparsh Hadryendo). The Ottoman Empire was greedy for new conquests, having already subjugated Albania, Greece, Venice and most of the Adriatic to the west, as well as large tracts east and south of Turkey itself. While my deceit is purely fictional, perhaps it is not beyond the bounds of possibility for a small delegation to have been dispatched to observe events and report back.

If Abu Abdullah, Isabel and Fernando had been removed, Spain would have been thrown into turmoil. A powerful army and navy could have exploited the subsequent confusion. Of course, these events never happened, and most likely never would, but it has been fun to explore the idea. It also gave me a hook on which to hang the mystery plot.

———

Many of the events described in *A Tear for the Dead* are taken from historical records, a few are made up, and a few more tailored to avoid repetition or confusion. I have also changed the chronology of a few events to make for a smoother plot-line. For those interested, the following list details some major events recorded during this period.

The fire in the Castilian camp is mentioned in several sources, including my primary ones for this book, *The Moor's Last Stand, by Elizabeth Drayson*, and *Granada 1492, by David Nicolle, illustrated by Angus McBride*.

Following the fire, Isabel moved the Spanish army to Santa Fe and began its construction.

The burning of the *vega* is well-documented and was a tactic used extensively by the Castilian army during the entire war.

I take the scene where a wooden board reading Ave Maria is nailed to the mosque door from several sources believed to be accurate. De Pulgar is mentioned as being the perpetrator, though I have changed his first name from Ferdinand to Perez to avoid confusion with Fernando.

Abu Abdullah's younger brother Tarfe is mentioned in most sources as dragging the sign behind his horse before fighting a duel with a Castilian knight who took his head.

I based the scene between Isabel and Thomas in the farmhouse on a brief excerpt I read during my initial research many years ago, before I had even started the first book in this series, and had to include it in this book. Unfortunately, I have lost any record of the source, so perhaps it is nothing more than a figment of my twisted imagination.

Olaf Torvaldsson is a creation of my imagination so I could do with him as I wished. I apologise to him for all the pain I have inflicted over the years. It would be foolish of me to make an enemy of Olaf. I hope he forgives me.

Several sources state that Columbus entered the Alhambra on 5 or 6 January 1492 only to be refused an audience with Isabel. He reached as far as the gate from Granada before he changed his mind and returned. The rest, as they say, is history. I took the liberty of involving Thomas in his change of mind. In fact, this scene was one of the first that ever came to me all those years ago when the idea for the series was born.

I have once again to thank the Viking sisters, Gee and Trish, in particular for the information I found in their recommended reference on herbal plants, *Culpepper's Complete Herbal*.

I have taken the title of this book from the phrase used to describe the expulsion of Abu Abdullah and his family from Granada. The story, first recorded in *The Conquest of Granada, by Washington Irving*, relates to when the exiles turned to take a last look at the wonder of the Alhambra palace and Abu Abdullah sheds a tear. His mother, the indomitable Aixa, is said to have berated him with the words "Do not shed a tear like a woman for that which you could not defend as a man."

―――――

Finally, *A Tear for the Dead* is intended to complete the series featuring Thomas Berrington and his rag-tag collection of friends and family as I envisaged it in a sudden moment of clarity in late 2011. It took me over two years to conduct my initial research and write *The Red Hill*, book one of the series, and over another year to edit it. *The Red Hill* appeared on 26 June 2014, and the release schedule has been a little over a book a year since.

As time went on, I realised I could not let these characters fade back into obscurity. Not to mention the many emails and comments I receive almost daily from readers who tell me I cannot stop writing about them.

So Thomas, Jorge, Belia, Will, Amal and Usaden will return, but it will not be in Spain. They will return to England to accompany Katherine of Aragon for her wedding to Prince Arthur.

For those who want to read more about medieval Spain, fear not. I plan two further prequels featuring Thomas and several sequels following the unification of Spain.

ABOUT THE AUTHOR

David Penny is the author of the Thomas Berrington Historical Mysteries set in Moorish Spain at the end of the 15th Century. He is currently working on the next book in the series.

Find out more about David Penny
www.davidpenny.com

Made in the USA
Middletown, DE
03 December 2024

65947964R00273